"IT'S AN INCREDIBLE VIEW BY NIGHT...."

Zachary's eyes were riveted on her mouth. "I'd like you to see it first thing in the morning...."

"I'd like that, too, dear," Ariel murmured, amber eyes glowing. His kiss was an electric response, his rough tongue flicking across her smooth skin, sipping at her. Closing her eyes, she savored her want of him, all of him....

"Ariel," Zachary groaned breathlessly, "I need to taste every inch of you."

"Yes," she whispered, and added simply, "I love you."

The hands clutching her shoulders were suddenly still.

"Zachary?" Ariel ventured tremulously.

He looked at her. His opalescent green eyes were strangely unguarded, entreating. His absurdly long lashes fluttered down. And when they lifted again, she wondered if she'd imagined that look of naked pain....

Books by Lynda Ward

SUPERROMANCES

3—THE MUSIC OF PASSION
33—THE TOUCH OF PASSION
89—A SEA CHANGE

These books may be available at your local bookseller.

For a free catalog listing all titles currently available,
send your name and address to:

Harlequin Reader Service
P.O. Box 52040, Phoenix, AZ 85072-9988
Canadian address: Stratford, Ontario N5A 6W2

LYNDA WARD
A SEA
CHANGE

A SUPERROMANCE FROM
W🌐RLDWIDE

TORONTO · NEW YORK · LONDON · PARIS
AMSTERDAM · STOCKHOLM · HAMBURG
ATHENS · MILAN · TOKYO · SYDNEY

For my parents, Jack and Edith Miller,
of Fort Smith, Arkansas.

———————————————◆———————————————

Published November 1983

First printing September 1983

ISBN 0-373-70089-X

CHAPTER ONE

Nothing of him that doth fade,
But doth suffer a sea-change
Into something rich and strange.
The Tempest
Act I, Scene 2

THE SALT-SCENTED BREEZE blew in gently through
the bathroom window, making the prismatic sun-
catchers twist and swing on their nylon cords, so
that they sprayed light in a shower of miniature
rainbows across the walls and Ariel Maclean's wet
naked body. Distracted as always by the play of
sunshine on the dangling faceted crystals, she
halted the vigorous strokes of her towel over her
voluptuous torso. She smiled appreciatively,
amber eyes sparkling. Then with a grimace she
turned her attention to the task of drying her
waist-length mane of gold-streaked brown hair.
When the thick terry cloth had soaked up enough
moisture to leave it damp but manageable, she
hung up the towel and ran a sinkful of warm clear
water, into which she dropped her scrappy bikini

to soak out the brine and sand. She padded naked into her bedroom, where she posed unselfconsciously in front of the oval, oak-framed mirror topping her dresser and began to brush the tangles from her hair. She was trying to tame one final errant tendril that persisted in feathering across her cheek, when a sharp knock sounded insistently on the front door downstairs.

"Oh, *merde*," Ariel muttered, startled, dropping the brush with a clatter. "He can't be this early." She squinted in exasperation at the clock on her nightstand to confirm the hour. No, she hadn't lost track of the time. It was only a little after eleven, and the appointment with the model was scheduled for midafternoon. The knock came again, louder and somehow imperative, and just for a second Ariel wistfully remembered the concierge in her apartment building in Paris. Madame Piaget had looked and acted like something out of Dickens, but at least she had known how to deal with unexpected visitors. Sighing, Ariel stepped out onto the landing to holler down the stairwell, "I'll be there in a minute!"

She leaned over the banister and peered down quizzically, wondering if a friend had arrived without warning. From her foreshortened angle she couldn't see the entryway directly, but the daylight that filtered through the ruffled curtains covering the glass door panel, falling across the polished planks at the foot of the stairs, was partially blocked, as if by a large body, masculine and unidentifiable. The knock sounded a third time, impatient, rather intimidating, and she realized the caller hadn't heard her. If it was a friend, the next step would probably be for him to try the doorknob, and she didn't think she'd locked it after returning from the beach. With a stifled yelp as she became acutely aware of her nudity, Ariel ducked back into her bedroom.

She jerked her head around frantically, long hair flying wispily as she searched for something to put on. When she heard the knock a fourth time, she snatched up the long calico prairie dress still lying across the bed, where she'd left it when she'd stripped for her shower. The voluminous tent-shaped gown of yellow sprigged cotton, with high yoke, ruffled collar and full cuffed sleeves, was an authentic nineteenth-century pattern. It had been a twenty-seventh birthday present from Ariel's friend Marie Ryder, a very talented seamstress who was currently into Americana. Although Marie wore such designs all the time—and by the standards of the northern California artists' colony of Mendocino the dress was rather conservative—Ariel preferred to use it only for lounging or as a beach cover-up.

More than once as she'd loped back up the hill from the bay, the gown flapping against her long legs and bare feet as she coped easily with the picturesque but uneven plank sidewalks bordering the narrow streets, she'd overheard childish tourist voices inquiring with awe, "Mommy, is that lady a hippy?" She'd always ignored those innocently rude remarks, figuring they were preferable to the kind of not-so-innocent comments that might have been generated by the sight of her Junoesque figure in one of the minuscule bikinis she preferred for swimming. . . .

With lithe grace she lifted her arms as in supplication to the turtle-shaped stain on the high ceiling and slipped the gown over her head, smiling ironically. In point of fact, the outward appearance of her hometown was as misleading as the antique style of the prairie dress on her. The brightly painted frame houses and dilapidated outbuildings, many of which dated back to the last century, clustered among misshapen pine trees and tall coastal redwoods fronting on a rocky bluff overlooking the dark blue green waters of the north Pacific. To anyone who really knew the village, its patinaed charm and New England-style quaintness were almost too studied to be quite real. Local businesses, of necessity, consciously catered to the growing tourist trade, cultivating the notion that Mendocino was a sort of aging hippie-commune relic from the sixties.

But away from the main street most of the residents were quietly serious about their work, and an increasing number were successful doctors and executives who had fled the big city for the peace of the country. Ariel's new next-door neighbor, for example, was an endocrinologist from San Francisco. Twice a week she commuted the hundred eighty miles southward to tend her practice, but the rest of the time she devoted to her flower-beds, setting out fuchsias in iridescent colors to mingle with the wild nasturtiums that twined along the picket fence separating the two yards. With wry envy Ariel admired the woman's industry. Since the onset of her father's final illness, Ariel's gardening had consisted of occasionally paying a local teenager a few dollars to run a lawnmower over the coarse salty grass.

Suddenly remembering the unknown man at the door, Ariel smoothed the gown over her bare body and lifted her heavy hair away from her neck, so that it flowed loose down her back like a river of caramel. Its damp weight was faintly annoying, and she wished she'd had time to secure it on top of her head in the casual but efficient knot she usually affected. With a resigned shrug she turned to run lightly down the stairs.

At the foot of the steps she swerved to avoid tripping over the large crates of dusty books that were all that remained of her father's sizable library, literary classics. Students from the junior college in Fort Bragg, where John Maclean had taught for so many years, had already come by to pick up the cream of his collection. He'd bequeathed the books to the school, and now only the last few cartons, mostly paperbacks and duplicate or worn hardcover editions, had to be disposed of. Ariel had stacked them by the front door, because someone was supposed to take them away in a day or two for a local church's annual rummage sale. She wondered abstractedly if that could explain the unexpected caller.

As she reached the door, through the translucent curtain of stiffly shirred organdy she could see that the man was just turning to leave. Evidently he'd concluded that no one was home, and despite her obscured vision, she could read irritation and fermenting anger in the set of his broad shoulders as he stalked away. With a squeak of alarm Ariel tugged frantically on the old-fashioned oval doorknob, cursing under her breath when, as usual, the damp-swollen wood stuck momentarily. The man had almost reached the front gate by the time she jerked open the door and wailed with artless huskiness, "Oh, please don't go!"

He froze. Even from the back, through the summer-weight gray gabardine of what was obviously an expertly tailored business suit, Ariel could see the wary tension stiffening that long straight spine. He was a big man, tall and athletic, the kind who gave the impression of maintaining absolute control over his body. Yet curiously she sensed that beneath the smooth flow of smartly styled, collar-length black hair the muscles of his nape must be knotted and throbbing. He exuded the nervy aura she often saw in tourists who flooded into Mendocino on weekends, their pallid city faces twitching and scowling as they paced around the little town, grimly determined to find a few hours' relief from the stress-filled tempo of their lives. But this wasn't a weekend, and he didn't look like a tourist.

Ariel forgot her dishabille, her own restiveness, caught up as she was in the puzzle of the caller's identity and errand. She frowned faintly as she became aware of a disturbing and unfamiliar air of disapproval, worry, that seemed to hang about him. It wasn't his size that troubled her. At five foot ten, Ariel rarely felt physically intimidated by men. During her years in France the male students in her art classes had been frankly awed by her stature. Some had called her *"Femme Miracle,"* Wonder Woman, and teased that she ought to escort them safely home after evening seminars. Only Matthieu—

Ariel pushed that memory aside and peered intently at the man who stood rigid by her gate, one hand poised over the rusty latch. Chiding herself for incipient xenophobia, she wondered if she really did feel threatened because he was so obviously a stranger. As a rule, local residents didn't go around costumed like walking advertisements for the dress-for-success philosophy, nor—her amber gaze slid past him to the dark blue car gleaming like a chromium dinosaur on the other side of her fence—did they drive gas-guzzling Lincoln Continentals. Mendocinans who could afford four-wheeled status symbols tended to favor the small but ostentatiously European. Mentally shaking her head, Ariel forced herself to call again, "Please don't go. May I help you?"

Slowly he swiveled on shining leather shoes, and Ariel found herself ticking off the items that reaffirmed her first fleeting impressions of power and wealth. The power was obvious in the heavy but taut muscular lines of his body. Although the touch of gray at his temples made Ariel judge him to be in his late thirties, he was built like a college football player. She would have been willing to bet money he worked out daily in a gym somewhere, perhaps in his office building, since he had the unmistakable air of a very high-level executive. Status and wealth were implicit in the understated elegance of his clothes: footwear by some Italian too recherché to plaster his initials all over his products; a three-piece business suit of sleek gray wool with an almost invisible pinstripe, expertly cut; a silk shirt of frosty white, with a glint of gold at the cuffs; and a rep tie, Ariel was suddenly certain, legitimately indicated the wearer's old school. As she cataloged the man's impeccably staid and utterly conventional attire, she thought dazedly, *I'll bet he sings Gregorian chants in the bathtub!*

Then his gaze caught hers, and her humor faded. For unexpectedly, he wore glasses—not businesslike horn-rims as she might have anticipated, but wide, wire-rimmed aviator glasses with big lenses, almost aggressively stylish. And behind those glasses he had the coldest green eyes Ariel had ever seen.

As he approached the porch once more, she could feel the chilly condemnation in his eyes as they raked intently over her, taking in every detail of her appearance—her stringy damp hair, her bare feet, the outlandish dress draping her statuesque body. Poised in the doorway, she shivered, and beneath the masking folds of cheery calico she felt her naked skin prickle with apprehension as he stared at her. He made her feel...immodest. With difficulty she fought down the impulse to shield herself with her hands.

He took a deep breath and muttered softly but audibly, "Good grief, an Amazon flower child."

Ariel bridled. She knew what she looked like, but this stranger's blatant rudeness set her teeth on edge. Her physical discomfort and disquiet turned to resentment at the instant erroneous conclusions he seemed to be drawing. Amber eyes narrowing, she snapped, "For your information, *no one* says 'flower child' anymore!" As he blinked at her retort, she continued in the same bristly tone, "May I help you with something? You got me out of the shower for this, so I do hope it's important."

His dark brows raised sharply, clearing the upper rim of his glasses, and he and Ariel regarded each other in charged silence for several seconds. He'd stopped on the step just below hers, but their faces were level, and Ariel noted curiously that behind the sexy glasses his green eyes were starred with almost effeminately long lashes—the only touch of softness she could detect in his craggy features. She was surprised he didn't trim them!

After a hesitation he said quietly, "I'm looking for...Ariel Maclean," and in the careful smoothness of his words she read a mild and grudging apology of sorts.

His voice was probably the most appealing thing about him, she thought, reacting despite herself to the caressing quality his well-modulated baritone imparted to her name. There was a certain transatlantic richness to his vowels, which puzzled her, since he was obviously an American. Her father, she remembered fondly, had striven—with questionable success—for that same tone whenever he read Shakespeare to his freshman literature classes, but this man's voice seemed quite natural. She wondered if the key to the riddle lay in that old school tie he wore. If he'd spent his formative years at boarding school in England, she supposed it would be entirely possible for him to have kept some of the accent.

"Do you know where I might find—" he began again, and Ariel, conceding she hadn't been terribly polite herself, decided to declare a truce. In her blandly Californian soprano voice she admitted, "I'm Ariel Maclean. How may I help you?"

Heavy lids veiled those jade-colored eyes, rather as if he were in pain. Then he looked squarely at Ariel. "Miss Maclean, my name is Zachary Drake. I've come from San Francisco in response to the letter from—"

Her mind seized on one word. "The letter!" she exclaimed in dismay. "You mean you're the one they sent? Oh, damn, how could they?"

He frowned, recoiling. "I don't understand."

Once again Ariel studied him comprehensively, looking past the exclusive splendor of his clothing to the heavy mass of long bone and solid, well-trained muscle, before she sighed in exasperation. "Look, Mr. Drake, I'm truly sorry, but it appears you've been sent all the way up here on a wild-goose chase. I don't know how it could have happened, because I was very definite about what I wanted, but you're just not the type at all.'' Her golden eyes raked him warmly, and she could see he was staring back at her blankly. She had the feeling that any second now he was going to explode, and thinking of the long and pointless drive he'd just made up the twisting shoreline highway—although on second thought she imagined he would have taken the more efficient inland route via freeway, which was dreary but faster—she couldn't really blame him. But it wasn't her fault! Some idiot in an office somewhere.... Hoping to placate him, she smiled and observed gently, ''You're...you're very attractive, of course.''

''Thank you,'' he drawled heavily.

But Ariel shrugged aside his sarcasm. She continued helplessly, ''For one thing, I'm afraid you're much too old. I specified someone in his early twenties at the most. I suppose I could work around that, other things being equal, but— Well, it's quite obvious that undressed you wouldn't be at all suitable to my needs.''

For a moment the silence between them was so complete Ariel could hear the distant pounding of waves against the tortured black volcanic rocks of the headland. Then the man who had identified himself as Zachary Drake grated, ''Miss Maclean, what the *hell* are you talking about?''

Ariel froze at his tone. For a few seconds she

couldn't breathe. Then she gulped uneasily, trying to swallow the acid sensation in her throat, the sickening certainty that she'd just made a colossal fool of herself. "You—you're n-not the nude model the Rand Agency was supposed to—to send today?" she stammered.

"No."

Until that moment Ariel had been unaware she was still capable of blushing. She'd thought that at the advanced age of twenty-seven such high-flown displays of emotion were as far behind her as her girlish fantasies of love everlasting.... But now, with just one word from an overbearing stranger, the condemnation and distaste in that terse monosyllable made hot color flood her face until her skin glowed vividly beneath the smooth gilding tan. She drooped her head so that her hair dangled forward, masking her features as she stared down at her bare toes and tried to regain her composure. God, what an ass she must seem to have made a mistake like that! Of course he wasn't the model she'd been expecting; she ought to have recognized that the moment she laid eyes on him. She wished she knew who he in fact was, what he wanted. If he'd appeared the least bit approachable, they could have smiled and joined in mutual laughter over this stupid misunderstanding. It would have made a hilarious anecdote each would treasure for years to come. Instead he stood there silently, cold and infuriating and superior, watching her struggle.

With considerable effort Ariel lifted her chin

and met his gaze evenly. As she brushed her hair out of her eyes, she said stiffly, her voice husky with embarrassment, "Mr. Drake, as I'm sure you've figured out, there's been a silly mistake. I'm expecting someone else later on today...."

"Someone more suitable to your 'needs'?" he inquired, his neutral tone at odds with the sly baiting of his words.

"Yes," Ariel responded through clenched teeth, refusing to react to his deliberate provocation. She didn't understand why this man seemed to enjoy sniping at her, but she wasn't about to let him see that his barbs hurt. "Naturally that need not concern you. Now if you'd be so good as to explain who you are and just what business brings you all the way here from—"

"Of course." He nodded, his glasses glinting in the noonday light, making his expression unreadable as he reached into the inner pocket of his well-cut jacket to draw out a leather card case and a long white envelope, whose ragged edge indicated it had been sealed and opened. He handed these over to Ariel, and she stared at them uncomprehendingly.

Ariel looked at the return address on the envelope and exclaimed in surprise, "But that's my father's attorney!" When Zachary said nothing, she turned her attention to the engraved card he'd given her.

"Seacliff Publications, Inc." she read curiously, noting the impressive address on California Street in the heart of the financial district, and area bustling with slick executive types who worked in lush corporate offices in architecturally exotic skyscrapers. The last time Ariel had had business in "the city"—as most San Franciscans thought of their hometown—she'd paid extortionate rates for the privilege of parking in the basement of one of those buildings, all the while trying not to think of what would happen to that lofty structure should there be a sudden recurrence of the 1906 earthquake.

"Zachary Drake, senior vice-president." Ariel's lips pursed thoughtfully. *Only a vice-president,* she wondered ironically. *I would have pegged him as chairman of the board at least!* She lifted her head. "I'm sorry," she said. "Is this supposed to mean something to me? I've heard of Seacliff Publications, of course. They produce some of the. . . prettiest art books on the West Coast." She wondered if her disdain for the merely pretty was evident in her words. She hoped not and quickly added, "I'm a painter, but I don't flatter myself that your company has heard of *me*. What is this all about?"

"You still don't know?" Zachary asked deeply.

Ariel regarded him through her lashes, wondering what he was driving at. All she knew was that it had something to do with her father's attorney and Seacliff Publications. She wrinkled her nose, considering. A publishing house. Was it possible that before his death John Maclean had finally written that book that he, like most scholars, had always claimed he would write "if he had time"—

a book to which Ariel, as his heiress, would now own the rights?

After a moment she rejected that notion. Her father would never have kept such a secret from her, and besides, during the last years of his life he'd grown incapable of reading his beloved books, much less writing. Although the successive strokes he'd suffered had never paralyzed him, they'd robbed him of more and more of his faculties, constricting his vision, his world, until in the end he knew only the comforting familiarity of the house he'd been born in, its narrow confines vibrating with the resonant words of Shakespeare and Milton as famous actors read the classics on tapes Ariel had ordered through the college in Fort Bragg.

In any case, Ariel decided, if her father had indeed ever written a book, most likely it would have been poetry such as he'd dabbled in in his younger years or else some kind of treatise on a recondite point of literary research. But Seacliff's specialty was art books, coffee-table books, big beautiful *expensive* compilations of exquisitely photographed paintings and treasures—the kind of books people gave as Christmas presents to not-so-close friends, books that were exclaimed over for a few minutes and then left to gather dust for the rest of the year....

Ariel said flatly, "No, I don't know what this is about."

Zachary glanced toward the door behind Ariel, and his voice darkened ominously. "Then I think we ought to go inside, Miss Maclean, if you don't mind. You and I have a great deal of business to discuss.''

Ariel hesitated, wary of this stranger, warier still of the as yet unrevealed purpose of his visit. Only her dislike of social lies prevented her from stalling him with the excuse that she had no time to talk because she was expecting a model at any moment. And besides, she added grimly, surreptitiously surveying the man from behind the shelter of her gold lashes, he didn't look like the kind of person who would let anything so minor as a prior appointment keep him from accomplishing what he'd set out to do. And he *had* driven all the way from San Francisco.... "Oh, very well," she muttered with minimum courtesy as she stepped back into the house. "Won't you please come in?"

Ariel had never been conscious of just how cramped the vestibule of her house was until she had to share it with Zachary Drake. Her father had been a tall man, but somehow his spare frame had never intimidated her as Zachary's did now. She felt suffocated by his nearness. When he closed the door behind him, his tall, broad-shouldered body seemed to fill all the available space in the little entryway, and Ariel, unused to men whose sheer stature could make her uncomfortable, retreated from him in confusion. He made her feel uncertain...vulnerable...small...and despite all the times in her girlhood when she'd longed to be dainty and petite, she wasn't sure she liked the feeling.

"The—the living room is—is that way," she stammered, waving toward the archway. "Make yourself comfortable. You'll have to pardon the swatches and the rest of the mess, but I've been working in there. If you'll excuse me for just a moment...." Propelled by an instinctive wish to put herself once more on a level with him, she inched backward toward the stairs, her eyes still trained on his face—but in her blind retreat her bare feet slipped on the polished floor, and she tripped clumsily over the stacked cartons of books.

With a squeal of dismay Ariel fell backward, flailing as she clutched wildly at the banister. Instantly Zachary lunged for her, powerful hands with irresistible strength shooting out to catch her arms. For half a heartbeat it seemed he'd saved her—but then the momentum pulling Ariel backward proved too strong for both of them, and she landed heavily on a heap of paperbacks, with Zachary sprawled on top of her.

She lay still, eyes closed against the spinning of the room, too stunned and winded by that precipitate fall to be aware of anything but the pounding of her heart beneath the considerable weight of his body, her constricted breath—and a fervent wish that she could crawl beneath the pile of books and quietly die. Death seemed preferable to the ignominious alternative! Having to open her eyes in a few seconds to face the consequences of her stupidity and clumsiness, having to face Zachary Drake.

As the dizziness subsided, other sensations seeped into her consciousness: the sharp corner of a gold tie tack digging painfully through the thin cotton of her dress into the softness of her unconfined breasts; buttons and buckles pinching her stomach; a knee clad in wool suiting brushing roughly against the bare skin of her leg.... Jolted by the cumulative force of those tantalizing impressions, Ariel blinked hard, her amber gaze opening to a world filled with the virid glint of lash-starred eyes behind polished lenses, eyes that just for an instant seemed warm with concern and—perhaps—a mutual awareness. She could feel his breath stroke her face, and at his temple, only partly hidden by the silver-frosted black hair, a pulse beat jerkily. Heat rose in her cheeks when she realized it must now be all too obvious that beneath the sun-colored gown she was naked....

She stared breathlessly at Zachary, and while she watched, his expression altered, cooled. He lifted his head, carefully untangling a long strand of Ariel's hair that had somehow become entwined in his tie. Quickly he rolled away from her with the economical movements of a gymnast. He bounded to his feet and towered over her, straightening his clothes with a calm that made Ariel wonder if she'd imagined that instant of physical communication between them. Peering down at her with an inscrutable frown, when she did not move immediately he asked, "Are you all right?" His words sounded perfunctory, clipped. "Did you hit your head?"

"N-no, I'm fine," Ariel said shakily as she pushed herself upright. "I-I think something cushioned me when I struck the floor." To cover her mortification when she realized exactly how much of her body had been exposed by her fall, she twisted so that she could look behind her. Spotting the black-and-yellow paperback lying just where her head would have made contact with the planking, she smiled awkwardly. "That's appropriate, I guess," she murmured as she stood up and smoothed her dress. "Providential, one might say."

She handed the book to Zachary, who perused it doubtfully. *Cliff Notes on The Tempest*?" After a second he said, "Oh, of course. 'Ariel.' I wondered about that. Your father's idea, I suppose?"

Ariel shrugged. "I know it's a funny name, but, well, he did teach English literature. He always told me he called me that because when I was first born I reminded him of a sprite. Of course he had no idea I would grow up to be so...so...."

Suddenly she floundered. The expression in Zachary's green eyes had changed yet again, and now he was watching her with a gravity that irritated her more than his obvious contempt had. It was none of his damn business that she'd always felt self-conscious about her height! With an effort she recovered, remarked brightly, "Actually, considering the way most newborn infants look, it's a wonder dad didn't name me Caliban." Biting her lip, she again gestured airily toward the archway that opened into the living room. "Mr. Drake, why don't you go sit down, and I—I'll finish getting dressed. Then we can discuss this business of yours. If you'll excuse me...." Without waiting for a reply, she turned and fled up the stairs.

After locking her bedroom door behind her, Ariel tore off the prairie dress and flung it on the floor, stifling a childish impulse to stomp on it. She jerked open the drawers of her oak dresser and grabbed underwear, jeans and an often washed T-shirt whose slightly faded motto declared CAPTAIN AHAB WAS PSYCHOTIC. It wasn't until she'd tightened the belt with its whale-shaped brass buckle so fiercely she pinched her skin that she dared ask herself why she was so agitated.

After she'd slipped flat-heeled sandals onto her long narrow feet, Ariel picked up her hairbrush and reluctantly faced her reflection in the oval mirror—and was startled by what she saw. Beneath the wild mane of sun-streaked hair her face was rosy, her smooth golden tan vividly tinted, a result of the myriad emotions that still shook her, emotions she hadn't experienced since leaving France.

When she'd returned from Europe at her ailing father's summons, she'd put aside her own needs in favor of his while she cared for him devotedly. She had never pretended to be a saint, but she'd loved her father, and she was determined to make the twilight of his life as sweet as he'd made the morning of hers. Ariel didn't regret those years of conscientious care, but she knew that in the process, by the time her father succumbed to a final massive stroke, she'd suppressed her feelings for so long she wondered sometimes if she would ever be able to react to anything again.

Now, within minutes of meeting Zachary Drake, she'd experienced anger, humiliation, suspicion, dread—emotions more varied and more violent than anything she'd felt in the past two years.

She had also felt the teasing pull of sexual attraction for the first time since Matthieu Bonnard walked out on her.

As she quickly pinned her hair into a thick knot on top of her head, Ariel tried to analyze her curious physical response to Zachary Drake. She'd always known that once her father's death, a release he had welcomed, signaled the end of her filial obligations, she would have to resume her own life again, with new work, new goals, new loves. She had already taken a challenging new direction in her career and now waited with a certain abstract anticipation for the man who would rekindle that fire long dormant in her. But certainly the last person in the world she expected or wanted to become interested in was a rude, overbearing, uptight businessman who had made it abundantly clear from the start that he despised her and everything he thought she represented!

As she jabbed the last pin into her hair, Ariel

swore in French. She was making a big deal out of nothing. She was a grown woman who knew perfectly well that physical attraction had little to do with liking someone, any more than her reaction to Zachary Drake automatically meant she wanted to go to bed with him. It simply indicated that since she was an artist, her eye was naturally sharp enough to recognize that beneath his punctilious exterior he was a very handsome specimen—strong, well-formed, physically fit to a degree few of the men of her acquaintance aspired to. Of course she enjoyed looking at him. The fact that he was obnoxiously prejudiced and had absolutely no sense of humor was neither here nor there.

With the air of one who had carefully put her priorities back in order, Ariel again descended the stairs.

Pausing in the archway, she watched Zachary as he stalked restlessly back and forth with silent catlike strides. He didn't notice her immediately, and she could see the faint frown furrowing his brow as he surveyed the fussy interior of the living room, crowded with cheap dark furniture: glass-fronted bookcases; stiff, scratchy, overstuffed sofa and matching chair; mass-produced imitation art-deco tables and lamps, all topped with ruffly doilies crocheted by Ariel's paternal grandmother decades before Ariel was born. The only touches of color in the room were the sketches and vivid fabric samples piled on the coffee table.

At least half the furnishings in Ariel's home

dated back to the house's construction, just after the First World War. In all her life she'd never seen one piece shifted even an inch out of place, except for cleaning, after which everything had always been returned exactly to the positions marked by deep dents in the faded carpet dotted with pink cabbage roses. When Ariel was a girl, she simply accepted her surroundings, and after she returned from France she never told her ailing father how depressing the house seemed to her. She'd limited her changes to her bedroom, which he was unlikely to see, because it was apparent he drew comfort from the dim musty familiarity she herself found so stultifying.

Now the entire house was Ariel's to do with as she wished, and although she fully intended to redecorate it as soon as she could afford to do so, she found herself annoyed by Zachary Drake's obvious distaste.

Ariel continued to observe him as he picked up a gilt-framed photograph from the sideboard and studied it intently, still unaware of her presence. His grim expression darkened, and she wondered what he found so disturbing about that picture, so familiar to her. It was a family portrait, a grainy snapshot that had been blown up from another photograph rather than a negative. Three people were posed stiffly in the front yard of the house: a man about as old as Zachary was now, tall, thin and ill at ease, with close-cropped dark hair and a bow tie; a petite pretty young woman half her husband's age, wearing a short straight dress and white gloves, with a matching pillbox hat placed on her heavily teased bouffant hairdo; and between them a little girl of about eighteen months, clutching at her parents' hands, so that the lift of her arms raised her pinafore dress and exposed the ruffled edge of her panties. The enlarging process had thickened and blurred the legend someone had scrawled across the bottom of the original picture: "This is John, Barbara and little Ariel, last Easter."

Ariel coughed, and Zachary set the photograph back in its place, then turned to regard her silently. When she announced, "All right, Mr. Drake, I'm dressed now and we can talk. Just what do you want from me?" His green eyes swept over her statuesque body once more, and she immediately wished she'd phrased her question differently. His gaze lingered on the voluptuous figure emphasized by her tight jeans and T-shirt, curves that the prairie dress had masked. Ariel ordered herself not to feel flustered by his intimate but oddly impersonal scrutiny. After all, only minutes earlier they had lain entwined in an embrace that, albeit unwilling, made further embarrassment rather pointless.

She waited, recalling all the things she needed to do before the model arrived, and when Zachary didn't speak at once, she repeated impatiently, "Mr. Drake."

He glanced back at the photograph he'd just set down, and astonishingly he said, "You know, you don't look a thing like Barbara."

For a moment Ariel stared in blank confusion. She wasn't sure she'd ever heard the name Barbara spoken aloud before, at least not in connection with the shadowy figure that was her mother. Catching her breath, she murmured uncertainly, "I—I suppose not. I wouldn't know for sure. She was killed in a car wreck when I was two, and that's the only picture I have of her. My grandmother gave it to me."

"Grandmother?" He watched Ariel suspiciously, as if expecting a specific response.

"My father's mother," Ariel said, baffled by the way he'd jumped on the word. "She died when I was ten. After that there were just the two of us."

Still Zachary probed, "And your father never married again? It was only you and he in this drab little house? That must have been lonely for you."

Ariel's volatile temper, which she'd been holding severely in check, skyrocketed. "Mr. Drake," she snapped indignantly, amber eyes flashing as she glared at him, "I don't know who you are or what the hell you want of me, but you have no right to storm into my home and begin interrogating me about my private life! For your information, I was not some pathetic little orphan. I had a very good childhood. My father was wonderful to me. He was a teacher and he never made much money, but we were happy. It didn't matter a damn that we lived in 'this drab little house,' as you call it, because the house was always full of the things that really mattered...literature and music and art and—and love.'' Her eyes narrowed assessingly as she surveyed that granite exterior once more, and in her face could be read the unspoken but scathing rider, *and I'll bet love is something you know little or nothing about.*

''I see,'' Zachary said without a trace of apology, his tone making it clear he'd interpreted her expression correctly. ''You seem to have been uncommonly fortunate in your choice of fathers.''

''Yes, I was,'' Ariel grated with deliberate sarcasm, ''but however edifying it might be to reminisce about my youth, right now I can't afford to waste the time. This afternoon I have an appointment with the professional model I've hired to help me with my new project, and there are a number of things I have to do to prepare before he arrives. So I'm afraid I must ask you to state your business as quickly and succinctly as possible, so I can get on with my work.''

Slowly Zachary unfolded his long frame from the scratchy sofa, and Ariel noticed inconsequentially that the gray gabardine that had been stretched tautly over his muscular thighs fell back into knife-sharp creases without his needing to brush it into place. When he straightened to his full height he towered over Ariel once again, and she retreated instinctively, realizing with surprise and dread that she felt intimidated less by his physical presence than by the icy glitter in those green eyes. His expression was only subtly colder than the chill in his voice when he spoke.

"So you want it 'succinct,' do you?" he rasped, that vaguely British accent she'd noticed earlier suddenly very evident in the way he clipped off each syllable. "Is this succinct enough for you, Ariel Maclean? I'm here at the request of your grandmother, my employer, who wants to know what in the name of God you mean by suddenly demanding money and support from her after you've totally ignored her existence for more than twenty-five years!"

ARIEL STARED, too stunned at first to be angry. "I knew there had to be some kind of mistake," she mused under her breath. Raising her voice, she said flatly, "My grandmother is dead."

"Apparently your paternal grandmother is deceased," Zachary responded with cool precision. "But people generally come equipped with two grandparents of each sex. I'm referring to your mother's mother, of course. Eleanor Raymond."

"Eleanor Raymond?" she repeated blankly.

"The head of Seacliff Publications." When Ariel didn't speak immediately, Zachary challenged, "You *are* Barbara Raymond's daughter, aren't you?"

Long gold lashes slowly veiled Ariel's eyes. "Eleanor...Raymond," she murmured with a curious sense of discovery. She'd always been vaguely aware that her long-dead mother's maiden name had been Raymond—it said so on Ariel's birth certificate—but she'd never really known anything about Barbara. When Ariel was a girl, the one time she questioned her father he had become uncharacteristically flustered and had hinted at some estrangement in the family.

Grimly Zachary watched the dazed look flitting across her expressive features. After a moment he demanded, "Are you trying to convince me you don't know the identity of your own grandmother? Under the best of circumstances I'd find that story rather implausible."

Ariel glared at him. All at once she'd had enough. The wistful tenderness she'd felt at the mention of those elusive women who were her mother and, even more nebulously, her grandmother, died, blighted by Zachary's withering skepticism. Her control was slipping badly. Drawing herself up to her full height—and trying with questionable success to forget that he still topped her by almost half a dozen inches—she declared with scathing deliberation, her voice growing more heated with each word, "Mr. Drake, it is a matter of complete indifference to me whether you find my story plausible or convincing. Although you apparently do seem to have some connection with my family, or at least my mother's family, you are a stranger to me—and I have no intention of trying to *convince* you of anything." Silently she added, *and you are also undoubtedly the rudest, most supercilious and downright hateful man it has ever been my misfortune to meet!*

Remembering how content she'd felt that morning, when she returned from the beach, how happy and at peace with the world for perhaps the first time in years, Ariel trembled with impotent rage. "How *dare* you come into my home and speak to me that way? Who the hell do you think you are? I want you to leave." She took a deep rasping breath, and when he showed no sign of moving, she concluded tremulously, "Right now...." Her regal air was spoiled by the audible quaver in her voice.

Without a word Zachary gazed down at her. Ariel stared back, tense and unblinking, noting his strong craggy features, his unfathomable expression. She was holding herself so rigid her jaw ached, and at his temple, beneath the smooth wing of silver-flecked black hair, a throbbing vein belied his apparent calm. She wondered just what she thought she could do if he refused to leave, how she could possibly hope to pit her limited strength against the force of that powerful body....

"No," he said.

At the cool determination in his tone Ariel fell silent again, her expressive face draining of all color. She was growing frightened. She could feel her heart racing, and her mind worked with equally desperate speed as she tried to analyze what she should do, what the situation called for. Like any single woman in the modern world, she had known moments of fear, the disturbing urban paranoia that enveloped her when circumstances forced her to walk alone down a dark street or board an elevator with a suspicious-looking stranger. But this man in the extremely civilized gray business suit alarmed her deeply in a way that was totally outside her experience. So far, despite his undisguised dislike, Zachary had made no overt move against her. At what point, she wondered helplessly, did his stubborn refusal to leave cease to be crass rudeness and become a threat? Dared she attempt physical action against *him*? Her gaze slid over him, once more gauging his daunting size, his strength. But she wasn't dainty herself, and in a self-defense class she'd taken years earlier she'd learned a few very elementary judo throws....

As clearly as if he'd spoken the words, Ariel read the warning in his eyes: *lady, I wouldn't advise you to try it.*

Ariel took a deep breath to still her shaking. Her gaze met his squarely. "Why won't you go?" she asked huskily.

In the depths of his murky green eyes something that might have been remorse flashed and was gone, like the phantom gleam of a shiny stone at the bottom of a mossy pool. His expression hardened, and he declared ruthlessly, "I won't go because yesterday I watched Eleanor Raymond, whom I love and respect more than any other woman I've ever known, collapse from a shock so severe we were afraid at first that it would bring on another heart attack."

Ariel gasped. *Heart attack,* she questioned in silent horror. Had this unknown grandmother, a miraculous blessing bestowed at a time when Ariel had accepted that she was now alone in the world, been revealed to her only to be taken from her before they'd even had a chance to meet? Oh, no. Life couldn't be so cruel. "Is—is she all right now?" she asked urgently.

"Yes," Zachary admitted after a moment. "Ellie is one very special, very tough lady, and it would take more than a conniving little—"

Gritting her teeth, Ariel interrupted with cold fury, "All right, Mr. Drake. That's the second time in five minutes you've accused me of some unspecified crime in regard to my grandmother. Unless you're prepared to state your charges clearly and show me proof, I'd advise you to shut up." As she glared up at him she wondered mirthlessly, *although what the hell I think I'll be able to do if you call my bluff....*

In answer Zachary indicated the letter from her father's attorneys.

Quickly Ariel slipped the single sheet of paper from the torn envelope and scanned it. It was addressed to Eleanor Raymond in care of Seacliff Publications, and in terse dry phrases it informed Mrs. Raymond of the death of John Maclean, her late daughter Barbara's husband. The law firm had been instructed by its client, the note continued with equal economy of language, to remind Mrs. Raymond she was now Ariel Alicia Maclean's only living relative. The firm was appealing on her behalf for Mrs. Raymond to forget the past and accept guardianship of her granddaughter.

Ariel raised troubled gold eyes to the man who

was regarding her intently. "And on the strength of this letter, my—Mrs. Raymond has immediately assumed that I'm some kind of con artist out to take her for all I can get?" When Zachary didn't respond at once, Ariel probed with sudden enlightenment, "Or is that idea something you've thought up on your own?"

"Considering there's been no contact between the families for well over two decades, I don't think my assumption is unreasonable," Zachary said stiffly.

Ariel read the letter again. "I know nothing about this," she averred quietly.

"You aren't in charge of your father's estate?"

"As a matter of fact, no. After my father's mother died, when I was ten, one of the law partners was named executor, and that was never changed. I can only assume that the instructions to contact my other grandmother were left about the same time. I guess my father didn't think to change that, either." She paused, smiling ironically. "I'm twenty-seven years old, Mr. Drake. I haven't needed a guardian for quite some time."

Zachary took a deep breath. "I...see," he murmured with grudging thoughtfulness, absently reaching up to adjust his glasses.

Ariel waited for him to continue, but when he remained silent, she suggested mildly, "I think you owe me an apology."

After what she had thought was a momentary easing of tension between them, the censuring glance Zachary shot Ariel stunned her. He said curtly, "I'll apologize to you when I become convinced my original impression was wrong—and not before. Whether you were the instigator of that letter to Ellie—and I have every intention of checking—is immaterial. I still find it uncommonly...opportune that after all these years you should suddenly evince an interest in your grandmother, who is, after all, a wealthy woman—"

Someone knocked on the front door.

CHAPTER TWO

ARIEL JERKED as if shot, the homely sound of knuckles on wood impinging with startling force on the strained scene being played out in her living room. Glancing sidelong at Zachary, whose graven features had settled back into hard impenetrable lines, she tried to call out a welcome, but she found her throat was so constricted she could only croak.

After a second she heard the creaking scrape of metal on wood as the recalcitrant doorknob was twisted and yanked impatiently. A light male voice sang out with easy familiarity, "Hey, Ariel, babe, are you home?"

She relaxed visibly, almost laughing with relief at the bolstering arrival of a friend. Turning away from Zachary, she answered warmly, "I'm just here in the living room, Sam. There's no need to shout."

She heard the glass panel rattle as the stubborn front door banged awkwardly against the jamb, and the sound was followed by a grunt as the newcomer shoved the door the rest of the way into position. "If you don't get that fixed pretty soon, the glass is sure to crack," he noted conversationally. As he crossed the entryway he added, "By the way, whose Lincoln is that out there, hogging most of the street? It looks like something left over from a Mafia funeral!"

"Sam," Ariel hissed through clenched teeth, not daring to look at Zachary as she sidled surreptitiously toward the arch to intercept her friend. They met at the entrance to the living room, and Sam threw his arms around Ariel, hugging her to his thin chest. Looking up at him, she realized with surprise that Sam Walsh was even taller than Zachary. But somehow his height had never made much impression on her.

A former college basketball star, Sam was wiry, almost skinny. He had light blue eyes set deeply beneath nearly colorless brows in a narrow sunburned face. He could have been any age from twenty to forty, although Ariel knew he was twenty-five. When, as now, he wore his usual anonymous summer outfit of comfortable jogging shorts and T-shirt, the only clue to his youth was his astonishing cascade of ash-blond hair—pale, moon-colored locks that tumbled gleaming to his shoulders. They were the despair and envy of every woman of his acquaintance. Since meeting Sam on her return from France, Ariel had lost count of the females, tourists and local residents alike, she'd seen dazzled by the mere prospect of touching those shining curls. Marie had fallen for him on sight. He'd moved in with her the day they met, and now, almost three years later, they were still living together.

"How's Marie?" Ariel asked with concern when she realized that the other woman hadn't come with Sam. Usually they were inseparable.

"She's okay," Sam said grudgingly, his mood darkening. "Just a little tired. She was up late last night trying to finish the embroidery on a vest she's making for her doctor's wife."

Ariel frowned. "She shouldn't be working so hard, especially not now...." She turned, acutely aware of Zachary's intent observation of them, and said lightly, "We'll talk later, Sam. Right now there's someone here to see me."

Sam's hands fell away from Ariel's arms as he glanced over her shoulder into the interior of the dim living room. Silently and assessingly he surveyed the other man, and Ariel saw his mouth tighten into a grim slit behind the mustache. In his pale eyes a strange new emotion she'd never seen previously flared, some instant antagonism that went beyond mere distrust of another person who pursued an obviously conflicting life-style. When she glanced apprehensively at Zachary, she recognized with a sinking sensation that the businessman was staring back at her friend with that identical expression. The hostility between the two men was so palpable Ariel felt like a civilian who had innocently wandered onto a battlefield. Anxious to get out of the crossfire of their locked gazes, she retreated to the far side of the living room, where, slowly and reluctantly, she made the necessary introductions. "Sam, this is Zachary Drake of Seacliff Publications. Mr. Drake, I—I'd like you to meet Sam Walsh, a—a dear friend of mine.''

Sam snorted acidly, ''Talk about bona-fide minions of the Establishment....''

Through the shining shield of his glasses Zachary regarded the younger man with weary contempt, his eyes lingering momentarily on Sam's long hair. He squinted thoughtfully, then commented, ''Walsh. Didn't you used to play professional basketball?''

Sam's surprise was obvious, but his expression remained surly. Bitterly he admitted, ''Yeah, I played pro—for about two games. Then I got injured, messed up my knee. They could have kept me on while it healed, but instead I was placed on waivers. It turned out that all the red-carpet treatment I'd received was a sham—they were just using me to keep the star forward in line at contract time. Once he signed up again, they didn't need me anymore, and I was dropped. The corporation that owned the team said it would have been bad business to keep me.''

Zachary inquired, ''If you were a good enough player to be a serious threat to their star forward, why didn't some other team snap you up?''

''After the medical report the team doctor trumped up about my knee? Are you kidding?'' Sam growled. ''And just because I made a fuss when I realized what they were trying to do to me....''

Ariel had heard Sam's grievances before, and she honestly didn't know how legitimate they

were, although she suspected his belligerent per-
sonality must have played some part in aborting
his sports career. Now she found herself looking at Zachary. Her amber eyes fenced with his
compelling green ones in a bright duel. His expression was deliberately unreadable, but as she
gazed at him, she felt herself coloring faintly. Her
blush deepened when he nodded in Sam's direction and agreed coolly, "Yes, that must have been
very frustrating for you. So what do you do
now?"

Good question, Ariel thought, recalling the way
Marie struggled to support both her and her lover
with her needlework. But loyalty to her friend
forced Ariel to rush to Sam's defense. "Sam is the
founder of Goodearth," she said brightly.

"Goodearth?"

"A local ecology group most of my friends belong to," Ariel explained, wishing Zachary
wouldn't keep stabbing her with his icy green
gaze, rather as if she were a hostile witness he was
interrogating. "You probably haven't heard of us
because we're still very small. But if it hadn't been
for Sam we never would have got started at all."

Sam smiled winningly, quirking his blond mustache, but Zachary seemed unimpressed. "Exactly
what kind of group is this...Goodearth?" he
asked. "The word *ecology* covers an awful lot of
territory, you know."

Ariel bridled, irked by his patronizing tone, but
before she could speak Sam retorted acidly,
"Ecology covers the whole world! All living things

are part of one great ecosystem, and if we don't take care to preserve it—''

Behind the shield of his glasses, Zachary's eyes narrowed. "Please," he interrupted tiredly, "spare me the lecture, both of you. I know all about modern technology and the way it's raping our planet. All I'm asking about now is the thrust of this group of yours. I'm presuming, of course, that your interests *are* concentrated on one particular problem? You aren't just generally determined to rescue the human race from its own folly, regardless of whether it wishes to be rescued? Saying you belong to a so-called ecology group could mean you favor anything from picking up trash in a park to picketing nuclear power plants."

Ariel thought her temper must be dangerously near the breaking point, but she knew any blatant reaction to Zachary's baiting would signal her defeat. Shaking her head faintly at Sam, she interposed sweetly, "Actually, I've done a little of both...."

Her composure seemed to startle Zachary, but after a moment he bowed his head slightly to acknowledge her riposte. When Ariel said nothing more, he began to survey her again, his eyes studying her figure with intent but impersonal curiosity, as if he were trying to analyze her mental and physical composition. With startling abruptness his gaze halted at her bosom. He stared at her so fixedly that even from across the room she felt her body begin to stir in unwilling response, hot color painting her cheeks as she felt her nipples hardening visibly beneath the stretched cotton of her old T-shirt.

Her blush deepened even more dramatically when she realized Zachary's attention was focused not on her voluptuous breasts but on the motto on the shirt that shielded them so inadequately.

"It figures," he murmured at last, his deep voice disgruntled. "I ought to have known without asking. You're a save-the-whales nut."

Before Ariel could reply, Sam challenged truculently, "You have something against whales?"

Ariel frowned in irritation, weighted down by the sinking feeling that any moment now she was going to have to eject *both* men forcibly. She waited breathlessly, and to her profound relief, when Zachary answered Sam his tone was mild, if not conciliatory. "No, of course I have nothing against whales. From what little I know of them they seem to be quite remarkable. My quarrel is with groups—such as your Goodearth, I suspect— that devote all their energies to the needs of animals, when there are human concerns that surely ought to take precedence."

The quiet sincerity of Zachary's words surprised and impressed Ariel, making her wonder suddenly if there was another softer side to the man, a side not immediately obvious to one dazzled by the polish of his hard-driving-executive facade. Her eyes slid over him, finding pleasure in the sight of his muscular, almost classically beautiful body. Her gaze was just lifting to meet Zachary's, when from the corner of her eye she saw Sam's blond brows come together sharply, his mouth twitching as if he were about to utter a squelching retort. Quickly she intervened, "I know there's a lot of truth to what you say, Mr. Drake, but there are those of us who happen to think that the senseless slaughter of any life form, particularly gentle and intelligent creatures like whales, diminishes us all as human beings."

"Naturally," Zachary murmured, nodding in a way that made her feel certain he'd recognized her diversion for what it was. His glance rested pensively on Sam for a few moments before he looked at Ariel again. "While it might be interesting to debate the issue at greater length sometime," he conceded, "right now that's not what I'm here for." And he reached up to adjust the wire frames of his glasses in a gesture that seemed to punctuate the subject under discussion—period. Briskly he continued, "Miss Maclean, you and I still have serious business to talk about—private business—and I think you mentioned something about an appointment of your own this afternoon...?"

"Yes, of course," Ariel said, flustered to realize that during her contretemps with Zachary she'd completely forgotten about the model. Glancing with dismay at her digital wristwatch, she muttered, "Oh, damn. The man from the Rand Agency is going to be here before too long, and I still haven't—"

"Hey, babe, don't worry about it," Sam interrupted with a laugh. "I completely forgot why I dropped by. The agency called Marie to say the model isn't coming after all. Since she's not feeling too great today, I told her I'd let you know.''

Ariel stared blankly at Sam. ''What do you mean, 'the model isn't coming'? I paid a deposit, for God's sake. And why should they telephone your house and not mine?''

Sam shrugged. ''Who knows? I'd gone out to get some beer when they called, but Marie said the agency said something about the guy changing his mind about driving all the way up here for such a short job. Apparently you gave our number for messages, and no one answered the phone when they tried here this morning.''

''That could have been while I was down at the beach,'' Ariel admitted. As she pondered the sudden change of plans, she began to pace around restlessly, not watching where she was going. ''I was gone for a couple of hours—'' Blindly she bumped into Zachary, and when he automatically caught her shoulders to steady her, her voice trailed off in husky embarrassment. Disturbed as much by the feel of his hands on her as by her own clumsiness, Ariel quickly backed away from him. She sank onto the arm of the scratchy sofa, only to rise again and swear stridently. ''Oh, damn,'' she again exclaimed indignantly. ''He can't back out now. I was counting on him!''

Forgetting the men who watched her, for a few heated moments Ariel cast vivid Gallic aspersions on the recalcitrant model's intelligence and ancestry before consigning him and his employers to

bleak and everlasting damnation. The fierce flow
of invective didn't stop until she chanced to look
up at Zachary, and astonishingly she glimpsed
behind his glinting glasses the first sparkle of
genuine amusement to warm those cold green eyes
since he'd materialized on her doorstep.

"Formidable," he murmured with a grin.

Ariel choked in dismay. "You speak French,"
she accused.

Zachary bowed his dark head in acknowledg-
ment. "I'm afraid so. Also German and Russian.
I'm considered quite fluent," he amplified lightly,
"but I don't think I can claim to be anywhere near
as...articulate as you obviously are."

Remembering exactly what she'd just said, Ariel
shrugged and smiled uncertainly. "Yes, well,
I'm...sorry about that. Usually it's a good way to
vent my anger without offending anyone. I
studied in Paris for a couple of years, and when I
first arrived, some of my classmates thought it
might be amusing to take me to Les Halles to
observe the, um, nightlife. It turned out to be
very...educational—and not just for my vocabulary."

Unexpectedly Zachary grimaced. "I should
think there were some kinds of education you'd be
better off without."

"Yes," Ariel said quietly, "that's what I decided, too." Her long lashes fluttered down, veiling
her golden eyes as she reluctantly recalled that
tour through the dingy streets surrounding the
bustling central market of Paris, where very late at

night, after burly laborers and truck drivers finished unloading the produce and meats that would
feed the city the next day, the students went in
search of relaxation and another kind of commodity.... At twenty-two, admittedly a late
bloomer, Ariel had been naive and still disoriented
by her recent arrival in a strange country. She'd
tried very hard to appear sophisticated, not wanting to give her fellow art students an excuse to
laugh at her by betraying that she was shocked by
what she saw and heard, that she was distressed by
the bedraggled women who strolled the sidewalks
with vacant determination. But it had all seemed
so sordid and terribly, terribly sad, especially the
sight of the large number of young girls whose di-
lated pupils and scarred arms showed they'd been
driven to the streets by hopeless drug addiction.

By the time dawn approached, Ariel had been
on the verge of tears—when suddenly her painting
instructor, Matthieu Bonnard, had appeared like a
knight errant, verbally blistering the other
students for their insensitivity and sweeping Ariel
off to an early breakfast of croissants and con-
solation in his apartment on the *rive gauche*....

Blinking hard, Ariel looked at Zachary. "I did
learn a lot in Paris." She sighed wryly.

Before Zachary could respond to that obviously
inadequate remark, Sam interrupted brightly,
"Ariel, honey, I know you're probably fuming
right now, the way you've been stood up by this
model from San Francisco. But I was thinking.
Maybe it's all for the best."

Ariel looked at him in surprise. "What do you mean?"

"Well, I know you were planning to pay an arm and a leg to get this guy to come all the way up here, and it occurred to me, why not use someone local, so you wouldn't have travel expenses on top of the regular fee? Half the guys in town would jump at the chance to take their clothes off for you."

Ariel shivered with irritation and stared down at her slim feet in their flat-heeled thong sandals. She wished Sam would shut up. As much as she admired his work for Goodearth, sometimes she found his teasing games more tasteless than funny. It was anybody's guess what Zachary Drake was making of it. When she felt she could speak without snapping, she said tightly, "No, Sam. You know I'd never ask a favor like that of a friend."

He persisted. "Well, how about me, love?"

Tawny eyes widening, Ariel laughed shortly. "Oh, sure. I'll bet Marie would just love that idea."

Sam smiled appeasingly. "Marie trusts me. Anyway, I doubt that she'd mind very much if you donated the money to the trawler fund."

"No, Sam!" she repeated furiously, glaring at him. "You know I do as much for the group as I possibly can. But don't you dare start trying to tell me how to do my work!"

At the anger sparking in her eyes he backed off immediately. "Sorry, babe, sorry," he muttered, his hands raised in surrender. "I just thought, since we're running short of time and money and since you've always been one of the biggest promoters of this project...."

"I'll talk to you later, Sam," Ariel said, her voice heavy with dismissal. "Mr. Drake and I have business to discuss right now."

Sam's pale eyes flicked between Ariel and Zachary, and after a moment he shrugged elaborately, the movement disturbing his shining locks. "Yeah, sure," he grumbled. "I'll tell Marie you send your love." Turning on his heel, he stalked out of the room. The front door banged shut behind him.

Ariel winced at the rattle of the glass panes. "If I don't get that door fixed, the panel really is going to crack one of these days," she noted to no one in particular.

Wearied by the tense confrontation between the two men, Ariel sank onto the sofa. When she glanced up at Zachary, he was still standing in the center of the faded carpet, observing her impassively. Closing her eyes momentarily, she motioned absently for him to be seated, and it wasn't until she felt the sofa cushions shift under his weight that she realized he was sitting beside her rather than in the chair opposite. Her lashes flew up in surprise.

Zachary nodded in the direction of the entryway and asked, "Just out of curiosity, why did you go all the way to San Francisco for a model? From what I could see on the streets here, there seem to be any number of men—*young* men, as I think you specified—for you to choose from." He paused, and not even his glasses could mask the warm gleam of appreciation in his hooded eyes as he surveyed her face, the long sweep of her neck bared by her pinned-up hair and low-necked T-shirt, the high full swell of her breasts. . . . Silkily he drawled, "Your friend is right. I wouldn't blame any man for wanting to undress for you."

She closed her eyes again and counted to ten in French, then, for good measure to twenty. When she felt she could face Zachary without blushing, she raised her thick lashes and said matter-of-factly, "Mr. Drake, that sort of attitude is the precise reason I will *not* use a nonprofessional as a model. Mendocino is a very small town, and even if I could find a man who would do the job without reading something personal into it, everyone else around here would draw their own conclusions. The new project I've started will be tricky enough without that kind of gossip interfering with my work, thank you."

Zachary glanced curiously at the pile of fabrics on the coffee table. "Didn't you say you were a painter?" he queried.

"Yes," Ariel confirmed, "but I'm hoping to get a grant from the Pacific Coast Regional Arts Council in connection with restoration of the Navarro River Opera House. In order to do that, I must switch over to a new medium. That's a very important reason why I can't afford personal distractions right now."

"What about the man who was just here?" Zachary persisted. "Surely he would understand? You already seem to be on rather close terms with him."

Ariel took a deep breath. She supposed she could explain she was on "close terms" with Sam only because he was living with her best friend, but she'd be damned if she'd offer him any explanations! "Sam's not suitable," she said shortly.

Zachary scowled. "Choosy, aren't you?" he muttered after a moment.

Ariel shrugged and replied quietly, "I hardly think that's any of your business, one way or the other. Wouldn't you agree?"

Zachary's mouth thinned. "Miss Maclean," he said tightly, "I assure you it is a matter of complete indifference to me how you and your fellow free spirits conduct your personal lives—but I did promise your grandmother I'd find out as much as I could so I could report back to her. Since receiving that letter, she is, of course, very curious about you."

Ariel didn't respond immediately. *Free spirits,* she thought in disgust as she turned to gaze out the window. That was a euphemism if ever she'd heard one! Why didn't he just come right out with it and call her a hippie, a term just as anachronistic and even more insulting. She sighed deeply. Above the bluff she could see sea gulls whirling and soaring, their weird scraping calls drifting back on the breeze, metallic yet oddly human, like the cry of an android in pain. Someone was flying a small kite with a long rainbow-striped tail, while nearby an impressive red tetra kite with triangular sails dipped and soared with ponderous grace in the sharp salty wind. The rainbow kite flitted agilely around the larger one.

At last she faced Zachary again. Her burgeoning irritation had suddenly been superseded by a peculiar feeling of... of pity for the man. He was so gorgeous, she thought with sadness as she met his gaze evenly. He had a big beautiful well-trained body that stirred her just to look at it—but that body seemed to house a mind more constricted, more insensitive than she would have dreamed possible for someone of his obvious intelligence. Of course she was aware that some of his remarks were quite deliberately provocative. For reasons she still couldn't begin to comprehend, he sniped at her, trying to rattle her. But still....

She surveyed his meticulously staid clothing again, the careful grooming, the hair that was neither too long nor too short; she thought about the car parked at her curb, all luxury and no flair. Finally she asked softly, "Mr. Drake, don't you ever get *tired* of being a walking caricature?"

Behind the shelter of the wide aviator glasses— the one anomalous element of his attire—his green eyes widened dramatically, fluttering the black lashes that looked so startlingly soft against the harsh planes of his face. "I don't know what you mean."

Ariel nodded, and a long tendril of sun-bleached hair worked loose from her casual top-knot and fell across her face. As she brushed it away, she smiled enigmatically. "I didn't think you would."

Noticing the letter lying on the coffee table, she thought about her grandmother, the woman who'd been so shocked to hear about Ariel that she'd almost had a heart attack. Good Lord, Ariel asked herself, suddenly chilled, was it possible that Eleanor Raymond had been as ignorant of Ariel's existence as she was of hers? If so.... She shook her head fiercely. No, the letter from the attorney, while ambiguous, seemed to assume that Eleanor was at least aware of having a grandchild, even if there had been no contact between them. "Forget the past," her father had appealed from the grave. What past? What was the bitter dispute that had so divided her family it had left Ariel, the innocent victim, estranged from the one person who might have been able to give her comfort and support during those last lonely, heart-wrenching years of her father's illness? There was so much she didn't know, so much she now needed to know.

Glancing around her, Ariel wondered at the brooding atmosphere that permeated her home. She'd lived all her life in this house, and she'd never felt so stifled, so confined as she did at that moment, sitting beside the impressive figure of Zachary Drake. But maybe that was it, she decided—the man was too big, the room too small. His physical presence overwhelmed her, and by some strange osmosis that sense of intimidation seeped into her brain and made her feel at a disadvantage mentally, as well. They needed to talk, but she couldn't function with him metaphorically looming over her the way he seemed to do. If she could just get him out into the open.... Suddenly Ariel asked, "Have you had lunch yet?" After a second she probed acutely, "For that matter, did you have breakfast?"

Zachary looked startled. "Just coffee," he admitted. His mouth twisted grimly. "I was in a hurry to get away."

Yeah, in a hurry to find and attack me, Ariel silently scoffed. "And you drove all the way up here from San Francisco without resting or eating? No wonder you're grumpy!" She stood up abruptly and gestured for Zachary to do the same. "Come on, Mr. Drake, I'll take you to lunch." When she saw his green eyes widen, she explained with arch sweetness, "Let's just say it's against my principles to let a fellow creature—*any* fellow creature—go hungry if I can help it." With a toss of her head she started toward the door.

AT ARIEL'S INSISTENCE they walked the few blocks from her home to the main street of Mendocino, which stretched along the bluff overlooking the beaches and the widening mouth of the optimistically named Big River. The breeze had died down slightly, and even in her light T-shirt and jeans, as she loped down the rough dusty sidewalks, Ariel felt uncomfortably warm under the early-afternoon sun. Zachary, she thought as she glanced sidelong at the tall man strolling beside her, his long legs more than a match for her quick strides, must be sweltering in that wool suit. Had she known him better, she would have suggested he discard the coat and tie before they'd left her house, but the tension between them seemed to preclude such familiarity.

Anyway, Zachary Drake was probably a man who rarely relaxed. Even when he ate—and especially during a business lunch, as she supposed this meal might be regarded—he would be very formal, very much the man in control. But oddly, when she'd invited him to lunch, he'd shown no reluctance to be seen with her, although she knew her attire couldn't possibly meet the standards of the elegant women he most likely dined with in San Francisco. Even in Mendocino their incongruity of dress would make them a rather startling couple, she decided as they wove through the ever-growing crowds of casually attired tourists clustered on the sidewalks. The visitors were snapping photographs of determinedly quaint storefronts, haggling with street vendors over the price of tooled-leather belts or sand-cast copper bracelets.

But perhaps more significantly, Zachary hadn't uttered conventional—and in Ariel's opinion, patronizing—protests when she'd indicated he was to be *her* guest for lunch at one of her favorite restaurants. Her invitation had obviously puzzled him. Yet his acceptance had been courteous and nondefensive, and Ariel couldn't help contrasting it with similar experiences she'd had in France. As besotted as she'd been with Matthieu Bonnard, she'd grown weary of his dogged insistence that he be the one to pay for, and therefore choose, their food and entertainment. Even on his birthday he'd refused to let her treat him.

In retrospect she supposed that all along Matthieu had been subtly reinforcing their relative positions in their love affair, had been preparing her for the day he would admit with a shrug that *oui*, it was indeed true that in three weeks he planned to marry the daughter of a wealthy industrialist. Ariel could still remember the reassuring smile in his warm brown eyes as he reached across the table to grasp her fingers, clenched around the stem of her wineglass. He'd pried them loose and kissed her palm, his lips moving sensuously across her skin as he murmured she must not bother herself, there would be no problems in the future, he knew of a furnished apartment in Neuilly, not expensive and *très discret*. . . .

Ariel conceded that there was a certain poignant justice in the fact that during all the months she'd dated Matthieu, the only drink she ever paid for was the glass of Dubonnet *rouge* she'd flung in his face that last evening.

"You're a million miles away," Zachary noted dryly when Ariel stumbled over a loose plank in the sidewalk.

"No, only about six thousand." As she steadied herself she looked up at him sheepishly. "I'm also not usually such a klutz. I guess I must still be upset over the change in my plans. I'm going to have to contact the modeling agency and complain. It came highly recommended, and I expected better service, especially after the deposit I paid. I presume they'll refund that."

"You say Rand was the name of the agency you contacted? I'm not familiar with them myself, but someone in Seacliff's advertising department might know something. They occasionally use models in publicity layouts. If you like, I can check around and find out if the firm is reputable before you make any further arrangements," Zachary offered unexpectedly.

Ariel blinked in surprise. "Thank you. I'd appreciate that," she said, her gold-tipped lashes fluttering over eyes wide with pleasure. She looked past his broad shoulders to a tall wooden water tower that fronted on the sidewalk, its huge square sides of rough redwood planking weathered to a soft silver gray by decades of exposure to sun and the salt-laden winds. Inside the framework rustic steps spiraled upward to an observation deck. "Here's where we're going," she remarked, and when Zachary looked puzzled, she pointed upward, explaining, "The restaurant is on the second floor of the building next to the tower. You have to take these stairs to get to it."

Zachary lifted his head and spotted the crowded dining tables set out under what at first glance appeared to be only an awning overhanging the sidewalk. "Of course," he said as Ariel started up the steps. "I hadn't noticed."

After they were seated at a round sunny table, its red-checked tablecloth fluttering in the breeze, Ariel peered across the top of her menu to advise, "Don't let words like 'hamburgers' and 'onion rings' make you think this is a fast-food joint. The food here is exceptional. I particularly recommend the burger with sliced avocado and Sonoma jack cheese, although if you prefer something a little spicier, the one topped with Ortega chilies and Swiss cheese is also very good." When she told the waiter, a college-age youth wearing an immaculate apron over his faded jeans, that she wanted her sandwich cooked medium rare, Ariel saw Zachary frown, and after he'd given his own order and the young man had disappeared back into the kitchen, he commented mildly, "I'm rather surprised you're not a vegetarian."

Ariel looked surprised. "Why should I be?"

"You're out to save the whales. Yet you have no deep-seated moral objections to killing?"

"Not for food," Ariel answered dismissively. "I accept the fact that man is by nature a carnivore. I also am not opposed to killing in self-defense or to protect one's loved ones or country." As she spoke, her bland California voice grew strident, more heated. "What I *am* irrevocably opposed to is killing for sport or using the profit motive as an excuse to drive any species to the brink of extinction, especially when there isn't one single product derived from that animal that can't be duplicated— and often more cheaply—from some other source, such as petroleum."

Quietly Zachary countered, "But there are some people who think the overuse of petrochemicals, with the resulting pollution and production of possible cancer-causing agents, is the greatest threat to mankind today."

The understated conviction in Zachary's deep attractive voice brought Ariel up short. Suddenly she was aware of the other diners around them, the tourists bustling on the sidewalk below them. Behind his shining glasses Zachary was watching her with grim wariness, and she realized that in her fervor she had come uncomfortably close to causing a scene. Abashed, she forced herself to calm down as she sighed, "I'm sorry. I didn't intend to make a speech. You're my guest, and I'm being rude. This is neither the time nor the place to discuss issues as complex and important as these."

Just then the waiter reappeared with a small wicker basket heaped high with hot crisp batter-fried onion rings, golden and savory, and a dip of sour cream seasoned with dill. Grateful for the interruption, Ariel smiled winningly at the young man, and her grin hadn't yet faded when she proffered the basket to Zachary. "Here, I hope you'll help me with these. I could eat onion rings by the bushel, but I'm fat enough as it is."

"You're not fat," he said, his eyes skimming over her, touching on her breasts, her throat, her mouth. "You're exactly right for your height."

Remembering Zachary's first words to her, Ariel tipped her head sideways and gazed evenly at him. Her wide mouth curved mischievously, dimpling her cheek as she prodded, "You mean you've decided you *like* Amazons?"

She wasn't certain how she'd expected Zachary to react to her teasing remark, but most definitely she hadn't anticipated the look of stunned surprise that washed over his hard features like a wave on sand, leaving his craggy intelligent face pale and smooth and vacant as the emotion quickly receded. As Ariel stared, she heard him mutter dazedly, "My God, *now* I believe you're Barbara's—" He broke off abruptly and shook his head. When he spoke again, his voice was as impersonal as if he were discussing the weather. "That's quite a smile you've got, Ariel Alicia Maclean. When you turn on the charm, you're really something. Tell me, do you flirt with everyone this way?"

Mildly shocked, Ariel protested, "I wasn't aware I was flirting." She held herself still with resentment. "I don't go in for game playing."

"Don't you? I'm supposed to believe that those half-veiled eyes, that funny little quirk of your lips...." His dark brows rose in polite contradiction, but before Ariel's temper could flare up, he relaxed and conceded, "Well, on the other hand, perhaps it's all unconscious with you. Some women are just born knowing how to wrap a man around their fingers. It's in their blood."

Suddenly he swiveled in his chair and squinted out at the breathtaking panorama that lay before him, the shingled roofs of the old frame houses and shops that fronted only on the leeward side of the street. Between the roadbed and the rocky bluffs, no buildings interrupted the view of the shore, the sky and sea and black twisted rock draped with ice plant and wild lupine. "That's quite a view," he noted with conscious inadequacy.

"Yes, isn't it?" Ariel agreed, grateful to switch to a less volatile topic. "Except for the years I studied in France, I've lived in Mendocino all my life, and I've never grown tired of it. I love to sit on the cliff for hours just watching the ocean. It's continually changing, continually fascinating, especially in the spring and fall, when the California grays migrate along the coast." She paused, smiling ruefully. "Sorry. I said we wouldn't talk about whales now, and here I am again, right back on my favorite subject."

"So tell me about them," Zachary said. "I'd be interested to hear how, in a world fraught with all kinds of evil, you chose to make the welfare of whales your special cause."

Ariel regarded him suspiciously, uncertain whether he was mocking her, but the glare of sunlight on his glasses rendered his expression inscrutable. After a moment she sighed and answered seriously. "I've been aware of whales all my life. They're part of life here on the coast. In September you watch the gray whales migrate south to their breeding grounds in the Sea of Cortez, off Baja California, and around April they travel northward again with their babies. It's an annual ritual that's very sure, very...serene in its regularity."

She hesitated, her face shadowed. With jerky movements she began to fidget with the silverware of her place setting. Hoarsely she continued, "Yes, it's all very serene—only sometimes things go wrong. A couple of years ago, shortly after I came home from France, I went down to the cove very early one morning for a short swim—"

"You swim here?" Zachary interrupted curiously. "I thought the currents in the bay were supposed to be treacherous."

"They are—to anyone who's unfamiliar with them. Cold, too. But I'm a very strong swimmer and I've swum in these waters all my life. I can take care of myself."

"I'm sure you can," Zachary replied deeply, a pregnant undertone edging his words. Ariel wondered how one simple phrase could carry so many meanings. As she pondered this, he prompted, "You were saying, about the whales...."

Ariel nodded. "I used to go swimming in the bay every morning. Most of the time I spent taking care of my father, but that morning swim was one luxury I allowed myself, no matter what. Only one morning when I walked down to the cove, I discovered that a pod of grays had beached themselves there." She hesitated, then continued bleakly, "I looked down from the top of the cliff and saw three of the most magnificent creatures God ever created lying stranded on the sand, helpless as newborn babies, their great barnacle-crusted sides heaving painfully as the sheer weight of their bodies crushed them to death—and I had to be the one who found them.'' Her long gold lashes fluttered damply over her cheeks, and she stared down into her lap, where her fingers twined and clenched convulsively.

Zachary said, ''That must have been incredibly difficult for you.''

Ariel nodded again, not looking up. ''Yes, it was. I felt so—so helpless. Everyone was helpless—the Coast Guard, the marine biologists who came up from San Francisco, the local people. We all tried, but in the end no one could do anything but watch those wonderful animals slowly die....''

From across the width of the table Zachary's deep voice probed quietly, acutely, ''The same way you had to watch your father die?''

Ariel jerked her head, her eyes wide and troubled as she stared at him, her face white with shock. ''H-how did you know?'' she stammered, gulping. ''How could you possibly know the way I felt when I—I—''

Before Zachary could answer their lunch arrived, and Ariel relaxed, grateful for the respite just when she feared she was about to become embarrassingly maudlin. She smiled disarmingly at the waiter as he placed a steaming platter in front of her, and after he'd served Zachary, the young man looked back at Ariel as if he recognized her for the first time. ''You're a friend of Sam Walsh's, aren't you?'' he ventured. When Ariel nodded, he shook his head and chuckled wryly, ''Funny guy, Sam. I hear that group of his is raising money to send a boat out into the Pacific to stop the whaling fleet this fall.''

"Well, we're trying," Ariel agreed seriously. "Unfortunately the money is coming very slowly. If you're interested, there's a meeting later this week. We can use all the help we can get.''

The waiter looked uncomfortable. "Nah, I don't think so," he muttered, backing away. "I'm not into whales." He glanced hastily toward the kitchen. "I've got to go now. It was nice meeting you." With a wave of his hand he was gone.

When Ariel returned her attention to the succulent hamburger before her, she found that Zachary hadn't yet touched his own lunch. Instead he was regarding her enigmatically, his green eyes unreadable in the afternoon glare. Ariel waited for him to say something, but when silence stretched thickly between them, she became uneasy. At last she said briskly, "You know, Mr. Drake, ever since you burst on the scene this morning, you've been grilling me on one subject or another, and you've given precious little information in return. I think it's time you answered a few questions yourself."

"Fair enough," Zachary complied smoothly. "Question away."

Startled by his easy acquiescence, Ariel stared at him. Somehow she'd expected him to put up more of a fight. When she'd had a moment to realign her thoughts, she leaned forward and said bluntly, "All right, the first thing I want to know is why I'd never heard of my grandmother. You blamed me for the lack of contact, but I don't think that's fair. After all, during most of the past twenty-seven years I've been a child. If Eleanor Raymond wanted to contact me, the overture would have to have come from her. So why didn't it? What caused a rift in our family so deep it kept her and me apart for more than a quarter of a century?''

Zachary took a deep breath. ''So you really don't know,'' he muttered, reaching for his napkin and spreading it precisely in his lap. ''You really don't know anything about your parents and the circumstances of their marriage?''

''I know my mother must have been very young when they met,'' Ariel said speculatively. ''She was only just twenty-three when she died, and daddy was around forty. I guess her family wouldn't have been thrilled about her marrying someone twice her age.''

''Barbara was nineteen when she met your father,'' Zachary said grimly. ''I happen to remember the occasion well. I was only ten, but Eleanor, who has always been like a mother to me, asked me to the party because she wanted me to meet John Maclean. Barbara and I were thrown together because we were the two youngest guests there, and I can still recall how the little 'princess' was about to go out of her tiny selfish mind, because for once her widowed mother was the center of attention instead of her.'' He paused heavily, his green gaze boring into Ariel, and it was as if that startling flash of communication the two of them had shared only moments earlier had never been. "You see," he rasped, his low voice jagged, accusing, "the celebration was an engagement party—for Eleanor Raymond and John Maclean. Even as a teenager Barbara thought she was God's gift to men, and to prove it, she deliberately seduced and eloped with her own mother's fiancé not two weeks before the wedding!"

CHAPTER THREE

THAT LAST RINGING CHARGE still reverberated in Ariel's mind several days later as she stuffed her suitcase into the luggage space of her old red Pinto station wagon. She glanced back toward the house, trying to remember if there was anything else she needed to do before she started on the drive south to San Francisco. She'd double-checked the doors and windows, and her neighbor, the endocrinologist, had promised to water the ragged grass before she made her own weekly commute to the city; Ariel expected to be back before the lawn needed further care. She was only going for a few days, she reminded herself impatiently, to a not-very-distant city she was already reasonably familiar with. So why, she wondered, did she feel as if she were about to embark on a perilous voyage into uncharted territory?

Ariel was going to meet Eleanor Raymond. As soon as Zachary Drake had made his shocking pronouncement that afternoon in the restaurant overlooking Mendocino Bay, Ariel had known she would have to see this woman. *Grandmother....* The word sounded strange to Ariel. It still meant Grandma Maclean, the tall raw-boned woman who, until the day of her death, had tried in her dour but loving way to make a home for her widowed son and his child. Grandma Maclean had been the one who found the old snapshot and had it enlarged and framed so that Ariel would have something to remember her mother by. She had also been the one who charged Ariel nightly to "remember your poor mother in your prayers and your father, who's so lonesome for her." Not once had that dear woman hinted at anything unusual or dubious about the brief marriage of John and Barbara Raymond Maclean.

So now Ariel was heading southward to meet the only person who might be able to enlighten her on what had happened when her parents met, how her quiet, gentle, rather abstracted father had managed to become one corner of what must have been a bizarre, not to mention scandalous, love triangle. Zachary's version Ariel dismissed, not because she thought he was lying but because his perception of the events he'd observed more than a quarter of a century earlier could have been distorted by his extreme youth. Although Ariel knew nothing of Zachary's personal background, in talking to him it had become clear that he'd always loved Eleanor dearly—in fact, still did—and that he blamed "that junior-grade nymphet Barbara" for all the anguish her mother had suffered as a result of her fiancé's defection. Surprisingly, Zachary didn't seem to consider Ariel's father culpable for his part in the episode, although it struck Ariel that a man in his late thirties, as John would have been then, was at least partially responsible for succumbing to the wiles of a seductive teenager.

But maybe it wasn't so surprising, she concluded wryly, shrugging as she shut the Pinto's tailgate with a bang. Zachary's attitude was just good old-fashioned male chauvinism rearing its macho head. After all, it was a time-honored excuse: "The woman tempted me...."

As Ariel walked around to the driver's side of her car, she heard quick light footsteps crunching on the gravel behind her. She turned just as a familiar feminine voice called breathlessly, "Hey, Ariel, don't leave yet. I have some stuff for you to take with you!" With a smile Ariel watched Marie Ryder walk toward her. Marie was twenty-four, a petite pretty redhead whose creamy-white skin was dusted all over with tiny freckles, like droplets of bronze. Her short, tightly permed curls were decidedly contemporary in style, at odds with the Victorian housedress she wore. The ankle-length skirt fanned up dust with each step as she scurried down the alley, but not even the voluminous feather-stitched apron she wore over it could disguise her advancing pregnancy.

In her arms she carried a brown paper grocery sack stuffed with fabric samples. "Thank goodness I caught you before you left," she exclaimed, gasping for breath. "I know that while you're in San Francisco you're mostly going to be busy meeting with your grandmother. But I did hear you tell Sam you'd check on a few of the arrangements for the Cetacean Celebration, and I thought that as long as you were going to be around Union Square anyway...well, I found a few dress lengths I'd really appreciate you seeing if you can match for me in that shop near there.''

"Dress lengths for what, elephants?'' Ariel commented with a laugh as she eyed the bulging sack. She wouldn't have been surprised if her friend had answered in the affirmative; she doubted there was anything Marie couldn't make with her needle. Although the younger woman rarely talked about her past, through the years Ariel had gathered that she came from somewhere in the Midwest, an area still rich in the tradition of quilting bees and county fairs. She'd been raised by two maiden aunts who'd taught her to sew almost as soon as she could walk. Ariel had no idea what family crisis had driven Marie from her home, but eventually she'd found her way to Mendocino, where her genius with a needle had earned her a steady income from the tourist trade. In Ariel's opinion, if Marie had the opportunity to develop her talents, she could become a recognized artist at stitchery. But at the moment she had no time to experiment and create, because she spent most of the time whipping out pillows and purses, bright simple items that were unchallenging but very salable, so that she could support herself—and Sam.

Ariel was grinning as she took the bundle from Marie, but her grin faded when she hefted it. "You shouldn't be lugging around something this heavy," she chided, eyeing the way her friend twisted awkwardly so that she could massage the small of her back with her knuckles. "I would have been glad to drop by your place to pick it up." When she saw the weariness scoring Marie's pale face, Ariel thought waspishly, *or Sam could have got off his lazy ass for a change and brought the bag over.*

She knew better than to speak the words aloud. As far as Ariel could tell, since the former basketball player had been dropped from his team—he always used a cruder phrase to describe the way he'd been treated—he'd shown little interest in anything, except, oddly, in Goodearth. Most of the time was devoted to "finding himself"—apparently at the bottom of a beer bottle—while Marie struggled to make a living for both of them. Ariel was deeply worried about Marie, but she'd learned long ago that Sam was the one subject on which the usually tractable woman remained adamant. Because Ariel valued Marie's friendship, she kept her opinions on her lover to herself. Gently she insisted, "You really must be more careful now."

"I needed the exercise," Marie said defensively, her blue eyes oddly defiant. "Anyway, the bag's not that heavy. Besides the dress fabric, there are some quilt blocks in there that someone traded me for a crewel vest I've outgrown." She glanced down ruefully at her swelling bosom. "The patterns are nice, rose of Sharon, mostly, with a few flying geese, and the workmanship is pretty good.

I thought that if I could locate the right fabric for backing, I'd like to piece together a quilt for the baby." She hesitated for a second before she sighed wistfully. "Of course, I know what I really ought to do is stitch up the blocks into purses. They're easy to sew, and tourists always buy them as fast as I can turn them out. I realize we need the money, but it's just...well, time is getting short and I've had my heart set on making something really pretty for the baby...."

Ariel shivered with suppressed rage. With great effort she kept her voice calm as she asked mildly, "What does Sam think about your working so hard now?"

Marie's red gold lashes veiled the expression in her eyes. "He hasn't said a whole lot," she admitted unhappily as she stared at the dusty ground. "Lately he hasn't said much of anything." When she looked up at Ariel again, Marie's blue eyes pleaded for understanding. "I—I know what you think of Sam, Ariel, but he's concerned about me, truly he is. The other night he told me it might be better if I stayed home when he goes to San Francisco for the Cetacean Celebration."

"So you can rest, you mean?" Ariel asked suspiciously.

"I guess—but I really do want to attend the celebration if I can."

Ariel forced herself to smile down reassuringly at her friend, but inwardly she wondered apprehensively, *but if Sam leaves Marie to go to San Francisco, will he ever come back?* The thought made her shudder. There was something appealingly dainty and fragile about Marie—whenever Ariel was around her, she felt a little like a bear who's adopted a kitten—and now she seemed doubly vulnerable. Not just because she was pregnant, but because she was deeply and blindly in love. Ariel knew what love could do to a woman, and she felt utterly helpless to spare her friend the disillusion that seemed inevitable.

Hugging Marie goodbye, she said roughly, "I'm sure it'll all work out. I worry about you, you know—not to mention that godchild of mine you're carrying. Promise me you'll take good care of both of you while I'm gone." She set the sack of fabric samples in the back seat of her car, and folding her long body into the constricted space behind the wheel, she sped away.

To reach San Francisco, Ariel had elected to drive south along the coast, following the tortuous shoreline highway. She much preferred this to the inland freeway route. The narrow oceanfront road had been literally carved into the high craggy bluffs overlooking the roiling Pacific, reminding her a little of the Corniche, which bordered the French Riviera. Heartstopping curves over sheer cliffs often slowed the traffic to no more than twenty miles an hour, but in Ariel's opinion, the panorama of sky and ocean and tiny half-forgotten seaside towns unfolding before her more than made up for the physical and mental strain of the drive.

Along the way she stopped at the Navarro River

Opera House, a crumbling Victorian structure that had once been a jewel of its kind, a gingerbread palace where famous entertainers like Lola Montez had danced and sung. For the past three-quarters of a century it had stood desolate and abandoned on its promontory overlooking the ocean, a moldering relic of a less cynical era. But now, under the direction of the Pacific Coast Regional Arts Council, the building was being restored. Inside, with half-closed eyes Ariel gazed at the empty stage framed by an elaborately carved proscenium arch, where a few flakes of gold leaf still clung stubbornly to the mildew-darkened wood. Mentally she filled the opening with rippling velvet and satin in glowing colors—the way it would be someday if she were awarded a grant from the arts council to make the new stage curtain.

There were other candidates for the project, of course, and although the arts council had expressed interest in Ariel's preliminary idea, before they issued the grant they wanted to see a more detailed proposal, with color drawings, sample cartoons, a notarized statement that she'd read and understood all applicable sections of the Mendocino County fire regulations and, of course, a firm analysis of projected costs. Ariel found the bureaucratic minutiae infuriating, but she plugged along because she wanted the grant. Not only would winning it guarantee her income for the next year—no small consideration for a free-lance artist—but the project, by far the most ambitious she'd ever attempted, would also mark the serious resumption of the career she'd put on hold while she cared for her father. Although her area of interest was murals and related large graphics, during the past two years Ariel's output, rather like Marie's, had been limited to small very commercial sketches and paintings that she could sell on consignment in Mendocino galleries. The only work she'd really enjoyed had been the posters she'd created for Goodearth.

In her mind's eye Ariel pictured again the stage curtain she wanted so desperately to make, wondering disconsolately if she would ever get the chance. Circumstances seemed to be working against her. Because of her father's recent death she'd already had to ask for an extension in submitting her final proposal. And just when she and Marie had begun stitching a sample section of the tapestry, Ariel had suddenly realized she hadn't taken into consideration the physical properties of fabric—a new medium for her—which could literally give her work a third dimension lacking in her sketches. In order to experiment with the draping qualities of cloth, she'd decided to use a live model, something she hadn't done since her student days in Paris. Arrangements for this had delayed her still further, and then, when he hadn't shown up the previous day. . . .

While she was in San Francisco Ariel intended to try again to procure a model, but as she waved goodbye to the security guard and drove out the opera parking lot, she thought wryly that it would have been a lot more convenient if she'd been able to persuade Zachary Drake to pose nude for her after all.

Zachary naked. The heated images evoked by that startling thought distracted her so much that, preparing to pull out into traffic, she almost headed her Pinto directly into the path of a speeding Mercedes. The other driver swerved and honked furiously, and Ariel could only shrug in lame apology, aware she'd been at fault. As she quickly backed her car onto the shoulder, she tried to concentrate on her driving, but the thought of Zachary's long strong body exposed to her view. . . .

What would he be like, she wondered. Oh, she could hazard a guess, of course; her life drawing classes had made her familiar with the human body as an abstract form, an impersonal collection of bone and flesh and muscle. And she wasn't without personal experience. Besides, after that doltish tumble she'd taken by the staircase on the first day she'd met Zachary, she knew all too well that his beautifully tailored suit didn't disguise any softness or flaccidity. No, she didn't need to see him naked to know he had a beautiful body. What she supposed she really wanted to know was whether his compelling aura was dependent on his clothes. Stripped of that pin-striped armor he wore, would he somehow seem more. . . *vulnerable*? Or would he prove to be the same kind of lover as he was businessman—very much in control, impatient, demanding. . . .

And why in God's name did it matter to Ariel in the first place?

Irritated with herself, she shook her head and glanced along the highway in both directions from the on ramp. No matter how attractive he might be, Zachary Drake was also none of her damn business. He was an emissary from her grandmother, his employer—nothing more, nothing less. If she were smart, Ariel wouldn't forget that. She had a long difficult drive ahead of her, and if she didn't keep her mind on what she was doing, she and the Pinto would probably end up going over a cliff right into the ocean. Spotting an opening in the lane of traffic, Ariel gunned the engine, and with a spray of loose gravel, pulled out onto the highway and headed her car south toward San Francisco.

As Ariel reached the singing strand of the Golden Gate Bridge, she caught a glimpse of the westering sun glowing orange rose across the choppy water, and she wished tiredly that she'd thought to pull off the highway at a nearby vista point in time to watch the spectacular Pacific sunset. Then with a sigh she returned her gaze to the road, aware that hours of driving had left her far too exhausted to appreciate anything but the prospect of a hot shower and a soft bed. By the time she checked into her hotel she was ready to collapse.

In her modest but comfortable room, Ariel kicked off her sandals and flopped across the coverlet. She arched her head over the far side of the bed, her hair escaping its restraining pins and streaming loose to the carpet. Extending her arms over her head, she stretched deliciously, relieving muscles aching and cramped from the day's journey. But when her amber gaze skimmed over the telephone on the nightstand next to her bed, she bolted upright, jerked back to her present predicament.

She wondered if she should try to call Zachary now. He'd insisted that she let him know the minute she arrived in San Francisco. At the time Ariel had been infuriated by the prospect of his monitoring her first meeting with her grandmother. Yet now that she was in town, now that that undoubtedly awkward meeting was imminent, she realized she would welcome his presence. Well, perhaps "welcome" was too strong a word, Ariel thought dryly. But if Zachary went with her to meet Eleanor, at least he would be able to make the formal introductions, and should the women become too overwrought, he'd be bound to cool things down. Slowly Ariel dialed the number for Seacliff Publications.

A few seconds later, after an arguably human voice had informed Ariel that it was sorry, the switchboard was closed for the day and if she wished to leave a message she should wait for the sound of the tone, she hung up and stared at the number Zachary had scrawled on the back of one of his business cards. Ariel felt peculiarly reluctant to call him at home, though she couldn't imagine the reason for her hesitation, especially since she knew he was expecting to hear from her. It wasn't, she was sure, because she disliked invading his privacy, even via wire. It seemed to her that Zachary's behavior toward her in Mendocino had forfeited him all right to have his own privacy respected. Rather, the thought of a personal call seemed just that, personal, and she found even an implied intimacy between her and the maddening Mr. Drake utterly ridiculous, utterly... disturbing.

Furious with herself for being so squeamish, Ariel dialed the number. When a low-pitched female voice murmured throatily, "Drake residence," she almost hung up again.

"I—I'd like to speak to Zachary Drake, please," Ariel stammered dazedly, trying to catch her breath. She wondered why it had never occurred to her that Zachary might be married. He hadn't been wearing a ring, of course—not that that necessarily made much difference, as she surely should have learned from Matthieu. While she distinctly remembered thinking that Zachary seemed a stranger to the gentler emotions, she ought to have realized that somewhere along the line a man of his age and conventional temperament would probably have acquired a glossily chic ex-debutante to act as his hostess and mother of his two-point-whatever children.

"Zack's in the shower right now," the woman on the telephone answered briskly, her husky undertone disappearing at the sound of Ariel's voice. "This is Laurette. May I take a message?"

"No," Ariel said quietly. "No, it's not important. I'll contact him at his office sometime tomorrow." Gently she replaced the receiver in its cradle.

BY THE TIME she went down to the hotel coffee shop for breakfast the following morning Ariel regretted hanging up on Zachary's wife. Dinner and an adequate amount of rest had revived her spirits sufficiently to make her see she'd behaved childishly. It was no business of hers if the man was married.

While she waited for her food to be served, Ariel sipped her coffee and studied the newspaper she'd purchased on entering the restaurant. She skimmed the society-and-entertainment section, looking for notices of any art-gallery showings that sounded interesting. When she turned a page, her eyes were captured by a familiar face staring back at her from a grainy photograph topping a gossip column. Ariel gasped. Even in blurry black and white with circles of light glaring off the rims of his wide glasses, Zachary was still Zachary, the force of his gaze unabated. He had obviously been caught unaware, his head jerking up as he assisted a fair petite woman from his car. Resentment and fury at the cameraman's intrusion flashed in his expression.

Ariel continued to study the photograph with frank curiosity. Zachary and his companion were both dressed impeccably and expensively in evening clothes, and even frozen in an awkward half-bent posture as he solicitously held open the Lincoln's door for the woman, his body looked powerful and compelling, reminding Ariel irresistibly of those provocative moments when she'd felt his weight pinning her to the floor....

With an effort she turned her attention to the woman, wondering if she was Zachary's wife. Pretty, Ariel noted grudgingly as she tallied the cumulative effect of very pale shoulder-length hair styled with deceptive simplicity, big eyes, dimples and a small sensuous mouth turned up in an arch smile that suggested the woman had spotted the photographer before Zachary had. Young, maybe only twenty-one or two, which surprised Ariel a little, since Zachary didn't strike her as the kind of man who'd be drawn to someone who could be his niece—or worse. Or was that just wishful thinking on Ariel's part?

But most aggravating of all to someone of her statuesque proportions, the woman was *little*. Although the poses in the picture made it difficult for Ariel to judge the subjects' relative heights, she would have bet that the dainty female extracting herself so gracefully from that luxurious automobile probably came up no higher than Zachary's shoulder, if that. Ariel chuckled with little humor as she remembered how she and her few girl-friends of similar size had constantly bemoaned the fact that, during their adolescent years, when tall boys were at a premium, big guys always seemed to be attracted to the smallest girls. With about half a bushel of sour grapes they'd concluded spitefully that the difference in height must flatter the insecure male's machismo or something. Sighing, Ariel decided things didn't change a great deal as one got older. Marie, for example, was a full eighteen inches shorter than her ex-basketball player.

Before she could read the caption accompanying the photograph, the waitress brought Ariel's breakfast, and she set aside the newspaper and busied herself with her mushroom-and-cheese omelet. When she finished, she reached for the paper again, but then glanced at her wristwatch and decided she'd stalled long enough; it was time to telephone Zachary. Picking up her check, she left the table and went in search of a pay phone.

The call was put through with such speed that Ariel suspected the switchboard operator had been alerted to expect it. Almost before she could tell the operator whom she wished to speak to, she heard a deep, disturbingly familiar male voice rasp, "Drake here. Is that you, Ariel?"

"Yes. I—"

"Where the hell have you been?" he demanded harshly. "You said you'd be down on Tuesday. This is Wednesday!"

She bristled at the anger that vibrated rawly through the receiver. "I didn't get in until yesterday evening," she retorted defensively. "Your office was closed."

"I gave you my home phone, as well," he persisted.

Ariel squared her shoulders, mentally bracing herself. She began awkwardly, "I did call your house, but—"

"But no one was there, either," he snapped before she even considered admitting she'd hung up on his wife. With an obvious effort he softened his tone of voice. "I'm sorry. The fault is mine. If I hadn't let Laurette talk me into going to that damned opening last night. She knows how I hate publicity that involves me personally. But she can be very persuasive when she— I do hope you'll forgive the inconvenience."

"I—I—well—" Ariel choked, disconcerted not only by Zachary's apology but also by the thought of someone of his inflexible temperament being *persuaded* to do anything. Laurette Drake, she concluded with a curious pang, must be quite a lady....

Briskly he continued, "You're here now. That's all that matters. Do you think you could come over to the office immediately? Fortunately when I told Ellie you'd be coming down to San Francisco, I didn't give her a firm date, just in case there was some delay. But of course she's anxious to meet you as soon as possible."

"Ellie," Ariel echoed softly, puzzlement in her voice. Ellie. Eleanor Raymond. Grandmother.... Laughter bubbled inside her. Her grandmother was waiting to see her! "I'll be right there!" she declared gaily, and hung up the telephone before she even thought to ask directions. As she paid her bill at the cash register, she glanced back toward her table. A new diner was sitting there, reading the paper. Ariel shrugged and left the coffee shop.

Thanks to a map—and the fact that in San Francisco no place is very far from any other place—despite steep hills, one-way streets and cable cars that stopped in the middle of blocks to disgorge crowds of jaywalking tourists, Ariel soon found herself pulling into the underground parking lot of the lofty high rise on California Street. There the business offices of Seacliff Publications were housed. With the sense of great relief she experienced every time she survived the city's dense traffic, Ariel halted by the attendant's kiosk and leaned out the car window to take her ticket. But instead of tucking the numbered stub under her windshield wiper, the elderly man regarded her narrowly for a moment and inquired tersely, "You Miss Maclean?"

"Yes," Ariel answered in surprise.

"Thought so," the man said, nodding with satisfaction. "You don't have to pay. Mr. Drake said you was to park in the private section over there to your left. Someone'll meet you in the lobby."

Rather bemused, Ariel carefully guided her Pinto wagon into the designated space between a Jaguar and a Porsche, noting apprehensively that except for Zachary's blue Lincoln, which she recognized at the end of the row, her old Ford seemed to be the only domestic car in the lot. She suspected the annual insurance premiums alone on some of those elegant vehicles amounted to more money than she'd paid outright for hers. The realization did nothing for her confidence.

She glanced down at the rose-colored suit that, after much deliberation, she'd chosen to wear. It's tailored styling was attractive and becoming, but nobody would ever mistake the linen-weave polyester for the real thing, nor would they assume that she'd found the ensemble anywhere except on a department-store rack, albeit a Parisian one. In keeping with her life-style, Ariel's taste in clothes was decidedly casual, with emphasis on comfort and practicality. Only occasionally did she feel a nagging need to be "fashionable."

After Matthieu's desertion, Ariel had known a few weeks of profound depression when her shattered self-esteem had almost convinced her that the fault had been hers, that he must have been ashamed of her looks. He might have married her if only she'd been chic, like the wealthy woman he did choose as his bride. Although Ariel would have denied she was trying to win back her lover, she had begun wearing inexpertly applied makeup. She had debated cutting and curling her hair. She had gone on an orgy of clothes buying that would have beggared her if her father's urgent summons hadn't stopped her in time.

Now, although she'd finally learned the proper way to use cosmetics, they'd been put away. Now each time she looked in the mirror she breathed a sigh of thanks that she hadn't chopped off the glorious mane of sun-streaked hair that had taken her years to grow. And most of the clothes she'd purchased in France—usually the pink suit, too—hung pristine and untouched in her closet in Mendocino, next to a couple of Marie's exotic creations and her well-worn jeans.

Ariel slid out of her car and slammed the door angrily. She didn't know what was wrong with her, why she was suddenly worrying about her appearance when she hadn't previously. She was dressed presentably, and that was all that mattered. She liked who she was, and if she had no intention of changing herself inwardly to suit anyone else, why should she bother with her outward image? She wasn't trying to impress anyone, not Eleanor Raymond and certainly not.... Sternly she marched across the parking lot to the lobby entrance.

Inside, the office building was a forest of huge tropical plants potted in giant urns. When combined with the milling crowds and the uncomfortably warm sunlight slanting in through the glass walls, the lobby made Ariel feel as if she'd wandered into a greenhouse. She was glancing around curiously, searching for some kind of reception desk, when an attractive young woman in a slim shirtwaist dress of jade silk approached her. "Excuse me," the woman said with a smile that sparkled against her coffee-colored skin, "you must be Ariel Maclean. I'm Gwendolyn Griffith-Jones, Mr. Drake's personal assistant. He asked me to locate you and escort you to his office."

"Thank you," Ariel murmured as she shook hands and turned to follow the woman to the packed express elevator, where they were squashed against the wall as it zoomed to the upper stories of the tall building. "I hope you haven't been waiting long," Ariel said, gasping when her stomach lurched as the elevator slowed. "With so many people around I'm surprised you found me."

"Don't worry. I only just came down this minute. The parking attendant called up to let us know you'd arrived, and after that it was easy. Zachary's been rather mysterious about you, but he did describe you very accurately."

"Oh, yes?" Ariel probed, regarding the other woman warily. She wasn't sure she wanted to know Zachary Drake's description of her.

Seeing her expression, Gwendolyn chuckled. The doors slid open, and they stepped out into a lushly carpeted foyer with a discreet bronze wall plaque that identified the headquarters of Seacliff Publications. She called lightly over her shoulder, "Oh, Zachary had you pegged perfectly. He just told me to keep my eye out for a big beautiful blonde with wonderful carriage."

Beautiful, Ariel thought in amazement as she followed Gwendolyn through a door marked simply Z. Drake. She'd known that he found her reasonably attractive, but to actually tell his assistant that Ariel was beautiful.... She was too stunned at first by the unexpected compliment to notice the man rising from his chair behind a massive walnut desk, and her attention focused on him only when Gwendolyn spoke.

"Well, here she is, all safe and sound."

"Miss Maclean," Zachary murmured with a formal nod. "Won't you sit down? I'll be with you in just a second." He turned to his assistant, and with a pang Ariel saw his green eyes shine warmly behind his glasses as he thanked Gwendolyn for fetching Ariel, his deep voice friendly and vibrant in a way it hadn't been when he'd spoken to her. Ariel listened as the other two exchanged pithy comments about someone named Tobias who was giving the Seacliff photographers a hassle about his netsuke collection. But as they bantered lightly, she lost thread of the conversation, less concerned with their words than with the ease of their relationship.

The Zachary Drake who chatted amiably with his co-worker was a different person from the tense belligerent man who'd charged into Ariel's life only a few days earlier. Physically he looked much the same, his muscular body once again faultlessly clothed in an expensive business suit—dark blue herringbone this time—with discreet but equally expensive accessories. He exuded the same aura of power and success she'd noticed the first instant she'd seen him, but his expression, his bearing, his whole attitude had changed. When he talked to Gwendolyn, he seemed—he seemed almost...nice, Ariel concluded inadequately. And as soon as the word had formed in her mind, she found herself wondering wistfully, *why can't he be nice to me, too?*

Zachary was nodding sagely at something his

assistant had said. "Yes, yes. I know Tobias is a certified crank, and he treats those ivory ornaments as if they were his children. But he does have some fabulous pieces, and we were damned lucky he agreed to take them out of the vault long enough for us to make pictures. All I can ask you to do is be your usual charming self and bear with him. Just try to be patient."

"Yeah, sure," Gwendolyn grumbled, but her mouth quirked as she spoke. Glancing curiously at Ariel, she looked back at Zachary and inquired with the familiarity of long acquaintance, "Now that that's taken care of, am I going to get to find out what's going on here, or are you going to make me depend on the grapevine like everyone else?"

Zachary shrugged with mock helplessness. "Soon, Gwen, soon," he soothed. "I'm sorry to act like something out of a bad spy novel, but before I can tell you anything, first Ariel and I need to talk to Eleanor."

Gwendolyn's brows lifted sardonically above her wide dark eyes. "And of course you never make a move without consulting the boss-lady first...." When Zachary frowned at her flippancy, Gwen continued, "Okay, okay. I get the picture. If you're going to be that way, I'll just have to use my feminine wiles and pry the information out of Ellie's secretary. I wonder if I can bribe him with lunch at Schroeder's.... I'll see you all later." She disappeared through the door, calling behind her, "It was nice meeting you, Miss Maclean."

"You, too, Miss—Miss..." Ariel faltered.

"Griffith-Jones," Zachary supplied. "Mrs.— or Ms., if you prefer. She's a very liberated lady— Griffith-Jones."

Ariel smiled blandly. "She seems very nice."

"Gwen is very nice," Zachary agreed affably. "She's also bright and ambitious, and if I don't watch out, she'll probably be running Seacliff before she's forty."

"If you don't watch out?" Ariel puzzled lightly, making conversation. "I thought this company belonged to my grandmother."

Instantly Zachary's eyes narrowed. "What are you doing?" he grated. "Trying to size up your inheritance already?"

Ariel gasped, shocked by the sudden attack just when she'd thought they were beginning to behave civilly if not cordially toward each other. Her temper flared. "Damn you, you have no right to say a thing like that to me! I didn't drive all the way down to San Francisco just to be insulted." She spun around and started to stalk toward the door.

Before she'd gone halfway, Zachary intercepted her, his big hand clasping her arm with gentle but irresistible force. "Please," he said quietly, awkwardly, "I'm sorry. You're right. I was totally out of line. After I saw you last week I talked to your father's attorneys, and they confirmed you had nothing to do with the letter that was sent to Ellie. It's just...." He hesitated, a pulse beating crazily at his temple, and the oddly husky note in his deep voice made Ariel realize he wasn't accustomed to explaining his actions.

She stared up at him, at that hard attractive face framed by prematurely silvered hair. Just for a second she thought his expression softened, seemed almost vulnerable, and that unexpected vulnerability, along with the caressing slide of his fingers on her skin, made her shiver with awareness. *No,* a voice wailed in the dark recesses of her mind. *No, I don't want to feel like this, not for someone like him!* Looking away, she deliberately fanned her resentment at the thought that he'd had the gall to actually check on her story about the letter. Acidly she demanded, "Well, if you know now that I was telling the truth the other day, why do you still dislike me so much?"

After another pause he insisted, "I don't dislike you at all, Ariel. If anything, I'm...afraid of you."

"Afraid?" she choked, staring at him again in astonishment. "My God, why? What could I possibly do to you?"

"To me, nothing," he said heavily. "But to Eleanor you could do a great deal of harm. No matter how innocent your motives in meeting her after all these years, I think the whole idea is a terrible mistake. In many ways Eleanor is a remarkable woman, Ariel, but she's not young anymore, and she's lived alone most of her life. But now, ever since hearing of your father's death, she's been obsessed with the idea of taking charge of her sweet little long-lost granddaughter, giving her all the love and affection Barbara threw back in her face so many years ago.''

"You make her sound like some kind of neurotic," Ariel said bluntly. "Is she? Is that the problem?"

Zachary shook his head impatiently. "No, of course not. Ellie is. . .Ellie, tough as nails on the outside but fragile inside. Between them, Barbara and your father broke her heart. She recovered, but that was a long time ago, and she's not nearly as resilient as she used to be. She has this fantasy about you now, Ariel. But it's just not going to work out—I know it. Maybe if you were still a child, there'd be a chance. But you're too old and too independent and—" He gazed steadily at Ariel, but his green eyes were curiously blank behind the glasses, as if he were seeing someone else. "God help us all," he groaned suddenly. "You're just too damned much like Barbara!"

Her jaw aching with tension, Ariel glared at him. If only Zachary weren't so big, she thought furiously, she might just give in to her overwhelming urge to slug him. Instead she demanded through clenched teeth, "Must I remind you that even if I never knew her, the woman you're talking about so scathingly was my *mother*? And besides, you're not being very consistent. The first day we met you told me I wasn't a thing like Barbara."

He shook his head again. "I didn't mean a similarity in looks," he said, surveying Ariel critically. "Barbara was a tiny thing, with dark hair, dark eyes, and she was never more than passably pretty. Whereas you...." He hesitated, and his deep voice softened subtly as he continued after a moment. "I assume you get your height from John Maclean, and your coloring is much more—more golden. You're much more the 'California girl' than Barbara...."

Ariel's lashes veiled her eyes as she looked away, deeply disturbed by his altered tone, the dark seductive timbre that stirred her in ways she refused to acknowledge. She cursed herself for her incomprehensible susceptibility, which, she supposed, was the result of living celibate for years. If she'd realized, since returning from France, that her nunlike existence was going to leave her vulnerable to the overtures of the first really attractive man she'd met in a long while, she might have gone ahead and accepted one of the numerous propositions she'd been plied with....

Inwardly she grimaced at the thought. Who did she think she was fooling? The blunt truth was that she hadn't made love with anyone since Matthieu because she simply hadn't met anyone who appealed to her. But Zachary....

Oh, damn, what difference did it make? Yes, yes, Zachary appealed to her, but he was also married, and besides, Ariel didn't think he even *liked* her. She didn't want him talking to her like that, paying her compliments. He had no right. Her lips tightened, and she interrupted stiffly, aggressively, "Thank you for your kind words, but I'd prefer you didn't call me a 'girl.' It's a small

point, I'll grant you, but I happen to think of myself as a woman.''

Zachary's hands rested lightly on her shoulders,
turning her to face him again. ''So do I, Ariel
Maclean,'' he murmured huskily, long fingers
sliding up to lift her chin. She blinked, startled
and yet not startled by the green fire leaping in his
eyes. With a sense of yielding to the inevitable she
watched his head slowly lower toward hers. She
could feel his warm breath tickling her face as he
whispered, ''Dear God, so do I. . . . ''

Absurdly her first thought was giddy wonder-
ment: *it's different when the man is taller.* Her
eyes closed, and as her head, cradled in one of his
broad palms, tipped back to make it easier for his
lips to stroke hers, she realized curiously that
neither Matthieu nor any other man who had ever
kissed her had been taller than average. She could
feel Zachary's fingers weaving into the thick knot
of her hair—and those other names, other images,
blurred, blotted out by the increasing pressure of
Zachary's hot mouth as it demanded entrance to
hers.

It's been so long, she thought dazedly, her
hands creeping up the front of his jacket to grasp
those beautifully tailored lapels as she rose on tip-
toe to meet him. But then, all at once, despite her
own need, his driving hunger seemed stronger, almost too strong; the force of it alarmed her. She
retreated slightly. *No, not like this—not yet,* she
protested to herself as she tried to pull away, to
evade his seeking tongue. When he sensed her re-

sistance, his free hand slid down her spine to the small of her back, clamping her tightly against him, reminding her of the weight of his body on hers when they'd fallen together that first day, making her aware once more of the tantalizing feel of his hard muscled chest crushing her breasts, thigh against long thigh.... Ariel gasped, giving Zachary access to the sweetness he sought. And then, as their open mouths joined and blended, she forgot why she'd resisted him.

Laurette, she remembered.

"No!" Ariel cried out, pushing his chest with all her strength.

Caught off guard, Zachary released her and staggered backward, steadying himself against his desk. "What the hell—" he exclaimed, breathing hard.

"I don't play around with married men," Ariel said flatly.

"Married?" Zachary stared at her. "I'm not married."

"But Laurette...."

Zachary's green eyes widened in surprise. "I had no idea my private life held such fascination for you," he rasped scornfully, his voice still hoarse from the passion they'd just exchanged.

Ariel retorted, "It's not exactly private when your picture is in the paper!"

"Just for the record," Zachary said grimly, "it was Laurette's picture that was in the paper. I just happened to be with her—and not that it's any concern of yours, but Laurette Masefield is a very close, very dear friend of mine—no, she is not my wife.''

Ariel hesitated, feeling her cheeks grow warm. *I must be growing conventional in my old age,* she thought ironically, wondering why she'd automatically assumed the other woman's apparent intimacy with Zachary meant they were married. They could be living together—they could be doing any number of extremely personal things without being husband and wife. With an effort at lightness Ariel said stiltedly, "You're right, of course. Your private life isn't my concern. But married or not, you still had no right to kiss me. Whatever the legal status of your relationship with Ms. Masefield, you must owe her some loyalty.''

"A remark like that cuts both ways, Ms. Maclean," Zachary mocked heavily as he straightened up and, with one long stride, stood in front of Ariel, towering over her.

"W-what do you mean?" she stammered uncertainly.

Zachary snorted at her discomfiture. "That kiss," he grated accusingly. "It wasn't exactly one-sided, you know. What about your loyalty to your hairy friend in Mendocino?''

Ariel was genuinely bewildered. "Sam? What on earth are you talking about?''

"You let him touch you," Zachary charged grimly.

Ariel frowned, trying to remember the day Sam had interrupted her first meeting with Zachary. She supposed she'd let him hug her, but that was a fairly standard greeting among all her friends in Mendocino, of either sex. "You must have misunderstood," she said slowly. "Sam lives with my friend Marie. Anything else is just his game."

Zachary's nostrils flared whitely. He caught her by the shoulders, his fingers digging into her soft flesh. His voice was as hard as his eyes as he exclaimed in disgust, "*Game*? You mean you're just a bunch of free spirits who sleep around at will?"

"*No!*" Ariel blazed, shock and outrage making her sputter. She tried to twist away from him, and when she couldn't escape his fierce grip, she pummeled on his chest with her fists. "Damn you, Zachary Drake, I—I don't mean anything of the—"

"Zachary!"

At the sound of the feminine voice issuing with quiet but imperative strength from across the office, the man holding Ariel froze, and Ariel took advantage of his distraction to twist out of his arms. With trembling fingers she brushed her tumbled hair out of her eyes. Then slowly she turned to face the woman who had intruded so opportunely on that virulent confrontation.

She looked about forty-five, Ariel judged, taking in the petal-smooth complexion; the pronounced bone structure; the deep-set, beautifully made-up brown eyes. She was of medium height, too slim, but her short dark blond hair had been expertly styled so that it fell around the woman's face in fluffy layers, softening the mannequin-gaunt hollows of her cheeks. She was wearing a gold silk blouse and a tailored beige skirt, obviously half of an expensive business suit, and in her hands she carried a pack of cigarettes and a slim silver lighter.

Despite her youthful appearance, the authority in her posture and voice would have identified her to Ariel even if Zachary had failed to do so. With restrained impatience she asked, "What's going on here? You two can be heard all over this floor."

"I'm sorry, Ellie," Zachary said curtly, the line of white edging his tight mouth the only visible evidence that his emotions were not yet completely under control. "I'm afraid things got...a little out of hand."

"I should say so," Eleanor Raymond drawled. "Please try not to let it happen again—at least not on company time. Of course, *I* know what you're like at heart, but after all the years you've spent refining that imperturbable facade of yours, it would be a real tragedy for you to disillusion the typing pool." She paused expectantly, her brown eyes surveying Ariel with impersonal curiosity. When Zachary remained silent, she asked with a smile, "Zachary, my dear, aren't you going to introduce us? I'd very much like to meet the young woman who has managed to disconcert my most unflappable executive."

Even without looking at Zachary, Ariel could sense the tension building in him, and she was surprised at how very calm she felt. *But maybe I'm not really calm,* she thought acutely. *Maybe it's*

too soon to feel anything. Maybe I'm just numb.
She tore her gaze away from the woman standing
in front of her and glanced sidelong at Zachary.
For a fraction of a second their eyes met in silent
communication, and with a faint nod he turned
back to Eleanor.

"Ellie, dear," he said gravely, his deep voice labored. "I'd like you to meet someone very—very
special. This is your granddaughter, Ariel Maclean."

CHAPTER FOUR

SILENCE LOOMED IN THE OFFICE, thick, almost tangible. Zachary was forgotten as the two women faced each other across the luxurious shag carpet that stretched like a bottomless chasm separating them. Eleanor spoke first. "Ariel," she whispered in wonder, her sable eyes studying her granddaughter intently. "How you've grown, so tall and beautiful.... The last time I saw you, you were barely two years old. You were wearing blue rompers, and you were tired and fussy and confused by all the people who kept calling at your house. I had brought you a princess doll almost as big as you were, and the first thing you did was spill chocolate milk all over its pink tulle skirt."

Ariel blinked in surprise. She vividly remembered that doll, with its bright gold curls and the ruffled dress that had been mysteriously and irradicably stained. For years it had gathered dust on the top shelf of her bedroom closet, too ornate to play with, too grubby-looking to be put on display. Hoarsely she replied, "I—I didn't know you gave that doll to me. I wasn't aware that you and I—that we had—had ever met."

"Oh, yes, we've met," Eleanor said ironically.

"We spent a few hours together some twenty-five years ago...the day of Barbara's funeral. That was the day I went to John, your father, and demanded that he give me custody of you, to make up for the daughter he'd stolen from me."

Shock left Ariel's expressive face vacant and slack. "You—you demanded...." She had difficulty even forming the words.

Eleanor nodded. The turbid silence was disturbed by the crackle of cellophane as her fingers spasmodically crushed the cigarette pack, but when she spoke again, her voice was calm, matter-of-fact. "Naturally your father refused to give you up, although he generously offered to let me visit whenever I wished. But I was too shattered by Barbara's death to realize that the situation must have been even more painful for him than it was for me. I stormed out, swearing I'd never have anything to do with either of you as long as he lived. Fool that I was, I abided by that vow."

"Ellie..." Zachary protested softly as she winced with remembered agony. He stepped toward her, one hand extended to comfort her, but she waved him back.

"No, my dear," she murmured, smiling wanly. "I know that ever since I had the—ever since I was sick, you've tried to shelter me from any kind of upset, but this is something I must deal with on my own." She paused again, her watchful eyes liquid with pain, and the fine lines that Ariel could now detect suddenly made her look her age. Thickly she added, "Ariel, I—I know what I did was stupid and arrogant and unforgivable, but do you think—do you think possibly now...please...."

As Ariel gazed at Eleanor, she was surprised by the fierce wave of resentment that flooded her at the thought of all those wasted years, years of loving companionship the two of them might have shared if it hadn't been for the other woman's inflexible pride. But almost at the same moment the resentment ebbed, replaced by swelling compassion. During all those years Ariel had always had her father—Eleanor hadn't had anyone. And even now, if Ariel wouldn't put aside her own considerable pride, they would both be alone....

Stepping forward hesitantly, she held out a trembling hand. "Grandmother?"

"Ariel!" Eleanor cried—and after that it was easy.

In the midst of the hugs and tears and incoherent murmurs of welcome and endearment, Ariel forgot about the man who silently watched them, and she didn't remember him again until Eleanor peered past her and said simply, "Thank you, Zachary. Thank you for bringing my grandchild to me."

Ariel twisted around to add sincerely, "Yes, Zachary, I want to tell...." Her words faded.

He was leaning against the side of his desk, long legs stretched in front of him as he scowled at the cigarette lighter that had fallen to the floor when Eleanor had leaped forward to embrace Ariel. He bent down to retrieve it, and when he held it out to Eleanor, the expression in his green eyes was curiously bleak. "Here, Ellie," he muttered, absently adjusting his glasses as he straightened. "I know you two will want to be alone, so if you'll excuse me, I have a few things to check over with Gwen."

"No, don't go," Eleanor protested. "I want you to stay with Ariel and me. We'll have something sent up from the restaurant downstairs so we can eat lunch in peace while we get to know each other—" suddenly her mouth curved impishly "—although from what I saw when I first came in, it seems to me you and Ariel already know each other pretty well...." Zachary's lips thinned, and Eleanor, who had also noted Ariel's rising color, squelched his protest by continuing briskly, "No, Zachary, I won't listen to any excuses. Contrary to popular opinion, I *am* still in charge around here, you know, and I insist that you eat with Ariel and me. Besides, I need you to help me welcome her to the family. After all, in addition to being my employee, you are also the closest thing to a son I'm ever going to have, so I guess that would make you Ariel's honorary uncle...."

Ariel winced at Eleanor's heavy-handed irony, but Zachary's tone remained carefully neutral when he spoke. "Whatever you say, Ellie. I'll join you in the conference room, but first just let me get a couple of things cleared up with Gwen, okay?"

"Of course, dear," Eleanor replied sweetly, and before Ariel could voice her own objections, her grandmother had ushered her out of the office.

In the privacy of Seacliff's mahogany-paneled

conference room they ate the delicious meal provided by the Japanese restaurant on the ground floor of the high rise. Ariel began to realize, with amusement, that her grandmother had a surprising talent for imposing her will on people—and that included Ariel and the indomitable Zachary Drake. She admired Eleanor's skill in directing the conversation, probing and subtly eliciting information without giving the appearance of prying. Ariel speculated that Zachary might learn a thing or two from his employer about the fine art of interrogation.

Although he'd repeatedly contended that Eleanor was "fragile," she struck Ariel as being about as delicate as a Sherman tank. Despite her coolly soigné and unexpectedly youthful appearance, Eleanor Raymond exuded an air of determination and drive. It was easy to believe that as a very young war widow she had single-handedly established a thriving business in the cutthroat world of publishing. It was also easy for Ariel to believe that Eleanor could have had the strength of will to sever relations with her last living relative and not weaken in her decision for a quarter of a century....

After Eleanor had lightly traced Seacliff's history from its humble inception—she had mimeographed a collection of recipes and household hints designed to help San Francisco homemakers cope with rationing—to its present notable position as one of the country's leading publishers of art books, she beamed at Ariel and concluded,

"But that's enough about me, my dear. Tell us what you've been doing all these years."

But you haven't told me a thing about you, only about your company, Ariel puzzled. Aloud she queried, "Describe my life in twenty-five words or less?" her smile softening what otherwise might have seemed like sarcasm.

"Well, maybe you can go up to fifty words," Eleanor teased. "I'm sure we'll be fascinated, won't be, Zachary?"

His head was tilted so that the overhead lighting reflected brightly off his glasses, making his expression unreadable. "Oh, yes, fascinated," he drawled.

Ariel sighed. For a moment she busied herself with her chopsticks, her fingers cramping as she clumsily tried to dip a fat batter-fried shrimp into the tempura sauce without dropping it. Zachary, she noted with grudging admiration, handled the awkward implements as if he'd been born in Tokyo. After she managed to guide the succulent morsel to her mouth without committing a messy blunder, she shrugged.

"Tell you about my life? I'm not sure there's all that much to tell. After Grandma Maclean died, my father and I...." Ariel hesitated, searching Eleanor's face closely for any visible reaction to the mention of her erstwhile fiancé. But there was none. She continued. "We lived very quietly. Father taught. I went to school. I drew the illustrations for the high-school yearbook, and for three years running I tried out for the swim team. But I never made it, because the coach told me I was built wrong for competitive swimming and should join the girls' basketball team instead. Eventually I went on to Santa Rosa State, where I majored in art with a minor in English literature. After I got my degree I spent several months doing both restoration work and some original murals for an 1890s-vintage hotel in Fort Bragg, among other less notable projects. When I'd saved enough money, I went to Paris for graduate study. I lived in France for two years, until my father had his first stroke and asked me to come home.'' Ariel paused again, aware that with the jerky phrases of her sketchy outline she had volunteered no more real information than her grandmother had. ''That's about it,'' she concluded tightly.

From across the table Eleanor watched her wryly. ''I...see,'' she said, and Ariel thought she probably did see. Regardless of their blood tie and their sincere mutual desire to establish a normal grandparent-grandchild relationship, the two women were strangers to each other, and it was going to take a while before they could lower their defenses enough to share confidences.

''And during all this travel and study, have you remained unattached, my dear?'' Eleanor asked quietly, ''I know you're single now, but are there any ex-husbands running around loose that I ought to know about? For that matter, is there some special young man who'll resent the time you spend with me?''

Momentarily Ariel remembered Matthieu. She

pushed the memory aside and shook her head.
"No, grandmother, there's...no one special."

For some reason she glanced up at Zachary
then. The cold accusation in his gaze shook her.
Ariel felt her cheeks tingle with embarrassment.
He couldn't possibly know about Matthieu....

When Zachary addressed Eleanor, his voice was
very clipped, very British. "Don't start counting
your great-grandchildren yet, Ellie, love. Ariel has
decided to dedicate her life to whales."

Eleanor regarded him curiously before she
turned, clearly puzzled, to Ariel. "Whales? I'm
afraid I don't understand."

Ariel stared down at her plate. Pushing around
grains of rice with the tips of her chopsticks, she
tried to control her temper. *Un...deux...
trois....* She counted slowly in French. If she
wasn't careful, she was liable to throw a bottle of
soy sauce at Zachary, and while the color might
not show on that suit he was wearing, she doubted
it would do his white silk shirt much good....

When she thought she could speak without hiss-
ing, Ariel explained to Eleanor, "When I'm not
busy with my own work, I'm very active in a Mendocino ecology group called Goodearth." Briefly
she described the organization and its goals. "I
know that substantial progress has been made
toward imposing a worldwide ban on the commercial killing of whales," she concluded, "but a
handful of countries—primarily Japan, Norway,
the Soviet Union—still refuse to abide by it, and
because of them many species of whales are in

grave danger of extinction. Goodearth is doing what it can to change that." She lifted her long gold lashes and stared challengingly at Zachary as she murmured, "I don't think Mr. Drake approves of money being spent for such things."

Eleanor looked surprised. "Oh, Ariel," she chided, "whatever Zachary may have said to you, I'm sure you've misunderstood him. Every year he makes substantial donations to any number of worthy causes—don't you, dear?"

"Ellie. . ." Zachary muttered repressively.

Eleanor ignored him as she continued blithely, "So tell me, Ariel, what exactly is your group doing to combat this problem? All I know about whales is what I've learned from watching Cousteau documentaries on television."

With an ironic smile Ariel said, "Well, the first thing you must understand is that Goodearth is basically a very small, loose-knit group—we artistic types have trouble blending in with the bigger, more regimented organizations—and to some extent our size limits our effectiveness. If we had more members, we could lobby for stricter laws, or we might try to organize some kind of economic boycott against those countries that won't respect the International Whaling Commission recommendation. But that sort of thing is only effective if you have virtually universal participation, and since there are so few of us, we all decided we'd do our cause more good by coming up with some idea that would make our statement in a really dramatic and newsworthy way."

Her eyes flicked in Zachary's direction, and she noted that one of his dark brows had arched upward until it cleared the rim of his glasses. His mouth was a thin skeptical line. Turning again to her grandmother, Ariel added defiantly, "So we're raising money to hire a boat, so that when the whaling fleets set out into the north Pacific in September we'll be there to meet and stop them."

When Ariel saw Eleanor's troubled expression, she instantly regretted snapping the way she had, but as she tried to frame her apology, it was Zachary who broke the heavy silence. "That's already been done," he said tersely.

Ariel nodded, mildly surprised that Zachary was familiar with the activities of the larger ecology groups. But then, she supposed, with their star-studded fund-raising events and their mailing lists that numbered in the millions, a person would have to be a hermit not to be at least marginally aware of their work. "Yes, I know that some of the international organizations regularly send trawlers out each fall, but in Mendocino we figured it would be much more meaningful if a handful of ordinary people showed they cared enough about the welfare of whales to work together at the grass-roots level to raise the money necessary for this project." She grimaced. "The trouble is, no one guessed exactly how much work it was going to be."

Eleanor poured green tea into a paper-thin cup and sipped it thoughtfully as she mused, "I understand. The trouble with doing things the most meaningful way is that it is rarely also the most efficient way. For all their paperwork and overhead, the very large charitable organizations still tend to be the ones with all the money and the political clout.'' She smiled encouragingly at Ariel, who looked vaguely depressed. ''So how much money have you raised, and how much more do you need?''

''I'm not sure of the exact figures,'' Ariel said. ''Sam takes care of finances. Until my father died, I had to limit my participation to things like telephoning, although I did create several limited-edition posters, which we sold in local galleries. I think those turned out to be rather popular....'' She sighed. ''I know there's still a long way to go and not much time to do it in. We're basing our hopes on the Cetacean Celebration that's coming up.''

''Cetacean Celebration?'' Eleanor queried, looking blank.

Zachary laughed unpleasantly. ''You mean you missed it, Ellie? It was in all the papers. The Cetacean Celebration—Lord, what a mouthful—is a highly publicized media event that will be staged in Union Square in a couple of weeks. A number of anti-whaling groups are joining forces to put on the show. There will be speakers and singers and politicians—don't forget this is an election year— all swearing eternal love for our brothers the whales and all asking for money.''

Ariel chose to ignore his sarcasm. ''It's going to be very nice, grandmother,'' she said seriously.

"The orchestra and chorus from one of the Bay-Area colleges is going to perform Ralph Vaughan William's *Sea Symphony*, which incorporates actual recordings of whale songs, and there will be a lot of artwork for display and sale. I've donated quite a number of my own things to Goodearth for this. Sam says—"

"This Sam," Eleanor interrupted again. "Who is he—or is it a she, as in Samantha?"

"Good question, if you've seen his hair..." Zachary grumbled under his breath as he scraped back his chair and stood up, stretching his long limbs as he began to stalk restlessly around the room. Ariel watched him a moment, reminded irresistibly of a caged panther.

With an effort she returned her attention to her grandmother and said lightly, deliberately closing her mind to her own qualms about Sam Walsh's sense of responsibility, "Since Marie, who is my best friend and who also lives with Sam, is expecting a baby this fall, I don't think there's much reason to doubt his masculinity. He used to play basketball, but now he's the guiding force behind Goodearth. By nature he's very laid back, but whenever the rest of us have been ready to give up in frustration because it seems we'll never be able to raise the thousands and thousands of dollars necessary for this project, Sam starts cracking the whip, reminding us what we're working for. We owe a lot to him."

Zachary halted his pacing long enough to glare down at her. "Don't be so free with your gratitude until you're sure you know what Walsh is getting you into."

"What do you mean?"

"Yes, Zachary," Eleanor echoed, "What do you mean?"

He regarded both women silently for a moment. With a pang Ariel watched the arresting craggy planes of his face, which had softened when he looked at Eleanor, become hard and implacable when he turned to her again. She wondered if this could truly be the same man who had kissed her so passionately less than two hours earlier. . . .

He stared critically at Ariel for several seconds, then addressed himself once more to Eleanor. "Since going up to Mendocino last week," he elaborated, "I've made a point of doing some reading on the subject of whaling, and the first thing that struck me was that the problem is much more complex than Ariel and her friends care to admit—a common failing with single-issue interest groups, although I don't propose to go into that now. I'd like to point out that great strides are being made on an international level to control both commercial and aboriginal whaling, and we can expect many changes in the next few years."

He paused, peering narrowly at Ariel. "But some people are never content to let matters progress at their own speed," he accused. "They cry out for equality and justice for all people, all creatures, but then they demand that everything be done their way, in their time. I'll grant you that sometimes people are impatient because they genuinely believe justice delayed is justice denied, but more often what they really crave is not justice but the tremendous ego trip of playing David to some faceless industrial Goliath.''

"Zachary," Eleanor exclaimed in dismay, drowning out Ariel's gasp, "don't you think you're overreacting just a bit?"

"Overreacting?" he shouted. "Damn it, Eleanor, have you stopped to consider exactly how dangerous your precious granddaughter's scheme really is? For the sake of some half-baked publicity stunt she and her long-haired companions intend to sail a leaky bathtub of a boat halfway across the Pacific to take on a whole commercial fleet, an *armed* fleet."

Ariel jumped to her feet. "All right, I've had enough of this—I don't have to take any more. It's been wonderful meeting you, grandmother, but I think I'd better be—"

"Ariel!" Eleanor cried, her smooth face seeming to age ten years as she watched Ariel pick up her handbag. She extended a hand in supplication. "Please, don't go. I—I'll take care of this." When Ariel hesitated, Eleanor spun on her heel and furiously confronted Zachary. "What's the matter with you?" she demanded, and Zachary recoiled instinctively. Ariel thought that in other circumstances the tableau the two of them presented— petite woman quelling a man about a foot taller and twice as heavy—might have seemed amusing. In other circumstances. . . .

Eleanor raged on. "Zachary Philip Drake, I've

known you almost all your life and I've never seen you like this. What's got into you? Why are you behaving like—like an obnoxious jerk?''

Ariel winced. She had the distinct feeling that if anyone else had dared to speak to Zachary in that fashion, he would have struck them. But Eleanor was different. Eleanor was like a much beloved mother, and even at the age of thirty-nine he felt hurt and embarrassed by her scolding. Ariel watched him turn away stiffly, muttering awkward apologies as he stared blindly at the framed book covers hanging on the far wall. From where she stood she could see, even if Eleanor couldn't, that his clenched jaw was blotched with patches of high color. Ariel knew very little about Zachary Drake, but she did know a great deal about pride—especially wounded pride—and she ached for him.

With an effort at lightness she chuckled, ''You know, grandmother, Zachary is right. We in Goodearth tend to be rather impractical at times, and I'm sure we would benefit from having someone with a level head to advise us, especially on financial matters. Perhaps if you're ever in Mendocino you could—''

''Mendocino?'' Eleanor queried, instantly distracted. ''But Ariel, my dear, I thought you were going to stay with me now.''

''She's become obsessed with the idea of taking charge of her little long-lost granddaughter.'' With a tingling sense of foreboding Ariel recalled Zachary's warning earlier that morning just before he'd kissed her. Surreptitiously she glanced at him, and although he was still facing the far wall, in the set of his shoulders and the way his raven-black head tilted slightly on top of that long straight spine she could read great tension, as if he were listening warily for her reply.

Awkwardly Ariel smiled at her grandmother. "If you'll have me, of course I'd love to stay with you a few days," she said with subtle emphasis.

Eleanor brushed one hand across her forehead, ruffling her beautifully styled and tinted hair, while her other hand fumbled for the new pack of cigarettes that lay unopened on the table beside her plate. As she tore open the cellophane wrapper she queried ironically, "Only a few days, Ariel? A few days to make up for all those lost years?"

Ariel could feel the pressure building, the gentle coercion, and she resented it. She was Eleanor's grandchild, but she wasn't a child. She cherished her independence too much to willingly relinquish any of it now, even for the sake of a woman she was sure she would soon come to love. Eleanor would just have to be made to understand. When she spoke her voice was soft but firm. "Grandmother, I think you misunderstood me. Now that we've met at last, of course I hope we'll continue to see each other as often as possible, but you can't just expect me to drop everything and—"

"Ariel!" Zachary interrupted sharply. When Ariel glanced at him in surprise, she found him scowling at her, his green eyes intent, as if he were trying to relay some message. "Ariel," he said again deliberately, "don't be so hasty about making a decision. You've plenty of time to think it over." After a pregnant pause he urged, "You will stay at Ellie's, at least for now?"

"Yes. I'd love to."

"Good." Zachary turned to Eleanor. "Now that that's settled, how about if I claim executive privilege and take off for a couple of hours to help Ariel check out of her hotel and move over to your house?"

"I can do—" Eleanor began, but Zachary cut her off.

"Now, Ellie, you know you can't. You have an appointment with the shop stewards from the graphic-arts department at two-thirty, and we'll need all that fabled charm and grace of yours to help us get through the meeting unscathed. Contract talks will be starting pretty soon, you know."

Eleanor's brows rose delicately. With a good-humored impatience she said, "Don't take that 'now, Ellie' tone with me, Zachary Drake! I've been finessing union people since before you could walk." She surveyed the two younger people acutely. "Go on, both of you. I'll call ahead so that my housekeeper will be expecting you. Zachary, you make sure Ariel gets settled properly. Don't worry about hurrying back here. I can always have Gwendolyn sit in on that meeting in your place. And of course you're welcome to stay for dinner."

"Thanks, Ellie, but not tonight. Laurette—"

Eleanor shrugged. "Another time, then." When she turned to Ariel, her smile was watery. "My dear," she said, "I can't tell you how. . . tell you. . . ." She gestured helplessly, her words trailing to a halt, her voice suddenly hoarse.

Quickly Ariel stepped toward Eleanor. "You don't have to explain," she replied soothingly. "I—I know just how you feel." She hugged her grandmother fiercely. Then, blinking hard, she turned to escape from the conference room, with Zachary close behind.

ZACHARY SWORE IRRITABLY as his foot accidentally slipped off the clutch pedal, causing the Pinto to lurch and stall for about the fourth time. "Damn it, there's no room to move around in this car!"

From the passenger's seat Ariel observed mildly, "I did offer to drive." Her mouth quirked at his furious expression. It didn't take much insight to figure out that Zachary Drake was one of those people who couldn't stand being driven by someone else. "Of course, you could have taken your car, and I would have followed. . . ."

Zachary turned the key in the ignition and revved the motor. "I told you, there wasn't any point in taking both cars. After I get you installed at Ellie's, I'll catch a taxi back to the office. Besides, I want to talk to you."

"So talk away. You've ensured yourself a captive audience."

Zachary didn't speak at once, instead watching a group of nubile teenagers uniformly dressed in cutoff jeans and tight T-shirts saunter across the street in front of the Pinto. He raised one black brow slightly at the motif ornamenting their shirts, a gaudy pink heart emblazoned with the legend I left it in San Francisco. When the traffic signal changed, he shifted into gear and crested the steep hill, braking slightly as they started down the other side. "I would think you'd find this car a little small, too, especially with a manual transmission," he commented.

Irked by his oblique reference to her size, Ariel said tightly, "I drive the wagon because it's inexpensive and still has room in the back for all my art supplies. And I prefer a stick shift because it allows me to maintain better control over my car and is also energy efficient. I consider automatics to be gas-guzzling frivolities."

Zachary glanced sidelong at her as he agreed quietly, "Yes, it's true that cars with automatics do use more gasoline, but I still think that after you've lived in the city for a while you'll discover coping with these hills makes them a near necessity, not a luxury."

Uncomfortably aware of how pompous her little speech must have sounded, Ariel shrugged. "Be that as it may, it won't make any difference to me, because I'm not going to be living in—"

"That's one of the things I want to talk to you about," Zachary interrupted. "But we'll discuss it later. Isn't that your hotel up there in the next block?"

By the time Ariel was checked out of the hotel,

she realized that when Zachary said "later," he meant it. He resisted all efforts at conversation, even when he accompanied her to her room. He peered silently out the window, his hands jammed deep into the pockets of his sleek trousers, while she swiftly repacked the few items she'd removed from her suitcase the previous night. Glancing at his broad back from time to time, Ariel found she was grateful for his taciturnity. She already suspected he was going to try to convince her to stay with Eleanor for an extended period of time, and she knew her refusal would probably spark a spirited conversation, if not an outright argument. Given the latent sexual awareness between the two of them—and she would have to be incredibly naive to deny its existence—an exchange of heated words and emotions within the intimate confines of her bedroom struck Ariel as dangerously provocative. . . .

Once Ariel's luggage had been stowed in the Pinto, Zachary again folded his long frame into the cramped space behind the steering wheel, and except for a few terse and grudging answers to Ariel's queries about the route they were taking, he didn't speak while he drove. When he turned off Geary into a district of San Francisco that had been called the Western Addition when it was developed but that was now actually part of north-central San Francisco, Ariel quit asking him questions.

He pulled the car to a halt at the curb. The house in front of them was set back on its corner lot just enough to permit it the luxury of a tiny lawn outlined with rose trees behind a low wrought-iron fence. "Here we are," he announced tightly.

Ariel eyed with pleasure the narrow but massive three-story frame building, noting the slanted bay windows and the colonnade. The walls had been painted a soft azure blue, except for the fanciful pediments that crowned the porch and roof, which had been picked out in white and darker blue. From the research she'd done when she first became interested in the Navarro River Opera House, Ariel was able to identify the architecture as a prime example of Italianate Victorian, a rather baroque style that had been very popular in San Francisco in the second half of the nineteenth century. Either the house had managed to survive in near-mint condition for the past century—an unlikely prospect, given the hazards of fire, earthquake and corrosive salt air—or else someone had gone to a great deal of work and expense to restore it to its former glory. She turned to Zachary with a dazzling smile. "Is this my grandmother's home?" she exclaimed. "It's—it's absolutely delightful!"

"Ellie will be pleased you approve," Zachary said dryly. "The house is her hobby. She fell in love with it at first sight twenty years ago, although at the time it was very run-down. In fact, it was about to be razed to make room for an apartment complex—that was before it became chic to restore old Victorians. The developer didn't want to sell, but then, as now, Ellie can be one very determined lady when she wants something. She turned on the charm, and at the last minute she was able to save the house by offering the man another property, a good commercial location, in exchange. Since then she's poured a tremendous amount of money and energy—and love—into making it the way it is now.''

''Well, it certainly looks as if it was worth the effort,'' Ariel commented truthfully. ''It's lovely. And if the interior matches the outside....''

She paused significantly, but Zachary made no move to get out of the car. He'd switched off the engine and now sat with his powerful body turned as far toward her as the constricted space would permit, one arm resting with studied casualness along the back of the seats. Puzzled by his silence, Ariel didn't realize until several moments later that he was staring fixedly at her mouth. She shivered. She was acutely aware of that hand only inches from her shoulder, the strong wrist covered with fine black hairs that curled over the cuff of his white silk shirt, the thumb that slowly stroked the vinyl upholstery as if he wished it were her bare skin.

Nervously she licked her lips, and she watched his eyes narrow, those effeminately long black lashes fluttering downward, almost brushing the lenses of his glasses. She wondered if he was going to try to kiss her again, and she retreated slightly, alarmed to discover she wanted a repeat of the sweet madness that only a few hours earlier had made them fall into each other's arms, momentarily declaring a cease-fire from their constant sparring.

She glanced at the house, where presumably a housekeeper awaited their arrival; at the street, where pedestrians strolled the steep sidewalk. With deliberate sharpness she asked, "Zachary, are we going to sit here all day?" and he blinked dazedly, as if wrenched from a dream.

He turned back in his seat so that he faced forward once more, and the hand that had rested so perilously close to her now reached up to remove his glasses. He wearily massaged the bridge of his long nose with his fingertips.

His obvious fatigue touched her, she supposed, because it seemed so removed from the indefatigable image he tried to project, and before he could replace his glasses she said his name again, more gently. "I'm sorry, I didn't mean to snap," she apologized. "It's just that....'' He peered curiously at her, his green eyes wide and soft with the other-worldly air peculiar to the seriously myopic, and her voice died away.

He really did have beautiful eyes, she noticed as she studied them for the first time without the intervening barrier of his glasses. Those mat black lashes were a frame, a stunning contrast to the irises that were almost opalescent in quality, confetti flecks of blue, hazel and yellow shimmering against the predominant jade color. Without the sophisticated aviator glasses to obscure his eyes he looked younger, less threatening somehow, and

Ariel wondered if that was why he'd never switched to contact lenses.

As if following her thoughts, Zachary slipped his glasses back into place and cleared his throat. "Ariel—" he began briskly, his deep voice that of a man prepared to embark on a lengthy debate.

"Zachary," she interrupted in matching tones, "I know what you're going to say, so there's no point in wasting your breath. You want me to agree to stay in San Francisco for as long as my grandmother wants me. Well, I'm afraid that's impossible."

"Why?"

"What do you mean, 'why'? The answer's obvious. Just try to imagine if the situations were reversed. Do you think you could drop everything and move to Mendocino if I asked you to?"

Zachary scowled. "The situations aren't comparable. I work here."

Ariel stared at him. "Just what the hell do you think I do in Mendocino?" she demanded, holding onto her temper with extreme difficulty.

His mouth tightened obstinately. "You're an artist. You can work anywhere."

Ariel stared down at her lap, and she was surprised to find her fingers digging into the soft flesh of her thighs. Her knuckles were lividly white against the rose pink fabric of her skirt. She tried to tell herself that Zachary's arrogant disregard for her work wasn't personal, that it was born of ignorance. There was no way he could possibly know the grueling hours she'd labored since her father's death, trying to restart the career that had been sidetracked for two years. He didn't know how many days she'd spent in dusty libraries doing background research for her stage-curtain design or how often she'd gone to bed with fingers aching and bleeding from her clumsy efforts to imitate Marie's facility with a needle....

And what about Marie and the baby, she suddenly thought, remembering with a pang how pale and tired her friend had looked the previous morning, when she'd handed over the bag of fabric samples. Marie was depending on her, too, not only because as Ariel's assistant she would benefit from the grant from the arts council—assuming Ariel got it—but also, Ariel was convinced, because sooner or later Sam was bound to let her down. When that happened, Ariel intended to be there to help cushion the blow.

In control of herself now, she said quietly, "I know you won't understand this, Zachary, but my work does depend on my remaining in Mendocino. In addition, I have several personal obligations I can't leave."

"I know," Zachary replied scornfully. "I've met one of them."

Ariel caught her breath. Blindly she turned away from him to stare at the neatly pruned rose trees lining the perimeter of her grandmother's little yard, and she was astonished and dismayed to find tears beading her lashes. Damn Zachary Drake, anyway! Who did he think he was to cast judgment on her like that? What right did he have to make her cry? After Matthieu got married she'd sworn no man would ever make her cry again....

When Zachary spoke again, she didn't look at him, although she sensed his hand hovering over her shoulder as if he would have liked to force her to face him. She prayed he wouldn't touch her; she was afraid she might shatter if he did.... His hand dropped away, and Ariel slumped slightly with relief.

"Ariel," Zachary began, quietly, sincerely, "I know you and I haven't exactly...hit it off well, but I want you to understand that Eleanor Raymond's happiness is the most important thing in the world to me."

"Why?" Ariel asked, biting off the word as Zachary had done only moments earlier. "Why do you care so much about her? She's not a relative."

"No," Zachary agreed. "Ellie isn't a relative...but she's the closest thing to a loving caring mother I've ever had. My father has never had time for me, and my real mother—" He broke off abruptly. "Forget about that," he said roughly. "My personal history is not germane to this conversation. What I want is your promise that once you move into that house, you won't leave it until Eleanor is willing to let you go—because if you walk out of there before she's ready for you to, the anguish might just kill her."

Amber eyes registering her shock, Ariel whirled around to confront him. "My God, what are you saying?"

"Your grandmother has a bad heart," Zachary

stated baldly. "She's had a heart attack—a fairly mild one, I'll grant you—but there's every reason to believe she might not survive another."

Ariel shook her head in disbelief. "But she looks so healthy, so—so young."

"The miracle of modern cosmetic surgery, my dear," Zachary drawled, although the expression in his eyes didn't match the lightness of his tone. "In fact, Ellie was in the hospital recuperating from her facelift when she had the attack, which was apparently induced by the strain of the operation. I remember hearing her joke with the surgeon that it was probably a judgment for succumbing to the sin of vanity." He hesitated, observing Ariel thoughtfully. After a moment he said, "The only people at the office who know exactly what happened are Eleanor and me—and now you. I hope you won't let it go any further."

"No, of course not," Ariel agreed automatically, "if that's what she wants." She puzzled a moment, remembered Eleanor's nervous movements, the shaky fingers that had clutched her cigarette pack as she chain-smoked. "Is my grandmother taking proper care of herself now. Does she try to relax? She struck me as rather jittery, although I realize that could have been brought on by the strain of our meeting. But surely her doctor doesn't approve of her smoking?"

" 'Aye, there's the rub,' " Zachary quoted dryly from *Hamlet*. "Ellie believes that if she acknowledges her health problems, it would be an admission that she's getting old. I don't think it's so much the fact of being in her sixties that she minds. It's more that she resents the necessity of slowing down. She's struggled for so long to get where she is that I'm not sure she even knows *how* to slow down anymore—and yes, the stress is definitely not good for her.''

He took a deep breath, pausing as if carefully considering his next words. ''I've tried to relieve Ellie of some of the burden of running the business, but when she realized what I was doing, she accused me of 'pampering' her.'' His expression grew tense, the harsh planes of his face shadowed as he continued with evident distaste. ''And certain other people at Seacliff who don't know about her illness seem to think I'm trying to steal the company from her.''

Ariel gasped in dismay. ''Oh, how awful for you!''

''I can take it,'' Zachary said tersely. ''I don't give a damn what people think of me as long as Eleanor is all right.''

With silent sympathy Ariel watched Zachary as he stared blindly through the windshield, green eyes narrowed against the bright afternoon light. His affected nonchalance didn't fool her for a second. She could guess that at a time when he was already worried about Eleanor the unwarranted suspicions of his co-workers must hurt him almost unbearably. In the few days she'd been acquainted with Zachary she'd come to know him as an astute businessman, tough and hard-driving, but under no circumstances would she ever have thought him dishonest. He might want eventual control of Seacliff, but he genuinely loved Eleanor, and besides, he was much too proud to resort to unethical conduct to achieve his goal; his self-esteem was far too important to him. And that same pride, Ariel realized, would prevent him from explaining his actions to those who questioned them.

Remembering the frustration and feeling of impotence that had plagued her during those interminable months while she watched her father's slow decline, Ariel said sincerely, "I'm sorry, Zachary. I know things can't have been easy for you lately, between the business and worrying about my grandmother. I—I wish there were some way I could help."

Zachary's expression was eloquent and faintly accusing. The unspoken words *stay here* seemed to reverberate in the silence of the car. Ariel met his gaze for a moment. Then her long gold lashes fluttered down over her eyes; without a word she turned to study the tall blue house again. She had thought it beautiful when she'd first seen it, but now she feared it might become a prison for her, as her home in Mendocino had been for the past two years, fortified with chains of duty, bars of love.... Was she selfish and heartless to resent this new appeal, which had come just when she was at last free to live her own life? Glancing back at Zachary, Ariel murmured, "Do you have any idea exactly what you're asking of me?"

"I'm asking you to curtail some of your...activities in order to devote a little time to a lonely woman who needs you.''

Ariel chose to ignore his sarcasm. Thinking of her work with Marie, and of all the other members of Goodearth, Ariel responded quietly, ''There are things, people.... Some of those 'activities' are very important to me.''

Zachary's mouth tightened grimly, and his eyes moved insinuatingly over her voluptuous figure. ''No doubt they are,'' he rasped. ''But maybe you ought to remember that a little abstinence is good for the soul.''

Ariel stared at him, her stricken expression quickly turning to blind fury. ''You—you pompous prig,'' she hissed. ''Who the—''

Zachary waved one hand impatiently. ''Oh, hell, forget I said that. Your private life is no concern of mine. All I care about is that Eleanor needs you. If living with her is going to cause some problems with your work, I'll make up any sales you lose. In fact, I'll make a hefty donation to that damned whale group of yours if you'll promise—''

''Dammit, you don't have to bribe me!'' Ariel retorted indignantly, shaking her head so that strands of her long hair fell loosely around her face. Glaring at Zachary, she came to a decision at last. ''Yes, even though it's bound to louse up my career again and possibly hurt a friend I care deeply about, I'll stay with my grandmother for a while—a while,'' she repeated with emphasis. ''I have no intention of moving to San Francisco permanently, no matter how much emotional black-mail the two of you try to apply. Incomprehensible as it may seem to you, I happen to like my life in Mendocino. However, since I was already planning to spend some time here in San Francisco helping with arrangements for the Cetacean Celebration, I don't suppose it will make much difference if I stay with my grandmother during that period.

"But I want to make two things very clear to you, Zachary Drake," she concluded, inhaling raggedly. "First of all, I *will* be going home again, after the ocean voyage if not before. And second, my giving in on this has nothing to do with your demands or your money or even Eleanor's money—in case you still think I'm trying to finagle a large inheritance out of her. The only reason I'm doing it is because...well, because she's the only relative I have left and...I love her."

For a long moment Zachary didn't speak, only observed Ariel intently. Returning his look, Ariel again wondered how it was possible to be physically drawn to a man who in every important respect was utterly different from her. She had always thought that sexual attraction should be the mirror image of a deeper emotional compatibility.

Suddenly, before Ariel could puzzle further, Zachary was galvanized into action. "Right, that's settled," he snapped dismissively, jerking open the car door. As he swiveled his tall body out from behind the steering wheel, he added, "We'd better get a move on. After I turn you over to Ellie's housekeeper I have to get back to work. There are a lot of things I have to do before I leave the office tonight, and I don't have time to work late. I've got a date.''

CHAPTER FIVE

"MY DEAR, is something wrong?" Eleanor asked, looking up from a computer listing just as Ariel set down the telephone receiver. "You seem upset."

Forcing a smile, Ariel slowly shook her head. "No, I'm not upset. Just...concerned."

Eleanor took one last drag on her cigarette before stubbing it out in the overflowing ashtray beside her. "Is your friend all right?"

"I...I'm not sure." Ariel's tawny eyes were troubled as she mentally played back the conversation she'd just had with Marie. Knowing her friend would worry if she didn't return to Mendocino the following day as scheduled, Ariel had called to explain her change of plans. She'd asked Marie if she would mind packing some extra clothes and art supplies—not to mention the papers that still needed to be completed before Ariel could submit her final grant proposal to the Regional Arts Council. Her obliging neighbor, the doctor, could bring everything with her on her next trip south to San Francisco. Although Marie muttered that of course she would be happy to do what Ariel requested, she sounded so worried and abstracted that after a moment Ariel demanded, "What's the matter? Don't you feel good?"

"Y-yes, of course," her friend replied shakily. "It's just—just. . . ." Her voice had trailed off. Then suddenly she wailed, "Oh, Ariel, I wish you were here. I need someone to talk to!"

Ariel groaned in dismay. From the distress in her friend's voice all Ariel could think was that Sam must have deserted her. Mustering as much control as she could she queried, "You mean Sam's left—"

"No, of course not!" Marie retorted indignantly.

Ariel scowled, baffled. "Then what?"

"The obstetrician at the clinic told me I have to quit working," Marie explained forlornly. "He says if I don't get some rest I'm liable to—liable to lose—" Her voice cracked.

Ariel drew a deep breath. "Oh, Marie, I'm so sorry." She hesitated a moment before asking, "What will you do now?"

"I'm n-not sure," Marie sniffled. "That's why I need to talk to you."

"Marie," Ariel protested, "you know I'll help you in every way I can, but isn't Sam the person you ought to be discussing this with?" Even as she spoke, Ariel knew how useless such a conversation would be. From what Marie had told her in the past Ariel had gathered that before Sam moved in with Marie, he'd eked out a living making ceramics for the tourist trade, although the few examples of his work Ariel had seen struck her as too amateurish to attract even the least discriminating buyer. But since he and Marie had been together, Sam had made use of other resources. . . .

Quite by accident, when she'd asked for an accounting of the whale posters she'd created and sold for Goodearth, Ariel had discovered that Sam had dipped into the Goodearth treasury several times to help pay the rent or buy groceries. With an embarrassment that had seemed out of character for him he'd promised to repay the money by taking odd jobs. For Marie's sake Ariel had kept quiet, reassuring Sam that his work for the group was worth far more than the petty cash he'd borrowed. . . .

Over the telephone Ariel asked again, "Have you told Sam what the doctor said?"

"N-no, not yet. I hate to bother him with something like this when he's already so busy with the celebration." Ariel remained silent. After a moment Marie continued wistfully, "Of course I'll be happy to get your things together for you, Ariel. You have a good time in San Francisco with your grandmother, and don't worry about me. Things will work out. It's just that I'm a little tired now, and with you gone and Sam getting ready to leave, too. . . ."

"But I thought you were going to try to come down with him," Ariel protested.

"I was," Marie sighed. "But now. . . I just don't know anymore. Everything's different, even Sam. For months, ever since the baby—" She broke off abruptly. When she spoke again, she sounded exhausted but composed. "Whether I go to San Francisco will depend on how I feel—and what Sam thinks."

"Of course," Ariel agreed sincerely. "The most important thing now is for you to take care of yourself." With that she and her friend had hung up.

Now, as she turned to Eleanor, Ariel reflected on what good friends she and her grandmother had already become in the few short days they'd spent together. Quite apart from their blood relationship, Ariel had discovered that she enjoyed Eleanor's intellect and admired her for the enterprise and daring that had made her a success in a highly competitive, male-dominated field. As yet, vast portions of their lives remained untouched in their conversations—Eleanor never mentioned John Maclean, just as Ariel remained silent on the subject of Matthieu Bonnard. But the two women were comfortable with each other, and when Eleanor had requested that Ariel call her Ellie rather than grandmother, Ariel complied easily. Now, when Eleanor asked if anything was wrong in Mendocino, Ariel felt no compunction about confiding in her.

Briefly she sketched her friend's situation, concluding helplessly, "I just don't understand how any man who can be so concerned about whales can be such a lazy, self-centered jerk when it comes to the person he supposedly loves."

Eleanor smiled sardonically. "But, my dear,

that's not hard to understand at all. It's always easier to love animals than it is to love people, because animals make no demands, pose no threats. They return your affection without question, they're always pathetically grateful for anything you give them, no matter how little it may be, and they don't reject you if you fail to meet their standards—a quality that I'll venture is uncommonly significant to a man still bitter over the abrupt termination of his sports career.''

Or to a woman still aching because her lover married someone else, Ariel realized with sudden insight. *A woman like me.*

Eleanor laid aside the papers she'd been working on and said, ''If your friend Marie loves her Sam, there's nothing you can do about it, regardless of whether you think she's going to be hurt. But it seems to me there are more pressing issues to be considered—namely the health of that young woman and her unborn child. From the way you describe her circumstances, it sounds to me as if she would be eligible for a number of welfare programs that would ensure her adequate food and medical care. Do you know if she's applied for any?''

''I'm not sure, Ellie,'' Ariel murmured. ''I suppose I can find out.''

''Well, why don't you do that, my dear, and then we'll see what else can be done.''

Ariel nodded absently, only half aware of her grandmother's words. She was still stunned by the uncanny accuracy of Ellie's casual remarks about

motivation—Zachary had said something similar-
ly perceptive the first day they'd met, when he'd
compared Ariel's frustration over not being
able to save those beached whales to her heart-
break as she watched her father die. Was it
possible, she wondered desolately, that since
returning from France she'd thrown herself into
the ecology movement not out of any inherent
love for her planet but because saving whales was
easier than coping with the mess she'd made of her
own life? If that were so, then she had a great deal
of rethinking to do about herself, about her future. . . .

Misreading the expressions playing across
Ariel's face, Eleanor assured her sympathetically,
"Yes, dear, I know. The hardest thing in the
world is to watch the suffering of people we love—
much harder than enduring our own trials. And
the hardest lesson of all to learn is that sometimes
you have to let your loved ones make their own
mistakes." She grimaced ironically. "Some people never learn that lesson. Zachary, for example. . . ."

At the mention of his name Ariel shifted uncomfortably. She hadn't seen him since the afternoon he'd driven her to Eleanor's house. After
he'd introduced her to Mrs. Fong, the housekeeper, he'd telephoned for a taxi and disappeared, leaving Ariel a little breathless at the speed
of his departure. Since then her days had been
spent checking on arrangements for the fast-
approaching Cetacean Celebration. In the eve-

nings, when Eleanor came home from work, Ariel had been too busy getting acquainted with her grandmother to worry about Seacliff's enigmatic second-in-command. But at night. . . .

Thoughts of Zachary were not so easy to avoid at night, in the privacy of the sumptuously comfortable bedroom Mrs. Fong had shown her to. The room was wide and gracious, with a thick plush carpet in a dusty pink color that was repeated in the flocked wallpaper. A heavy Victorian dresser and stately four-poster were made alluringly feminine with draperies of white lace edged with matching pink ribbons. Although the decor was more traditional than Ariel would have chosen herself, she thought it one of the loveliest rooms she'd ever seen, graceful and appealing and hopelessly romantic. She wondered if that almost tangible atmosphere was the reason she'd tossed restlessly in that big bed each night, wishing she weren't alone, wishing a certain man were lying beside her, a man with ebony hair and opalescent green eyes. . . .

Eleanor was busy lighting yet another cigarette, but when she saw Ariel's instinctive shudder, she exclaimed, ''My Lord but we've grown somber tonight, and here I was so determined that you should enjoy your stay with me! I'm afraid I've been a very poor hostess so far. For the past few days I've been wrapped up in the opening round of contract negotiations with the graphic-arts union—as much as I hate to admit it, it's taking a bit more out of me than it used to—and it com-

pletely slipped my mind that you might get rather
bored spending every moment ensconced here,
just chatting. How would you like to go out somewhere tonight?''

Ariel recognized this as a change of subject and
forced herself to pay attention. After all, there
was nothing she could do about Marie—or Zachary—that night. "Out, Ellie?" she inquired
brightly. "You mean to a movie or something?"

Eleanor smiled. "Actually, I was thinking more
of a nightclub. Today, for some reason, I've been
thinking of a place in North Beach I used to be
rather partial to. I haven't been there in years, but
it might be fun to see if it's changed any. How
does that sound to you?"

"Fine," Ariel said. Then she hesitated, eyeing
the shirt and figure-molding jeans she was wearing. The jeans bore the distinctive stitchery of
a well-known designer on the hip pocket, and
the shirt was red silk crepe, flowing loosely,
V-neckline allowing an interesting glimpse of the
full bosom beneath. The outfit had been ridicu-
lously expensive, purchased on a whim. Yet the
total effect remained provocative while decidedly
casual. "Ellie," Ariel ventured uncertainly, "of
course I'd love to go out tonight, if that's what
you want. But until my other clothes arrive, I'm
afraid I don't have anything very formal to
wear."

"Formal for North Beach? Don't be silly,"
Eleanor exclaimed, surveying her approvingly.
"You look perfectly lovely the way you are—so

lovely, in fact, that on second thought I believe it would behoove us to take along some nice strong man as protection. If you'll excuse me, I'll make a phone call.''

Against her will Ariel blurted out, ''Oh, please, Ellie, don't ask Zachary to escort us!''

Eleanor frowned, clearly astonished. ''Whatever made you think I was going to call Zachary?''

Ariel bit her lip uneasily. Her cheeks were flaming. ''I—I....''

Eleanor surveyed her shrewdly. After a moment, sighing, she commented, ''Ariel, I hope you know what you're getting into....'' She shrugged and admonished mildly, ''My sweet child, I was only about to suggest that I telephone a very dear friend of mine who might enjoy accompanying us to the club.''

Ariel's color deepened even further at the way she'd betrayed herself, and Eleanor chuckled, her brown eyes softening. ''Listen, when you get to be my age, the shortage of presentable men puts enough of a strain on one's social life without having to worry about arranging dates for someone else, especially someone as young and beautiful as you are.'' Her grandmother paused again, waiting for Ariel to speak, but when she didn't, Eleanor shook her head in exasperation and declared hardily, ''For Pete's sake, girl, you're only twenty-seven. If you want Zachary Drake, you can bloody well catch him without any help from me!''

WITHIN FIVE MINUTES of meeting James Dunhill, a retired stockbroker, Ariel realized that Eleanor's "very dear friend" was very much in love with her. But she wondered if her grandmother was also aware of his feelings. James was an attractive charming man in his sixties, long since divorced, with grown children and grandchildren, and Eleanor introduced him with a casual intimacy that seemed to imply a deep, long-standing relationship between them. At the same time her smiles were offhand and complacent in a way that was almost rude when compared to the wistful hunger that darkened James's expression whenever he thought she wasn't looking at him. Because Ariel liked James on sight, she felt troubled by Eleanor's apparent blindness.

They drove down to North Beach in James's car, but on account of the traffic, they had to park several blocks away. When they strolled onto Broadway, Ariel suddenly realized where all the traffic they'd encountered earlier had been headed. After the quiet of the side streets, where most of San Francisco's extensive Italian population lived, the contrast of the main street was dizzying. Ariel stared around her, rather shocked at the sleazy garishness of her surroundings. The sidewalks bustled with people in all stages of dress and sobriety. Beneath gaudy neon signs and theater marquees that blinked messages bordering on the obscene, raucous brassy noise spilled from curtained doorways.

Beside most of those doorways outlandishly

costumed barkers beckoned to passersby, loudly and crudely promising all sorts of unspeakable delights to those who dared venture within. When one of the barkers shouted a vulgar invitation to James, Ariel winced, her mind dragged back unwillingly to that night in Les Halles, before Matthieu had rescued her. Shuddering, she demanded of her grandmother only half-jokingly, "Heavens, Ellie, what have you got me into?"

Eleanor and James exchanged meaningful glances before she grimaced apologetically. "I'm sorry, my dear. I think it's been even longer than I realized since I was last down here. I know what I've read in the papers, but I guess I thought they were exaggerating. Broadway has always been loud, but I don't remember everything being so— so blatant. I'm sure the club will be quieter, but I suppose if you prefer we could just go home," Ellie added uncertainly.

At the embarrassment and genuine regret in Eleanor's voice Ariel steeled herself. She wasn't an overage adolescent anymore, not like she'd been when she'd gone to Europe. If she didn't want to spoil the entire evening for her grandmother and her escort, she'd better get hold of herself. Shrugging elaborately, Ariel said, "Oh, Ellie, forgive me for acting like a goose. I was just...a little surprised, that's all. And no, I don't want to go home. I have my heart set on enjoying an evening out." She scowled teasingly as she drawled, "But you must admit, this isn't exactly the sort of scene in which one expects to find one's sweet little grandmother...."

Matching Ariel's tone, Eleanor declared, "My dear girl, when you get to know me better, you'll find that I may be little, but by no stretch of the imagination can I be called sweet—right, James, darling?"

"Oh, I don't know about that," James contradicted quietly, smiling down at Eleanor with such warmth that Ariel quickly glanced away, feeling an intruder. She tried to remember if any man had ever looked at her in quite that way.

The smoky interior of the nightclub was rather seedy, characterless and dim. There was no barker, though, and as Eleanor had predicted, the room was quiet except for the clink of glassware and the muted hum of conversations held around plastic-topped tables. The flickering red candles on those tables provided fitful illumination, but after the blinding blaze of neon in the street, the shadows were a welcome relief. It took Ariel's eyes several seconds to adjust to the poor light, but when they did, she noticed a handkerchief-sized dance floor in one corner of the room. Behind it stood a darkened bandstand, where instruments and sheet music strewn casually on chairs indicated the musicians were taking a break.

A hostess was showing the three of them to a table toward the rear of the room when suddenly, from next to the dance floor, someone called Eleanor's name. Squinting in the direction of the voice, Ariel spotted a portly but well-dressed middle-aged man just rising to his feet. Eleanor and James exclaimed with delight and turned to wend their way toward him, with Ariel and the hostess bringing up the rear.

When they reached the table, the man asked jovially, "What on earth are you two doing here? Slumming?"

"No. James and I just wanted to show my granddaughter a little of San Francisco's night-life," Eleanor explained. "Unfortunately things have changed a bit since I was last here. . . ."

"Well, you'd know that if you read my column once in a while," the man chided.

"I will—when you start writing for a quality newspaper," Eleanor retorted good-naturedly. Noticing her granddaughter's puzzled expression, she explained, "Ariel, I'd like you to meet Don Fielding, who is actually rather a nice person, despite the fact that he writes the Nightlife column for one of San Francisco's more scurrilous scandal sheets. You'd never guess it to look at him now, but aeons ago, when we were all a lot younger, Seacliff published a fine volume of short stories he wrote."

Fielding laughed as he shook Ariel's hand. "You'll have to ignore your grandmother. She'd never forgiven me for going 'commercial.' She thought I ought to starve for the sake of my art." He gestured toward the table. "I'm here to review the show tonight. Won't the three of you join me?"

"We'd be delighted," James readily agreed. He

glanced uncertainly at the vacant chair beside Don before he turned to the hostess. "We'll need two more chairs—or is it three?"

"Three. Zachary Drake's here, too, but he's gone backstage. He should be back any minute."

Ariel stiffened with the effort not to react outwardly to that casual announcement, but she knew her grandmother's eyes were skimming lightly over her face, trying to read her expression. As Ariel seated herself in the chair James gallantly proffered, she smiled reassuringly at Eleanor. But her smile became rather brittle when from just behind her a deep voice apologized, "Sorry, Don, I didn't mean to— Ellie, James! What on earth are you two doing here?"

As the other three people murmured greetings, Ariel slowly twisted around to face the man standing beside her, and she caught her breath at the change in him. The Zachary Drake towering over her was someone she'd never seen before—smiling, relaxed... *casual*, dressed in a black turtleneck sweater and jeans that molded his long thighs almost too explicitly. In the tailored business suits she'd seen him in up till then, Ariel had thought him one of the most attractive men she'd ever met, yet even when he'd kissed her, he'd seemed somehow aloof. This evening, dressed as informally as the rest of the group clustered around the little table, he looked less intimidating, younger, more approachable. He stunned her.

In the murky light the wavering flame from the

candle on the table reflected off Zachary's polished lenses, obscuring his expression as he noticed Ariel. "Ariel," he acknowledged her, nodding tersely as he seated himself in the vacant chair beside her. "How nice to see you again. I hope you're enjoying your stay in our city." The hackneyed phrases seemed to imply just the opposite.

"I've been having a wonderful time," Ariel answered with equal lack of imagination. "Ellie and everyone else have gone out of their way to make me feel at home." *Everyone but you,* she finished silently.

Oblivious to the unspoken tension between Zachary and Ariel, Don asked curiously, "So how's Laurette?"

"Oh, a little nervous," Zachary replied, shrugging. "But she'll be fine once her set starts."

"I didn't realize Laurette..." Eleanor began. Then she brightened. "Oh, of course. I overheard you discussing it at lunch, and that's what made me think of this place for the first time in years. But tell me, how did Laurette Masefield wind up singing in the wilds of North Beach? I'm surprised her parents—"

"Her parents had nothing to do with this," Zachary said. "She got the opportunity to fill in for one of the regulars who came down with the flu. I've been delegated to act as bodyguard, and Don was kind enough to offer to listen to her."

"He means he threatened to break my arm if I

didn't," Don interjected dryly. "It wasn't enough that I got her picture in the society column the other day. I have to review her act, as well."

Eleanor frowned, observing seriously, "Zachary, I realize you're very concerned about Laurette, but sometimes I wonder if you don't pamper her rather too much. If she wants this career, she's going to have to fight for it herself. She's not a little girl anymore, you know."

"I'm well aware of that, Ellie," Zachary murmured. Without further comment Eleanor turned to address the cocktail waitress who had appeared to take their orders.

As Ariel listened to this exchange, she was startled by the wave of jealousy that washed over her at the thought of Zachary catering to another woman. With an effort she forced herself to look squarely at him. A faint huskiness in her voice was the only sign of her agitation. "I didn't realize your... friend was a professional singer."

"Only time will tell if the 'professional' appellation sticks," Zachary said. "Laurette's mother was a professional, a contralto with the Houston Civic Opera Company, but Laurette prefers pop music. That's one of the reasons I asked Don to give us his opinion. Basically Laurette's just a sweet kid, very vulnerable. Apart from the family opposition she faces, I'm not sure she has the drive and the sheer ruthlessness necessary to succeed in something as competitive as the music industry."

Only the fact that the rest of their party was

preoccupied with their drink orders gave Ariel the courage to persist. "And that's why you're so protective of her, as Ellie mentioned?"

In the candlelight Zachary's brows, beneath a drooping lock of equally black hair, were a black line slashing his forehead. He regarded Ariel narrowly, then quietly replied, "Some people need to be pampered."

She stared back, noting the way his sweater emphasized his broad shoulders, the strong column of his neck, those arresting features. It really did stir her just to look at him.... Ariel felt an unwilling tightening deep in her bosom and, glancing down, blessed her choice of shirt, since the blouson style hid her body's response. To distract herself she mocked lightly, "Pampered? Are you sure you don't mean patronized?"

Zachary shrugged. "Call it what you will—although now perhaps you'll understand why I wouldn't dream of trying to pamper *you*...."

Their gazes met and locked, his faintly satanic, hers inexplicably hurt, and when the cocktail waitress approached them, Ariel was deeply grateful for the interruption.

After their drinks arrived, Ariel toyed idly with the frosty, salt-rimmed margarita glass. When the quartet casually wandered back onstage, turning on music lights and tuning their instruments, she didn't know whether she felt relief or renewed anxiety at the thought that in a few moments she would have to face the woman who was Zachary's lover.

The return of the band signaled the end of general conversation in the darkened club, and the sudden silence was punctuated only by the scrape of chairs being moved into position. When the pianist reached for the microphone clipped to his music rack, a teeth-shivering squeal of feedback arced through the room.

"Idiot," Don Fielding growled under his breath, writing something in a small notepad.

While the pianist fumbled with the microphone, Eleanor, puzzled, commented quietly, "I can't get over how much this place has gone downhill. Of course, it has changed hands a number of times since I first came here. That was with your parents, Zachary, and that was a few years ago...."

"Quite a few," Zachary agreed sardonically.

After a couple of minutes, during which the pianist's muffled curses and those of his fellow musicians were clearly audible to the increasingly restive audience, he mounted the microphone in place and began playing a desultory riff on the bass keys. In a smoky voice invested with false enthusiasm he announced, "Ladies and gentlemen, tonight North Beach's finest nightclub—" someone just behind Ariel jeered "—is proud to present San Francisco's society songbird...."

"'Society songbird'? I thought patter like that went out with hula hoops," Don snorted, making another note.

"Our very own Laurette Masefield!"

The bandleader's inept introduction was drowned out by a strident squeal from the clarinet when Laurette bounced onstage, grabbing the nearest microphone. Her youthful energy contrasted markedly with the jaded musicians accompanying her. Ash-blond hair fluttered around her shoulders, and her petite body, draped tantalizingly in a silky pantsuit of gold-shot orange, glittered in the single spotlight that followed her as she began to sing an up-tempo rendition of an old ballad. Ariel glanced uneasily at Zachary. He was watching Laurette raptly through hooded eyes.

Surprisingly, the entire audience quieted down soon after Laurette began to sing—or perhaps the audience's reaction wasn't so surprising, Ariel admitted grudgingly, because the young woman's performance was impressive. Her husky soprano voice sounded unusually full-bodied for someone of her diminutive stature, and her delivery was so true and dramatic it seemed to inspire the musicians, whose accompaniment livened up noticeably as the song progressed. From across the table Don glanced at Zachary and murmured, "I guess I owe you an apology. When you dragged me down here I figured— Well, I was wrong. The kid's not bad, not bad at all." Zachary smiled fondly.

Something twisted deep inside Ariel, and to conceal her welling agitation she stared down at her hands. When she thought she could speak calmly, she lifted her amber eyes to Zachary. "Yes, your friend is very good. I know you must be proud of her."

With a faint frown Zachary turned to Ariel. "We're all proud of Laurette," he said inscrutably.

At the conclusion of the first half of her act, Laurette acknowledged the enthusiastic applause with a graceful bow and flashed a glowing smile in Zachary's direction before she retired backstage. The band began playing quiet dance music, and Don grimaced. "I'll make a lot of sacrifices for a friend, but listening to that band all by itself is not one of them! If you'll excuse me for a couple of minutes...." He disappeared in the direction of the restrooms.

Eleanor and James rose immediately and headed for the dance floor, leaving Ariel and Zachary alone at the table. Ariel watched wistfully as the couple fell into each other's arms, frankly clinging to each other. They seemed enthralled, and Ariel found herself wondering why her grandmother didn't marry the distinguished gray-haired man. They obviously cared deeply for each other.

The silence at the table persisted. Ariel toyed uncomfortably with her empty glass, acutely aware of the man who sat beside her, not touching her and yet so close that her denim-clad thigh tingled with the heat radiating from his, so close that she could smell the dry citrus of his cologne and the deeper, more subtle man-fragrance of his body.... She was afraid to look directly at him, fearful he might think she expected him to invite her to dance, also. And she didn't want him to do that. Zachary's presence was disturbing enough without her feeling his arms around her again, touching her, holding her—when she knew his actions were motivated by nothing more than social obligation, when she knew he would rather be holding Laurette.

A large hand reached out and captured her wrist, stilling the fingers that nervously twirled the stem of her glass. Ariel glanced up in alarm as Zachary asked tightly, "Shall we dance?"

She took a deep breath. Her face ached with the effort to shape her lips into a semblance of a smile. "Sure. How kind of you to ask."

The minuscule dance floor was so crowded Ariel wasn't sure just how another couple was supposed to fit on it, but somehow Zachary made room, grinning when he hauled her into his arms. His grin faded as he peered down at her, and his eyes darkened with a deep brooding expression Ariel couldn't interpret. She stumbled slightly, and automatically her hands clung to his broad shoulders to steady herself, her fingertips shaping the heavy muscles through the black wool of his sweater. Zachary's arms tightened around her waist, pressing her explicitly against his body, breast to chest, thigh to thigh, and she stiffened, jolted by the awareness that sizzled through her. Zachary frowned. "Relax," he murmured, his warm breath brushing her ear.

"I'm sorry to be so clumsy," she muttered lamely, not daring to meet his look. Her eyes focused on the hard line of his jaw, where a muscle twitched. "It's just been a...long time since I danced with anyone."

Zachary didn't speak, but his grip tightened, one hand pressed flat between her shoulder blades while the other traced down her spine until it rested provocatively just below the waistband of her jeans. Ariel closed her eyes and literally clenched her teeth. She felt feverish. She was burning inside and out, scorched by Zachary's nearness, her flesh heating from the friction of their two bodies moving against each other in time to the slow, smokily seductive music whose rhythm matched the pounding of Ariel's heart. Or was it Zachary's heart she felt, she wondered. Wrapped in his arms, she sensed every tremor, every movement of his body as if it were her own.

The drummer struck the cymbal with a clash, and abruptly the interlude was over.

"Here she is again, folks!" the pianist announced brightly, and almost before the startled crowd on the dance floor realized what was happening, Laurette again popped onstage. She'd changed costumes, and she looked dazzling, almost luminescent. Murmuring conventional thanks for the dance, Zachary quickly escorted Ariel the few feet back to their table. All his attention was now centered on the woman in the white-sequined jumpsuit, and Ariel thought that if he'd slapped her, his rebuff couldn't have been more pointed. Silently she cursed herself for feeling hurt. They had danced, nothing more. She was behaving like a romantic fool—or worse, a repressed spinster suffering from overactive hormones.

With superhuman effort she forced herself to watch Laurette, never permitting her eyes to wander even a millimeter in the direction of the man seated beside her. This she managed quite well, for no matter how much Ariel might spitefully wish it otherwise, Laurette really was a talented singer. Ironically, she would probably have enjoyed the show much more if only Laurette hadn't repeatedly cast melting blue glances in the direction of their table.

Eventually, after loud applause and two encores, Laurette left the stage, and once she was gone, a general air of exodus seemed to fill the club. The studied silence that had hung over the room was suddenly replaced by a cacophony of scraping chairs, clinking glassware and raised voices as people summoned the waitresses for their checks. At the table by the dance floor, Eleanor and James glanced at each other and then turned expectantly to Ariel, but not before she'd seen the intimate look that passed between them. When Eleanor asked, ''Ariel, dear, are you ready to move on to someplace else? It's early yet, and James was just suggesting—'' Ariel quickly shook her head.

''Oh, Ellie—'' she yawned elaborately ''—you know I can't keep up with you! The past few days have been rather hectic, and I think I'm ready to call it a night. Why don't you and James go on, and I'll catch a taxi back to the house.''

Eleanor frowned. "No, of course not. I can't let you do that. If you're tired, we'll just—"

"Ellie, no!" Ariel protested. She didn't miss the look of consternation that passed over James's face when Eleanor proposed cutting the evening short, so she was more determined than ever not to intrude further on her grandmother's date. She knew that no man, no matter how old or how nice he might be, would really appreciate having a chaperon tag along with him and the woman he loved. "Don't be silly, Ellie," she insisted. "There's absolutely no reason for you and James to—"

"I'll take Ariel home," Zachary said quietly.

Flabbergasted, Ariel turned to look at him. "No," she declared breathlessly. "I wouldn't dream of imposing on you, and I'm sure Miss Masefield. . . ."

Zachary's mouth tightened. "Don't worry about Laurette. She and Don are going to a party being given at the Fairmont by a producer she knows. Do you want a ride with me or not?"

Ariel's eyes widened at both Zachary's words and his sharp tone. He seemed to be saying he trusted the columnist to watch over Laurette while she made contacts that might prove valuable to her career, but the terse way he clipped off each syllable implied he wasn't too happy about letting her out of his sight. Either way he was bound to be in a lousy mood, and Ariel didn't feel up to dealing with his ill humor.

She was about to refuse his offer, but when she

glanced again at Eleanor and James, she hesitated. She knew that if she declined, her grandmother would insist that James take them both back to the house. Surely for Ellie's sake she could endure Zachary's company a few moments longer.... Grudgingly Ariel relented. "All right, I'll go with you." Belatedly remembering her manners, she forced herself to add, "Thank you."

Eleanor kissed Ariel's cheek and departed on James's arm. After they'd gone, Zachary regarded Ariel ironically and inquired, the gleam in his eye not entirely due to the reflection of candlelight on his glasses, "Did it really hurt so much to give in to me on something?"

Ariel shrugged. "I suppose not." She gazed steadily into her near empty glass and began picking salt crystals off the rim, dropping them into the dregs of melting ice and diluted tequila.

From across the table Don asked curiously, "Do you two always snipe at each other this way?" Ariel looked up just in time to see Zachary's face flush oddly.

As they waited for Laurette, Don tactfully diverted the conversation. He asked Ariel how she'd been occupying her time during her visit, and Ariel launched gratefully into a long and mildly humorous tale about the frustrations inherent in opening a San Francisco bank account for Goodearth. "Time is running short before the Cetacean Celebration, and we need someplace to put whatever money the group makes off the event. Also, since we'll be setting sail at the Golden Gate, it will be much more efficient to go through a local bank for the hiring of the boat and buying supplies. The trouble is, when Sam asked me to go ahead and get things taken care of down here, he neglected to give me the paperwork that proves we're an established nonprofit organization. He also forgot the check to cover the minimum deposit, so I had to use my own money to open the account.''

She sighed impatiently. ''Of course, I'm sure everything will be straightened out once Sam comes down for the celebration, but sometimes I get extremely tired of all the hassle. It seems so...so far removed from protecting whales.''

Don thoughtfully rubbed the bridge of his nose. ''I've heard quite a bit about this celebration lately. Sounds like there will be a lot of media exposure, free publicity for anyone who gets involved.'' He glanced at Zachary. ''You might suggest to your girl friend—''

''I'll think about it,'' Zachary replied quellingly, ''but I don't know that this is the sort of publicity Laurette needs. In addition to the well-known entertainers, these things invariably attract a lot of kooks, and I can't say I'm eager to have her classed with the kind of spaced-out ecology freaks that—'' He broke off abruptly, watching the hot flags of color unfurl along Ariel's high cheekbones, her eyes gleam metallically in the dim light. His jaw clenched. ''Oh, hell,'' he ground out. ''I didn't mean that the way it sounded. Believe me, I wasn't trying to get at you.''

"That's a switch!" Ariel snapped, and Zachary spread his hands in a gesture of concession.

"Yeah, maybe it is...." He sighed gustily, the muscles of his broad chest expanding under the clinging fabric of his sweater.

Ariel tried not to remember how those hard muscles had pressed against her soft sensitive breasts while they were dancing, the way his hands had stroked the long line of her spine.... Her eyes narrowed against the tantalizing images forming in her mind, and she exclaimed. "Look, here comes your friend."

When Laurette reached the table, her blue eyes were still glowing with the excitement of her performance. She looked, Ariel thought dispiritedly, quite beautiful, and both men hastened to congratulate her. When Ariel added her own words of approval, Laurette looked at her, puzzled, then glanced at Zachary. He said neutrally, "Laurette, I don't think you've met Ellie's granddaughter, Ariel Maclean."

The younger woman frowned. "Miss Maclean," she responded formally, "how nice to meet you. Zack has told me a lot about you."

"Nothing good, I'm sure," Ariel responded, her flippant tone belying the accuracy of her statement. She didn't want to think about Zachary discussing her with his lover.

Conversation became desultory until Don Fielding announced, "It's time for that party. Laurette, if you're ready...."

"Yes, of course," she murmured. Turning to

Zachary, she exclaimed naively, "Oh, Zack, I'm so nervous I could just die. To meet a real live *producer*. Are you sure you can't come with me?"

He shook his head firmly. "No, honey. As you and everyone else keep telling me, you're not a little girl anymore, and you don't need me to stand guard. After all, if you're going to become a professional entertainer, you'll have to learn to face meetings like this on your own." He paused for half a heartbeat. "Besides," he drawled significantly, his eyes glinting behind his glasses, "I can't go with you because I've already made plans to go home with Ariel."

Ariel didn't speak until the blue Lincoln was gliding through the dark streets now shrouded in summer fog. Watching the headlights glare against the mist, she said bitterly, "I didn't appreciate the way you were trying to play me and your girl friend off each other."

Zachary scowled, his eyes never leaving the roadway. "What do you mean?"

"I'm talking about the crude way you told Laurette you were driving me home. It was obvious you were just getting back at her because you were angry she was leaving you to go to that party with Don Fielding. You had no right to inject me into your relationship that way."

"Since you know nothing at all about my *relationship* with Laurette," Zachary retorted coldly, "*I'd* appreciate it very much if you'd quit making assumptions about things that don't concern you." He paused before continuing. "For that matter, while we're on the subject, I'd also advise you not to go weaving romantic fantasies around Ellie and James Dunhill!"

Ariel twisted sideways in her seat to stare at him. "What do you mean?"

"I'm talking about your heavy-handed efforts to play Cupid tonight, tactfully offering to take a cab so the two of them could be alone. I could almost hear the Wedding March playing in your head...." His voice remained low and tense. "Forget about matchmaking, Ariel. It's not necessary. If Ellie and James want to spend time together, they'll do it, regardless of whether you're there, just as they always have."

"You mean they're lovers?" Ariel asked candidly.

Zachary grimaced. "Who said anything about love? Don't start cluttering up the situation with hearts and flowers. I mean they have a relationship that's continued off and on for the past ten years. They're both busy independent people who get together when it's convenient. By all indications their affair is comfortable and undemanding, and it seems to suit their needs. Presumably it will continue to do so as long as you don't interfere."

Troubled, Ariel turned away again, unable to look at the dark brooding man so achingly close to her. She began toying with the buttons of her red silk blouse, trying to imagine an affair that continued for years for no better reason than it was "comfortable and undemanding." The notion was incomprehensible to her. Ariel was certainly no prude, but she'd been in love with Matthieu Bonnard, and she couldn't imagine ever again becoming involved sexually with someone, no matter how absurdly attractive he was, unless they were first committed to each other on an emotional level....

Which brought her right back to Zachary. Sternly she suppressed all reaction to his nearness. *"That way madness lies,"* she thought wryly, resorting to her father's old habit of seeking refuge in Shakespeare. She smiled tenderly at the memory of her gentle, hopelessly romantic father, wondering what he would have made of a cynic like Zachary Drake. Unfortunately, she suspected the two men would have been utterly alien to each other.

She was unaware that Zachary had interpreted the expression on her face as she silently fingered the soft fabric of her blouse—until he demanded harshly, "What's the matter, Ariel? Have I demolished your naive little dreams of rice and white lace and love everlasting?"

Her eyes were sad, almost pitying as she glanced up at him. "No, Zachary," she answered firmly. "Try as you might, there's no way I'll ever let you destroy my faith in love."

Behind his glasses Zachary's black brows came together sharply. "Lady, sometimes you baffle me."

Ariel said nothing. After Zachary had pulled his

car to a halt at the curb in front of Eleanor's house, she silently walked up to the dark porch with him, handing him her key. He opened the door and quickly glanced inside, flipping on the light in the entryway. "All clear," he commented tersely as he handed the key back to her.

Ariel forced a polite smile as she thought desolately of the empty rooms awaiting her, lonely and cheerless without Eleanor's comforting presence. How differently the evening might be ending if only Zachary liked her, if only she dared.... Perfunctorily she said, "Thank you for driving me home."

Zachary peered down at her, his green eyes intent as he studied her forlorn expression. When she moved as if to step inside, he laid a hand on her arm to prevent her. "Oh, Ariel," he sighed, "forget what I told you about Ellie and James. There's no need to worry about them."

She supposed she ought to be grateful he could so misconstrue the cause of her sagging spirits, but at the same time his obtuseness angered her. He just couldn't seem to understand feelings— hers or her grandmother's. "I'm not worried," Ariel insisted doggedly, "because I think you're wrong. Yes, Ellie and James are both 'busy independent people,' but they obviously care deeply about each other, and although my grandmother does seem to take him a little for granted, it's abundantly clear to me that James is in love with her."

He snapped, "Then you ought to feel sorry for

James, because apparently he's had to settle for what he can get.''

Ariel took a deep breath, and quietly replied, ''If you're right—and I'm not convinced you are—then I think I feel sorry for both of them.'' With painful clarity she remembered the way her pride had deafened her to Matthieu's importunings once she'd become aware of his true feelings, or lack of them; how she'd refused to settle for something less than love. She'd never regretted that decision, but suddenly her eyes clouded as the thought formed in her mind, *I would settle for an affair with you, Zachary if I had to....*

At her obvious distress his anger seemed to leach out of him. He stroked her cheek lightly, and she quivered at his touch. ''Don't worry, Ariel,'' he murmured. ''I promise you everything will be all right.'' He bent down to kiss her.

His breath was warm against her cheek, his lips soft and caressing, brushing over hers with great gentleness. But Ariel needed much more than gentleness, and at the touch of his mouth she exploded. The first time Zachary had kissed her, that day in his office, he'd been the one driven by a compulsive need that frightened her with its power. Now, with a hunger she knew would shame her later, Ariel overtook and surpassed him, leaning forward, lifting her face, her arms sliding around his waist to hold him when he would have retreated. She felt him hesitate as if startled by the strength of her desire—then his arms were around her, too, crushing her against his broad chest as they came together equally.

When they parted reluctantly, Ariel drew a deep rasping breath and glanced down, deliciously aware of her fingers splayed over the bronzed skin beneath the black wool of Zachary's sweater, relishing the heat that radiated from damp resilient flesh stretched taut over hard muscles. Her own blouse was unbuttoned, the silk falling away to reveal her full breasts in the flimsy bra. As she watched, mesmerized, one of Zachary's hands stroked across a swelling mound, teasing the nipple through the sheer lace until Ariel groaned and arched against him to deepen the embrace. When her body rubbed intimately against his, she felt with intense clarity that he was as aroused as she was.

For a moment she leaned her forehead against his chest, shaking. Then, with a breath that was almost a sob, she gazed up at him again, her eyes wide and golden and defenseless in the spill of light from the open door. She knew the chance she was taking. She knew that against all reason she was perilously close to falling in love with Zachary Drake. It made no sense for her to be drawn to a man markedly different from her in taste, in values; a man, moreover, who was already emotionally committed elsewhere. But she was. He aroused her just by looking at her, and she realized wistfully that their fierce physical attraction was somehow easier to accept than the equally strong but even more bewildering mental appeal he also held for her.

She wished she could find solace in the undeniable irony that, against his will, Zachary wanted her as much as she wanted him. Instead she felt only hurt at his resentment.

Driven by a need she couldn't explain and knowing she was making herself vulnerable to his rejection, she whispered huskily, "W-would you like to come inside for . . . coffee?"

For endless seconds Zachary didn't speak, his craggy features shadowed and unreadable. At last he shifted restlessly, turning slightly in the light, and Ariel could see his mouth curl up in a rueful smile. "There's nothing I'd like better than . . . coffee," he murmured wryly, "but I'm not sure this is the place. Somehow I don't think either of us really wants to take a chance on Ellie. . . ." He paused meaningfully.

Ariel's face fell, and aching with frustration, she stared blindly at his sweater. She'd forgotten all about Ellie—just as momentarily her hunger had driven away all thought of Laurette. Disconsolately she sighed. "No, of course you're right. I'm sorry. I didn't think."

His long fingers curled under her chin and lifted her face to his again. His eyes were dark, enigmatic. "Ariel," he suggested with soft purpose, "we could drive to my house in less than ten minutes."

Her silky lashes fluttered down over her eyes, veiling her expression. Less than ten minutes, he'd said. Only a few hundred heartbeats from now she could be at his home, alone at last with this man she wanted so desperately, safe from all interruptions.... A bolt of sheer sensation coursed through her, but as she got control of herself she knew what she had to say. She was surprised at how steady her voice sounded as she mouthed the words. "No, Zachary. Not tonight. I don't think it would be...wise."

For a long moment he studied her in silence; then he nodded. "Perhaps not," he agreed slowly, dropping his hand. He cocked his head toward the open door. "You'd better go inside now. The fog's coming in, and you'll catch cold in that thin blouse. Don't forget to lock the door behind you." With a brief salute he turned and strode back to the waiting Lincoln.

CHAPTER SIX

ARIEL MADE A FEW TENTATIVE STROKES with her charcoal pencil, peered critically at the result and wadded the paper into a ball. She tossed it into the cut-glass bowl in the center of Eleanor's gleaming Victorian dining table, where it landed on top of a growing heap of spoiled sketches. Sighing deeply, she covered her face with her hands and groaned.

She had to face the sobering fact: she was losing the inspiration for this project. Her difficulties sprang from more than just the frustration of dealing with the Rand Agency. After learning that Ariel was temporarily based in San Francisco, the company had readily offered to find her another model. But realizing she would have to engage a new collaborator if Marie truly couldn't continue with her work, Ariel told the agency she preferred to wait until she knew exactly what her plans would be before committing herself further.

Only to herself was Ariel willing to admit that her reluctance sprang from deeper, more insidious doubts about the project, about her ability to carry it through. The creative forces that had led her to design a magnificent tapestry symbolizing the mountains, the sky, the sea and the man-creature who was at once caretaker and destroyer were drying up. She's been robbed of her vitality by the many traumatic events that had occurred since she'd submitted her original proposal to the arts council: her father's death, her reconciliation with her grandmother, her growing love for Zachary.... The emotional shocks, good as well as bad, had left her feeling drained, burned out. Ariel prided herself on her professionalism, and now she was beginning to wonder if it might not be better for all concerned if she simply contacted the arts council and told them she was withdrawing her application.

In the hallway the telephone burred stridently. Automatically Ariel pushed back her chair, but before she could stand up she heard Mrs. Fong switch off her vacuum cleaner in another room and go to answer it. A couple of seconds later the housekeeper popped in from the hallway. "It's for you," she said, smiling, then paused, glancing in surprise at the bowl full of crushed paper.

Feeling like a naughty child, Ariel flushed guiltily. "I'm sorry for the mess. I'll clean it up in just a minute."

Mrs. Fong shrugged. "Don't worry about it. You'd better get the phone. I think it's Mr. Drake."

Ariel's color deepened. "Z-Zachary?" she echoed unsteadily. At the woman's nod Ariel stepped quickly into the hallway.

She picked up the receiver with trembling fingers. Too few hours had passed since that scene on the porch. She was still feverish with the memory of how he'd held and caressed her, how they'd held each other.... "Zachary," she said with unconvincing casualness. "How good of you to call. What can I do for you?"

Although his words were unimpeachably courteous, the dry chuckle underlying his deep tones told her he'd thought of several other responses to her artless question. "Actually...I was wondering if you might be free to have lunch with me today."

"Lunch? You mean eat at the office with you and Ellie?"

"No. Ellie's having a working lunch with some union people. I thought perhaps you and I...."

Ariel felt oddly breathless. "I—I'd like that very much," she said huskily.

Zachary's response was briskly approving. "Good. It'll give us a chance to talk about your save-the-whales rally. I've been thinking over Don Fielding's suggestion that Laurette sing during the festivities—maybe you could give me some more details on what's involved."

WELL, WHAT DID YOU EXPECT, Ariel asked herself angrily for about the twelfth time as she and Zachary crossed the street into Union Square. *A declaration of love?* And for the twelfth time she admitted abashedly that yes, that was exactly what she'd expected. She had thought.... She had thought that the passionate episode at Eleanor's front door the previous night had meant something to Zachary, had indicated that, like her, he felt a mutual attraction on more than just the physical level. What that incident had really meant, she realized bitterly, was that she'd shamelessly thrown herself at him, and like any red-blooded male, he hadn't been averse to accepting her blatant invitation.

But it wouldn't happen again, she vowed with silent conviction, deliberately turning her attention to the activity in the park. Hammers banged, their metallic clang dissipating into the perpetual din as carpenters nailed together the portable grandstand they were erecting at the base of the tall Civil War monument. Where Northern sympathizers had once held mass meetings, workers from nearby shops and office buildings ate their paper-bag lunches, oblivious to the noise and the college students who were plastering every vertical surface with posters announcing the Cetacean Celebration. Ariel stared around her, momentarily distracted from her personal problems by the thought that soon the relatively peaceful square would be jammed with—hopefully—thousands of people united in one cause, their fervent determination to end the senseless slaughter of whales.

Most of them, anyway, she amended acidly, looking at Zachary and noting with pleasure that the smooth line of his perfectly tailored jacket was slightly spoiled by the sheaf of papers he'd tucked into his breast pocket, papers designating Laurette Masefield as one of the featured performers in the upcoming celebration.

After an elegant lunch, which Ariel had been incapable of enjoying, she'd taken Zachary to the office serving temporarily as celebration headquarters. There she'd watched him use potent charm—and a hefty donation—to cajole the entertainment committee into scheduling his girl friend on the program. Standing on the sidelines, silently observing the ease with which he manipulated both a stodgy society matron and an intense young man, Ariel didn't know whether she ought to feel impressed or cynical. Mostly she felt pain at the thought that he was doing all this for Laurette, always Laurette. . . .

She sincerely hoped none of her hurt showed as she described to Zachary the way Union Square would be laid out for the rally. Gesturing like a tour guide, she explained airily, "Speakers and individual entertainers like Laurette will address the crowd from the grandstand. You'll be able to hear her from any place in the park, since there'll be a sound truck and plenty of PA equipment—but of course that won't be set up until the morning of the celebration. When it comes time for the orchestra and chorus to perform the *Sea Symphony*, they'll be seated directly in front of the grandstand, and they'll take their chairs and instruments away just as soon as they've finished. Other than that, individual groups like Goodearth will have their booths or tables or whatever arranged all around the perimeter of the square."

Zachary nodded, scanning the park through

narrowed eyes as he commented, "You seem to have everything surprisingly well organized."

"You mean surprisingly well for a bunch of 'spaced-out ecology freaks'?" she queried tightly, longing for an excuse, any excuse, to hate him.

He glared down at her. "I mean for any group of amateurs attempting to organize an event of this size. Damn it, Ariel, I apologized last night for saying that!"

Already she was regretting her pettiness. After all, she was the one with the emotional problem, not Zachary. He'd never asked her to love him.... "Yes, I know you apologized," she agreed quietly, then assessed him frankly, her golden eyes shadowed with a reproach directed as much toward herself as him. "I just wish it was because you'd changed your attitude toward us and our goals, rather than simply because you regret that you were rude."

"Ariel," Zachary said flatly, "I refuse to apologize for believing that Goodearth and most of the other groups participating in this rally are seeking simplistic and impractical solutions to highly complex problems."

"I don't expect you to," she said, peering ahead. In their path a flock of brown-and-gray pigeons ruffled and cooed as a couple crumbled up the remains of their lunches. The woman was dressed very conventionally, whereas the man was wearing a pink tutu. The banjo case slung across his burly shoulders identified him as one of the street musicians who roved downtown San Francisco. Ariel cut sharply sideways, not to avoid the couple but to put some distance between her and Zachary. After she'd schooled her expression she observed dryly, "No matter how impractical you may think us, Zachary, I couldn't help noting that you were eager enough to whip out your checkbook and make a donation to buy Laurette a spot on the program."

"And the committee was just as eager to accept it!" Zachary countered sharply.

Ariel wheeled around so suddenly that Zachary almost collided with her. Now that the morning mist had burned away, the noonlight was unusually bright and clear, and when he jerked to a halt, his raven hair gleamed, catching the sunshine. To subdue the hunger that welled up in her at the sight of him, Ariel demanded, "Why shouldn't we take your money? Self-interest or true belief—one pays the bills as well as the other!" Out of the corner of her eye she observed the man and woman staring at her and Zachary, and she turned away again, embarrassed.

For a moment her furious words hung thickly between them, the charged silence punctuated by the pounding hammers. Then Zachary said calmly, "Speaking of money, I'm curious to know more about what you've arranged for Goodearth. I gather you do expect to earn something from the event?"

Staring at the ground, Ariel nodded, grateful for the change of subject. Speaking of practical matters would give her a chance to calm her overwrought nerves, a chance she desperately needed, since she'd already made enough of a fool of herself where Zachary was concerned. "Although most of the money raised will be used to help influence legislation in Washington," she explained, "each group that participates in the celebration will get a cut. And of course Goodearth will be selling artwork and crafts, as well. All in all we hope to raise the balance of what we'll need to hire the trawler to take us out into the Pacific."

"And how much is that?" Zachary asked.

Ariel shrugged. "I'm not sure of the exact figure. Sam handles all the paperwork."

"Your friend with the hair?" Zachary muttered, scowling.

Puzzled by his tone, Ariel said, "You know who Sam is."

"Yes—unfortunately. But I thought you were in charge of banking."

"No. I only just opened an account for the group because I happened to be the first person to come south for the celebration. As soon as Sam arrives along with the rest of the members, I'll turn everything over to him."

Zachary's scowl deepened. Behind his glasses his dark brows came together in a thick skeptical line. Spacing his words deliberately, he demanded, "Are you telling me you intend to let Walsh handle all the money—and it must be a substantial amount, if you seriously plan to charter a boat for an ocean voyage—without requiring a bond or even asking for a simple accounting?"

Looking up at him, Ariel gestured nonchalantly. "Sam's always handled the money. There's never been any problem."

Zachary persisted. "How do you know?"

"Mon Dieu," Ariel swore softly, her tawny eyes flashing with impatience. "You executive types never trust anyone, do you...." With a belligerent sigh she lifted her chin, the weight of her heavy knot of sun-bleached hair tilting her head back regally. "Zachary," she asserted, "I'm all too aware you and Sam didn't hit it off very well the day you met, which I guess isn't surprising, considering.... But you have to understand, the man is my friend. I've known him ever since I returned from France, Marie even longer, and while I can't pretend I approve of the way he treats her, I've never had any reason to question his integrity in money matters."

For a moment she paused, suddenly remembering Sam's petty thievery from the Goodearth account, seriously considering Zachary's tacit doubts about the other man. Then she nodded to herself, reaffirming her own contention that Sam's only real problem with money was his reluctance to earn any. And he'd regretted that earlier incident. Aloud she continued firmly, "We owe Sam a lot. He practically started Goodearth single-handedly."

Zachary was silent, but his expression indicated he didn't think much of Sam's accomplishment. In an effort to convince him, she went on fervently, "When that pod of California grays I told you about beached in Mendocino, the incident made TV newscasts all over the state, even a few network spots. It happened that my name was mentioned as the person who'd found them, and some people who saw the report sent me money—not a whole lot, granted, but 'a little something to help save the whales,' they said.''

She hesitated again, her emotions so volatile that moisture beaded on her skin as she remembered that long desperate and ultimately futile effort to rescue the pathetically helpless sea creatures. For weeks after the Coast Guard cutter had towed the huge carcasses out into the Pacific for disposal, Ariel had felt shattered, although she'd tried to hide her distress from her ailing father. Huskily she continued, "After it was all over, I was just going to return the checks to the people who sent them, but Sam said no. He said if strangers cared enough to donate their hard-earned money, then we owed it to them to do something really important to justify their concern. He suggested the trawler idea. We knew it would take a long time, but everyone agreed. Since I was busy taking care of my personal responsibilities and Marie was working, it was left to Sam to get things moving." Taking a deep breath, she concluded firmly, "I think he's done a fine job."

She stared up defiantly at Zachary, who was staring enigmatically at her. As his gaze slid upward over her long stately figure, lingering momentarily on her voluptuous breasts, his gem-colored eyes flashed and darkened, but when at last he spoke, he still sounded dubious. "Yes, well, that's all very touching, but I think you're being incredibly naive. Even in the best of circumstances—"

Ariel exploded then. Fueled by hurt and frustration and heedless of the public park in which they stood, the passersby who were beginning to gawk as they strolled through the square, her voice cracked dangerously as she shouted, "You don't trust anyone, do you—not Sam, certainly not me! You think everyone in the whole world except Ellie and—and possibly Laurette is just out to get—"

"Ariel..." Zachary admonished, his voice low as he crossed to her in one long stride that brought him so close they were almost touching.

She faltered, briefly recalled to awareness of their surroundings. Then distress made her plunge on fiercely. "I mean it—you don't trust anyone. You don't believe anyone acts for any reason but self-interest. I'm not blind. I can see you've convinced yourself that Sam's and my involvement in Goodearth is just a front for—for—"

Zachary hauled her into his arms and kissed her.

Her lashes flew up in astonishment, almost brushing his glasses, and she squawked as the flow of hot indignant words was stoppered against his mouth. When she tried to pull away, he laced his hands into her hair and held her head immobile. Breathless wild seconds passed as she stared at him, his green eyes filling the universe, his hungry lips seductive now, making a mockery of every kiss she thought she'd experienced previously. Against her will she felt her resistance fading, and her own lips softened, opened to him, warm and welcoming as her body—

As abruptly as he'd grabbed her, Zachary let her go.

She stumbled backward a step, straightening her spine and trying not to notice the people in the square watching them with frank speculation. She looked at Zachary. Her emotions were written on her rosy cheeks, as clear and fragile as tears. "W-why did you do that?" she stammered hoarsely.

His smile was indulgent. "It was the best way to shut you up," he drawled outrageously. When her eyes grew round with fury, he added in an undertone, "Ariel, you were perilously close to hysteria."

She turned away without speaking, knowing this wasn't true but mortified to think he was laughing at her. She stared up at the tall buildings surrounding the square, their height amplified by the steep hills on which they were built. Way up on the gleaming glass walls of one of the newer skyscrapers she could see reflected the dark blue waters of San Francisco Bay, which was invisible from the ground observer's perspective, and she told herself that before she returned to Mendocino she really must go on a sketching tour of the city.

Behind her Zachary touched her shoulder caressingly. "The fault was mine. I've always been susceptible to beautiful women...."

She shrugged his hand away without looking at him and declared, "God, I hate it when you patronize me!"

"Is that what you think I'm doing?" he asked quietly. Suddenly he sounded genuinely puzzled.

"I *know* it's what you're doing," she countered in subdued tones. "You're not susceptible to me. You don't even like me—or anything I stand for, either. From the first day we met you've positively radiated disapproval of my friends and all we're trying to accomplish. I'm well aware that the way the committee let you use your checkbook to buy your girl friend a spot on the program has just confirmed everything you think you know about us—you've forgotten that that donation you made this morning is money earmarked for a very worthy cause."

"But, Ariel—"

At last she turned to face him. She felt as if her heart were physically breaking, but her voice, though tired, remained firm. "No, Zachary, don't say anything—don't do anything. I've had all I can take. I have enough problems of my own without enduring your rudeness and your insults, as well—especially when you seem to think that a quick grope now and then is all it takes to keep me pacified." As she spoke, she saw his face flush dully, the harsh planes distinct. He looked about to burst, but when he didn't speak at once, she continued with more control than she'd thought herself capable of at that moment. "Of course I want you, Zachary—after all, you're probably the most attractive man I've ever met—but I refuse to succumb to that attraction. I am not some pathetic, sex-starved spinster so hard up for attention that I'll make love with a man who despises me." She took a deep rasping breath. "So I'm telling you here, now—*don't ever touch me again*. As far as I'm concerned, you can save it all for Laurette." Without waiting for a response, she turned and strode out of the park.

"YOU NEVER TOLD ME you had rich relatives," Sam accused her.

Ariel, carefully clipping pen-and-ink drawings to wires strung behind the card tables serving as Goodearth's booth, ignored him. She glanced nervously toward the sky, thankful that the early-morning fog had burned away before the damp could damage the delicate artwork. Now the only problem was to ensure that direct sunlight didn't fade them. When Sam sidled closer and repeated his petulant charge, Ariel turned on him impatiently.

"Damn it, Sam, I wish you'd quit harping on my so-called 'rich relatives'! Oil sheikhs are rich. My grandmother is just a woman who's worked very hard all her life to earn what she has." And Eleanor was still working hard—perhaps too hard, Ariel thought with concern, her amber eyes darkening at the memory of her grandmother's obvious exhaustion each night when she dragged herself home from Seacliff. Contract talks with the graphic-arts union had apparently hit some sort of snag, and for the first time, the previous evening, Eleanor had hinted that a strike might be possible.

"Then how come you never got around to introducing me and the others to this hard-working lady?" Sam persisted.

"There hasn't been time. Now just leave it, will you? I don't want you to hit her up for a donation to Goodearth."

Sam's eyes narrowed. "Why not?" he asked bluntly. "Don't you think she'd be delighted to help out on a project that's important to you?"

Ariel shook her head, silencing him. She was rather puzzled by his attitude. She'd encountered a monomaniac intensity in other members of the ecology groups she frequented, but she couldn't recall ever having seen Sam react quite so strongly previously. Forcing herself to answer calmly and seriously, she explained, "That's just it. Ellie cares about *me*. She feels this—this compulsion to try to make up for all those years we didn't know each other." Her voice and her expression softened as she said gently, "Please try to understand. Goodearth is supposed to be a group of knowledgeable and concerned citizens who are trying to prevent an ecological tragedy. We may be small, but our strength derives from the fact that we *know* our cause is just. My grandmother doesn't know or particularly care anything about whales. She'd show an interest in whatever I happened to be doing, for no better reason than just because I was involved in it—and I won't ask that of her.''

Beneath his sweeping blond mustache Sam's mouth thinned. ''Not even if it would make the difference between our reaching our goal or not?''

''What do you mean?'' Ariel demanded. ''Are you saying we won't be able to make the trip after all? Has something happened since I left Mendocino that I don't know about?''

Sam wove his fingers into the bright hair at his temples and brushed it back away from his face. Boyishly he scuffed his toes together before he looked at Ariel again. ''It's money,'' he said flatly. ''There's just not enough.''

''I don't understand. We've been working so hard, for so long. You said— I thought—''

''Inflation,'' he explained tersely. ''As soon as I got into town I contacted the charter line that owns the boat we wanted, and they tell me now that the cost of the trip has gone up fifty percent from the estimate they gave us when we started two years ago. I don't see any way we can possibly raise the extra.''

Ariel felt as if she'd been struck. ''No! Why didn't you tell me this earlier?'' she gasped, growing pale at the memory of all the endless frustrating hours she, Sam, Marie and the others had spent working toward their goal, all the posters she'd drawn, the phone calls she'd made. She thought again of the pod of whales she had watched die and the anonymous benefactors from around the state who had cared enough to send donations to help in some small way. "No," she repeated hoarsely. "You must be wrong. It can't end like this. It's not *fair*...."

Sam's pale eyes were oddly opaque. "Facts of life, babe," he muttered unanswerably.

Looking over her shoulder, Ariel watched in silent distress as her other friends in the booth blithely went about their business. Quietly she asked, "Do they know?"

"Sort of—only I think they're hoping for a miracle, like maybe finding a backer to sponsor the trip...." He paused. "Look, Ariel, I wouldn't expect you to ask your grandmother to dig into her own pocket for the money. I was thinking more along the lines of seeing if that company of hers would back us. They'd probably jump at the chance for a fat tax write-off. After all, what's a few thousand dollars to a big corporation, right?"

He looked hopefully at Ariel, but she was still skeptical. "I still think you're missing the point, Sam. We've always maintained that Goodearth's greatest strength was the fact that we *didn't* have corporate—"

"Don't preach at me!" he interrupted harshly. "I'm the one who got this group together, remember, and if I say—" At the expression on Ariel's face he broke off abruptly. After a moment he declared, "I don't know what the hell you're so self-righteous about. Your grandmother runs a big business, and you know as well as I do that all those people make their profits by ripping off the little guy, anyway.''

Her eyes shimmering with fury, Ariel simply stared at Sam. ''I'm going to try to forget you said that,'' she stated with deadly control, ''because I know you're upset about the money situation. But don't you *ever* speak like that about my grandmother again!''

Resolutely she turned away. After she'd hung up the last of the drawings she stepped over to one of the card tables, where another member of Goodearth was setting up a display of crafts and stitchery for sale, intermixed with leaflets describing the group's goals. Ariel surveyed the items on the table with a frown. ''Is that all? I thought Marie was contributing some things. I distinctly remember a crewel pillow and a couple of handbags.''

''So do I,'' the girl agreed, ''but this is all Sam brought.''

Both women looked at Sam, who shuffled uncomfortably. ''Yeah, well. . . .'' He shoved his hands deep in the pockets of his well-worn jeans. ''Since the doctor says she can't work anymore, I decided it would be best if—that is, she thought— Hell, we need the money as much as the whales do!''

Ariel's eyes widened, and she gazed in consternation at the other woman, who shrugged helplessly. After a moment Ariel muttered, ''I need some air,'' and without waiting for a response she stalked out of the makeshift booth.

Restlessly she wandered around Union Square, observing the hectic activity as the long-awaited Cetacean Celebration got underway. Her long legs carried her easily through the lively throng already filling the park. Most of the people seemed to be of college age, and most were as casually dressed as Ariel, in jeans and T-shirts with logos proclaiming their devotion to the cause, although some demanded the closure of all nuclear power plants—and one declared defiantly Nuke the Whales! Seeing the looks others were casting his way, Ariel hoped the man wearing that last shirt knew how to defend himself....

She strolled toward the grandstand, which was now draped with bright banners. A garishly painted sound truck with the logo and call letters of a Bay Area rock station was parked beside the stand, and the platform itself appeared to rise from a thicket of electrical cables and amplifiers. A television cameraman was focusing on a small group of people huddled together at one end of the grandstand, conversing seriously. Ariel recognized a nationally known ecologist talking to two women, one a state senator and the other a popular actress currently playing the sultry villainess of a nighttime soap opera. She looked remarkably ordinary and nonthreatening in daylight.

Ariel glanced at her wristwatch. Eleanor was due to arrive soon. It was Saturday, but she'd gone to her office very early that morning. Remembering how late her grandmother had worked the previous night, Ariel frowned, troubled. Eleanor wasn't a young woman anymore; she was setting herself a pace that would have flattened someone thirty years her junior. She seemed incapable of relaxing. Misled by Ellie's remarkably youthful appearance, Ariel had been reluctant at first to accept Zachary's assessment of her grandmother's precarious health, but she admitted now that he must be right. Since the onset of the contract talks Eleanor had begun to look increasingly tired. She looked her age. Ariel knew Eleanor was very sensitive about her position as head of Seacliff, but she wished the woman would relent and allow Zachary to handle the negotiations. The last thing Eleanor needed was to become involved in a marathon bargaining session.

In a few moments Ariel spotted her grandmother strolling hand in hand with James, and just behind them walked Zachary and Laurette. Ariel forced the corners of her mouth up in a smile of welcome as, sauntering forward, she waved to catch their attention. "Ellie, James!" she called, weaving through the thickening crowd. "Over here!"

Eleanor embraced Ariel. "Good morning, darling," she said. "It looks as if there's going to be quite a turnout for your celebration. I'm sure it's going to be a great success. You seem to have picked a lovely day for it."

Ariel pushed aside her apprehensions about Goodearth and agreed, "Yes, it is nice. I'm so glad you could come."

Eleanor sighed wearily. "I wouldn't have

missed it for the world, but I'm afraid I won't be able to stay too long. I have to get back to the office as soon as possible.''

Ariel studied her grandmother's shadowed face. Even her expertly applied makeup couldn't disguise the fatigue bruising her sable eyes. ''Oh, Ellie,'' she chided lightly, affecting good-natured impatience to mask her concern, ''this is Saturday, and you promised. If you're not careful you'll turn into a worse workaholic than I am! Don't you ever take time off?'' She turned to Eleanor's companion. ''James, you make her forget about going back to work. She's supposed to stay here and enjoy the fresh air and listen to the music and unwind a little, isn't she?''

When James spoke his tone was teasing, but the expression in his eyes as they met Ariel's was not. ''Honey, I've never been able to make your grandmother do anything she didn't want to.''

With uncharacteristic rudeness Eleanor cut in waspishly, ''Then I guess it's lucky you and I usually want the same thing, James!'' She jerked open her handbag and rifled nervously through the contents. ''Damn, where are my cigarettes....''

Ariel said nothing, startled by Eleanor's anger, which she'd never seen previously. Obviously her strong-willed grandmother resented even the most oblique reference to her health. Over Eleanor's bent head Ariel looked anxiously at James, who smiled ironically, then scowled in silent warning. Nodding faintly, Ariel glanced past him to the big powerful man standing behind him. Surely Zachary, Eleanor's second-in-command, her son in all but fact, could succeed in making her take his advice, when no one else could.

Ariel watched hungrily as Zachary surveyed the scene. She hadn't seen him since that afternoon when she'd told him not to touch her again, but perversely her whole body ached just to look at him. His dark head was tilted slightly to one side, so that the bright sunlight caught and emphasized the sprinkle of silvery hairs frosting his temple, making him appear older and yet so heartstoppingly handsome that Ariel's were not the only eyes that picked him out of the crowd. In a red shirt that hugged his broad shoulders and dark cords that emphasized his slim hips and muscular thighs, he looked elegantly casual, a striking contrast to the throng surrounding him.

Ariel saw with a pang that he tipped his head to better hear the whispered comments of the petite blonde who clung to his arm, her blue eyes wide and dazzled, like those of an excited child—a very sexy child, Ariel amended, assessing the halter-top jumpsuit of clinging turquoise crepe Laurette was wearing. *But she's still too young for him,* Ariel silently insisted, aware of how unjust she was being. After all, she herself was only five years older than Laurette. And yet, despite her provocative exterior, she did strike Ariel as being very immature for her age, especially when she pointed out the actress Ariel had recognized and gushed guilelessly, "Oh, Zack, will you just *look* who's standing over there on the platform! I watched her on television last night! Do you think I dare ask for her autograph?''

Zachary patted the small hand that clutched his arm. "She looks rather busy right now, sweetheart,'' he observed. "Why don't you just calm down and wait awhile. Who knows, after you've sung maybe she'll ask you for *your* autograph.''

A bolt of fierce scorching jealousy jolted through Ariel at Zachary's casually murmured endearment, but she schooled her expression as she approached the couple and greeted them. "Yes, Laurette,'' she said brightly. "I'm sure you're going to be a tremendous hit.''

The other woman looked up in surprise and smiled, extending a hand in welcome. "Oh, hi, Ariel. I'm sorry, I didn't spot you at first. I'm so nervous—all I can see is those cameras and all these people. . . .''

Ariel chuckled benignly. "Come on, now, Laurette. You handled the crowd at a nightclub without a qualm, and I'm sure we whale lovers can't be anywhere near as intimidating! After all, you're a fine singer and you're helping us with something that's very important to us. I've been telling Sam and the others about you, and they're all looking forward to hearing you.''

Laurette colored becomingly as she frankly admitted, "It's very kind of you to say that, but, well, actually it was Zack who arranged everything.''

With great effort Ariel forced herself to look

directly at Zachary. His expression was hidden from her behind the glare on his glasses. "H-hello," she said huskily. "I—I'm glad you could come, too.

His strong shoulders twitched in a slight movement, which she interpreted as a shrug. "Anything for a good cause," he answered laconically, his words clipped in that half-British accent Ariel was beginning to recognize as his "angry" voice. She realized with a pang that this was the first time he'd used it on her since she'd moved in with Eleanor. If he was still upset because she'd told him to keep his hands off her, then that was just too bad. As far as she was concerned, if anyone was owed an apology, she was.

Ariel jumped, startled, when loudspeakers all over the square suddenly spit out a dissonant thunk-thunk noise as someone on the grandstand tapped one of the microphones and said, "Testing, testing." Deliberately turning away from Zachary, Ariel addressed her grandmother. "Ellie, it looks like things are about to get started finally, so I guess I'd better go back to the others. Why don't you relax and enjoy the program, and then maybe you can join me a little later on?" Without waiting for a reply, she fled back to the Goodearth booth.

As she slipped behind the card tables, Sam looked at her oddly. "Hey, I'm sorry," he muttered grudgingly. "It's just— Well, a lot of things have been getting to me lately."

Ariel sighed and nodded noncommittally. "For-

get it. I guess we're all a little uptight these days.''
She glanced past him to a woman studying a display of watercolors. Pasting on an encouraging
smile, Ariel said cheerfully, "The one with the
rock and the sea lions, ma'am? As a matter of
fact, I did paint it. The view is from the point at
Mac Kerricher State Beach, just north of Fort
Bragg.''

The woman decided to take the painting, and
after Ariel had handed the money to the girl acting
as cashier, she turned her attention to another cus-
tomer and then another. Ariel was encouraged by
the fairly brisk business, but then after the first
flurry of sales, most people who wandered past
the booth seemed to be "just looking"—except
for one very clean-cut young man who priced
Ariel's most expensive painting and then invited
her to join him in the back of his van, where they
could share some really primo grass he'd just
scored in Sausalito.... After she politely declined his offer he suddenly lost interest in the
painting.

Despite a hedge of tall junipers that made the
grandstand invisible from Goodearth's booth,
Ariel could hear the master of ceremonies introducing the opening speakers, whose impassioned
talks were punctuated by enthusiastic applause.
When the first entertainer, an aging folksinger
who'd been famous during the early sixties,
stepped onstage, he was greeted by whistles and
cheers that carried clearly through the crisp air,
masking the drone of traffic from the surrounding

streets. In the booths Sam asked, "So when's your friend come on?"

"I'm not sure," Ariel replied. "Soon, anyway. Most of the less well-known acts are scheduled for the late morning—or at least that's what the entertainment committee told Zachary the other day." Her eyes darkened as she recalled that day, the strained lunch she and Zachary had shared, the kiss, the angry words.... She added unsteadily, "I believe the plan is to save the really big names for this afternoon, after the slide show and before the keynote speaker."

Sam eyed her curiously. "Makes sense," he muttered. When Ariel didn't speak again, he moved away to supervise the craft table.

Ariel was engrossed in a discussion with a gay couple over the most striking way to mat a trio of small seascapes for their breakfast room, when suddenly she realized that the soprano voice blaring throughout the square, its husky tones blurred and distorted by amplification, belonged to Laurette. She paused in her conversation, momentarily distracted by the memory of that night in the North Beach club, the way Zachary's green gaze had followed the woman with such intensity. She wondered if he was watching her that same way now.

"Ariel!" a familiar masculine voice called imperatively from a few feet away, and she glanced up to see James solicitously leading a slumping Eleanor toward the booth. "Ariel," he called again, more quietly, "is there someplace Ellie can sit down? She isn't feeling well."

Quickly Ariel apologized to the two men she'd been talking to and hurried toward her grandmother. She saw with dismay that Eleanor looked unnaturally pale, her skin faintly clammy. "My God, Ellie," she exclaimed, "what have you done to yourself?"

Eleanor smiled wanly and stroked her manicured fingertips across her brows, as if smoothing away a headache. "I'm sorry, darling," she answered breathlessly. "I don't mean to be any trouble. It's just, the—the crowd must have got to me. I can't imagine why."

"I can," Ariel said severely, motioning for someone to bring over a folding chair. "The pace you set would be enough to fell a rhinoceros." After James had settled Eleanor into the chair with tender care Ariel asked, "Would you like some water or something?" Without waiting for an answer, she glanced at the other Goodearth people, who were watching anxiously. "Did anyone bring anything to drink?"

"I know there's cold beer," Sam volunteered as he began to sift through the items in the big plastic ice chest hidden behind one of the card tables. "Let's see what else there is...." After a moment he looked up and said, "Beer seems to be about it—unless you like unfiltered organic carrot juice."

Eleanor grimaced but smiled gamely, and Ariel said, "We'll take the juice." When Sam produced a cup brimming with the murky orange brown liquid, Ariel teased, "Here, Ellie, just hold your nose and think of all that vitamin A. . . .'' After her grandmother had downed most of the juice and handed the cup to James, who carefully dumped the dregs into a nearby flowerbed, Ariel asked worriedly, ''Is that better? Do you need anything else?''

Eleanor shook her head. Although she still seemed pale, she insisted, ''No, dear, I'm fine, thank you.'' Looking past Ariel to Sam, hovering nearby, she murmured, ''And thank you, Mr.— Mr. . . . .''

''I'm sorry,'' Ariel apologized, surrendering to the inevitable. ''You've never met face to face, have you?'' Quickly she introduced Sam to Eleanor and James.

Even though Ariel had been aware Sam was eager to meet Eleanor, still the unctuous gallantry he displayed when he stepped forward and took her proffered hand startled her. James seemed to react to Sam with the same guarded suspicion Zachary had shown, but Eleanor appeared too tired to do other than take Sam at face value when he said, ''Mrs. Raymond, Ariel has spoken of you with such affection I feel as if I already know you.''

As she studied Sam assessingly, Eleanor absently pressed her cheek against James's hand, which was resting on her shoulder. After a moment she said, ''Ariel tells me you're the driving force behind this organization she loves so much. I'd like to hear more about it.''

''Ellie, don't bother with that right now,'' Ariel protested. ''You should just—''

One of the other women in the booth called, "Hey, Ariel, could you come here a moment and tell this lady about your sketches?" Reluctantly Ariel stepped away.

By the time she returned to her grandmother's side, Sam was concluding earnestly, "So that's why those of us in Goodearth feel it's really important we make this voyage our statement to the world."

Despite Eleanor's unnatural pallor and the weakness of her voice her dark eyes sparkled with rising interest. "And all you need is someone with money who's willing to back your trip?" She glanced up at Ariel. "Darling, why didn't you tell me your group needed help?"

Ariel froze. Sam's hand was clamped tightly around her arm, and she could feel him shaking, but she didn't look at him as she croaked, "I . . . didn't want to bother you."

Eleanor looked hurt. "You think it would bother me to help my only relative achieve something that's very important to her?"

Ariel felt torn between her love for her grandmother and her loyalty to the group she'd worked with so tirelessly, but in the end she knew what she had to say. "No, Ellie. I appreciate the thought, but we're talking about thousands and thousands of dollars here. You can't possibly—"

"Can't possibly what?" Zachary asked teasingly as he strolled up to the booth, his arm flung casually around Laurette's shoulders. As she had been at the nightclub, the singer was flushed and triumphant in the aftermath of her performance, and Ariel was struck by the unbidden thought that this was how Laurette would look after making love. She wondered how often Zachary had seen her like that....

Sensing the tension in the air, Zachary scanned the group hovering around Eleanor's chair. When he recognized Sam, he nodded curtly and asked again, less brightly, "So what's going on here?"

Quietly James said, "Eleanor has just offered to provide financial backing for this boat trip out into the Pacific."

Only the slight flaring of Zachary's nostrils indicated his agitation. Straightening his shoulders, he stepped away from Laurette, who was obviously mystified, and said, "That's very generous of you, Ellie, but I don't think it's a very good idea."

"Why not?" Eleanor demanded belligerently.

Zachary remained outwardly imperturbable, but Ariel, watching him with the heightened sensitivity of a woman in love, was certain he was furious. "Well, for one thing," he said mildly, "with the labor situation at Seacliff as volatile as it is right now, it would hardly be prudent to commit yourself—or the company—to a venture of this sort."

Eleanor rose shakily to her feet, pulling away from James's supporting arm. The flush of color on her cheekbones was a shocking contrast to the clammy pallor of her skin. She said tensely, "But since it *is* my company, I think I should be the one to make that sort of decision, don't you agree, Zachary?''

He took a deep breath. "You're the boss," he conceded tightly.

"Also the majority stockholder—don't forget that." She turned to Sam, who was watching her avidly, expectantly. "Mr. Walsh," she stated clearly, her voice carrying across the booth with surprising strength, so that all the Goodearth members paused in what they were doing, "if after today's activities are over your group finds it still needs funds in order to finance the voyage you hope to make to intercept the whaling fleet, if you will tell me how much money you need, I hereby pledge that I and my company, Seacliff Publications, will donate the balance."

For endless seconds no one stirred. Ariel stared helplessly at her grandmother, bewildered, elated, dismayed. Beside her Sam gaped, his mouth opening and closing fishily beneath his drooping mustache. Then suddenly pandemonium reigned. Several group members began to applaud and cheer, and the woman at the crafts table whooped shrilly, tossing a handful of leaflets into the air. They drifted slowly back to earth, startling passersby and attracting the attention of a wandering television crew.

"We did it! Oh, God, Ariel, we *did* it!" Sam shrieked, and he pulled her into his arms and began to jump around, kissing her lustily.

Knowing he was acting out a harmless exuberance, Ariel suppressed the feeling of revulsion that coursed through her at his touch, her body's instant instinctive rejection of arms that were too thin, lips too soft. In the midst of the noisy commotion she forced herself to stand still, to endure his enthusiastic response, his mustache that tickled her skin unpleasantly. As soon as his excitement subsided somewhat, she pushed lightly against his narrow chest and chided teasingly, "Now cut that out, Sam. What would Marie say?" His grip loosened, and without waiting for him to reply, she pulled away and turned to speak to her grandmother. She needed Eleanor's reassurance to still her nagging fear that the woman had been pressured into making a rash promise that might, at this crucial time, hurt both her and the company she'd struggled for so many years to build.

The elegant woman was almost invisible behind the clamoring throng of well-wishers who clustered around her to thank her, jostling her, grabbing at her arms to shake her hand. But the gaze that met Ariel's over the heads of the crowd was as green and stark and cold as moss on the tundra. Ariel gazed back. She knew what Zachary was thinking. She knew that the possibility troubling her mind was a harsh certainty in his—and that he would never forgive her for exposing her grandmother to such stress. Staring at Zachary with her heart in her eyes, Ariel pleaded silently, desolately, *Don't blame me. I didn't mean for anything like this to happen. Oh, God, I love you so much. Don't hate me. . . .*

She knew her pleas never reached him, because

just then she heard a strangled gasp of horror
shudder through the unruly crowd surrounding
her grandmother. Zachary turned abruptly in that
direction. Someone screamed. With a paralyzing
sense of predestination Ariel watched the group
fall back to reveal James Dunhill crouched ashen-
faced on the sidewalk, Eleanor lying in his arms,
her slim body still and limp except for the hand
that even in unconsciousness clutched at her heart.

CHAPTER SEVEN

"YOU SAVED MY LIFE," Eleanor said again, her voice stronger now but filled with the same wonder and gratitude that had marked her words when she'd first made the observation several days earlier.

Ariel glanced up from the piece of tapestry she was stitching and smiled at her grandmother, grateful to see healthy color returning to those parchment-pale cheeks. Propped against a mound of pillows in the center of her huge tester bed, Eleanor still looked incredibly small and fragile, rather doll-like in her fluffy chiffon bed jacket, though she was obviously feeling better.

Ariel's mouth quirked ironically. She and Zachary had both objected vigorously when, despite her doctors' advice, Eleanor had insisted she be allowed to recuperate in her own home once the crisis was past. They ought to have realized their protests would be in vain. No matter how frail she was in body, Eleanor's will remained as strong as ever. James, too, had been horrified at her precipitate departure from the hospital, but at least he'd been able to convince her she should engage a private nurse until she was back on her feet. Only Ariel knew that the nurse spent most of her time downstairs in the kitchen, where Mrs. Fong was teaching her the art of cooking with a wok.

When Ariel didn't speak, her grandmother persisted, ''My dear, I'll never ever forget what you did.''

Ariel sighed. ''Ellie, I only did what anyone would do in that kind of situation. I just thank God I've had CPR training.'' She shrugged with affected casualness. She still didn't want to think about that day. She hadn't yet fully recovered from the sheer terror that seized her when, kneeling beside the stricken Eleanor, she realized that the woman who had been so vibrant and forceful only moments earlier wasn't breathing, had no pulse. . . .

But typically for Ariel, fear gave way to determination. Knowing that even a few wasted seconds could spell disaster, Ariel pushed James roughly aside and began cardiopulmonary resuscitation at once, trying not to remember that the slack body beneath her crossed hands, the mouth she breathed into, belonged to her grandmother, the only person left in the world who loved her. . . . Her arms were already aching with the effort to maintain the steady beat, when from somewhere over her head she heard Zachary shout for someone to call an ambulance. But she deliberately blanked out all but the life-and-death rhythm that pumped blood through the heart, oxygen to the brain.

That evening, while she sat in trembling silence on a vinyl couch in the hospital waiting room, patting James's hand absently, Ariel saw it all again on television, captured in brutal detail on videotape by the camera crew that had wandered by so opportunely. "Unexpected drama at today's save-the-whales rally in Union Square, when prominent San Francisco businesswoman Eleanor Raymond..." the newscaster intoned gravely, and Ariel watched numbly as Ellie jerked in pain and collapsed. "Paramedics attribute the victim's survival to prompt action by her granddaughter, Mendocino artist Annabelle Maclean." Somehow the incorrect name seemed appropriate, for the livid set features of the woman bent over that inert body bore no resemblance to the face Ariel saw each morning in the mirror. Near catatonic with delayed shock, Ariel stared at the screen until Zachary, who unknown to her had slipped into the waiting room, muttered grimly, "God, we can do without that!" Stalking across the floor, he snapped off the television.

Zachary, Ariel thought now with a sigh. When would she see him again? Since Eleanor had come home, although James was still a daily visitor, Zachary communicated mostly by telephone. For the first few days while her grandmother was in intensive care, Ariel had stayed at her bedside continuously, except when she was relieved by James. Zachary had come to visit at frequent but irregular intervals, whenever he could snatch a few minutes away from work. With Eleanor's illness the labor situation at Seacliff had become more unstable than ever. The task of trying to mollify union negotiators without jeopardizing the company's uncertain future had fallen to Zachary, while at the same time he oversaw the day-to-day running of the publishing house. Each time Ariel passed him in the cool antiseptic corridors of the hospital she thought he looked thinner, more strained, almost haggard. She longed for the right to comfort him. . . .

From her nest of pillows Eleanor noted curiously, "You never told me how you happened to know CPR."

Glancing up in surprise—she'd been so deep in her thoughts of Zachary that she'd lost the thread of the conversation—Ariel shrugged again. "It's just something that, ideally, all adults should know. I took a training course at the Red Cross. It's no big deal."

"My dear girl, it certainly is to me!" Eleanor exclaimed, the return of her customary dry humor cheering Ariel immeasurably.

"Yes, I guess it is," she agreed with a smile, but after a moment the corners of her mouth drooped, and her gold eyes darkened with remembered pain. "I took the CPR class right after I came home from France," she explained hollowly. "The doctor advised me that I'd better know the technique if I was going to care for my father. In the end it wasn't necessary."

Eleanor's forehead wrinkled pensively, and Ariel, distressed, wondered if she'd been less than tactful to have mentioned her father at all. But after a moment Eleanor sighed sorrowfully. "Poor John," she murmured.

Looking directly at Ariel, she asked bluntly, "Do you know anything about your father and me?"

Ariel recoiled inwardly. She wasn't sure she wanted to hear any unsavory revelations from the past. She loved Eleanor, and her father and mother were both gone now. There seemed little point in digging up three-decades-old secrets that might smirch their memory. But Eleanor was watching her steadily, and after a moment Ariel reluctantly admitted, "Zachary told me some things I find hard to believe."

Eleanor nodded. "I'm sure you do. On the face of them the cold facts do sound a trifle...melo-dramatic."

Ariel studied her grandmother's face closely. Eleanor looked thoughtful but impersonal, as if she were debating some abstract intellectual puzzle, and in her voice Ariel could detect no undertone of lingering rancor. The events of almost thirty years earlier no longer seemed to have the power to hurt her. With that thought in mind Ariel asked, "Then it is true you were engaged to my father before he eloped with your daughter, my mother?"

"Oh, yes. Stated baldly, it sounds rather kinky, doesn't it? Shockingly Freudian...." She smiled wryly. "Actually, the only thing shocking about our little ménage was that I'd actually convinced myself I ought to marry John Maclean."

Ariel bristled defensively, and her grandmother quickly soothed her. "Darling, I'm not denigrating your father. John was one of the dearest people I've ever known—a true gentleman, a *gentle man*. We met when he came to Seacliff to see about publishing some of his poetry—that was long before we started to specialize in art books—and I liked him at once. After the Philistine cutthroats I had to deal with every day it was so refreshing to meet a man who loved music and literature, who could converse for hours, learnedly and without any embarrassment on some obscure essay by Donne or the possible interpretation of one of Sidney's sonnets. I loved talking to John, and because I found his old-fashioned gallantry and his innate innocence so endearing, I mistakenly thought I loved *him*, too...."

Ariel found herself nodding at Eleanor's assessment of her father's character. John Maclean had been warm and sweet and kind—and never quite in tune with the world he lived in. As affectionate as he'd been toward Ariel, she'd always known he was happiest when immersed in his books, more at home with an Elizabethan poet than his own child. "But what about him?" Ariel protested in confusion. "There must have been some real feeling—at least on his side. After all, he proposed to you."

"*Who* proposed?" Eleanor challenged. When Ariel's brows rose, Eleanor explained dryly, "I was in my mid-thirties, head of a flourishing business. I'd been a widow almost half my life, and I thought it was time I got married again. So I presented it to him quite logically—if John would marry me and help me run my company, I'd make sure Seacliff published all the poetry he cared to write. Besides, I had decided, a trifle belatedly, that Barbara needed a father.''

Ariel muttered, ''My God, that's cut-and-dried. It's a wonder he didn't run away in terror.''

''But, child,'' Eleanor replied softly, ''that's exactly what he did do. . . .''

After a long moment Ariel demanded, completely bewildered, ''Then how did my mother become involved in all this? I still don't understand.''

Instead of answering right away, Eleanor began to toy with the sleeve of her chiffon bed jacket, trailing her long nails over the soft fabric until it appeared in danger of snagging, and Ariel realized that her grandmother's control was a sham. When at last Eleanor looked up at Ariel again, her brown eyes were bleak. ''I told you—'' her voice was husky ''—Barbara needed a father. She was nineteen years old, but still she needed someone to give her loving care and guidance—all the things she certainly had never got from me because I was far too busy playing the hotshot lady executive to take time to be a mother.''

Ariel could hear the real guilt and anguish behind her grandmother's words, and she knew she didn't want to listen to any more. Setting her tapestry on a table, she stood up abruptly and moved restlessly around the room, her statuesque body graceful even in her agitation. Pausing at the window, she peered down at the street. The rose trees edging the lawn were in full glorious blossom. "It's a beautiful day," she noted neutrally.

Eleanor watched her for several minutes before she said, "You don't want to hear this, do you, Ariel?"

"No," Ariel answered without looking back. "I don't think it's any of my business. Besides, after the things Zachary said—"

"Zachary was a child at the time," Eleanor asserted impatiently. "He doesn't know anything."

Flushing faintly, Ariel turned to face her grandmother. "He may have been only ten then, but he seems to remember a great deal. He told me Barbara was a spoiled brat who—who seduced your fiancé because of some kind of...perverted rivalry between the two of you."

Eleanor's retort was swift. "I'm going to have to have a talk with that young man," she grumbled. Looking squarely at Ariel, she added, "Listen to me. More than just my daughter, this is your *mother* we're talking about, and if you don't try to understand now, the uncertainty could eat at you for the rest of your life. I know. It took me years before I began to see things clearly."

Ariel hesitated, gazing at the woman huddled in the stately bed, her youthfully styled hair seeming to mock the weary age now more visible on those smooth features. It took very little insight to realize Eleanor wanted more than to merely explain a long-dead scandal to Ariel; she needed absolution for her own role in it. Ariel sighed. "All right, Ellie, I'll listen."

"Good." Eleanor sat up straighter and adjusted her bed jacket around her thin shoulders. With feigned nonchalance she declared, "First of all, if Barbara was spoiled, it was because I made her that way. I indulged her with things to make up for the discipline and affection she really needed. . . ." She paused, muttering irritably, "Hell, Zachary Drake ought to understand better than most people what that can be like!" Then she said, "And there was nothing 'perverted' about the rivalry between the two of us. Mothers and daughters are often jealous of each other—I know I was. I resented Barbara's youth, her budding sexuality. I realize now that temperamentally I'm probably the kind of woman who should have had sons, rather than a girl, but at the time I only knew that I felt vaguely guilty because. . .because I didn't love her as much as I thought I ought to. She made me feel old—which is probably one reason I suddenly decided to marry again. I thought if I were a bride, I'd feel young again. I thought if I found Barbara a new father, that would somehow make her a child again. . . ."

Once more Eleanor hesitated, and when she spoke again her voice was heavy with irony. "My ingenious plan backfired. Barbara was almost a woman, seductive in the way adolescent girls who are emotionally deprived often are, and John. . . ."

"Yes, what about my father?" Ariel probed quietly. "He was in his late thirties at the time. Didn't he understand what her problem was—or do you think he was genuinely in love with her?"

Eleanor's face became shadowed. "I don't know," she replied slowly. "I'm inclined to believe John felt more like a mentor to Barbara than a lover—at least at first. She was quite intelligent, you know."

"No, I didn't know. I don't know anything about her."

"Oh, yes," Eleanor remembered, smiling fondly, "Barbara was very bright. She taught herself to read at the age of four, and she adored literature. Sometimes when I'd come home from work, the housekeeper would complain that Barbara hadn't set foot out of doors all day long, she was so busy reading.... " Eleanor winced slightly. "And of course, as I said earlier, John could talk enthrallingly for hours on his favorite subject—"

"He was always a very good teacher," Ariel interjected.

"Yes, I'm sure he was," Eleanor agreed. "And while I was off being the hard-nosed businesswoman—an aspect of my life that alarmed him deeply, although he tried not to show it—he talked to my daughter. After we became engaged he wanted to get to know her better, so he began to tutor her. She was young for her age, nonthreatening and eager to learn—everything I wasn't—and I suppose that to someone of John's romantic temperament, the circumstances must have reminded him of Dante with Beatrice or Abelard and Héloïse. . . . ''

Her voice trailed off again, only to return harsh with conviction. ''I don't know how things would have worked out for John and Barbara if she'd lived longer, whether they could have sustained a relationship once she matured and ceased to be the worshipful student. I only know I would have been an abysmally bad wife for him—I would have destroyed him. I'm too hard, too selfish to be anyone's wife, even—'' She broke off abruptly, only to continue self-deprecatingly, ''Of course I didn't see it that way at the time. Then I felt humiliated and betrayed. It took me years before I realized that, quixotic as his action may have seemed, eloping with Barbara was probably one of the smartest things John ever did—for all of us.''

She sighed deeply. ''I can't honestly say which hurt worst, being spurned by my lover or abandoned by my child—or having to face the people who knew what had happened—but in the end, when Barbara died in that car wreck, it was the mother in me that grieved. . . . ''

Ariel listened impassively, her ears catching that oblique, quickly stifled reference to James Dunhill. She speculated that, in a roundabout way Eleanor's guilt over her treatment of her daughter might be part of the reason why now, so many years later, she refused to marry a man who loved her deeply, whom she obviously loved in return. If only she would relent, she and James could easily spend fifteen, twenty happy years together. Didn't Eleanor think she deserved to be happy?

Then she recalled something Eleanor had said, one word heavy with implication, and heart pounding, she asked frankly, "Ellie, did you ever sleep with my father?"

Eleanor started, frowning. After a long breathless moment the corners of her mouth began to curve up in a wry impish smile. Her dark eyes brightened, making the years drop away, as for the first time since her attack she began to look something like her old self. "Does it matter?" she murmured mildly.

Ariel thought over the question seriously. "No, Ellie," she said at last. "No, it doesn't matter at all." Pushing herself away from the wall she'd been leaning against, she crossed briskly to her grandmother's side and plopped down into a chair. She grinned and asked easily, "Well, now, since we seem to be sharing all our deep dark family secrets, did I ever tell you what happened to me while I was in France?"

SAM SHIFTED UNCOMFORTABLY, the upholstery of the cut-velvet sofa obviously itchy against his bare thighs below the hem of his brief jogging shorts. "I need to talk to you about something, babe, but while I'm here I'd also like to thank Mrs. Raymond again for all she's done for us. I can't get over the fact that a businesswoman would take the time to authorize that donation, especially when she's so sick."

As she settled in a chair opposite him, Ariel sighed. "It's really sweet of you to want to thank Ellie in person, but unfortunately she's napping right now. The nurse finally put her foot down. Her doctor nearly had a stroke when he dropped by here last night and found out Ellie had started working again. He threatened to rip out every telephone in the house if she didn't promise to stay off the line and quit trying to run Seacliff from her bedroom." She paused, her gold eyes darkening pensively. "And I do wish you'd get over this fixation you have with business people, Sam. Running a corporation doesn't automatically make someone a monster, you know."

"Oh, yeah?" Sam retorted as he slumped forward awkwardly, so that his thin but unusually long legs stretched away from the irritating velvet. He looked as if he were about to slide off the sofa, and he dug his running shoes into the carpet for better purchase. "Tell that to your friend Drake. Was he in a foul mood yesterday when I dropped by his office to pick up the check!"

Knowing Zachary's less-than-favorable opinion of Sam, Goodearth's proposed expedition and Eleanor's underwriting of it, Ariel thought with grim humor that he would probably be in a foul mood no matter when he had to hand over the money. But tactfully she dismissed Sam's complaint. "Well, I imagine things have been very nerve-racking for Zachary lately. Not only has he been worried about Ellie, but he's had the company to contend with almost single-handedly. Although I know he's a very capable businessman, I'm sure the strain has been—''

"We're all under a strain," Sam interrupted irritably. "Hell, think of what it's been like for me the past couple of weeks! Since the celebration I've had to do all the work, make all the arrangements for the trip itself. You're ensconced in this house all day, and everyone else in the group has split for Mendocino. And whenever I call home, Marie sounds worse.''

Ariel stiffened with concern. "Worse? How do you mean? Is she ill? Has something happened with the baby?''

Sam's brows came together in a thick silvery line as he rubbed the bridge of his big nose. Absently he brushed his long hair away from his face as he admitted, "No. As far as I know, the kid's still all right. But Marie's really tired and cranky, and I guess a bit scared. She's worried about money, too—bills. Last night on the phone she told me the grocer is threatening to take her to small-claims court.''

"Oh, no," Ariel groaned, appalled. With the precarious state of her health the last thing Marie needed hanging over her head was a lawsuit. "Is there any way I can help?''

"You got a few thousand bucks you can spare us?'' Sam rejoined with leaden irony. When Ariel shook her head, he muttered, "Don't worry. I didn't think you did." Glancing around Eleanor's lovingly restored living room, studying the obviously expensive antique furniture, Sam remarked distantly, "You know, Ariel, as much as I care about Goodearth, it really gets to me sometimes the way people will jump at the chance to spend money to do something like save the whales but still not...." His voice trailed off, the thought unfinished.

For several minutes Ariel watched him in brooding silence, thinking idly how out of place he seemed in the Victorian parlor, a misfit, his long hair and jogging clothes like something from another dimension. Oddly, whenever Zachary was in Eleanor's home, style of dress wasn't a consideration. It was the house that seemed out of synch, not him.... Pushing aside that puzzle, Ariel ventured tentatively, "Sam, you have a college degree, don't you? Have you ever thought of—I don't know—maybe becoming a teacher or something?"

He jerked upright and gaped. "A teacher?" he sputtered, his drooping mustache jumping with each outraged syllable. "For God sake, Ariel, I'm an athlete. I'd go crazy cooped up inside a classroom all day long! Anyway, I can't stand kids—" Ariel's gleaming eyes turned cold and metallic, and he amended quickly, "All right, scratch that last remark. I guess I'll have to learn to like them, won't I?"

"Looks that way."

Another strained silence prevailed, broken only when Sam stood up abruptly and said, "Besides thanking Mrs. Raymond, there's something you and I need to work out. I've run into a snag with the Goodearth bank account."

"A snag? What do you mean? Weren't you able to put the Seacliff check in the bank?"

"Sure. There was no trouble putting the money *in*. It's getting it out again that's the trouble. When I tried to put down a deposit on that boat we want, I discovered that since you were the person who opened the account, you're the only one with authority to write checks on it."

Frowning, Ariel recalled, "Oh, of course. We were supposed to get that all taken care of as soon as you came down from Mendocino. I'm sorry. There've been so many things happening lately that I forgot all about it." She glanced at her wristwatch. The bank would be closing in half an hour. "I'm not sure there's enough time to go get your signature authorized today. We'd be cutting it pretty close, and anyway I really did want to be here when Ellie woke up...." She shrugged. "I guess we'd better plan on going to the bank first thing in the morning."

Sam shook his head. "We can't wait that long. The guy at the charter company told me they've had a better bid on the boat for the same time we want it. He said he'll still honor the terms we agreed on, as long as we get the deposit paid today. But otherwise he's going to take the other offer."

"Oh, *merde*. If it's not one damned thing, it's another." Ariel glanced around hurriedly for her handbag. "Just let me grab my purse and we'll run to the bank now, before it—"

The telephone rang.

Jarred by the strident summons, Ariel headed automatically for the telephone in the hallway. But just then she spotted her handbag, and she decided to let the housekeeper answer the call. It was probably for Eleanor, anyway.

"Miss Maclean, it's for you," Mrs. Fong announced. "It's Mr. Drake."

Ariel froze. Zachary was calling *her*? Oh, God, it had been days since she'd even seen him, much less had him deliberately seek her out—

"Ariel," Sam interrupted impatiently, "come on! We've only got a few minutes before the bank closes."

Why would he want to talk to her, she wondered abstractedly, her body already reacting instinctively to the mere prospect of hearing that rich deep voice. She knew his reason must be something important. Did he have some news about Eleanor that he thought Ariel needed to know?

"Miss Maclean, shall I tell Mr. Drake you'll call back later?"

"*Ariel*, damn it, we're—"

She felt like the rope in a tug-of-war. Muttering an oath that Matthieu had once primly advised her to expunge from her French vocabulary, Ariel called over her shoulder, "Mrs. Fong, please tell Zachary to hold on for just a moment. I'll be there as quick as I can." She turned back to Sam. Whipping her pen and the Goodearth checkbook from her purse, Ariel scrawled her name at the bottom of a blank check. "Here," she said, shoving the slip of paper into his hands. "You fill in the rest. If you hurry, the bank will have time to verify it for the charter company today. You'd better run. I'll see you tomorrow. Bye, now." Sam was already forgotten as she raced into the hallway.

"H-hello, Zachary," she gulped, telling herself she felt breathless because she'd been hurrying.

"Ariel, is that you? You sound as if you've been running."

Her spirits rose mercurially at the sound of his voice, and she laughed. "Oh, no, nothing like that. I was just saying goodbye to Sam."

There was a long pause before Zachary spoke again. "I see," he said tersely. "I'm sorry I disturbed you. Perhaps I should call later."

"Oh, no, you weren't disturbing us!" Ariel protested quickly. "Sam was leaving anyway." For a moment there was silence on the line, and she asked apprehensively, "Z-Zachary, are you still there?"

"Yes, Ariel, I'm here." He sounded very British.

She wanted to growl with frustration. His rudeness would have been infuriating except that, absurdly, his awkward hesitations reminded her of nothing so much as a teenager asking a girl out for the first time.... She tried again. "Zachary, is there anything I can help you with? Did you want something?"

With apparent effort he explained, "Actually, I'd been hoping you might be free to go out with me tonight—dinner, possibly the theater, if I can get tickets this late. I realize this is rather short notice, but until today I had no idea when or if I'd ever be able to get away from Seacliff—I was beginning to think I'd become rooted to that bargaining table—but now, thank God, the talks finally seem to be easing up a little. The union has agreed to an extension of their current contract, at least until Ellie's better, and frankly that's such a load off my mind that—that I felt like celebrating. Of course, if you and Walsh already have something planned...."

Ariel was sure her face must be beaming like a Japanese lantern, her cheeks aglow with the light of her happiness. Zachary wanted to celebrate. He wanted to celebrate with *her*.... "Oh, no, I'm free," she reassured him at once. "Sam just dropped by for a minute to see about some Goodearth business." She huskily added an outlandish understatement. "I'd love to go out with you tonight."

"I'm glad," Zachary said, and in those two short words Ariel thought she heard the warmth and affection she'd given up hope of him ever showing her.

SEVERAL HOURS LATER Ariel splayed her fingers over the flowing, hand-embroidered silk of her gown and asked hesitantly, "Will I do, Ellie?" While she was bathing and dressing, she had felt confident that for once Zachary was going to see her looking her absolute best. But now, only minutes before he was due to arrive, she was seized with the sudden fear that he would think her outfit too bizarre, too artsy.

Eleanor glanced up from her book and gasped, her brows peaking in astonishment. "Good Lord, girl," she breathed in awe, "I never knew you could look like that." She studied the topaz-colored gown with obvious appreciation. The simplicity of its classic styling—shimmering silk smoothly draped from one shoulder, falling in gentle folds to the floor—complemented Ariel's tall splendid figure. The richness of the bands of jewel-toned butterflies stitched in floss on the bodice and hem was impressive—even more so because of the extraordinary workmanship.

"I think that's the most beautiful dress I've ever seen," Eleanor complimented her truthfully. "Where did you get it?"

"My friend Marie—you know, the girl I told you about who's having a baby—made it. When it comes to needlework, she's really something of a genius." Relaxing slightly at Eleanor's approval, Ariel grinned sheepishly. "I even put on makeup for a change." With an artist's hand she'd outlined and emphasized her eyes until the irises shone as big and bright as newly minted gold coins. "Do you think I used too much?"

"No," Eleanor judged firmly. "With a dress like that you need dramatic coloring. I like your hair, too." Ariel had brushed her long sun-touched mane until it also gleamed. Then she'd pulled the thick strands all to one side and looped them through a plain gold clip so that they fell forward over her bare shoulder and curled at her breast. Her only other ornament was a wide bracelet of antique gold filigree that she'd pushed high up on her uncovered arm, an ornate design of interlocking butterflies, their wings set with tiny green, yellow and red garnets. Looking closer, Eleanor noticed with surprise that the butterflies on the gown matched the bracelet.

Seeing her grandmother's reaction, Ariel traced the delicate lines of the engraved gold with her fingertips as she explained, "I found this years ago at the Marché aux puces in Paris. Although I've always loved it, I never really knew what to do with it because I hardly ever wear jewelry. But then one day, not long after I came back home, I showed the bracelet to Marie. She looked at it for a while and said, 'You know, I could make a dress to go with this. . . .' "

"Any woman who can create clothes like that could make a fortune as a couturiere."

"Yes, I know," Ariel agreed. "Except that Marie tends to think of her art as a labor of love rather than a business. I had to twist her arm to get her to take any more than just enough money to pay for the materials in this gown, and even then the amount was nowhere near what she should have got for all the work she put into it." She smiled. "Frankly, I couldn't have afforded to pay what the dress is worth. Of course, to top it all off, it's been hanging in my closet ever since. This is the first time I've ever worn it or the bracelet." Giggling suddenly, she caught the skirt in her hands and twirled around like a little girl, the silk billowing upward to reveal flat-heeled strapless gold slippers. "Oh, Ellie," she exclaimed. "Do you really think I look pretty?"

"Not pretty—beautiful," Eleanor said sincerely.

Ariel halted awkwardly, her laughter suddenly uneasy. "I'm not sure I can cope with being beautiful if this is what it does to you. I hope I don't make a fool of myself in front of Zachary tonight. I feel weird, almost...drunk."

Eleanor's smile grew tender and indulgent. "Child, the word is 'giddy,'" she said gently. "And it has nothing to do with the way you look, except perhaps inversely. That wonderful bubbly feeling you're experiencing right now is a very common symptom of being in love."

Ariel stared at her grandmother for a long moment. She wondered dismally if her feelings were so obvious to everyone, especially Zachary.... In a feeble effort to salvage her pride she protested, "Ellie, I've been in love before, and I never felt like this."

"Maybe you were never in love like this."

The words hung in the air, reverberating with meaning, until Ariel gave a wistful sigh. "Maybe not. I thought I was." Then with a liberating chuckle she reminisced teasingly, "You know, it's too bad Matthieu never saw me looking like this. If he had, maybe he would have offered to set me up in style in my very own townhouse instead of just a furnished apartment. Oh, well, I guess now

I'll never know what it's like to be a kept woman.''

Suddenly from the street below, Ariel heard the loud purr of a powerful engine drawing up to the curb. She paled, her amber eyes darting with alarm toward the window, then back to her grandmother. "Ellie," she whispered breathlessly, "I—I.... Why do I feel as if I've never been on a date before in my life?''

"Because you haven't—not one that counted," Eleanor answered brusquely, waving her arm impatiently. "Now go on, go on. You have better things to do than talk to me!" When Ariel still hesitated, Eleanor persisted, "Silly girl, can't you tell I'm just waiting tactfully for the coast to be clear so I can ask James to come over?" Ariel fled.

She'd just reached the top of the stairs when she heard Zachary's hard imperative knock, and glancing down toward the entryway, she was reminded so forcefully of the day they first met in Mendocino that she laughed aloud. How long ago that seemed. And yet it had only been weeks, a few dozen days during which her perception of Zachary Drake had changed absolutely. She had thought him the stereotypical "corporate man," unfeeling, unimaginative, narrow-minded, but those erroneous first impressions had gradually faded. With something approaching her late father's facility with a quotation Ariel mused whimsically, 'Nothing of him that doth fade, But doth suffer a sea-change Into something rich and strange....'

Strange, indeed, she thought. Now she realized what a deep, very complex character he was, a man with emotions and drives that were all the more intense for being so ruthlessly contained. She couldn't begin to understand why Zachary should wish to be thought a cold-blooded pragmatist, either, when he was in fact caring and highly sensitive to the needs of others. He had demonstrated this quality repeatedly in his treatment of Eleanor and Laurette—if not Ariel. . . .

She wondered if perhaps the answer to the riddle might be locked somewhere in his background, that as-yet-unexplained amalgam of cultural heritages that made him sometimes seem a very typical San Franciscan and yet at other times peculiarly British. Eleanor had hinted that Zachary's childhood had been unhappy, but Ariel supposed that unless he someday relaxed enough to tell her himself, she'd never really know. The only thing she knew for sure was how she felt about him.

When he knocked on the door again, Ariel shook herself and rushed forward to answer it. She didn't care about Zachary's background now. None of it was important—not his past, not her own past, not even his present rather ambiguous relationship with Laurette Masefield. Nothing mattered to Ariel except the fact that this evening for a few hours she and she alone was going to be in the company of the man she loved.

With fingers that trembled she opened the door. He stood there tall and proud, vibrant with impatience, wearing his impeccable dark evening clothes with a grace that should have seemed incongruous in a man of his muscular build. Ariel caught her breath at the spasm of indescribable need that twisted deep inside her at the sight of him. "Good evening, Zachary," she said huskily.

The yellow porchlight reflecting off his glasses masked his expression as he gazed down at her, but curiously she noted a slight involuntary movement of his strong jaw, as if he were swallowing in surprise. He didn't speak. His silence disturbed her, threatening her fragile self-confidence. With a sinking sensation she wondered if, despite all Eleanor's enthusiastic reassurances, Zachary didn't like the way she looked, thought Marie's wonderful creation too...exotic or something, her makeup and hairstyle too blatant. Smiling uncertainly, she retreated into the bright hallway and motioned for him to follow. When she turned to close the door, he loomed over her alarmingly, and she was torn between equally overwhelming urges to plaster her body against the wall in a feeble attempt to escape him or to fling herself shamelessly into his arms. Instead she hovered nervously, waiting for him to speak. When at last he did, his voice sounded oddly thick. "You look...magnificent."

Tension seeped out of her, and her eyes half closed, veiling the relief that shone in them. "Thank you," she murmured. After a moment, when she was certain she had control of her composure once more, she looked up at him again and grinned impishly. "So do you."

She could see his eyes now, and something flashed in their virid depths as he took a deep ragged breath. "I ought to kiss you for that," he growled.

Ariel felt her woman-powers revived by the warmth of his admiration, growing in strength and confidence at a rate that would be frightening were it not so exhilarating. Tilting her head to one side so that the thick, honey-colored swath of hair stroked seductively across her bare throat, she flicked her tongue over her dry lips and challenged, "So why don't you?"

He seemed mesmerized by the sheen of moisture her tongue had left, and it was only after a visible effort that he again lifted his gaze to meet hers. "Oh, I will," he promised, his voice deep and gravelly. "But not here, not now when we might be hurried. I haven't forgotten that crack you made about me taking a 'quick grope' every now and then...."

Ariel blushed fiercely as she remembered that afternoon in Union Square, Zachary's rough embrace and the bitter cutting charge she'd spat at him in her anguish. She regretted the words she'd used but not the sense of them. With a defiant lift of her chin she declared, "I can't apologize for what I said, Zachary."

"I didn't expect you to," he replied surprisingly. "I admit I was being my most high-handed and patronizing that day. I have a bad habit of always wanting to be in control of any given situation." He paused, and when he spoke again his tone was

heavy with ironic, self-deprecating humor. "Ellie
says it's a throwback to my empire-building fore-
bears, this tendency of mine to march in and immediately try to. . .subdue the natives."

Disarmed by his teasing, she smiled up at him as
she pointed out, "But I'm not a native San Franciscan."

"I know," he said softly. "Are you going to
make me wait until you go back to Mendocino?"

"Are you going to try to subdue me?" she par-
ried.

"Actually, I had something a little more mutual
in mind. . . ."

Suddenly the entryway was airless, oppressive
with the weight of unanswered questions, abeyant
desires. Biting her lip, Ariel tore her eyes away
from him and stared blindly at the spindly,
marble-topped console table where she had laid
her shawl and purse. "W-would you like to—to go
up and say hello to Ellie before we leave?" she
stammered.

Zachary seemed to recognize her retreat for
what it was. He nodded and murmured easily,
"Of course. I talked to her on the telephone
earlier today, but it will be good to see her for a
moment. Then we'll have to run. Our dinner reser-
vation is for eight."

They ate in a very good French restaurant, hovered over by a personable young man with a continental accent so patently fake Ariel couldn't
resist the impulse to tease him. Flashing her most
beguiling smile, she began to ask him various

items on the menu in fluent French. To her astounded delight, after a moment Zachary also joined the game. She noticed that his accent, while very good, was a trifle stilted, indicating he'd learned French in the classroom rather than on the streets of Paris, as she had. The waiter listened to them in consternation for several moments before dropping his obsequious act and pleading good-naturedly in very Californian tones, "Hey, you guys, have a heart, will you? I'm a computer-science major at Berkeley, not a language expert!" Grinning, Zachary and Ariel reverted to English, and after they'd finished their meal she noticed that the tip he left looked as if it would probably make a start toward buying the young man's textbooks for the next semester.

Apologizing because he'd been unable to obtain the theater tickets for the show he'd chosen, Zachary instead took Ariel to the penthouse lounge on top of one of the famous old hotels on Nob Hill, where through wall-sized windows they admired the incredible view as they discussed their plans over drinks. "We could go dancing, of course," he said, unaware of the frisson that shivered through Ariel at the heated memory of Zachary's arms around her while they swayed in time to sultry music.... "Or I was able to locate a couple of art galleries with showings you might find interesting."

"That sounds lovely," Ariel said, smiling, genuinely touched he'd gone to so much effort to please her. But then, she remembered, even on the first day they'd met, despite the fact that he'd been generally irritating and pigheaded, she'd realized he was a man who felt no qualms, sensed no subtle affront to his masculinity, in letting a woman decide what they should do. Sipping her white wine, she sighed and said again, "Yes, it all sounds perfectly lovely, but would you mind terribly if we just stayed here for a while? It's so relaxing just sitting here looking out at the bay and all the lights."

"Whatever you want, Ariel," Zachary said affably. "There's no hurry."

From their table Ariel could see the double-decked arches of the Oakland Bay Bridge to the east and the lofty towers of the Golden Gate Bridge to the west. With an artist's eye she appreciated the luminous sheen those light-spangled ribbons of steel and concrete painted on the dark waters below, and she wondered if she could capture the scene in a way that hadn't been done a hundred times already. After several moments of mutual silence she murmured inadequately, "It really is a beautiful city, isn't it?"

"Oh, yes," Zachary agreed. "Despite all its many problems, San Francisco is the most beautiful exciting cosmopolitan city in the world."

"I know some Parisians who might disagree with that."

Zachary shrugged. "I'm sure they would. Every man is a chauvinist about his home." He paused for several seconds, then turned in his chair so that he was facing the windows that looked away from the water, inward toward the hills to which the city clung precariously. "Do you see that transmitter tower up there?" he asked abruptly, pointing toward the highest peak.

Puzzled, Ariel followed his direction above the aurora of the streetlamps, not sure what he was leading up to. Her eyes settled on three red signal lights flashing, topping what she recognized as the three prongs of a huge, futuristic-looking structure. Bright orange by day, the tower loomed over the city like the trident of Roman mythology transplanted there by some slightly avant-garde sea god. "Yes, I see it. What about it?"

After the easy camaraderie they'd shared for the past few hours Zachary's voice sounded curiously strained as he elaborated. "My house isn't far from there, just a little way down the hill. Near the end of Stanyan Street, in the Upper Haight-Ashbury."

"Haight-Ashbury?" Ariel echoed, smiling involuntarily at the thought of the sober Zachary Drake living in a district whose name, for many people, still evoked visions of hippies, "flower power" and all the social turmoil of the sixties. Her expression clouded when she realized he wasn't returning her smile. "Zachary?" she asked uncertainly.

Staring down at the table, he said stiffly, "I'd like you to see my house, Ariel. I've put a lot of work into it, and I. . . admit to being rather proud of it." Suddenly he lifted his head, and his green gaze met her amber one directly. For once the shining lenses of his glasses formed no barrier between his mind and hers. She knew what he would say before he spoke, and his lips hardly moved as he asked quietly, "Ariel, will you come home with me tonight?"

She took a deep breath. All at once she was conscious of the weight of her long hair lying across her bare shoulder, curling enticingly over her full breasts—breasts already growing taut with anticipation, pressing against the clinging silk of her gown. "Yes, Zachary," she replied huskily, reaching for her evening bag with slim fingers that trembled slightly. "Yes, my dear. . .oh, yes."

CHAPTER EIGHT

LEANING AGAINST THE BALCONY RAIL, Ariel gazed over the rooftops at the city below. It was a very clear night, the view not obscured by the evening fog usual at this time of year. From this elevation San Francisco was an undulating panorama of light and color, with flowing white-and-scarlet ribbons of traffic and the window-checkered thrust of lofty high rises. Out in the bay, the revolving beacon on Alcatraz swept the dark water, and the twin towers of the Golden Gate looked compressed and foreshortened, the shining span between them a reverse silhouette against the hulking land mass to the north, Marin County. Behind Ariel, Zachary said quietly, "You ought to come back inside now. It's getting rather chilly out there."

Startled, she whirled around. He was standing at the open sliding glass doors, a balloon-shaped snifter in each hand. "Oh, I didn't hear you," she said breathlessly, her hand at her throat.

"Sorry. I didn't mean to sneak up on you." They stepped into the house, and he held out one of the glasses to her. "Brandy?"

"Thank you," she murmured as she accepted it.

She stared down into the glass, cradling it between her palms and tilting it so that the liquor swirled and warmed, wafting fragrantly to her nostrils. Silently she savored the scent. Zachary stepped behind her to pull the sliding door closed and draw the draperies. Ariel turned to watch him, and as she raised the glass to her lips she commented casually, "That's an incredible view. I'd love to see it in the daylight sometime."

Zachary's eyes seemed riveted to her mouth as she drank. "How about when you wake up tomorrow morning?" he asked.

Ariel's hand trembled. The brandy splashed slightly, and a drop trickled from the corner of her mouth, the alcohol stinging her skin. Automatically she reached up to wipe it away with her fingertips, but Zachary stopped her. "No," he said hoarsely, quickly setting his glass on a side table. "Let me." And before she could reply he bent his head to hers and caught the errant droplet with his tongue.

Only his mouth touched her. Clutching the snifter in front of her, she gazed, mesmerized, into his sparking green eyes as his rough tongue flicked across her smooth skin, sipping at her. She wasn't sure which burned hotter, the brandy on her own lips or Zachary's lips on hers, but when she closed her eyes against sensations that had suddenly become too intense, she felt her need transmitting like electricity across the inches that separated them. She was only vaguely aware that he rescued her glass, which was in peril of spilling, and set it beside his own. Then he pulled her to him, closing the dynamic gap between them, and the kiss that had begun so softly raced out of control.

Her hunger was more than a match for his. Her fingers slid upward along the starched pleats of his shirt to explore his strong neck, the hard line of his jaw. She wanted to touch him, she wanted to... do everything with him. She wanted to make him want her in return. When she probed a pulse point and realized his heart was pounding as rapidly as her own, the knowledge of her effect on him made her dizzy.

She stroked the silver-frosted black hair at his temples, and her fingers accidentally jarred one of the earpieces to his glasses, which by now seemed so much a part of him she was usually unaware of them. When he reached up to reposition the frames, she stilled his hand. "Why don't you take those off?" she suggested lightly.

Momentarily distracted, he frowned. "I really do need these glasses, you know. Without them I tend to walk into walls."

She hadn't realized until that moment what an overwhelming image of strength he presented, but now she found the thought of this weakness strangely appealing, even...stimulating. "Don't worry, Zachary, I'll lead you," she said.

He chuckled uneasily. "But I may not even be able to see you."

Huskily she countered, "You will if you get close enough."

With great care she removed his glasses and

folded them shut before handing them to him. When he slipped them into the inside pocket of his dinner jacket, with her fingertips Ariel smoothed the faint red mark they left on the bridge of his nose. Then she drew his mouth down to hers once more.

They kissed as if they starved for each other, probing, nipping, licking, but each sharp bite seemed to tantalize them, only making them hunger for more. When they were both breathless, Zachary buried his face against her throat and groaned, "Oh, God, Ariel, I'd like—I'd like to taste every inch of you...."

She pulled away slightly, smiling up at him dazedly. "Me, too," she whispered. Then, compelled by an emotional need even more intense than the physical desire that scorched and throbbed within her, she added simply, "I love you."

Zachary said nothing. The hands that clutched Ariel's shoulders were suddenly motionless, so utterly still. She gazed anxiously at him, unnerved by his silence. "Zachary?" she ventured tremulously.

He looked down at her. For one long moment his opalescent green eyes were unguarded, revealing a vulnerability and entreaty so in contrast to his usual self-assurance she wanted to call back her words, beg him to forget she'd ever said them. Then his absurdly long lashes fluttered down over his eyes, and when those lashes lifted again, she wondered if the naked pain she thought she'd seen had been an illusion, if she'd imagined it because she was unused to him without his glasses.

As if he were deliberately trying to divert her thoughts, Zachary took control of the embrace. He slid his arms around Ariel and pulled her close against the hard contours of his body, while he nipped at her earlobe, at the sensitive hollows of her throat. She shuddered convulsively and arched away from him, trying to catch her breath, but he allowed her no respite. Insistently he cupped and caressed her full breasts through the clinging topaz fabric of her gown. Under his teasing fingertips she could feel the nipples firming, growing so tender that even the gossamer silk was an unbearable weight on them, and she sobbed aloud in agony and delight.

The guttural moan that escaped her lips seemed to jolt through him, and with an answering cry he scooped her into his arms so quickly her gold slippers dropped from her feet as he stalked toward the staircase.

For several dizzy seconds Ariel clung mutely to him, seduced into silence by the unique and astonishingly heady sensation of being carried as if she were a doll, a *little* doll. Then common sense reasserted itself, and she squealed, "For heaven's sake, Zachary, put me down. I weigh a ton!"

"Be quiet and quit squirming," he growled, bounding up the stairs.

"But you're not even wearing your glasses! We'll both be—" He stopped her protest with his mouth.

When he set her on her feet again, she was completely disoriented, stunned by the force of his kiss. Still trying to catch her breath, she closed her eyes and leaned weakly against Zachary as she reproached him. "You claimed you'd get lost."

"Not in my own house, sweetheart," Zachary replied with a laugh, his lips ruffling the long strands that had worked loose from the gold clip. He removed the clip, so that her thick hair fell like a mantle across her shoulders as he began to comb it with his fingers. "Besides," he added huskily, "with a woman like you in his arms even a blind man could find his way to the nearest bedroom."

"Bedroom?" she echoed dizzily. She lifted her lashes just enough to glance around. In the subdued light she could barely make out the interior of the room, which seemed to be decorated with luxurious simplicity in rich, very masculine earth tones, one wall completely masked by drapery. Beneath her nylon-clad feet she could feel the thick shag carpet that covered the floor and the unusual pedestal of the vast, wood-framed bed. She mused dreamily, "Oh, a waterbed... how nice," and with a sigh she closed her eyes again and rested her head against his jacket.

She could feel laughter rumbling deep in his chest as he queried, "Ariel, did that brandy go to your head or something?"

"No, of course not," she murmured. "I hardly touched the stuff." She knew she wasn't drunk, but she wasn't sure how to explain that she was drugged by his nearness, that it was his comforting strength that intoxicated her, the warmth and pressure of his hands splayed across her back, the intimate heat of their bodies molding together. No man had ever affected her this way, not even Matthieu.... She inhaled deeply, trying to clear her mind. Zachary's elusive man-scent mixed with that of crisply starched linen as she nuzzled his throat. His impeccable black bow tie tickled her nose, and her questing fingers crept up the front of his shirt to capture one end of it. As if fascinated, she tugged slowly until the loop slipped through the knot and dangled sloppily from his collar. "There," she murmured with satisfaction, pulling back to survey her handiwork. "That's much better. You're always too perfect."

"The result of my unfortunate upbringing, I suppose," Zachary volunteered cynically. "At the prep school I attended in England, whenever we were caught with improperly knotted neckwear we got our knuckles rapped with a ruler."

Ariel frowned, disconcerted by his casual reference to a past he'd never mentioned previously. She hadn't missed the grim note in his deep voice. "So what happened if you forgot your tie altogether?" she inquired hesitantly.

"Don't ask." Casually he removed the offending black ribbon and tossed it onto a chair. Then he shrugged out of his dinner jacket. After he'd unfastened his collar stud and cuff links and dropped them into a leather box on his dresser he looked at Ariel and suggested lightly, "Well, my dear, would you care to finish the job?"

Her amber eyes were avid and appreciative as she gazed at him. Surveying those wide powerful shoulders and arms encased in white linen, the absurd half vest nipping his slim waist, the tight black trousers so sleek on those long muscular thighs, she thought with a touch of whimsy that the only thing sexier than an attractive man in evening clothes was that same man half out of them.... Desire stirred insistently within her, and she began to fumble clumsily with the buttons on his vest.

She was still trying to resolve the intricate mysteries of the shirt stud when he grew impatient and caught her fingers in his own, pushing them gently aside. Quickly he pulled his shirt from his waistband and dispensed with the remaining studs. When he stretched out an arm to drop them into the box on the dresser, his lapels gapped open, revealing a broad chest darkly furred with curling black hair. Irresistibly Ariel's hands reached up to touch him. His tanned skin was warm and resilient under her fingertips, the muscles beneath it solid and rippling. She buried her face hungrily against him and sighed plaintively, ''Oh, Zachary, I've needed you for such a long time!''

She could feel him shudder as her lips brushed his bare flesh. And then his hands were on her again, loosening the single knot of yellow silk at her shoulder, sliding deftly over her while he searched out and located the invisible side zipper that held Marie's creation in place. With a grunt of triumph he tugged gently. The dress slithered downward over Ariel's voluptuous curves and formed a shimmering pool at her feet, leaving her naked except for her sheer panty hose and the antique jeweled bracelet on her upper arm.

For endless moments he stared at her in silence. Basking in the emerald fire of his gaze, she lifted her chin regally and straightened her shoulders, so that her full breasts were exposed proudly to his view. "You're beautiful," he breathed.

"You still have too many clothes on," she said. She slid her hands under the flapping lapels of his shirt and eased it over his shoulders, in the process forcing his body forward, so that his hair-roughed chest rubbed erotically against her swollen nipples. She thought he groaned, but she knew that harsh cry of need could as easily have risen from deep in her own throat. When his shirt hit the floor, Zachary caught her by the waist and hooked his thumbs into the elastic band of her panty hose. With trembling fingers she groped for the fastener on his trousers....

When they stood nude before each other, Ariel surveyed his long athletic body in awe. Stirred and elated by his desire, as obvious as her own, she whispered, "I wondered what you'd be like. From the first day I met you that's all I've been able to think about."

One dark brow arched sardonically as he reminded her, "But when you mistook me for the model you were expecting that afternoon, you told me that undressed I wouldn't be at all suitable for your needs...."

With a provocative smile she murmured, "Anyone can make a mistake. . . ."

He started to reach for her, but his eyes were attracted to the glittering stones on her bracelet, which she'd forgotten about. "Do you mind if I remove this?" he asked, she shook her head. Gently he slipped the gold circlet from her arm and smoothed out the imprint the filigree had marked on her soft skin. When he set the bracelet on the dresser next to the box holding his cuff links and shirt studs, he paused as if he'd just remembered something. One hand lingering on the pull of the top drawer, he asked quietly, "Ariel, is everything all right with you, or shall I. . .take precautions?"

She smiled tenderly at Zachary, loving him even more because he'd cared enough to ask. Aloud she said, "Don't worry, everything's fine"—and with a rasping cry he swept her into his arms. Locked in a heated embrace, they fell together onto the undulating surface of the wide waterbed.

Suddenly, as she felt the tickling ripple of the mattress beneath her and Zachary's mouth closing greedily over her breast, Ariel wondered if, despite the fond teasing of their foreplay, they were not both too powerful, too intense to be gentle in their loving. So many conflicts hovered unresolved between them, and she was afraid their lovemaking might turn into a battle for dominance, for control.

"What's wrong?" Zachary asked, lifting his head when he sensed her hesitation.

Ariel bit her lip uncertainly. "You—you're so strong...." she whispered.

Zachary recoiled. "My God, do you think I'm going to hurt you?" he grated.

"No!" she reassured at once, seeing the anguish that obscured his expression. "I wasn't talking about your physical strength. I *like* that...." Her voice trailed off as she was momentarily diverted by the feel of the muscles of his back, sleek and supple under her fingertips. "I trust you...completely," she continued with an effort, her welling hunger making coherent speech difficult. "It's—it's just...."

Zachary stared at her, his black brows coming together as he surmised acutely, "It's just that you're afraid I may try to...subdue you sexually, take advantage of your feelings."

Ariel nodded. "It wouldn't be difficult," she admitted, a quaver in her voice. "I do need you so much."

For answer Zachary threw one lean leg heavily across Ariel's thighs, pressing himself explicitly against her. "Did you think I didn't need you?" he asked deeply.

Reveling in the hard glory of his body, she smiled with whimsical candor, her amber eyes growing murky. "I—I guess you do, at that," she conceded unsteadily.

Gently Zachary brushed her thick hair away from her face and kissed her nose. He chuckled. "Don't you know there can't be—or shouldn't be, anyway—contests in bed? When two people want each other, they are both equally vulnerable, equally strong...." He curled his fingers possessively over her breast, moving his hand in tiny circles so that the nipple grew erect in his palm as he murmured, "Don't you feel it, Ariel? When my flesh presses against your yours, yours presses against mine with just as much force, as much sensation. Here, whatever happens to one happens to both of us, because there are no barriers. We share everything...."

We share everything, her mind echoed as she gazed at him in silent rapture, their faces so close her lashes fluttered against his cheekbone. *Share,* she thought again, and she realized then that even though Zachary had been distressed when she'd told him she loved him, he was touching her with more consideration, more real emotion, than Matthieu Bonnard had ever shown her in the two years of their affair. Oh, her painting instructor had been a skilled lover, of course, his technique imaginative and very polished. But now she understood that Matthieu's expertise had been inspired not by any affection for her but by his own self-esteem.

Lacing her fingers together, Ariel placed them over Zachary's cupped hand. Her heart was beating so violently she was surprised the buffeting didn't bruise his palm. Huskily she said, "I want to give you everything, Zachary. I...want...to give—" His mouth covered hers.

Lips, teeth, tongues met and exchanged their riches before moving on with searing intent to greater treasures. When Zachary's hot breath scorched the delicate skin of Ariel's breasts, she writhed spasmodically and began to fondle the taut muscles of his buttocks. His hand slipped tantalizingly down over her flat belly, and she arched against him, moaning in wordless delight. Arrows of sensation buried themselves deep in the core of her being, leaving her vibrant, alive. Zachary smiled as he watched her catch her breath. Idly she wove her fingers into the crisp hair matting his chest, and then, when she felt capable of controlled movement once more, she took advantage of the still rocking motion of the mattress and levered Zachary over onto his back.

For long exultant moments he allowed her the freedom of his body, stroking, tasting. But then, while she was distracted by the virile wonder of the flesh she caressed, without warning he caught her in his arms and hauled her on top of him. Ariel gulped with surprise and choked out his name.

"My turn again," he laughed as his sharp unexpected action made the mattress surge and billow beneath them, amplifying his movements, urging her closer, so close.... Ariel grasped his broad shoulders to steady herself. She had never felt like this, never, never, and she was helpless to fight the sensations his touch was rousing in her. She saw his face flush with triumph as he stared up at her, his green eyes almost black with desire at the sight of her naked body poised above him, her honey-colored hair that cascaded down over her full breasts to brush his chest. "Zachary, please," she wailed, her voice high and faint, her head whirling. "Please stop—you're making me dizzy!"

"I won't let you fall," he reassured her quickly, his hands stretching up to encircle her rib cage and prop her upright. "I just want to be able to look at you—at us—together...."

"Together," Ariel repeated hoarsely, aflame. Hampered by her straddling position, she suffered in exquisite torment as he lightly caressed her mouth with one fingertip, teasing and skimming her sensitive lips, outlining the curve with his nail until she began to shake, all sensation, all arousal seemingly elicited by that square centimeter of rough skin on the end of his finger.

Then, when she could stand no more, almost reflexively she nipped at his fingertip, catching it between careful teeth and drawing it into her mouth to suck on it. She could feel Zachary tremble beneath her, and the knowledge of his own loss of control elated her. He was right; in this they were equal.... At last his hand stroked with moist coolness down over her chin, throat, breastbone, caressing her heated flesh, until one hand joined the other, splayed across her waist. Ariel's eyes widened incredibly as, with a fierce groan, Zachary lifted her upward and back. She gasped as he held her poised precariously. Then with great care he lowered her over him again, making them one, and she cried out in welcome and wonder.

IN THE EARLY HOURS of the morning Ariel awakened, languid and content. Zachary's hard arms were possessively around her, even in his sleep.

She snuggled against him, relishing the protective cocoon of his warmth, the delicious dampness of his flesh against hers. She could feel the even tenor of his breathing against the back of her neck, the slow throb of his heart that matched her own, and her kiss-drenched lips curled up in a smile as she marveled at the ecstasy they'd shared.

She stretched languorously, mildly puzzled to discover that her usually well-behaved body felt oddly stiff in a number of places. The slight movement wakened him. He murmured a wordless invitation, and the water mattress rocked gently under their combined weight when she rolled back toward him. Her head rested on his shoulder as she curled into the compelling contours of his body, wriggling still closer, passion stirring anew as she felt how beautifully they complemented each other, smooth and rough, soft and hard.... Flicking her silky lashes upward, she met Zachary's gaze, the carnival-flecked green eyes that were already growing opaque with renewed desire. She quivered as once again his strong clever hands began to explore and claim the now familiar regions of her body. His tongue brushed across her hardening nipples, and when he spoke his words were muffled against the slope of her breast. "Is everything okay?"

Relaxing against her pillow, she arched upward to deepen his caress. "Everything's fine. Everything's...just perfect," she reassured him, and with a little moan of delight she trailed her fingertips down the long sweep of his spine....

"ZACHARY, PLEASE, not again," she mumbled, burrowing deeper into the bedclothes. "I need to sleep!"

"You've been sleeping all morning, lazybones," he replied vigorously. "Come on, now. Get up. It's after ten." Grabbing the sheets, he yanked them down to the foot of the bed, leaving Ariel sprawled naked to his view.

She pulled herself into a sitting position, blinking against the sunlight that poured in through the glass wall that had been covered with drapes the previous night. "Sadist," she grumbled as she swept her thick hair away from her face and gazed up at him. She was surprised to see him dressed in jogging gear—a faded Stanford sweatshirt with cutoff sleeves, which adhered damply to the broad muscles of his chest, and brief shorts that revealed almost too much of his long bronzed thighs.... Wisps of black hair were plastered to his sweating brow above the rim of his glasses, and as he loomed over her, she could smell the pungent musky scent of overheated male flesh. "You've been out running?" she queried.

Zachary chuckled. "No woman who admits to rising at the crack of dawn every morning to go swimming in the icy waters of Mendocino Bay has any right to sound so amazed!" he declared. "Anyway, I brought back some breakfast for us." Casually he tossed a small paper sack at her, which she caught with ease. The bag was warm, and as soon as Ariel curiously uncrimped the top, the room filled with the yeasty aroma of fresh-baked bread. She peered inside, and when she saw the flaky golden crescent-shaped rolls, she began to laugh.

Zachary frowned in confusion. "What's the matter? Don't you like croissants?"

"I love them," Ariel said as she quickly stifled memories of Paris and the Left Bank, memories that suddenly struck her as more amusing than anything else.... "I'm sorry I laughed. It was just a private joke."

With a growl of mock menace he lunged at her, forcing her back down onto the bed. Balancing above her, he pinioned her with one hand on either side of her head and said hoarsely, "I didn't think it was possible for you and me to have secrets from each other anymore...."

Ariel caught her breath as she looked up into his craggy face. The skimpy clothes he wore made her own nudity seem more blatant somehow, provocative, and while he didn't actually touch her, in this posture she was as aware of him, of the curves and muscles and bones of that hard body surrounding her, as if his weight crushed her into the mattress. His scent was strong in her nostrils, and she felt her own body begin to respond with revived hunger to his nearness. She could see Zachary's eyes darken as he, too, noticed the flush of color flooding down over her throat, her breasts growing taut and inviting. "No secrets," she agreed huskily, wishing the words meant to him what they did to her—a promise for the future, a commitment.

Still poised above her, Zachary lowered his head to kiss her lingeringly. She rose on her elbows to meet his lips, which were warm and salty. After a few moments he said reluctantly, "I really do need to take a shower, darling."

The sensitive skin rimming her mouth stung slightly, and she lifted her fingers to test the sharp black bristles stubbling his chin. "You'd better shave, too," she murmured.

His eyes narrowed as he noticed the irritation his whiskers had caused. "Damn," he muttered darkly. Soothingly he bathed the pink marks with the tip of his tongue, each moist stroke sending temors of sensation radiating throughout her body. Ariel shivered as he whispered, "I was going to invite you to share the shower with me, but now...I'm afraid you're right about that shave. Do you mind very much if you wait for me?"

If I have to, I'll wait for you forever, she answered silently, but she knew in her heart he wasn't ready to hear that pledge. When he bounded abruptly to his feet, pulling her with him, she asked nonchalantly, "How about if I make coffee?" She glanced at her long silk dress, now neatly draped across the back of a chair, and added, "Do you have something I can put on before I go downstairs?"

"Oh, why?" Zachary teased, eyeing her bare torso appreciatively. "I rather like you the way you are."

His face grew still, and once more Ariel could feel a fierce ardor welling palpably between them.

With an effort she shrugged and commented, "I'm glad you like looking at me—but unfortunately, with all the windows in this house, if I'm not careful, so will your neighbors!"

"Prude," Zachary snorted with pretended disgust, gently caressing her cheek. Then his hand skimmed softly but possessively down over breast and waist, circling her nipples, stroking the concave plane of her belly...and beyond. She could feel the tension in him, and the soft fabric of his brief jogging shorts hid little of his increasing arousal. "God, woman," he breathed, "the things you do to me...." At last he pressed her gently away from him at the hips as he sighed reluctantly. "Go get the coffee, and I'll finish up in here as quickly as I can." Ducking into the bathroom, he grabbed a robe of thick brown terry cloth, which he tossed to her. While she cinched the bulky tie belt around her narrow waist, she could hear him turn on the water in the shower stall.

Ariel found her gold slippers lying at the bottom step when she padded barefoot down the stairs. Slipping on the shoes, she smiled reminiscently, hardly daring to believe, in the clear light of day, the turbulence that had engulfed them both the previous night. She went into the kitchen. After she'd set the automatic coffee maker to brew, she relaxed against the ceramic-tile counter and tried to think seriously about her relationship with Zachary.

There were so many things to consider, to

analyze, so many points that had yet to be cleared up between them. She needed to know what the previous night had meant to him. She knew what it had meant to her: she was in love with Zachary and she had made him a gift of her heart, handing it over to his keeping as surely and willingly as she'd wanted his supple, well-trained body to love hers. Even when their passion had been at its most unrestrained, Zachary had touched her with generosity and consideration, but still Ariel wasn't sure whether the rapture they'd shared had derived from mutual affection—or whether, like Matthieu, Zachary had simply pleasured her with the calculated skill of a man who prided himself on his prowess in bed. . . .

That possibility—that their lovemaking had been no more to him than any other casual encounter, perhaps even a one-night stand chilled her, and for her own peace of mind she refused to consider it. His emotions were involved in some way. They *had* to be. But how? She was still haunted by that look of unguarded distress clouding his eyes when she'd told him she loved him, and she didn't think she would begin to understand him until she knew exactly what had caused that look.

A dull click caught Ariel's attention, reminding her that the coffee maker had finished its brewing cycle. Rich aromatic steam wafted through the kitchen, and methodically Ariel began to search the cupboards for cups and saucers. By the time she mounted the stairs again, tray in hand, she had vowed she wouldn't be impatient. After all, she wasn't an adolescent trying to force love, childishly demanding instant everlasting commitment from the object of her affections. She was an adult, and she knew she would have to allow Zachary's feelings to burgeon and develop at whatever pace was comfortable for him. For the moment it ought to be enough that she was very sure of her own.....

When Ariel returned to the bedroom, Zachary was still in the shower. Beneath the gush of water rattling the glass stall doors, she could hear him humming deeply, tunelessly; she thought it the most poignantly domestic sound she'd ever heard. Ariel bit her lip as she wondered with curious longing what it would be like to have the right to hear that friendly sound every morning, every day.... The cups jiggled alarmingly on their saucers, and she quickly searched for a place to set down the tray.

She was just stirring cream into her own coffee when the telephone on the nightstand rang. Zachary called, "Will you get that for me, please?" and Ariel picked up the receiver.

"Drake residence," she said.

She could sense the presence of someone on the other end of the line, but for several seconds all she heard was charged silence. At last a feminine voice that sounded quite familiar asked carefully, "Miss Maclean, is that you?" When Ariel, puzzled, answered in the affirmative, the voice hesitated again. "Miss Maclean, this is Gwen Griffith-Jones. May I speak to Zachary, please?"

"Zachary's in the shower," Ariel replied automatically, and this time the silence stretched so long she began to feel apprehensive. Suddenly she remembered the first time she herself had telephoned Zachary's home, when Laurette had answered with almost those identical words. She wondered if Gwen, who had always been cordial and friendly to Ariel, was speaking in this peculiar stilted fashion because she was used to encountering another woman when she called her boss early in the morning. . . .

Gwen said, "I'm sorry, but I must speak to Zachary at once. It's urgent."

"Of course," Ariel answered. "I'll get him right away." She set down the receiver and loped across to the bathroom. Steam billowed out when she pulled open the door, and through the fogged glass panels of the shower she could just discern the dark outline of his tall bronzed body. She felt her own body stir yet again, and when she spoke, her voice was thick. "Zachary, your assistant is on the phone. She says it's important."

Immediately he turned off the water and slid open the shower door. "Toss me a towel, will you?" he said, squinting against the droplets of water that dripped into his eyes from the sodden curls dangling over his brow. Ariel stood motionless, mesmerized by the sight of him, wet and glistening before her, those broad shoulders, that muscular chest. She watched water bead in the blue-black hair plastered slickly against his tanned skin; she followed the shining rivulets that trailed down over his narrow hips, strong loins, powerful thighs.... She could feel her face growing warm, and his eyes glowed with answering heat as he said throatily, "Darling, I really do need to dry off so that I can see what Gwen wants." Reluctantly she handed him a towel.

The towel was anchored around his hips, his glasses perched on his long nose, when Zachary strode to the telephone. He motioned for Ariel to come to him, and when she approached, his free arm snaked out and caught her by the waist, pinning her against the hard contours of his body. She could feel his fingers stroking the side of her breast through the terry robe as she nuzzled her face against his shoulder, once again losing herself in the clean masculine scent of him, the faintly soapy taste of his skin. She was paying only minimal attention when he spoke briskly into the receiver.

"Hello, Gwen. I'm sorry I didn't warn you I wouldn't be at the office today, but after finally getting the labor situation reasonably squared away, I decided to claim executive privilege for once and sleep late. What can I do for you?"

Ariel snuggled closer, running her fingertips along the upper edge of the towel, watching fascinated as the muscles of Zachary's flat stomach clenched reflexively under the tickling brush of skin against skin. She heard Zachary say darkly, "Yes, Gwen, I took care of that a couple of days ago, exactly as Ellie specified. What about it?" For several seconds he listened carefully, and Ariel glanced up at his face, and she was dismayed to find that his genial smile had disappeared completely.

Realizing that Gwen's call obviously concerned some matter that required all Zachary's attention, Ariel tried to pull away, but to her surprise his grip tightened, his arm clamping around her rib cage. "Zachary!" she protested with a stifled hiss.

He didn't look down at her, but as she squirmed against him, his arm squeezed harder. Ariel began to struggle in earnest. Zachary barked into the telephone, "*What?* Are you sure? You've confirmed it? *Shit!*" She could hear Gwen speaking excitedly, and Zachary muttered in reply, "Yes, yes, I see.... No, not right away. Let me think about it for a while." He paused, and suddenly he seemed to become aware of the woman he held caged in his arms. He glared down at Ariel with a face as harsh and forbidding as the volcanic rocks that rimmed the Mendocino headland, and his eyes remained riveted to hers as he spoke curtly into the mouthpiece. "Look, Gwen, I'm going to have to get back to you later. There are some... things I need to take care of on this end. Thanks for letting me know." He slammed down the receiver.

Ariel gazed up at him, bewildered and apprehensive. "Zachary, what's the matter?"

"You bitch," he husked as the hand that had held the telephone now bit into her upper arm, trapping her against his bare chest. "You miserable greedy bitch! So you had to do it—you couldn't for once in your sordid little life put someone else's needs above your own.'' He was shaking with an anger so fierce he could hardly form the words, and the contempt that flamed in his eyes made the blood drain from Ariel's face.

Something was heinously wrong. This couldn't possibly be the same man who had teased and caressed her only moments earlier, the man who had loved her all during the wild wonderful night.... "Zachary," she cried, "please tell me what's happened!"

For endless moments he stared down at her, his mouth curling with distaste as if the very sight of her sickened him. Then suddenly he shoved her away. With a squeal she toppled backward. Before she could catch herself she landed with a muffled splash on the mattress's surging surface. The force of her fall and the undulating movement of the water beneath her loosened the belt of the brown robe, exposing her body and making it arch jerkily in an obscene parody of invitation. Zachary's eyes darkened at the sight of her naked torso, and he grated thickly, "For God's sake, cover yourself!"

She felt the heat of her blush clear down to her toes as clumsily she sat upright and silently tugged the lapels of the robe across her full breasts. When she looked up at Zachary again, her wide amber eyes were shimmering. With great effort she swallowed the lump in her throat and asked simply, "Why?"

Just for a second she thought he hesitated, uncertainty flickering across his adamantine features. But when he spoke again his words were icy with conviction, and Ariel thought he'd never sounded so British.... "You know why, Ariel," he stated flatly, biting off the syllables. "But what you obviously didn't expect was that word would reach me so soon. Although the owner of the boat-charter service had told Walsh he'd give the boat to his other client if Sam didn't get back to him right away, he knew how much Goodearth was counting on him, and he decided to give the group another chance. So this morning he called his hotel, and when he couldn't reach him there, he contacted Seacliff—Walsh had originally given him Ellie's name as a handy reference. Gwen started checking around. It would appear, Ariel, that your lover has disappeared—taking with him every penny from the Goodearth bank account, including the donation Eleanor made!"

AT FIRST the only thing that formed in Ariel's staggered mind was, *but I thought* you *were my lover.*

Then, when the sense of his words began to penetrate her stupor, caused by the shock of Zachary's inexplicable fury, Ariel repeated dully, "Disappeared?"

"Disappeared, vanished, fled—Ariel, the man is *gone!*" Zachary exclaimed harshly. "He checked out of his hotel late yesterday afternoon, less than an hour after he'd raided the group's bank account."

"But—but I don't understand. Everything was arranged—"

"I'll bet," Zachary snorted, swearing viciously. "I was right about you all along, wasn't I? From the beginning you've been planning to take Ellie for everything you could get—only when you met her you found out that not only was your long-lost grandmother not quite the malleable little old lady you expected her to be, but also she had me to look after—" He stopped, stunned, his stony features suddenly slack and livid, as if he'd been dealt a physical blow. "My God," he choked, slowly looking at Ariel, who sat in the middle of the tumbled bed, eyeing him warily, "was that what *that* was all about? You were just keeping me occupied while Walsh—"

In anguish Ariel cried, "Zachary, no! I *love* you!" He didn't speak, but the distaste in his eyes stabbed her. She tried to appeal to his reason. "You're not thinking clearly—you know you're not. You *can't* believe what you're saying! There was no way I could have planned for last night to happen. After all, you called *me*." She studied his dear face searchingly, but he appeared unmoved. At last she said again quietly, tiredly, "Zachary, I do love you."

She was unprepared for the vehemence of his reaction. Looming over her like some avenging Titan—and despite her distress Ariel couldn't help noting that, wrapped in his loincloth of a towel, Zachary really did look like an ancient deity, the near nakedness of his body somehow girding him. "Oh, God, I loathe that word!" he spat.

Her eyes widened. "What do you mean? What word?"

"Love," he snorted. "The ultimate excuse for any lie, any betrayal. When all else fails, tell the person you've wronged that you acted out of love, and instantly he *has* to forgive you!"

"Zachary..." Ariel began uncertainly, but he wasn't listening to her. Suddenly she realized he wasn't even thinking about her anymore. She watched as he began to pace the length of the room, his movements jerky and stiff. In the bright sunlight that poured in through the picture window she could see his eyes were shadowed with acrid memories.

"I can still hear my mother's voice during those arguments," he rasped. " 'Philip, you know the only reason I flirt with the consul is to help you with your work, because I love you.' 'Philip, darling, those other men don't mean a thing. It's you I love.' And of course, the biggest lie of them all. 'Zachary, sweetheart, you don't really want to move back to gloomy old England with daddy, do you? Mommy *loves* you!' " He closed his eyes and took a deep breath. "God help me, I believed her," he groaned. "And my father never forgave me for believing her, for choosing her over him...."

Ariel listened in anguish. Since meeting Zachary she'd been blinded by the facade of his big, very adult body, the executive armor he habitually wore. Now, beneath the strength, the intelligence, the overwhelming sensuality, she found the vulnerable heart of a child, wounded and defensive, deathly afraid of the emotion that had hurt him.... "My poor darling," she murmured.

Zachary whirled around, green eyes glittering. "Damn you, Ariel Maclean," he growled. "I don't want your pity. I don't want anything from you except a fast rundown on the plans you and Walsh made. What was the scenario to be? Were you going to tell Ellie that something pressing that required your presence in Mendocino had cropped up and then meet Walsh at—"

Ariel recoiled from his fury. In a voice as steady as she could manage she insisted, "Zachary, you're angry and you're not thinking clearly. If you'll just stop and consider for a moment, you'll realize there's still no proof that anything has in fact happened to Sam, and certainly no way I could know what's become of him. There must be any number of logical explanations. I'm sure it will all turn out to be just a—"

Scathingly Zachary interrupted, "Spare me your innocent act, because I don't buy it. According to the bank manager, the check Walsh used yesterday had *your* signature on it!"

Ariel froze. Suddenly a succession of bright images flashed through her mind, repeating faster and faster, until they were a blur of color, vivid—and damning: Eleanor's smile when she announced Seacliff Publications would fund Goodearth's trip into the Pacific, Sam's long pale mustache drooping with sullen despair as he told Ariel that creditors were beginning to harass Marie, Ariel's own hand scrawling her name on the bottom of a blank check.... "Oh, my God," she whispered brokenly.

Grimly Zachary scanned her expressive features. "Well," he demanded, "are you going to deny you wrote Walsh the check?"

"No, of course not," Ariel muttered abstractedly, her mind working rapidly, "But...." *Marie,* she thought, and she lunged for the telephone.

Before she could touch the receiver, Zachary caught her wrists with hands like manacles and pulled her against his chest. "And just what do you think you're going to do?" he drawled silkily.

He was hurting her, but Ariel didn't try to escape him. Her tawny eyes challenged him as she said evenly, "I have to call Mendocino."

His grip tightened. "Trying to warn your lover?"

"Damn it, Zachary," Ariel hissed, "how many times do I have to tell you? *Sam Walsh is not my lover!*"

"Then why the hell did you give him the money?"

"I didn't—at least not the way you mean," Ariel protested unhappily. As she spoke, she realized with regret that she was already yielding to Zachary's interpretation of Sam's mysterious disappearance. No matter how much she would like to believe otherwise, the evidence seemed overwhelming. Tersely she explained the frantic sequence of events of the previous afternoon, omitting nothing—except the irrelevant fact that her love for Zachary was so strong that when he'd telephoned, her delight at the prospect of speaking to him had blotted all other considerations from her mind. . . .

He listened enigmatically. The blind rage seemed to seep out of him, only to be replaced by stunned disbelief as he demanded, "My God, woman, are you trying to tell me you blithely handed Sam Walsh a blank check?"

Ariel shrugged awkwardly, her eyes veiled. Now that Zachary's air of menace had subsided somewhat, her disquiet was rapidly changing to irritation. Jerking her hands out of his grasp, she retorted, "I didn't do it 'blithely' or any other way. It just happened." She slid off the bed and stood up, rubbing her aching wrists.

Zachary's mouth tightened at her action, but when he spoke his voice still sounded impatient and accusing. "I've never heard such deplorable ignorance of even the most basic tenets of sound business practice," he declared. "Don't you know that you must never ever give a person access to money or any other negotiable commodity without also establishing some kind of safeguard on his behavior? Given carte blanche, even the most honest employee can succumb to temptation if—"

Through gritted teeth Ariel stated, "I'm not a businesswoman, Zachary. I'm an artist. And Sam was my *friend*.... I trusted him,'' she finished feebly.

"A hell of a lot of good your trust has done you," Zachary pointed out relentlessly. "Your group is broke, and unless the money is recovered, you have no indemnity. As I recall, you became quite scathing on the subject when I tried to warn you about putting some kind of bond on—"

"All right!" she interrupted hotly, wanting to hate him, glaring up at his arrogant arresting face with eyes that tended instead to soften caressingly.... She looked away again. She didn't want to feel her body's overwhelming response to him. She didn't want to remember that last night, while she'd been making blissful passionate love with Zachary, Sam had been destroying a dream,, absconding with the fruits of two years of hard work by her and all the other members of Goodearth. "All right, Zachary," she repeated wearily. "I admit it—you were right, and I was wrong. Does that make you happy?"

He laughed mirthlessly. "Right now I think about the only thing that would make me happy would be to feel my fingers around Walsh's scrawny neck!" When Ariel didn't respond, he caught her chin lightly with his fingertips and tilted her face up toward his. Quietly he asked, "Do you have any idea where Walsh might have gone?"

She sighed. "No matter what Sam's plans might be—assuming he actually has plans and isn't just running scared—the first place he would go would be back up to Mendocino, to get Marie."

Zachary's mouth curved skeptically. "Ah, yes, the mysterious Marie. . . ."

Ariel looked baffled. "What on earth is that supposed to mean?"

"I was merely taking note of the odd coincidence," Zachary replied smoothly, "that while to date I've never met Sam Walsh's alleged lady friend, I have frequently seen the man with you, usually with his hands on you."

Shrugging aside the temptation to interpret Zachary's jealousy as evidence that he harbored deeper feelings for her, she said impatiently, "Well, whether or not you've met Marie she does exist. And even if Sam hasn't returned to Mendocino, I think he would have let her know where he was headed." Her expression softened, and she pleaded, "Zachary, you must let me telephone her. Marie has been my best friend for years, and I know her very well. She loves Sam, but she would never purposely abet him in the commission of a crime. If I tell her what's happened, she may be able to help us locate him."

Zachary stared at her searchingly, his gaze opaque and unreadable behind his glasses. Returning his gaze, Ariel remembered wistfully how, only a few pathetically short hours earlier, she'd felt as if she could swim in those shimmering emerald depths. . . . Zachary exhaled explosively, as if he'd been holding his breath. "Very well," he conceded through lips that hardly moved. "You can make your call—not that I think it will do you much good. I'm going to get dressed." Turning on his heel, he stalked across the luxurious carpet to his closet.

He was lounging in an easy chair, the collar of his sportshirt unbuttoned, his long gabardine-clad legs crossed indolently, when Ariel at last hung up the telephone and turned away in defeat. He swallowed the tepid dregs of his coffee and grimaced as he asked, ''Any luck?''

Ariel shook her head, ruffling the mat of sun-bleached hair that lay tangled across her shoulders. She glanced sidelong at Zachary, admiring as always the grace with which he wore his clothes, the way his well-formed body lent a certain style to even the most conservative tailoring. She looked away, unconsciously cinching the terry-cloth belt tighter around her waist. She glanced unhappily at the evening gown that lay draped across the bed, where Zachary had moved it just before he sat down. In the bright daylight the gleam of jewel-toned embroidery on topaz-colored silk seemed inappropriate, almost gaudy. She didn't relish putting that gown on again—she didn't think she would ever be able to bear wearing it again—but she knew she had no choice. Now, she thought dispiritedly, her own near nakedness had ceased to be provocative, seemed only slatternly....

Again Zachary asked about the telephone calls, and Ariel replied woodenly, ''I tried Sam and Marie's house several times. There was no answer. Then I called one of the other women from Good-earth who lives just a couple of doors down from them, and I asked if she'd seen Marie. She said no. She also told me that late last night, when she and her husband got home from a movie, she thought she spotted Sam's car outside their place—only she thinks now that she must have been mistaken, because there doesn't seem to be anyone at home this morning.''

Ariel paused heavily, and Zachary said, ''That seems to be it, then. What do you plan to do now?''

''I don't know,'' Ariel admitted helplessly. ''I've never in my life been in any situation remotely similar to this. I guess—I guess I should call the police or something—not that I could tell them very much. I don't even know the exact time my friend in Mendocino spotted Sam's car. I was afraid to probe too deeply for fear I'd make her suspicious. After all the work everyone in the group has done for the past two years, all the dreaming and planning, I—I'm just not ready to tell them that the ocean voyage will have to be canceled.''

''Sooner or later they'll have to find out,'' Zachary pointed out unanswerably.

''Yeah,'' Ariel murmured. She gnawed on her lip. ''Unfortunately, so will Ellie! I think I could face what's happened a lot more easily if only I didn't keep remembering how happy and excited Ellie was at the celebration when she promised to help us. . . .''

Her voice trailed off, and with grim irony Zachary finished the sentence for her. ''You mean how happy and excited she was—just before her heart attack! By some perverse twist of fate that's been pretty much the pattern of Eleanor Raymond's whole life. Joy—followed almost instantly by tragedy or disillusion. She lost her husband within a year of their marriage. When at last she found another man to love, her own daughter eloped with him. She was reunited with her long-lost granddaughter, and now it turns out that she's been conned by—"

"Zachary, no!" Ariel shrilled in horror, going to him, leaning intensely over him as her hands gripped the arms of his chair. "No," she repeated, her eyes luminous with distress. "You can't honestly believe that I had anything to do with it, that I would deliberately set out to embezzle money from my own grandmother!"

He stared up at her intently, piercingly, as if he were plumbing the depths of her glimmering gold eyes for her soul. As silence stretched between them, she began to tremble. At last he acknowledged grudgingly, "No, Ariel, I don't believe you had any willful part in what happened. . . ." She went limp with relief. Yet he continued pitilessly, "But I do blame you for your criminal negligence in permitting a character like Sam Walsh free access to the Goodearth bank account!"

Ariel closed her eyes. When she opened them again, her trembling had stopped. She squared her shoulders. "Okay," she announced tonelessly, "I accept the responsibility." Pushing against the arm of the chair, she straightened and brushed her hair away from her face. She walked to the bed and collected her gown and underclothes before heading for the bathroom. Zachary watched her movements in brooding silence.

At the door to the bathroom she paused and glanced back at him. "If you'll excuse me for a few minutes, I'd like to get dressed," she explained politely. "After that I'll need to make a few telephone calls. Whether I want to or not, I'm going to have to let the other members know what happened. I'll worry about what to tell Ellie later.... I'm assuming, of course, that it's all right with you if I use your phone?" *Lord,* she thought in disgust, *after all we've just been through, what an asinine thing to say!*

Zachary seemed to agree. "Be my guest," he muttered wryly.

She hung Zachary's robe on the hook on the back of the bathroom door and then with quick compact movements slipped into her rumpled dress, carefully avoiding her reflection in the wide mirrors. She didn't ever want to see herself in the yellow gown again. She didn't want to remember the way she'd preened happily before her grandmother, giddy as a young girl, slightly disoriented by the change in her appearance. She ought to have recognized then that she was inviting disaster by acting so completely out of character. In the life-style of Ariel Maclean, struggling free-lance artist, there was no place for silk and jewels, anymore than there was a place for—

As she tugged awkwardly on the side zipper, she noticed a smudge on the bodice, a small brown smear that she identified after a moment as a drop of *sauce bordelaise*. Wistfully she recalled the moment during their dinner the previous night when, just as Ariel was taking a bite of succulent filet, Zachary had said something so witty she'd sputtered with laughter, only just managing to clap her napkin to her mouth before she disgraced herself completely. Smiling fondly at her discomfiture, Zachary had reached across the table to take her hand....

I guess last night we were both acting out of character, she thought sadly, and with a sigh she went back into the bedroom.

CHAPTER NINE

THE FIRST THING SHE NOTICED was that Zachary hadn't moved from the armchair; in fact, he didn't seem to have moved at all. He sat in unnerving silence, his long legs stretched before him, his eyes focused on some invisible point just past his toes. Ariel, glancing uneasily toward the telephone beside the bed, asked cautiously, "Do you mind if I make my calls from downstairs? I—I'll use my telephone credit card, of course."

Without looking at her, he said, "You don't need to make the calls, Ariel. I'll finance your voyage."

She didn't think she'd heard him correctly. When he repeated his statement impatiently, she gaped at him and choked, "You'll *what*?"

Letting out his breath in a hiss, he demanded harshly, "How many times do I have to say it? I'll back your trip. I'll be Goodearth's backer."

He was joking—he had to be—and the very idea that he would make light of problems that devastated her hurt so much that her eyes shimmered. But she felt too emotionally exhausted to do more than say, "Don't be silly, Zachary. It was one thing for Seacliff to provide the funds—quite another for a private individual! Have you any idea exactly how much money you're talking about?''

He shrugged. ''I think so. You needn't worry. I'm good for it.''

''That's not the point.''

''That's exactly the point,'' he countered. ''It happens that I have some stock my broker thinks is shaky, which he's been pressuring me to unload. I don't need the cash, so I've been planning to make donations to a couple of charities I'm rather fond of. But now....'' He paused, then concluded cynically, ''I suppose one tax deduction is as good as another.''

Ariel was staggered. ''I—I had no idea,'' she said inadequately. After a moment she continued in confusion, ''What I don't understand is why, despite all the tax write-offs, you should want to help Goodearth in the first place. Why us, of all groups? You've never made any secret of your low opinion of our work.'' Gazing down at his dark head, she watched the sunlight glinting off the silvered hair above his ears. During the night her fascinated fingers had returned repeatedly to his temples, drawn back to those gleaming strands as if their metallic brightness were somehow magnetic.... *Oh, Zachary. I wish I could believe you wanted to help Goodearth because of me, but I know your opinion of me and my friends is even lower than your opinion of what we're trying to do....*

At last he looked up at her with gem-hard eyes

as he contradicted, "You're wrong, Ariel. I have no particular objection to saving the whales. I just think you're going about it the wrong way."

"Then why did you say you would finance our trip?"

"Because," he explained tightly, "if I don't do it, Eleanor will."

Ariel gasped at his implied accusation. "I would *never* ask her to—" she began heatedly, only to break off abruptly. "But I wouldn't have to ask her, would I?" she whispered.

Zachary smiled grimly. "No, you wouldn't have to ask. All that would be necessary would be for Ellie to find out you needed the money. She'd willingly beggar herself to see that you got anything you wanted—and I don't want her to do that."

"Whether or not you believe me, neither do I," Ariel said. She fell silent again, chewing on her lip as she considered the many things that had yet to be done, all the tasks that Sam was supposed to have carried out, which would now land squarely on her own aching shoulders if they continued with their plans. So little time remained, time she had hoped to devote to finishing her grant proposal before the group embarked. She realized fatalistically that if she took over the preparations for Goodearth's voyage, she would in effect be abandoning all hope of ever winning the job at the Navarro River Opera House. Her career seemed continually to be put on hold while she dealt with other things that were equally important to her:

she'd abandoned her studies in France in order to care for her father, and now, just when a prize commission appeared almost in her grasp....

And yet, she admitted, in the greater scheme of things her personal ambitions mattered very little compared to the ecological tragedy she and her friends were trying to prevent. Fall was fast approaching, and in the north Pacific the whaling fleets would soon set sail for their voyages of government- and business-sanctioned slaughter. Soon the haunting songs of the great whales would be drowned out by muffled booms and tortured cries as the harpoon cannons found their targets, and the billowing waves would run red.... Ariel clenched her fists tightly. It had to be stopped. It *would* be stopped.

"Thank you very much, Zachary," she said with humble sincerity. "I know I speak for everyone in Goodearth when I say we'll always be grateful to you for your generosity."

He made a curt gesture of dismissal. "I'm not being generous. I expect to be repaid in full."

Ariel faltered. "I—I beg your pardon," she began uncertainly. "I must have misunderstood. I thought when you said—I'm sorry. That puts an entirely different complexion on the problem." Her mind worked rapidly for several minutes before she conceded with regret that there was no way she would be able to persuade the other members of the group to accept Zachary's terms. Many of Goodearth's original participants had dropped out during the two grueling years they'd spent working toward their goal, and the ones who remained had held on only because their grail seemed at long last within reach. Even in the best of circumstances it took very little perspicacity to foresee that once the journey into the Pacific was over, the group would dissolve—and these were hardly the best of circumstances. No, it was hopeless—unless. . . .

Drawing a ragged breath, Ariel ventured, "Look, you must realize I can't agree to any arrangement that would obligate my friends to repay your loan. What I could do is give you a mortgage on—on my home—assuming you're agreeable, of course. . . ." She paused, momentarily distracted by a vision of the weathered frame house that had been home to three generations of Macleans. Oh, God, what she wouldn't give to be there right now! When she saw Zachary's green eyes widen with astonishment, she rushed on, "I know you weren't terribly impressed with the place that day you came looking for me, but in today's market Mendocino property is considered very val—"

Zachary cut in, "You really care that much?"

Ariel blinked. "Yes, I care that much," she asserted flatly, puzzled by his tone. She could see a curious flush of red creeping up over the angular sweep of his hard jaw. "It'll take a little time to arrange, but I'm sure I can get a note for at least—"

"Ariel, I don't want your house," he said quickly.

Still she didn't understand. "But you just told me—"

He shook his head impatiently. His eyes stroked her voluptuous body, caressing her with languid heat as he said deliberately, "I had a different type of payment in mind."

Ariel recoiled. Her mouth felt as if it were full of ashes, caustic and suffocating, and for a long moment she couldn't speak. "Oh, Zachary, that's—that's cheap," she finally choked in distaste.

He shrugged unrepentently as he drawled, "Sweetheart, considering the amount of money we're talking about, I hardly think 'cheap' is the right word. . . .

Gasping with pain, she turned away. Hot tears stung her eyes as she fumbled blindly for the doorknob, but before she found it, two large hands gripped her shoulders gently but irresistibly from behind, stilling her. Only his hands touched her, but his warmth reached out to her. She could feel his breath tickling her nape. She waited warily for him to speak.

She knew what he was doing. During the night he'd let her get too close to him, breaching all his carefully erected defenses, making him vulnerable. And now in the cold clear light of day he was rejecting her as crudely as possible in order to push her away again, back outside the barriers. Yes, Ariel understood all that—and pitied him for it—but even so, his words hurt so much she thought she might just possibly die. One fat salty droplet trickled silently down her cheek, catching on the corner of her mouth. As she licked it away, she tried not to remember the sensual abrasion of his tongue when he'd sipped brandy from her lips. . . .

His deep graveled voice continued roughly, "I thought I understood how it was between us. I thought *you* understood that we were just— I was wrong, and I apologize."

She winced. *Apologize.* He apologized. What a feeble anodyne for the agony of knowing that Zachary preferred to think of their coming together as only a mutual satisfying of needs by two consenting adults, like—like scratching an itch— or worse, striking a bargain. She recalled bitterly how earlier that morning she'd wondered what their lovemaking had meant to him. Well, now she knew—and wished she didn't. Suppressing a sniffle, she replied stiltedly, "Don't worry, Zachary. I do know the score. I assure you I won't read anything into what happened that you don't. . . that you don't. . . ." Her voice died out in a strangled sob.

His fingers tightened on her shoulders, digging into her soft skin. "Damn it, Ariel," he grated. "I'm sorry, but I don't know how to give you what you want!"

Ariel thought it was the most tragic statement she'd ever heard in her life.

When she turned around to face him, her composure amazed her. Her amber-shining eyes were shadowed but steady as she softly insisted, "But that's what's so pathetic. I don't want anything from you. I never did. Instead I had a present for *you*, a gift of love—and now I don't think I'll ever be able to forgive you for changing my gift into something tawdry, like payment for services rendered...."

She could feel the shudder that coursed through him as he stared back at her, but when he spoke once more, his voice sounded as even as her own, punctilious with courtesy. "Again I must apologize. I never meant to hurt you. I just hope you'll remember that, as you reminded me so winningly last night, anyone can make a mistake...." He captured a long strand of hair that dangled over her eyes and brushed it back away from her face, his fingertips lingering in the sensitive depression behind her ear. Then he said briskly, "Let's get your things together, and I'll take you home to Ellie. I expect by now she's beginning to wonder what's happened to you."

ARIEL STUDIED the provision list with a frown. "Two cases tortilla chips," someone had penciled in. "Maybe some bean dip." She sighed impatiently. Goodearth was supposed to be planning an extended cruise into the north Pacific, though whoever had composed the original list was treating the voyage as if it were an afternoon jaunt around the bay. The last thing they needed was a galley full of junk food! She slashed her pen across the entry. Just then she heard Eleanor and James walk in through the front door, and setting aside the list, she pasted a grin on her face as they came into the living room. "Hi!"

she said brightly. "Did you two enjoy your stroll?"

Eleanor flashed a rueful glance at James, who was helping her remove her light jacket, before she answered Ariel. "Stroll?" she chuckled dryly. "Hike would be more like it. The last time I took a walk that long I got a Girl Scout merit badge."

Her charming, gray-haired companion laughed. "Well, this time, darling, you'll just have to settle for Brownie points from your doctor. You know he wants you to begin regular mild exercise, now that you're back on your feet."

Eleanor murmured teasingly, "I can think of other forms of exercise I'd much prefer...." James's answering smile was so intimate and meaningful that Ariel quickly looked away. When Eleanor sank gratefully onto the couch, her color high in the hollow cheeks that had been pasty white for weeks, James hovered over her, and Ariel, feeling distinctly de trop, started to excuse herself. Her grandmother forestalled her. "No, don't go, please," she said plaintively.

"But, Ellie, you need to rest."

Eleanor shook her head. "No, dear, I just have to catch my breath for a few minutes, and while I'm doing that, you can tell me all about how your preparations are going for the sea trip." She looked up at James again. "Would you mind asking Mrs. Fong if she would fix us a cool drink? And while I'm thinking about it, wasn't there something in the mailbox for Ariel?"

Ariel thought she saw something flash in

James's eyes at Eleanor's rather curt command, but dutifully he fetched a fat manila envelope from the table in the entryway and, after handing it to Ariel, disappeared into the kitchen. Through the long veil of her lashes Ariel regarded her grandmother uncertainly. "You shouldn't order him around like that, you know." She reproved mildly. "The man cares about you."

Eleanor's mouth thinned. "And James knows how I feel about him," she retorted, visibly agitated. Grabbing her handbag, she riffled clumsily through the contents, at last retrieving her cigarettes. As she repeatedly flicked the balky wheel of her lighter, she said with asperity, "Ariel, dear, I would appreciate it very much if you would stay out of matters that don't concern you. After all, as much as I love you, I have avoided probing into the rather erratic nature of your affair with— Oh, damn, I think I just broke a fingernail!"

Ariel retreated into the soft cushions of the chair, recognizing that for the first time she'd been scolded by her grandmother. Oh, well, maybe she deserved it. Eleanor and James were both adults, and whatever went on between them was certainly none of her business, just as it wasn't really any of Eleanor's business that Ariel's so-called affair with Zachary had turned out not to be an affair at all.

Because she knew she would only wallow in despair and self-pity if she permitted her thoughts to continue along that path, Ariel resolutely turned her attention to the large envelope James had handed her. It contained her mail, forwarded down from Mendocino, and she tore it open raggedly, dumping the contents in her lap. After she'd separated out the various window envelopes that obviously contained bills, she was left with two letters and the quarterly report from an Oakland-based ecology group she belonged to. The first letter was from the head of the English department at the college in Fort Bragg where her father had taught. The professor told her that the alumni association had decided to establish a small scholarship fund in memory of John Maclean's many years of dedicated service. The man asked if she might be able to attend the dinner organized to announce the scholarship. Ariel smiled tenderly. Her father loved his work, and she couldn't think of any honor that would have pleased him more. Glancing at the date for the dinner, which was after the time she ought to return from the ocean voyage, she vowed to be there.

The second letter was from the Pacific Coast Regional Arts Council. She'd written to them as soon as she'd finally accepted the fact that she wouldn't be able to complete her grant proposal. Yet she knew that seeing the final rejection in black and white was going to hurt. Apprehensively she burrowed her nails under the gummed flap and yanked it open.

Her fingers shook slightly as she held the single sheet of paper that fell out in her hand. "Dear Ms. Maclean," she read, her tawny eyes darkening as she skimmed the concise phrases. "It was with regret that we received the notice withdrawing your application...we were very enthusiastic about your proposal...hoped by allowing the extension you requested earlier.... In conclusion, must agree that further delay would be unfair to the other applicants...." Blinking hard, she crushed the letter into a tight ball between her palms and gazed blearily at the floor.

Eleanor's eyes narrowed as she watched Ariel. Drawing smoke deeply into her lungs, she asked in measured tones, "Bad news?"

Ariel shrugged with feigned lightness. "A job I rather had my heart set on didn't pan out, that's all," she murmured. "It was inevitable, but still, it's a setback...."

Eleanor stared pointedly at the glowing tip of her cigarette. "This job you wanted," she probed shrewdly. "Does your failure to get it have something to do with the fact that you've been staying with me all this time?" When Ariel shook her head quickly, too quickly, Eleanor sighed contritely. "Oh, child, I'm sorry. Having you here has meant so much to me I've deliberately ignored the fact that you have work and a life of your own elsewhere. Can you ever forgive me for being so selfish?"

Ariel could feel her face growing warm with the effort to keep her lips curved into a reassuring smile as she calmly explained, "The difficulties began long before I met you, Ellie. Basically I think they developed because it's been so long since I worked with large graphics. I just got a little...overambitious...." When she saw that her grandmother remained unconvinced, Ariel concluded with a halfhearted chuckle, "If you don't believe me, you can always ask Zachary. I'm sure he'll be glad to regale you with the saga of my search for the perfect model...."

Perfect, she thought in anguish, her voice trailing off as she remembered ardent whispers in the heated darkness. "Everything's just perfect.... Excuse me," she said roughly, jumping up, scattering the lists she'd been working on. "I have to—I must— Excuse me." When she fled from the room and ran toward the staircase, she almost collided with James in the hallway.

Galloping up the stairs, she'd just reached the landing when her flight was arrested by the sound of an indignant male voice carrying clearly from the living room. "Eleanor, what the *hell* are you doing with that cigarette?"

Ariel froze, stupefied by the fury coarsening James's words. She had never heard him raise his voice, had certainly never heard him address her grandmother in anything but loving, even adoring tones. But now he sounded beside himself as he shouted, "Damn it, Eleanor, I'm not interested in hearing your excuses! You know as well as I do what your doctor said about taking care of yourself from now on. Doesn't it *matter* to you whether you live or—"

"But, James—" Eleanor started to speak, but just then Ariel's attention was diverted by Mrs.

Fong, who appeared in the hallway carrying a tray with glasses and a frosty pitcher of something iced. From her vantage point at the top of the stairs Ariel could see the housekeeper hesitate, uncertain whether she ought to intrude on the scene in the living room. Ariel cleared her throat, and Mrs. Fong glanced up at her. For several seconds the two women exchanged bewildered speaking glances. Mrs. Fong retreated to the kitchen.

Ariel knew she probably ought to discreetly make her own swift departure to her bedroom, but, concerned that her grandmother might need her, she instead hovered on the landing, listening in shock as James raged on. "Damn it, Eleanor, you *are* my business. You have been for the past decade! For ten years I've loved you, but because I've always known you were skittish about making a commitment, I've done things your way, catered to your whims, accepted whatever crumbs of affection you've seen fit to toss in my direction, followed you around like some goddamned puppy."

"James, no!" Eleanor gasped. "You know you mean more to me than that!"

"Do I?" he continued implacably. "How? You don't want to marry me. You don't seem to need me for anything but a social convenience—good ol' James, your pet dinner partner, your pet *bed* partner...."

Eleanor seemed to be recovering somewhat from her initial shock as she retorted, "Don't you like being my bed partner, James?"

There was a long pause, and when James answered her, his voice was quieter, more controlled, but to Ariel's ears, the very softness of his response made him sound only that much more resolute. He said, "Of course I enjoy being your lover, Eleanor—but I'd rather be your husband. I want the right to live with you, cherish you, take care of you, since you obviously don't know how to take care of yourself. And unless you give me that right *right now*, that's going to be the end of it—forever. The pleasure of making love to you occasionally is not sufficient recompense for what I went through a few weeks ago when I watched you almost die...."

Ariel slipped off to her bedroom.

She threw herself across the white eyelet bedspread and stared at the rose-colored wallpaper, her eyes swimming with unshed tears as she thought about the concern, the incredible tenderness that had throbbed in James's voice even when he was hollering at Eleanor, the love that transcended his anger, his fear. Oh, Lord, how could Ellie be so obtuse, so stubborn? Didn't she know that what James was offering her was precious beyond measure, a treasure so rare that most people went their whole lives without ever guessing that such love even existed? *Oh, please, Ellie,* Ariel prayed desperately, *don't reject his gift of love. Don't be like Zachary....*

She thought she must have dozed, because the next thing she knew, her cheeks were sticky with tracks of dried salt, and Mrs. Fong was tapping gently on her door. "Mr. Drake would like to speak to you on the phone,'' the woman announced when Ariel stumbled across the room to answer her summons. Ariel thanked her and automatically headed for the extension upstairs but as she passed the top of the staircase she paused and looked back at the housekeeper quizzically. Mrs. Fong smiled, her impassive mask dissolving as she murmured reassuringly, ''Don't worry, they're not yelling anymore. Whatever's going on in the living room, it does *not* sound like an argument....'' Ariel grinned in relief and went to answer the telephone.

Scarcely acknowledging her tremulous greeting, Zachary came straight to the point. ''I want you to add another name to the passenger list.''

His brisk tones irritated her. ''In addition to yourself, you mean?'' she said coolly. ''I've known all along that you would expect to go with us so that you could protect your—''

Zachary interrupted impatiently. ''I wasn't talking about me. Laurette will also be accompanying us.''

Just for a second Ariel was too flabbergasted to speak, made mute by a vision of the petite blond singer in one of her spangled jumpsuits, posed incongruously against the backdrop of a ramshackle fishing boat. ''W-why should Laurette Masefield need to come along on Goodearth's expedition?'' she asked unsteadily.

Zachary shot back, ''She doesn't 'need' to come. She'll be there because I want her there.''

Her fingers clenched the receiver so tightly she

was sure she must be denting the hard plastic. She knew Zachary didn't love her, didn't even like her very much. Yet the degree of his callousness left her gasping with near physical pain. Despair, jealousy, rage clawed at her, until she thought she could literally taste the sour tang of blood in her mouth. Then she realized that her teeth had savaged the soft inner lining of her lip.

"Ariel, did you hear what I said?"

She swallowed hard and answered gruffly, "Yes, I heard you. You're bringing Laurette with you. I guess that's natural enough, wanting to make use of a few of the little extras your money entitles you to, like the private cabin I've assigned you. I suppose I'd better check it again to make sure it will be big enough for both—"

"That won't be necessary," Zachary snapped icily. "Laurette will bunk with you and the other women on the cruise. She's making the trip because Don Fielding thinks the publicity will help her singing career through greater exposure—*not* because I need another warm body in my bed!"

Ariel blushed scarlet. *A warm body in his bed,* she thought miserably. *That's all I was, just another warm body.* "H-how very frustrating for you..." she husked, and quietly set the receiver back in its cradle.

Instantly the telephone rang again. Ariel debated not answering it, but she knew that if she let it ring, Mrs. Fong would only pick it up downstairs. With great reluctance she lifted the receiver, and before she could even raise it to her ear she heard

Zachary roar, "Damn it, Ariel Maclean, don't *ever* hang up on me again!"

With deceptive calm she asserted, "I'll hang up on you whenever I feel like it, Zachary."

For several seconds he was silent. When at last he spoke, he sounded once again like the man Eleanor had characterized as her "most unflappable executive." As composed as if he were addressing a point of order at a board meeting, he inquired, "You mean you don't want to know what the private detective I hired has found out about Goodearth's erstwhile leader?"

Ariel's heart began to pound alarmingly. "Sam?" she gasped. "You've discovered what's happened to Sam? And what about Marie? Is she with him? Is she all right? Has she had the—"

Sharply Zachary cut into the rush of questions. "The detective didn't say anything about... Marie, but so far Walsh has been traced to Sacramento, where he sold his car to a dealer. From there he could have taken a plane, or he might have purchased another car elsewhere and headed off in any direction. We don't know yet, but the detective is sure he'll soon find someone who remembers Walsh. After all, a guy six and a half feet tall with shoulder-length platinum blond hair isn't exactly inconspicuous...."

Ariel grimaced. Detectives, fleeing felons—it all sounded so unreal, like something out of a movie. Certainly it bore no relation to her peaceful, well-ordered existence in Mendocino, where life had been as predictable as the tide, the migration of whales—or the weekend influx of tourists. Even the painful events of the past few years—her father's death, her concern over Marie's difficult pregnancy—had seemed part of the natural cycle. If only she could go home now.... She sighed and murmured unhappily, "It's all so—so sordid."

"Crime usually is," Zachary said laconically.

Silence stretched between them, chilly and uncomfortable. Longingly Ariel remembered the night he'd taken her to the French restaurant, where every moment had been so filled with conversation, with laughter, that they'd hardly found time to eat. Now she searched for something, anything, to say. At last she concluded with an effort, "Well, I guess I wish your detective luck in locating Sam—and please, if you hear about Marie, let me know, will you?"

"Of course," Zachary replied smoothly. "The instant there's any news." After a significant pause he queried lightly, "And, Ariel, if you should accidentally happen to hear from Walsh, you will let *me* know, won't you?" His tacit insinuation hurt so much that it scarcely impinged on her when he hung up the telephone.

THE PAIN STILL SHOWED several days later when Eleanor studied Ariel's drawn face with concern and asked, "Darling, do you mind about James's and my getting married?"

Ariel looked up from the duffel bag she'd been packing and exclaimed, genuinely astonished,

"No, of course not, Ellie! Where on earth did you get such a ridiculous idea?"

Eleanor sat down on the edge of the bed and picked up one of the thick thermal-weave undershirts that lay in a pile on the lace bedspread. After folding it into a tight roll, she handed it to Ariel and commented, "Maybe I'm a silly old woman, but I suppose I expected you to...react more when we told you the news."

As she stuffed the undershirt deep into the bag and reached for another, Ariel chuckled dryly. "Come on, Ellie, it's hardly news. I've known since the first moment I laid eyes on James that he was mad about you."

Eleanor smiled reminiscently, the skin around her dark eyes crinkling into a network of fine lines. Watching her, Ariel realized that no one would ever again mistake her grandmother for a woman twenty years her junior. Her near-fatal seizure had aged her considerably, nullifying the rejuvenating effects of expensive dressing and skillful makeup—not to mention plastic surgery. But, Ariel decided judiciously, in an odd way Eleanor looked lovelier than ever—no longer young, but relaxed and happy.

"Mad," the older woman mused, seizing upon Ariel's earlier statement. "Yes, James certainly was mad that day! I've never seen him lose his temper the way he did when he saw me with that cigarette. I didn't know he had that much fire in him!"

"Oh, yeah?" Ariel probed teasingly, regarding

her grandmother through half-lowered lashes. "That's not the way I heard it!"

Blushing like a young girl, Eleanor floundered, "Well...that is...I mean...." Her words died out in a mirthful giggle, her joy so abundant that Ariel, torn by envy and happiness for her grandmother, had to look away quickly, trying to hide her pain from Eleanor's sharp eyes. But Eleanor had spotted Ariel's expression, and she said seriously, "James made me see how very selfish I'd been all these years, thinking of our relationship only in terms of my own feelings. Am I being selfish with you now, dear, expecting you to share my happiness when it's obvious there's something deeply wrong between you and Zachary?"

Ariel gave up the pretense of packing. Folding her long body onto the edge of the bed, she admitted glumly, "There's nothing wrong between Zachary and me. There's nothing at all between Zachary and me. Things...just didn't work out."

"I can't believe that," Eleanor countered flatly. "I don't think I've ever in my life seen a woman as deeply in love as you are."

Ariel shrugged stiffly, gazing at the flocked wallpaper as she declared, "But my being in love isn't enough. Zachary doesn't love me. Oh, he wants me, all right. He likes making love to me— but when it comes right down to it, he doesn't *like* me. He doesn't even trust me!"

Eleanor frowned. "You mean because of this business with your ecology group's money?"

Since the morning Sam's embezzling had been

detected, Ariel and Zachary had scrupulously avoided all mention of it in Eleanor's presence. "How did you find out about that?" she demanded.

Eleanor sniffed impatiently. "Really, child! Don't you repeat Zachary's mistake of assuming that my illness has affected my mind. I may be a little fragile these days, but I'm certainly not senile! When I see you running yourself ragged making arrangements that only a few weeks earlier you claimed had already been taken care of, when your friend with the remarkable hair is no longer in evidence, when Zachary suddenly shows a profound interest in an expedition he's always vigorously opposed—how much intelligence is it supposed to take to figure out that something drastic has happened?"

Ariel smiled sheepishly. "We just didn't want to worry you, Ellie." Briefly she outlined the sequence of events that had led to Sam's disappearance, making no attempt to excuse her own carelessness.

Eleanor scowled. "Are you telling me that Zachary blames you for the theft?" When Ariel nodded disconsolately, her grandmother sighed with exasperation and muttered, "That idiot." Then she commented, "Still, I suppose it's to be expected, if he thought you'd been using him in some fashion. After the way his mother treated him and his father, Zachary has an almost paranoid mistrust of manipulative women."

Ariel stared. "What did his mother do to him?"

"She made his life hell, that's what she did," Eleanor said, grimacing. At Ariel's look of horror she amended, "No, I don't mean in the sense of physically abusing him. There was never any of that that I know of, nor do I think she was aware of causing psychological damage. Frankly, I doubt that she cared enough about her son to *want* to harm him. It was more impersonal than that. He was just a handy tool for whenever she needed to coerce her husband into something."

"She didn't love Zachary?" Ariel asked in helpless confusion, picturing a small sturdy boy with curly black hair and green eyes. She wondered how any woman could fail to love him. . . .

"I doubt that Davina Farrell Drake ever really loved anyone, be it her husband, her lovers or her child. She was too shallow for such emotions, interested only in whatever was the current fad— what Truman Capote once defined as a 'sincere phony.' Women usually saw through her instantly, but men. . . . She was quite pretty—Zachary gets his coloring from her—and outwardly she was very dainty and feminine in all the old stereotypical meanings of the word. But Lord, how she used that apparent frailty! Some invalids are like that. They become household tyrants no one dares contradict for fear of endangering their health. It's a time-honored ploy that I find utterly reprehensible."

"What about Zachary's father? He was English, wasn't he?"

"Still is," Eleanor said surprisingly. "He and

his second wife live in Surrey. I think he raises roses. Every year like clockwork I get a neatly engraved Christmas card from Mr. and Mrs. Philip Drake, but the only message ever included was a note several seasons back announcing that he'd retired from the diplomatic corps.''

''I had no idea either of Zachary's parents was still alive.''

Eleanor shook her head sadly. ''Zachary and his father quarreled bitterly when Zachary turned twenty-one. Philip never forgave him for choosing his U.S. heritage over his British.''

''How...tragic,'' Ariel murmured, remembering the loving relationship she'd always shared with her own father. After a moment she asked, ''So how did Zachary's parents meet? I gather his mother was a Californian?''

''Yes. Davina was a native San Franciscan, from one of the families who used to live in palatial splendor up on Nob Hill back before the earthquake. The Farrells had come down a few notches by the time Davina made her debut, but they still had money and position. Long before I ever met her, I knew her name from the society columns. Philip was a career diplomat—a protocol officer or something like that—one of those jobs where success or failure depends on wearing the right school tie. San Francisco was his first posting. As I understand it, Davina met Philip at some kind of reception and they were instantly attracted. The only problem was, in every way that really mattered—temperament, ideals, interests—the two of them were absolutely incompatible.''

"But still they married?'' Ariel probed.

Eleanor nodded in a gesture of resignation. "It was a whirlwind courtship. War had just broken out in Europe, and Philip was eager to return home to enlist. In those circumstances people often make grave mistakes. It was literally years before they had a chance to cohabit long enough to realize they had absolutely nothing in common and couldn't even agree on where they should live. Philip had decided he could best pursue his diplomatic career in England, while Davina was determined to come back to California. They shuffled back and forth several times. Unfortunately, by then they already had Zachary, and the child was pulled in both directions.''

Ariel drew her bare feet up onto the lacy bedspread and rested her chin on her knees. For several minutes she sat in pensive silence, thinking about what Eleanor had just told her. "So how did you get to know Zachary's parents?'' she then asked curiously.

Eleanor chuckled dryly. "It was well after the war, during one of Philip's rare sojourns in San Francisco, and, would you believe, I met them at a cocktail party when Davina tried to get me to publish a book for her. If you ever want to gain instant popularity, just tell people you're in publishing! Magazines, books, fiction, nonfiction—the particular genre you deal with is immaterial. Instantly they'll fawn all over you as they tell you about the book they've written, the book they're going to write, the crazy thing that happened to their great-aunt Harriet that they just *know* could be turned into a bestseller. . . .

"Davina Drake was no different, although what she wanted to peddle was a volume of 'beat' poetry, patterned after Kerouac or Allen Ginsberg. I actually read some of Davina's work, and as best I can recall, she'd managed to parrot the profanity of those other writers, while at the same time she totally missed the power of their observations."

"That sounds like an. . .unusual style for the wife of a budding diplomat," Ariel said.

"My dear, it was. Philip found it appalling—especially when Davina took to entertaining at consular functions with her half-baked poetry and her coffeehouse philosophy on 'free love'—or whatever the hell it was called then. They had some horrendous rows, and finally Philip's superior ordered him posted back to London permanently. Davina refused to go, and worse, she deliberately used Zachary to try to coerce his father into staying with her. It didn't work. She filed for divorce, and of course she got custody of her son—mothers always did in those days. Afterward she went back to her bongo-playing friends and left poor little Zachary in the care of whatever housekeeper was handy. . . ."

"And that's when you took it upon yourself to become sort of a surrogate mother to him?" Ariel asked acutely.

Eleanor's face twisted with remorse. "Ironic, isn't it, considering that my treatment of my own daughter wasn't much different.... But of course, Barbara was nine years older than Zachary, and when she and I communicated at all, we usually ended up arguing violently, either because she was trying to get my attention or because I was jealous—I did *not* like being the mother of an almost grown woman! In contrast, Zachary was still a child, the son I had always wanted, so sweet, handsome, loving and intelligent...."

She sighed deeply and stood up, restlessly pacing the dusky pink carpet of Ariel's bedroom. "Soon everything changed," she continued wearily. "In very short order I lost both my daughter and my fiancé, and then I lost Zachary, too. Our circle of friends had scarcely stopped reeling from Barbara's and John's elopement when poor Davina decided to give up being a beatnik and became a believer in homeopathy and taking ocean swims in the dead of winter. Unfortunately the first time she tried it she contracted a chill that almost instantly turned into pneumonia. Within forty-eight hours she was dead."

Eleanor paused, the corners of her mouth curling up in a sad smile. "It sounds almost funny, doesn't it? Actually it was pointless and pitiful, especially for Zachary. I took care of him until Philip came to fetch him, and I remember how devastated and bewildered the child was, torn between tears and rage at his mother's stupidity. When his father took him back to England, he apparently decided that Zachary's mood swings were lingering remnants of Davina's 'contaminating' influence, and he promptly put him in a boarding school that sounded like something out of a Victorian nightmare, where he could be literally whipped into shape as a proper British gentleman. It didn't work. It only served to alienate father and son. As soon as Zachary came of age and inherited his mother's money, he flew back to San Francisco, finished college at Stanford and then came to work for me at Seacliff.''

"And he's been with you ever since," Ariel concluded quietly.

Eleanor nodded. "Yes. He's been a great joy to me." She turned and looked squarely at her granddaughter. "Ariel," she said, "nothing would give me greater joy than to see you and Zachary together in some meaningful way."

Ariel pressed her forehead against her knees, her long hair shielding her expression from her grandmother's watchful eyes. Biting her lip, she whispered, "But there's not a chance of that, Ellie, don't you see? Everything you've just told me confirms it. Zachary and I are too different— as different as his parents were. He may have quarreled bitterly with his father, but there's still a great deal of Philip Drake in him. Those years in English boarding schools left their mark. You know how conventional and punctilious he can be at times, and in contrast he sees me as some kind of shallow nonconformist, like his beatnik mother—or else a selfish little flirt, which is the way he remembers my own mother...."

She lifted her head again, and her eyes bored into Eleanor's. "And as if that weren't enough," she continued, trying not to react visibly to the words that pricked dartlike at her heart, "you and I are both conveniently forgetting that Zachary appears to be already involved 'meaningfully' with Laurette Masefield. In fact, she strikes me as exactly what he needs—someone young and malleable whom he can shape to suit his requirements." She took a deep breath. "No, Ellie," she finished resolutely. "There's nothing at all between Zachary and me, meaningful or otherwise."

Nothing, she echoed silently, *except the memory of the ecstasy we shared one warm summer night....*

THE NIGHT was anything but warm as Ariel waited in the predawn darkness for the taxi that would take her down to the harbor. Wisps of fog floated like jaundiced specters beneath the yellow streetlamps, and Ariel pulled the collar of her down-filled jacket high up under her chin, trying to block out the cold clammy air. Beside her, shivering in her velour bathrobe, Eleanor asked anxiously, "Are you sure you have everything you need?"

Ariel glanced at the canvas duffel bag lying on the porch beside her feet. Across it, wrapped in black plastic sheeting for protection against the damp, were two packages: a large square flat one, containing her portfolio and drawing papers; and a smaller box holding pencils, oil pastels and the other materials she would need to keep an illustrated journal of the voyage. She smiled reassuringly. "Yes, Ellie, I've remembered it all. There's not that much to take. We'll be gone two, three weeks at most. During that time we won't exactly be dressing for the captain's table. This isn't a pleasure cruise, you know."

Eleanor frowned uncertainly, her dark eyes somber and concerned. "Yes, I do know," she said quietly. "And I can't pretend I'm not worried. I'm aware I've supported you and Goodearth in the past, but the more time I've had to think about it, the less convinced I am that what you're doing is...wise. You don't know what you might run up against out there!"

"I think I have a fair idea," Ariel replied, smiling grimly. Far Eastern observers who sent word back to West Coast ecology groups reported that the whaling fleet that had set out from Vladivostok the previous week had been as strong as ever. "We've always known what we were up against...."

Eleanor looked troubled. "Promise me you'll be careful?"

Shaken by her own growing fears, Ariel retorted curtly, "Of course I'll be careful. I'm not a fool!" When she saw the way Eleanor recoiled from her rudeness, Ariel was contrite, "Oh, Ellie, I'm sorry I snapped. I guess I'm a little nervous myself. Hell, I've never even been out on the ocean in a boat!"

Eleanor's brows came together. "In that case," she suggested practically, "I hope you're carrying lots of Dramamine with you."

"Lots," Ariel agreed dryly, and for a moment the two women fell silent, succumbing to the awkward and embarrassed tension characteristic of leave-taking. Ariel glanced at her wristwatch. "The taxi should be here any minute now."

"I would have been happy to drive you down to the docks."

"No. I told you, that's not necessary. There wouldn't be anything for you to do. Besides, you still need your rest, especially if you're going back to work while Zachary's gone. You ought to be in bed right now."

"Then Zachary could have picked—"

"No!" Ariel repeated sharply, her voice high and distressed. Swallowing carefully, she explained in a more normal tone, "Zachary's taking Laurette."

"Oh."

Just then a taxi rounded the corner and pulled smoothly to the curb in front of Eleanor's wrought-iron fence. Before the driver could honk the horn and disturb sleeping neighbors, Ariel forestalled him with a wave of her hand. The man returned her signal, and Ariel looked anxiously at Eleanor.

"Ellie—"

"Ariel—"

Both women spoke at once. They broke off, exchanged sheepish glances, and then Eleanor cried, "I wish you wouldn't go!"

Ariel regarded her grandmother steadily, her tawny eyes sad but determined. "But I have to go, Ellie," she said quietly, firmly. "No matter what happens, this is something I must do." Leaning down, she brushed her lips across Eleanor's lined cheek, which felt cold and suspiciously damp in the morning air. "You'd better get back inside," she ordered huskily. Then, taking a deep breath, she hefted her duffel bag and packages into her arms and quickly strode down the walk to the waiting taxi.

CHAPTER TEN

As the trawler *Melinda May* chugged westward into the north Pacific, the prow lifted over a rising swell and dipped sharply, spraying a shower of fine salty mist across the upper deck. In the stern, huddled beside the ladder leading up to the bridge, Ariel paused in her work long enough to zip her Windbreaker all the way to her throat. She was balanced precariously on a shapeless bale of reinforced rubber. When inflated, it would become one of the large life rafts Goodearth members would deliberately sail into the path of the whaling ships as they tried to come between the hunters and their prey.

Ariel picked up her charcoal pencil again and sketched rapidly, her hand moving in smooth sure strokes as she tried to rough out the contours of Vancouver Island while they were fresh in her memory before the island, the whole continental land mass, sank below the horizon. When errant droplets of water spattered the top sheet of the tablet of paper she'd been drawing on, she grumbled under her breath and glanced up, wondering if the ocean was becoming too choppy for her to continue. So far the voyage had been exceptionally smooth, but now that they were at last heading out into open sea, she wasn't sure what to expect.

Gary Gruenwald, one of the Goodearth members, leaning against the stern rail, stared glumly out to sea and complained crankily, ostensibly to his companion but in a voice loud enough that it carried clearly to Ariel. "I don't understand why we had to waste time sailing up the coast when we could have left from Seattle in the first place. We would have been starting out a hell of a lot closer to our destination."

Ariel's fingers curled tightly around her pencil. Lowering her head so that her billed cap shaded her face from the glare of the late-morning sun, she tried to ignore his whining. When he repeated his remark, louder, she felt her cheeks grow hot. Her temper was rising alarmingly, and she waited several seconds before she felt able to force her lips into a commiserating smile as she glanced up from her sketch pad. To prevent her long hair from frizzing in the dampness, she'd plaited it into a single fat braid that fell heavily over her shoulder. With a casual flick of her head she tossed it back as she agreed blandly, "Yes, Gary, I suppose we could have cut our time in transit by almost half if we'd embarked from Washington or even British Columbia. Too bad you didn't suggest it at one of the meetings when we were planning the trip."

Gary turned to face her, but his eyes fell away before her challenging gaze. Sullenly he admitted,

"All right, so I didn't think of Seattle then. But I'll bet Sam would have...."

Sam, Ariel thought bitterly. The name hung in the brisk salt air, heavy with suspicion and resentment. As if it weren't bad enough that he'd robbed her grandmother and perhaps endangered the health of Marie and her unborn child, his disappearance had soured Ariel's relationship with the other members of Goodearth, people whose opinion she valued. The trip already showed signs of winding up a total disaster, and Ariel was the one being blamed. Although she'd wanted to tell her friends about the way Zachary had rescued them, he refused to let her. He'd reminded her that if Sam's embezzlement became public knowledge, it would probably spell the end of the group and all they had worked so hard for—not to mention the fact that Eleanor would be certain to find out. Eleanor, on the other hand, told Ariel wryly that Zachary seemed to be deriving such pleasure from his efforts to protect her from the awful truth it would be a shame to disillusion him. Caught between the conflicting good intentions of two people she loved and her concern for the Goodearth mission, Ariel had reluctantly agreed to keep silent, or least until after the trip was finished.

Unfortunately, in the meantime the other five members making the trip, three men and two women, felt baffled and confused when Sam vanished just as their years of struggle were about to pay off. They'd begun to conjecture—and the conclusion most of them had drawn was that Sam and Ariel must have quarreled and that she'd used the influence of her grandmother's money to oust Sam and replace him with Zachary. Their erroneous opinions were reinforced by the fact that the captain of the *Melinda May* had taken one look at the ragtag group and immediately pegged Zachary Drake as the man in charge of the expedition.

Ironically, Ariel's predicament called to mind something Zachary had once confided to her about the way his fellow employees at Seacliff had misinterpreted his efforts to relieve Eleanor of some of her work pressures; his colleagues had assumed he was trying to steal his mentor's job. Although she was certain that if she explained the situation frankly to Zachary, he would release her from her promise to keep silent, she now found that, like him, she was too proud to make excuses to the group.

"If Sam were still running things—" Gary began huffily.

Gritting her teeth, Ariel said quietly, "This is supposed to be a group project. We would have been delighted to have some help." With an effort she returned her attention to her drawing.

A large shadow fell across the paper. Ariel's heart lurched in her breast when she glanced up to find Zachary looming over her, gazing down at her enigmaticially. His long legs, encased in tight jeans, were spread for balance on the rolling deck. Below the ribbed hem of his natural Irish wool sweater, the bulky design emphasizing his broad shoulders and heavy muscles of his chest, his hands were jammed deep in his pockets. His belt buckle was at about Ariel's eye level, and she tried not to stare at the way the taut fabric of his jeans explicitly outlined his hips and thighs, but when she craned her neck to look up at him, she felt her face growing warm as a wave of sickening hunger, epic in proportion, washed over her. She smiled wanly and waited for him to speak, praying that this veritable tsunami of desire didn't show.

Because he wore dark sunglasses to protect his sensitive eyes from the glare off the water, she couldn't decipher his expression. She was astonished when he nodded in Gary's direction and murmured outrageously, "Annoying, isn't he? I suppose if you like, I could toss him overboard for you...."

His comment was totally unexpected. Although she assumed Zachary was teasing her, she was almost afraid to take the chance he might be serious. She couldn't tell about him anymore. His attitude toward her seemed continually to take polar swings: he was either ignoring her or making love to her. One moment he would treat her with the distant courtesy appropriate to the granddaughter of an old friend. Then suddenly those cool green eyes would grow warm with languid insinuation, as if he were deliberately reminding her of that night there had been no distance between them, no distance at all.... Worried that Gary Gruenwald might soon find himself taking an unscheduled swim, Ariel tried to match Zachary's tone as she said lightly, "Oh, please don't toss Gary overboard. He's our photographer, and we'll need him to record whatever confrontation we have with the whaling fleet."

She shook her head as she continued seriously, "It's not his fault he's feeling irritable. He's like everyone else in the group—they all know something has happened, but they're not sure what. In addition, everyone's a bit bored and frustrated cooped up on this boat and unable to do anything. When we boarded in San Francisco, that was supposed to be *it*, the moment we'd been waiting for for two years. It's rather anticlimactic to discover that before we can do anything, first we have to sail for days and days just to get to our destination. It's enough to make anyone jumpy."

"Anyone except you," Zachary noted quietly.

Hoping he wouldn't notice the way her hands trembled, Ariel pointed out, "I have my work to keep me occupied."

He glanced down at the sketch pad. "What are you doing now?"

"These are notes and color studies that will help me recall the scene once I'm back in my studio in Mendocino. I'm starting a new project, a series of paintings covering this trip from our departure the other day until such time as we return to San Francisco. If it turns out well, I hope I'll be able to interest a gallery in giving me an exhibition."

"Sounds ambitious."

Ariel shrugged. "I am ambitious. Art is my life—not to mention my livelihood—and it's vital to my spiritual well-being that I keep finding new challenges.'' Momentarily she wistfully remembered the Navarro River Opera House; then she put the disappointment behind her—permanently. ''Of course things don't always work out quite the way I'd like, but I can't afford to waste time crying over my failures, any more than I can sit back and rest on those few laurels I've acquired. For an artist there's no such thing as remaining static. Either you forge ahead toward new goals, or else you fall back.''

''Not a bad philosophy for anyone, wouldn't you agree?'' Zachary commented.

Instead of replying at once, Ariel looked away, squinting out at the ocean, the sun-glittered blue green water that stretched endlessly, eternally. Yes, she did agree with Zachary—but she didn't want to. She didn't want to think about those things the two of them had in common: their pride, their attitudes toward their work, their taste in food and music, in sex.... The pain of losing him to Laurette might be slightly more bearable if only she could concentrate on the differences, numerous and profound, that separated them.

Mentally shaking herself, Ariel turned back to Zachary and chuckled uncomfortably. ''My God, this sounds terribly intense, like some of the conversations I used to have over a glass of Dubonnet back in my Paris days!'' She closed her portfolio with a snap. Glancing past him to the other people clustered resentfully at the rail, she concluded dismissively, ''Anyway, the drawing keeps me busy, for which I'm grateful. It's becoming very clear to me that we really didn't plan this trip well at all, and most of the group is growing discontented because they won't have anything to do until we actually make contact with the whalers.''

Zachary, still staring down at her, seemed unwilling to change the subject. Studying her drawn features intently, he murmured, ''It's an odd thing about you. For someone so highly emotional, I'm continually amazed at how calm you remain in a crisis. Ellie's heart attack, Walsh's disappearance—nothing much rattles you, does it?''

You do, Ariel thought, wondering if he was conveniently forgetting the unbridled passion they'd shared that night, when her responses—and his—had been anything but controlled.... Her gaze remained steady as she observed, ''Actually, I'm not all that emotional. Like anyone else there have been times I would have liked to yell and scream and throw things, but I've never been able to see the point of a display of temperament if it's not going to change anything.''

Zachary's mouth quirked in a mocking smile. ''Is that the way you see yourself? Funny...I recall things differently. In any case, that's a curious comment from someone willing to spend two years of her life organizing a demonstration that at best can have only marginal success.''

Ariel bridled at his allusion to their early volatile encounters. She refused to answer him on that score. Yet she responded tightly, ''What we're doing may be quixotic, but it is most

definitely *not* pointless!'' She picked up the sheet
of black plastic that had been lying at her feet and
methodically wrapped it around her portfolio.

The boat pitched, and Zachary grabbed awkwardly for the ladder to steady himself, his long
legs flexing with the movement of the deck. When
a shower of droplets spattered lightly over them,
he grimaced and muttered, ''Damn, it's getting
rougher.''

Quickly Ariel laid aside her artwork and scoot-
ed sideways on the rubber raft. ''Here,'' she
offered without thinking. ''You'll be more comfortable if you sit down.''

Zachary's black brows arched above his sunglasses. ''Are you sure?'' he asked dryly. ''I was
under the impression you'd been carefully avoiding all contact with me—no small accomplishment
on a boat that's less than a hundred feet long.''
Without waiting for her reply, he lowered his
bulky frame beside her, so that their denim-clad
thighs and hips were pressed together provocatively.

The flexible material sank under their combined
weight, causing their bodies to slide closer, and
Ariel flushed heatedly, remembering how on the
waterbed.... With an effort to maintain that
deceptive composure Zachary had admired she
glanced around and inquired mildly, ''Where's
Laurette? I haven't seen her since last night.''
After dinner in the main cabin the other woman
had entertained the group with an impromptu
recital, and Ariel, distraught over the way Lau-

rette sat curled up beside Zachary on the vinyl couch as she sang, had made her excuses and retired early. When she'd risen before dawn to watch the *Melinda May* chug into its refueling dock in the Strait of Juan de Fuca, Laurette and the other two women she shared a compartment with had been no more than dark, blanket-draped figures huddling in their berths. She'd taken care not to disturb them.

Removing his sunglasses so he could rub the bridge of his nose, Zachary scowled. "Laurette's lying down," he said, the concern in his deep voice tearing at Ariel. "I don't think she's got her sea legs, poor kid. She was all right while we were traveling up the coast, but now that we're in open water she's feeling a little under the weather."

"I'm sorry to hear that. Is she taking medication for it?"

Zachary snorted impatiently. "No one seems to have thought to bring any."

Ariel replied in surprise, "I did. It was one of the few things I did plan for properly. I got a prescription from Ellie's doctor just in case, only I haven't needed medication. I guess living beside the ocean all my life has made me immune or something. I'll go dig the capsules out of my duffel bag right now." Gracefully she got to her feet, shaking the heavy braid back over her shoulder as she stretched her long limbs to relieve the kinks her cramped sitting position had caused.

When she reached down to retrieve her drawing supplies, Zachary's strong fingers curled lightly around her arm to detain her. "Ariel, I really appreciate your concern," he said quietly.

She could only stare at him, at the beautiful confetti-flecked green eyes with their astonishingly long lashes, and she marveled at how naked and vulnerable they looked without the protective shield of his glasses. The last time she'd seen them that way.... Her voice was curiously gruff as she declared, "Think nothing of it, Zachary. Laurette's a nice girl, and I'm glad to be of help. And why not? After all, I'm the one who's always so calm in a crisis." Twisting her arm away from him, she grabbed her portfolio and scurried along the deck, in her haste almost colliding with Gary, who along with the others was heading forward to seek shelter from the spray.

The stateroom was dark except for the tendrils of light that filtered through the curtained porthole, and in the gloom Ariel could just discern Laurette's petite figure hunched on her bunk, shivering in silent misery. One quick sniff disclosed that she'd already been sick, and Ariel could see that her bed had been stripped of its sheets, which lay wadded on the floor, while she sobbed chokingly into the bare mattress. Shaking her head ruefully, Ariel flipped on the light and touched Laurette's shoulder.

With great effort Laurette lifted her head. "Oh, it's you," she rasped, blinking against the brightness. Her pallor was shocking, her usually rosy complexion tinged with gray, pale as the lifeless hair that dangled in dull unkempt strings over her red-rimmed eyes. The boat pitched, and Laurette moaned miserably, "Oh, Ariel, I feel so awful. I think—I think I'm going to die. . . ."

"No, you're not," Ariel reassured her gently, too full of pity to find the melodramatic words amusing. "I'm going to give you some medicine that will make you feel better in no time." As she soothingly brushed Laurette's blond hair out of her eyes, Ariel's compassion was quickly superseded by intense anger, directed at Zachary. "A little under the weather," he had said unfeelingly. How dared he leave Laurette alone in this condition?

Before she could tell Zachary what she thought of him, Ariel decided, surveying the mess with a grimace, she first had to make Laurette more comfortable and then clean up the compartment. The smell was enough to make anyone nauseous. Sliding a strong arm behind Laurette's back, she said, "Come on, honey. Sit up and I'll help you move over to my bunk. You're going to be chilled, lying here without any cover."

"My bedclothes got. . .dirty," Laurette admitted unnecessarily, blushing sheepishly as she struggled into an upright position. "I—I started to feel queasy and I couldn't make it to—to—"

"Forget it," Ariel replied briskly. "It could happen to anyone."

"Not you," Laurette sniffled querulously, making the words sound almost like an accusation. "Not Zack. . . ." As she stood up unsteadily, her eyes suddenly widened into troubled blue pools. She clutched at Ariel's arm and pleaded hoarsely, "Promise me you won't tell him!"

"Why on earth not?" Ariel demanded. "I think he ought to—"

"You don't understand!" Laurette wailed. "He didn't want me to come on this trip, so I promised him I wouldn't be a nuisance. That's why I couldn't tell him how sick I was when he knocked on the door earlier. If he finds out I've been throwing up all over the place, he'll be so angry with me."

As Ariel helped Laurette settle into the clean bunk, she murmured reassuringly, "Oh, I can't imagine Zachary being angry with—" She stopped abruptly. Breathlessly she repeated, "He didn't want you to come?"

Laurette shook her head. "No. It took me forever to talk him into it. He said he was afraid there might be trouble when we meet the whalers, and he didn't want me to get hurt."

"I see," Ariel murmured, her mercurial spirits subsiding as quickly as they'd risen. She was silent for a moment as she pulled her duffel bag from beneath her bunk and located the bottle of motion-sickness medicine. She checked the label carefully and noted that the compound was liable to have a sedative effect, probably a benefit in Laurette's overwrought state. After she'd given one of the capsules to the patient, she waited until Laurette relaxed, her petite body straightening into a more comfortable position on the bunk as her nausea eased. When a few minutes had passed,

Ariel asked curiously, "Doesn't the possibility of trouble worry you at all?"

Laurette settled wearily against the pillow, burrowing her pretty face into the ticking as she yawned. "Of course not, silly. People make these expeditions every year, and all that happens is that they get their pictures in newspapers and magazines—and sometimes even appear on television shows. That's what I want—a chance to make my name known. It's important if you're going to succeed as an entertainer, you know." She hesitated. "Anyway, whales aren't dangerous, are they?"

Ariel said dryly, "Well, once upon a time fishermen called the California gray 'devil fish,' because it was so fierce...." Laurette's blue eyes flew open, and Ariel added with a chuckle, "Of course, that was a hundred years ago, when whalers invaded Scammon's Lagoon in the Sea of Cortez, where the grays bear their young. Whales can be quite ferocious when protecting their calves. Usually they're harmless, even affectionate."

"I thought so," Laurette said drowsily, relaxing once more. "I told Zachary there couldn't be any danger, or else *you'd* never make this trip. You have too much sense to do something foolish. You're a very together lady, Ariel, and I admire you so much for...."

Her voice trailed off; her even breathing indicated she was asleep. Gathering up the soiled sheets, Ariel started to slip from the stateroom. At the door she paused. Looking back at Laurette's sweet, rather immature features, she thought ironically that it was no wonder Zachary felt so protective toward her. Lord, she made Ariel feel protective herself....

ON THE FIFTH DAY OUT they reached the fishing grounds.

The first sighting came at a time when the unrelieved tedium of the journey had stretched nerves almost to the breaking point. Not long after the reassuring outline of the North American land mass had sunk below the horizon, the trawler passed through a weather front, and while they hadn't yet encountered rain, the sun was now lost behind the overcast. They were enveloped in a cold gloomy world of unending gray—gray sky meeting gray sea at a horizon that was only a variation in the grayness. The lack of any focal point was disorienting, and to escape the vertiginous effects of looking at the ocean, most of the passengers had fled indoors, killing time with books or cards or handheld video games—or petty squabbles. Zachary seemed to spend each day on the bridge, conferring with the captain, while Laurette, who had rebounded with surprising vigor from her attack of seasickness, locked herself in her cabin with a portable cassette recorder to polish her vocal technique. Ariel preferred to remain on deck, alone except for the occasional crewman who walked by. Undisturbed, in the quiet and the fresh briny air, she could lose herself in that otherworld that was birthplace to her artistic vision.

She was designing a new mural, shapes and colors shifting kaleidoscopically in her mind while her hands tried with the frustrating inadequacy of all translators to transfer the vision to the sketch pad. Suddenly, from the bow of the boat, someone bellowed theatrically, "Thar she blows!" Shaking with excitement, Ariel dropped her paper and pencils and rushed to the rail to peer expectantly out to sea. She held her breath tensely as she waited, and at last, at about the two-o'clock position, rising above the swells, she saw the distinctive plume of mist that indicated a great whale had surfaced several hundred yards to starboard.

From all over the trawler a commotion arose. The handful of people on the boat ran from their cabins and huddled in the bow, clamoring and whistling and pointing as a second spout was sighted. When two pairs of huge flukes flipped up into the air as the whales sounded, a collective "ooooh" rose from the group like a slightly off-key lullaby. Ariel didn't realize that she herself had begun to squeal with exhilaration, until from behind her a sinewy hand clamped lightly around her nape and a deep voice murmured teasingly, "Easy, now. If you jump any higher, you're liable to fall overboard."

She twisted so she could see over her shoulder. "Oh, Zachary," she sighed, her golden eyes burnished with wonder, "aren't they magnificent?"

He stared intently at her, frowning, as if stunned by the look of soft rapture that shone from her face. But before he could speak, Laurette squeezed into the gunwale beside Ariel and gabbled excitedly, "Have I missed them? I couldn't hear over that tape recorder of mine, and if someone hadn't knocked— Where did they go? What kind were they?"

Answering Laurette's last question first, Ariel said, "In these waters they could be humpbacks, fin whales, sperm whales, even grays, although those tend to stay closer to shore." She pointed in the general direction of the sighting. "They were out there when we spotted them, but there's no telling when they'll come up again. Depending on the species, they could stay down as long as an hour." She lifted her head and quickly surveyed the crowd. "Gary," she called forward to the photographer, who was struggling in the crush to fit a telescopic lens on his camera, "did you get a good look?"

"They were sperm whales," Gary answered, "The biggest one fifty, maybe fifty-five feet long. Look, there's another smaller one, and she seems to have a calf with her! I think we must have sailed right in among a bull and his harem."

Ever conscious of Zachary's body pressing her against the rail, his warm hands steadying her shoulders, Ariel watched awestruck as the great sea creature exhaled a wide puff of mist and then, only a few dozen yards from the boat, slowly and gracefully rolled onto her side, her upper flipper waving jauntily in the air. "What's she doing?" Laurette asked.

Ariel's eyes were shimmering. "She's getting

ready to nurse her baby,'' she explained hoarsely. ''She lies on her side like that so the calf can breathe normally. . . .''

Gary approached Zachary. ''Mr. Drake,'' he asked, for once failing to display his habitual resentment, ''do you think you could get the skipper to cut the engines for a while so I can get some pictures?''

''Of course.'' Zachary excused himself and stalked back to the bridge.

In a few minutes the thrum of the engines silenced for the first time since the trawler had stopped for refueling. The only sound was the murmur of the wind and the gentle slapping of waves against the hull as the boat slowly yawed with the swell. Even the people crowded on deck were quiet. Now that their initial exuberance had subsided, they spoke in hushed, almost reverent whispers, as if aware that they stood in the presence of one of the miracles of creation.

''I can't imagine anyone wanting to kill something so beautiful,'' Laurette said plaintively.

As Ariel gazed out over the water, she laughed sardonically. ''Who knows who will win in the end? Maybe it will be as Melville said: 'If ever the world is to be again flooded. . .then the eternal whale will still survive and spout his frothed defiance to the skies.' ''

''Are these the kind of whales the hunters will be after?''

Ariel nodded. ''All species are hunted by someone, but the sperm whale is the most commercially valuable. A full-grown male produces eighty barrels of oil.''

"What's the oil used for?"

"Cosmetics, soap—pet food," Ariel replied bitingly. "Moby Dick was a sperm whale. I wonder how many high-school students studying that book realize that Captain Ahab achieved literary immortality trying to feed someone's cocker spaniel."

Conversation between the two women became desultory as they watched the cow and her calf, Laurette asking an occasional question, Ariel answering if she could. When at last the calf finished suckling and the two whales disappeared beneath the water with one final salute of their flukes, Laurette moved forward to join Gary and the rest of the group.

Sighing, Ariel left the rail and headed for the stern to retrieve the sketching materials she'd dropped when the whales were first sighted. She wondered if she could possibly capture on canvas the heartbreaking beauty of the scene she'd just witnessed. Just as she passed the ladder leading to the bridge, Zachary leaned over the top and called her name softly. She glanced up in surprise. "Could you come here, please?" he requested gravely. "There's something we need to discuss."

When Ariel's deck shoes faltered on the slippery-damp rungs of the ladder, Zachary reached down and caught her wrists, hauling her over the top with the easy strength that always astonished her. As he pulled her upright, she stumbled, and his arms wrapped tightly around her, pressing her face, her breasts, against the hard wall of his chest. Just for a second she relaxed and closed her eyes, breathing in his warmth through the heavy sweater he wore, the tantalizing man-scent of his body that was so achingly familiar.... Then with an effort she levered herself away from him and asked a little unsteadily, "You had something you wanted to talk about?"

Zachary nodded. He led her into the shelter of the bridge, where the skipper and one of his sailors glanced up just long enough to nod courteously before they returned their attention to their charts. After guiding Ariel to a stool in one corner of the compact, instrument-lined compartment, Zachary stood and stared at her for endless seconds. Behind his glasses his green eyes were shuttered. Drawing a ragged breath, he announced bluntly, "We've located the Soviet whaling fleet. Since yesterday we've been monitoring radio broadcasts between the various ships, and we've found a catcher boat only a few hours' sail from here. My college Russian is a bit rusty, but I heard the radio operator tell a friend on another boat that they haven't had much luck so far. He says his captain is getting frustrated and irritable, so they've wandered eastward from the main body of the fleet in search of better game."

He paused, and Ariel inhaled raspingly. Staring down at her lap, she was surprised to find her hands clenched tightly together, the knuckles straining whitely against her creamy skin. Until this very moment she'd had no idea of how apprehensive she felt. Letting her breath out slowly she said, "Thank you, Zachary. That sounds like exactly what we're looking for—a lone ship suitable for a one-on-one encounter."

Zachary's fingers curled gently around Ariel's chin; he tilted her head upright so that she gazed directly into his face. Studying her wan features caressingly, his thin sensual mouth curled up in a persuasive smile as he murmured. "You know, Ariel, it's still not too late to call it off."

Her eyes widened. "Call it off?" she repeated blankly, as if he'd suddenly spoken in a foreign language.

His fingers tightened into her soft flesh as he grated, "Yes, Ariel. I want you to think seriously about this before you take the final step. Do you truly realize how dangerous what you propose to do is?"

"We've always known there would be opposition," she said stiffly. "The whole point of this voyage is to show the powers that be that—"

Abruptly Zachary released her and stepped back, his arms crossed. "Damn it, Ariel, we're not dealing with some nebulous 'power' here. We're talking about *people*—something you visionaries tend to forget about in your haste to save the world!" Clipping off each syllable, nodding in a vaguely western direction, he declared, "Out there somewhere is a ship, a whaler if you will, filled not with kill-crazed monsters but with men, ordinary human beings just trying to do the job they're paid for. We know already that their voyage is off to a bad start.'' He shook his head in exasperation as he continued tiredly, ''Laurette told me what you said about the way the California grays attacked fishermen who hunted their young in Scammon's Lagoon. Well, I want you to stop and think for a moment. If a *fish* can react so violently when threatened, just what the hell do you think a boatload of sailors is going to do when you and your friends blunder in and try to make them give up their livelihood?''

She gazed unwaveringly at him, at his long muscular body, that rugged but beautiful face, and she felt the old familiar stirrings tingle through her. Again she asked herself how it was possible to love someone whose goals and beliefs were diametrically opposed to her own. Quietly she said, ''Zachary, you've always been aware of what we intended to do. You even paid for the trip....'' Her eyes narrowed shrewdly as she queried, ''Or could it be that you didn't think we'd go through with this?''

His smile was bitter as he conceded, ''I suppose I did hope you would come to your senses before it went this far, before I had to step in and stop you.''

''*You* step in and...'' Ariel choked. She slid off the stool and stood up, stretching her statuesque frame proudly to its full five feet ten inches as she glared challengingly at him. Out of the corner of her eye she noticed that the sailor who'd been going over the charts with his captain retreated to the far end of the bridge, where he suddenly evinced extreme interest in some gauges mounted beside the wheel. "Zachary," she demanded, "do you honestly think you *can* stop me?"

She watched his eyes flick sidelong toward the skipper, who'd given up reading his charts and was now frankly listening to the confrontation between his two passengers. She guessed that Zachary was trying to decide which of them the man would favor in a showdown. After all, although Zachary was the person paying for this trip, Goodearth had engaged the captain and his boat in the first place. With an ironic quirk to his brows Zachary at last commented mildly, "Ariel, my dear, I have the distinct feeling that nothing short of physical violence would ever stop you from doing whatever you'd set your mind to."

Ariel shuddered. He thought she was being contrary just for the hell of it. He thought she was some kind of fanatic—and the pain caused by his incomprehension was almost worse than the agony of loving him. Dispiritedly she said, "Well, I'm glad we understand each other now," and turned to the captain. "Despite Mr. Drake's gloomy predictions," she reassured him, "I don't think there's any need to worry about the safety of your vessel or your crew. We do know what we're doing. Now if you don't mind, I'd like us to get under way again. The sooner we get this over with, the better."

"WE KNOW what we're doing," Ariel murmured with a reassuring laugh when, in the predawn darkness, she and her cabinmates bumped clumsily into one another as they struggled into their thick thermal-weave underwear. It would protect them from the chilling spray while the motorized rafts skimmed over the choppy water to form a barricade between the whalers and their quarry. "We know what we're doing!" she exclaimed again more forcefully later, watching the shapeless bales of rubber unfold like blossoming jungle flowers when inflated.

Beside her Gary checked his cameras and said, puzzled, "Of course we know what we're doing, Ariel. We're going to stop those bloodsuckers in their tracks, just the way we always planned."

Ariel pulled her bulky parka closer around her neck. "They're not bloodsuckers, Gary," she sighed, her breath forming a little cloud that was instantly blown away by the freshening breeze. Drawing the hood up over her tightly coiled hair, she commented, "You know, I read once that in Japan alone, more than eighty thousand people are employed in the whaling industry. I wonder what will become of them if we succeed in what we're trying to do."

"They'll find work somewhere else," Gary dismissed, frowning. "That's not our problem." He looked at her strangely. "Something wrong with you this morning?" he asked. "You're acting weird." Ariel shook her head and walked away.

In the bow she found Zachary and Laurette.

The younger woman was warming her fingers around a steaming thermos of coffee, while Zachary peered into the distance through binoculars. At Laurette's bright greeting he lowered the glasses and turned to Ariel. "There's your target, riding at anchor," he said, indicating a point low on the horizon where white-and-red lights shone, haloed by the mist. He passed the binoculars to Ariel, and when she took them, she could feel the warmth of his hands on the leather-covered barrels.

In the rising light she could just discern the outline of a vessel that resembled a tugboat except for a curious platform mounted in the bow. On that platform she recognized the lethal harpoon cannon. Shivering with a chill that had nothing to do with the frigid air, she returned the glasses to Zachary. "Do they know we're here?" she asked.

"The radio is silent, so I suspect most of the crew is still asleep. But I should imagine their watch has noticed us by now. Before long we ought to be hearing from them, if only to demand that we identify ourselves."

"*Then* what do we do?" Laurette asked.

"Then we wait for something to happen," Ariel answered gravely.

By the time the sun lifted over the horizon the two boats were less than a hundred yards apart, bobbing in silent antagonism as their respective passengers leaned over the rails and exchanged surly glares. Over the gunwales of the *Melinda May* two Goodearth members suspended a long homemade banner that fluttered and pleaded *Don't kill them. The Ocean is big enough for all of us!* The hooted response from the Soviets sounded obscene even to those who didn't understand Russian. Soon a sailor reported that the whaler had requested they leave the area. "They say they're operating legally in international waters and we have no right to interfere with them."

Ariel retorted, "Tell them we'll be happy to leave them alone, just as soon as *they* agree to leave." She choked off her words when suddenly, on the port side, a huge gray black sperm whale breached.

It broke through the surface in a smooth perfect arc, as if perfecting its technique, and it brought with it the dank musty odor of the deep. Water streamed from its enormous blunt head as it rose clear of the waves and then fell back with a resounding splash so large its wash rocked the trawler. Forgetting Zachary and Laurette, Ariel watched raptly. The whale bobbed easily among the swells, issuing moist blubbery snorts every few seconds as it spouted wide puffs of mist and air. Heedless of the two boats, it floated with serene grace, motionless except for the blinking of its low deepset eyes, the gentle stroking of the flippers that seemed absurdly small to propel such a massive body. She breathed reverently, "Oh, Lord, have you ever *seen* anything so—"

Behind her one of her friends gave a strangled shout. "No—*no*!"

On the catcher boat a stocky muscular man in

pea jacket and knit cap mounted the gun platform and began methodically to ram black powder and wadding into the muzzle of the harpoon cannon.

On the *Melinda May* the cry went up, "This is *it*!" and in a body the three men and two women of Goodearth rushed aft, where the two rubber boats were lashed to the stern. As Laurette turned to follow them, she looked questioningly at Zachary, her wide blue eyes suddenly tense and wary. He shook his head. "Forget it, sweetheart," he said, the tender note in his voice belying his obdurate expression. "Getting dumped in a subarctic ocean wouldn't do your singing voice one bit of good." Laurette relaxed visibly.

Gary, who was snapping photographs continually, glanced up from his camera long enough to call forward, "Hey, Ariel, you'd better hurry!" and Ariel, wincing at the casual affectionate way Zachary had addressed Laurette, started toward him.

Zachary caught her by the wrist, his long fingers constricting her pale flesh like metal bands. "You're not going, either," he insisted.

Ariel stared at him, speechless. When someone in the stern yelled her name again, she said impatiently, "Let go of my hand, Zachary."

"No."

"Zachary," she hissed through clenched teeth as she twisted and tried to squirm from his grasp, "you're hurting me! Now let me go. They're waiting!"

He released her hand only to pinion her against

the rail, his strong arms hard and inescapable on either side of her. His eyes sparked with emerald fire. "I don't give a bloody tinker's damn who's waiting for you. I'm not going to let you risk your life!"

She wanted to lash out at him, but aware of Laurette's bewildered gaze trained on the two of them, Ariel mustered her ebbing control and stated flatly, "It's not your decision, Zachary. You have no rights over me."

For endless moments they stared at each other, Zachary's craggy features oddly pale beneath his tan, Ariel's smooth face still and remorseless. One of the women hollered, "Hey, Ariel, are you coming or aren't you?"

Quickly clamping one hand over Ariel's mouth, Zachary swiveled his dark head and called back, "Go on without her!" The first rubber boat slid over the side and settled lightly onto the water, bucking slightly in the breeze, and Gary and the four others tumbled in. The small outboard engine on the back fired instantly, and the boat skipped over the waves, its nose kicking up spray as it rounded the bow of the trawler and headed toward the floating whale.

When Zachary released her, Ariel, glaring at him with tear-glossed eyes, snarled, "Damn you. I hope you rot in whatever conformist chauvinistic corporate hell you happen to believe in!"

"Maybe I will," he responded relentlessly. "But just don't expect me to apologize for trying to save your fool neck!"

Shivering with fury, Ariel turned away to watch the progress of the raft. When it crossed the short span of water between the *Melinda May* and the catcher boat, the gunner on the cannon platform looked up from the barbed harpoon he was arming and screamed gutturally with outrage. From throughout the vessel his companions rushed forward. They sounded, banged on things, waved their fists. Someone threw an empty bottle with remarkable accuracy. The people on the Goodearth craft ducked and chugged on.

Turning her attention to the whale, Ariel saw that it was displaying no apprehension and little curiosity about the strange intruders drawing near. When the motor was cut so that the boat could glide within touching range of the animal, Ariel watched, fascinated, as the huge sea creature drowsily blinked one large piggy eye; otherwise it didn't stir. The rubber raft drifted nearer and at last nudged gently against the beast's wall-like flank. For a long moment no one moved, anywhere, and Ariel covered her mouth with her hand to keep from sobbing aloud. Then, as Gary delightedly snapped pictures, one of the women on the raft reached out trembling tentative fingers and petted the whale.

"Oh, Zack," Laurette breathed, struck, "have you ever seen anything like that?" He didn't answer. "Zachary," she persisted when his ominous silence continued, and he swore viciously under his breath. When Laurette gasped, Ariel turned reluctantly to see what was wrong. She, too, caught her breath.

On the harpooning platform of the catcher boat, a second man had joined the gunner, a ramrod-straight figure in an overcoat who wore the peaked cap of an officer and carried a bullhorn. Just behind him stood three ordinary sailors, each holding a high-powered rifle.

Cold with dread, Ariel watched the Russian officer lift the bullhorn and call out in halting English. She broke away from Zachary and Laurette, climbing up onto the prow rail so she could hear better. Swaying with the rising wind, she perched precariously on the damp slippery metal and listened with difficulty as the words floated back piecemeal across the water, rendered almost unintelligible by the speaker's pronounced Slavic accent and the distortion of the microphone. "Go away... whale is ours... treaties... quotas.... Go *away*!"

The five people in the rubber boat didn't seem to hear him. The whale's huge side sheltered them from the breeze, and Gary blithely continued taking photographs while the others stroked and caressed the animal's dimpled leathery skin. Even from a distance Ariel could tell that not only the wind but their own emotions had deafened them. They had succumbed to the rapture of their quest, so absorbed in the near-religious ecstasy of this moment of communion with the great whale that they'd forgotten their avowed purpose was to protect that whale. Now they seemed incapable of even protecting themselves....

"Leave now...no one will be harmed...last warning...."

Ariel's heart raced. Fear rose in her throat, acid and burning, as she watched the Russian officer angrily lower the bullhorn. He rapped out some kind of instruction to the gunner, who nodded tersely and took his position behind the harpoon cannon. The armed sailors shouldered their rifles. "They can't *hear* you!" Ariel screamed, but her words were blown back in her face. She began to shake. She'd seen films made in other years, when other whalers had fired on other demonstrators. Those films were always greeted with cheers and applause at save-the-whale rallies, where they were usually shown just before the collection was taken.

This was no movie. These were no flickering shadows on a screen, and the five people on that pathetically fragile rubber boat were her friends. She would have been out there with them herself if Zachary hadn't prevented her....

She glanced back over her shoulder at him. He was holding Laurette tightly in his arms, stroking her curls comfortingly as she shielded her eyes, her head against his chest, sniffling in fright. His head was bent low over hers.

Biting her lip, Ariel turned away. The people in the boat were still petting the whale, which appeared to have rolled slightly onto its side as if to help them reach a more sensitive spot on its huge body. The Soviet officer had disappeared, and the harpoon gunner was buckling a safety line around his waist, to prevent the cannon's recoil from knocking him overboard when he fired. One of the riflemen took careful aim. From this angle it looked to Ariel as if he was hoping merely to disable the raft, forcing its passengers back to the trawler before the boat sank. But she couldn't be sure. She studied the murky water separating the *Melinda May* from the Soviet vessel, and with her eyes she quickly estimated the distance. Less than a hundred yards. Even on her lazy mornings she swam several times that far in Mendocino Bay. . . . She kicked off her deck shoes and unzipped her parka.

Behind her she suddenly heard Zachary cry hoarsely, "For God's sake, Ariel, *don't*!" And then she was in the water.

The force of her expert racing dive carried her away from the trawler, and the swift powerful strokes had propelled her almost halfway to the catcher boat before the shock of the icy water hit her, before she realized the enormity of the mistake she'd just made. Her outraged muscles began to ball up in knots of pain. She gasped, breaking her rhythm. The instant she lost her forward momentum her sodden clothing began to drag at her, while a backwash of saltwater splashed into her face, the corrosive brine stinging her eyes, her throat. . . . Retching and disoriented, she treaded water with leaden arms as she jerked her head around, trying to see through the hair that had come loose and covered her face like a wet shroud. *Keep calm,* she told herself sternly. *You're the one who's always expected to be under control—don't panic!* She didn't have time to panic. She had to find the Soviet vessel so she could use the one Russian word she knew and tell them *nyet*, not to hurt her friends. She had to make them understand. . . .

Where was that damned boat—the whaler, not the little rubber one some daredevil was speeding in her direction. God, she had thought she was closer to the Soviets than *that*! And why were all those men hanging over the rail gaping like goldfish? Even the harpoon gunner seemed to be staring in her direction. Now that she had their attention, maybe she could explain to them about endangered species. Only she didn't speak Russian. Zachary spoke Russian. He could have made them understand, but he wouldn't, because he didn't care. *Don't panic,* she told herself again with less vehemence; she felt too tired to be vehement. What on earth was the matter with her? She was a strong swimmer, could have been Olympic caliber if only that stupid coach in high school hadn't tried to pressure her into going out for basketball instead. There was a voice, hollering. And there it was again, that funny-looking thing looming over her, brown and rectangular with tentacles like a man's arms, snatching out bruisingly to grab. . . .

SHE STRUGGLED TOWARD THE SURFACE through a sea of exhaustion and pain, until at last she pried open one gummy lid and peered around blearily. Green eyes regarded her steadily over the rim of a steaming coffee cup. The coffee was hot; the eyes were cold.

"Feeling better now?" Zachary asked, his tone indifferent.

She frowned, oddly surprised that he spoke in English. She seemed to recall him using another language, bellowing one word over and over.... "Yes, I—I think I am," she croaked. Every muscle in her body protested as she lifted her head from her cocoon of thick blankets and glanced around the dark unfamiliar room. Unlike the compartment she shared with the other women, this one was outfitted with only two wide bunks. She lay heavily bundled on one, and across a narrow space Zachary sat on the bare mattress of the other. "Where am I?" she asked.

"My cabin. It was the only private one."

"Oh. Thank you." She leaned back against her pillow and became aware of low vibration and the continual hiss of water passing under the hull. She looked questioningly at Zachary. "We're under way again?"

"I suggested to the captain that perhaps we ought to get the hell of there. He seemed to think it was a good idea."

Apprehensively Ariel asked, "Are my friends all right?"

"Yes," he reassured her with a grim smile. "You caused so much commotion they finally broke out of their trance and made a tactical retreat before anyone could get hurt."

Ariel sighed with relief. "Thank God!" She

hesitated, squinting as she tried futilely to remember what had happened after she'd dived overboard. She attempted to swallow, but the residual salt in her throat made her cough harshly. "What—what happened to the whale?"

"It swam away." Zachary set down his coffee cup and picked up the thermos from the floor beside the bunk. As he carefully poured the black scalding brew into a fresh cup before refilling his own, he pointed out, "Kind of anticlimactic, don't you think? All the years of work, all the money—just so one whale can swim away."

"One whale is better than none," Ariel said doggedly.

Zachary held out Ariel's cup to her. "There will be other whales, other whalers, too, you know."

"I know." She heaved herself into an upright position to accept the coffee. As she did, the bedclothes slipped down over her body, and for the first time she realized she was naked. Flushing deeply, she tried to pin the sheet under her elbows. But hampered as much by her lethargy as by the steaming cup in her hands, she could only watch helplessly as the sheet fell away from her full, rose-tipped breasts. When she looked quickly at Zachary, she saw his nostrils flair faintly as he gazed at her. "Z-Zachary," she pleaded shakily. "Please...."

But he held his ardor in check as he reached across the space between the bunks and with silent precision adjusted the sheet so that she was covered again. She thought it must have been an accident that his fingers brushed the slope of her breast, but she felt her nipples swell in revealing response, and she lowered her eyes quickly, unable to face his rejection yet again.

"Did Laurette undress me?" she asked hopefully, already knowing—and hating—the answer.

"Of course not," he snorted. "I did. You think someone Laurette's size could have wrestled you out of your waterlogged clothes?" He hesitated, and when he spoke again, his deep voice had lost its chilling impersonality. "Dear God in heaven, Ariel," he muttered, "what possessed you to dive in like that?"

"I had to stop the whalers from shooting at my friends," she replied simply.

He took a deep steadying breath. "Of course I understand that," he said slowly, as if addressing a child. "But why didn't you think to launch the second raft—or better yet, ask me to?"

Ariel's answer was soft but uncompromising. "I didn't think you gave a damn."

For a very long time, it seemed, Zachary didn't respond. Ariel tried to drink her coffee, but the liquid was too hot to take more than tiny sips, so she closed her eyes and savored the rich aroma. When she lifted her lashes again, she saw that the rugged beautiful planes of his face were tinged with gray, and a white line of strain edged the hard mouth that could be so soft, so coaxing.... Suddenly he exploded, "For God's sake, woman, the water was near freezing, and considering how absorbant thermal underwear is, it's a wonder you didn't sink like a rock!''

In matching tones Ariel retorted, "Damn it, Zachary, I'm not an idiot! I knew it was risky, but it didn't matter.''

"It would have mattered to Ellie. Did you ever stop to think about that? Didn't it occur to you just what it would do to your grandmother or to— or to the other people who care about you if something were to happen to you?" His eyes narrowed. "Or have I been right about you all along, thinking you're as selfish and self-centered as—" He broke off abruptly.

Growing cold with rage, Ariel asserted through gritted teeth, "I did what I had to do.''

Sarcastically he countered, "A fat lot of difference your nobility of purpose would have made to Ellie if you were to contract pneumonia or drown, or worse!''

Ariel was bewildered by his reaction. Contempt for her supposed selfishness she clearly heard in his tone, but beneath the anger she could also sense pain, acute and inexplicable. Then suddenly she remembered that Zachary's own mother had died of pneumonia, pneumonia contracted during an imprudent ocean swim. Oh, Lord, she thought with remorse. No matter what he thought of her or her beliefs, that precipitous plunge must have brought back tragic nightmarish memories, and she'd never ever meant to wound him like that.

In an effort to distract him she asked with deliberate whimsy, "So what's worse than drowning?''

"Don't be flippant," Zachary rebuffed her grimly. "You could have got yourself shot out there, too, you know. You didn't see the way the whaling crew was watching you as you approached their boat. I did. And if I hadn't managed to convince that Soviet captain that you were...."

Ariel eyed him thoughtfully. "If you hadn't convinced him I was what?" she probed, her brow wrinkling as she struggled to remember. "I seem to have a very fuzzy recollection of your yelling some Russian word over and over," she ventured. "*Be...bye*—something that started with a 'b'...."

"*Byezumnaya,*" Zachary supplied reluctantly. "I told them you didn't know what you were doing, that you were...crazy."

Ariel's hands shook so hard she had to set down her coffee before it splashed and scalded her. Leaning over the edge of the bunk, she put it on the floor, uncaring that the movement bared her torso. She knew Zachary was watching her, but it didn't seem to make much difference anymore. The mere sight of him might still be enough to make her ache with feverish frustration, but her body, which had delighted and inflamed him one unforgettable night, now apparently stirred him about as much as a department-store mannequin. When she sat erect again and adjusted the sheet modestly across her breasts, she quietly asked, "Do you think I'm crazy?"

"Every now and then I wonder."

The silence in the cabin was marred by the roar of the boat's engines and the continous racket of water spraying the thick-planked hull. In her bunk Ariel pulled the bedclothes up around her neck in a subconscious attempt to shield herself from the brand of Zachary's scorn. *Keep calm,* she ordered herself when she felt her throat constricting with suppressed tears. *Don't lose your cool. Remember, you're Wonder Woman, Femme Miracle, and you can take anything, anything and everything....*

Seated on the bare mattress, Zachary gazed at her across the narrow aisle, as still and solid and implacable as a stone god. Only the infinitesimal flutter of his absurdly long black lashes softened his flinty expression. Meeting his eyes with her own, Ariel finally said hoarsely, "I'm sorry my impulsiveness has disturbed you, Zachary. It wasn't deliberate, you know. It's just that I—I feel things deeply, and when I see something that needs doing, I tend to rush right in and try to do it—not always very effectively or efficiently, I admit."

She realized with alarm that her voice was on the verge of cracking, and hastily she continued, "I see now that you're quite right, and I have selfishly neglected to consider the effect my rash actions might have on those people who care about me, people like Ellie or—or even James or.... I promise it won't happen again...." Suddenly exhausted by both the physical and emotional stress her battered body had endured in the past few hours, her eyes drooped shut wearily. When she opened them again, Zachary was gone.

CHAPTER ELEVEN

WATER SLAPPED softly against the kelp-covered pilings, a sea gull shrieked metallically and Eleanor asked with concern, "Are you certain you don't want to stay for the press conference? James and I are in no hurry. We'll be happy to wait for you."

Ariel glanced toward the black sedan idling at the foot of the pier, the driver scowling as he surveyed the jammed parking lot. "You'll wait double-parked in a loading zone?" she questioned dryly.

"Well, of course we would have to try again to find a space. Not that there's much chance of success this close to Fisherman's Wharf. But if necessary, James and I...."

James and I, Ariel echoed silently. From the first moment she'd stepped wearily off the gangplank into Eleanor's welcoming arms, Ariel had grown acutely aware of how often her grandmother repeated that telling phrase. James and I. It had a pleased, proud, loving sound about it that warmed Ariel, even as it aroused more than a touch of envy. While she'd been out on the ocean watching her dreams die,

Eleanor and James had at long last become a couple.

She looked past her grandmother to the *Melinda May*, which was once again at rest in the slip belonging to the charter company. On the pier beside the gangplank an untidy mound of luggage lay heaped, signaling Goodearth's departure from the vessel that had been the group's home for almost two weeks. On the trawler one of the sailors had already hung a sign over the upper deck, announcing that the boat was again "available for bay and ocean cruises." Through the glass front of the bridge Ariel could see Zachary, the captain and a Coast Guard officer gesturing like figures in a silent movie, and she wanted to know just how Zachary was describing that encounter with the Soviet whaler, whether he'd thought it necessary to mention her impetuous dive overboard.

As she gazed longingly at him, he looked down, and just for a second their glances dueled as if they were trying to read each other's minds. Since that afternoon in his cabin they'd spoken very little. Ariel had malingered in her compartment, trying to combat her growing apathy by concentrating on the preliminary sketches for her new art project. According to Laurette, Zachary had spent a great deal of time in mysterious conversation with Gary Gruenwald. Drearily Ariel had wondered what on earth Zachary and Gary could have to say to each other.

The Coast Guard officer addressed a question

to Zachary, and he turned away. Feeling oddly bereft, Ariel diverted her own attention to the group farther down the dock, where Laurette and Gary and the other passengers huddled together and discussed the best way to make use of the limited press coverage their arrival had attracted. After their less than impressive performance at sea Ariel had been frankly surprised to find any reporters at all waiting for them when they limped into home port. But when she heard one of the newspapermen casually mention Don Fielding, she realized Zachary must have asked his friend to pull a few strings for them—or rather, for Laurette, she amended ironically. After all, the only reason Zachary had allowed his girl friend to join the ill-fated voyage was so that she could get some of the publicity she craved so much. And if it helped Laurette to be portrayed as the heroine of the adventure, that was fine with Ariel. She was glad someone would get some good out of it.

Handing her portfolio to Eleanor, Ariel hefted her duffel bag under one arm and assured her, "There's no reason to bother about finding a parking space, Ellie. I don't have to stay here with the group any longer. They won't need me to help make a statement to the press. I wasn't even on the raft that went out to the whale."

"I'm glad to hear that," Eleanor declared with a sigh of relief. "I realize you'll think I'm acting like a grandmother, but I did worry about you the whole time you were gone. I know how strongly you feel about the whaling issue, and I was so afraid you would take foolish risks to make your point. I don't think I could have borne it if anything had happened to you, now that we've just found each other after all these years...."

Ariel gazed remorsefully at Eleanor. Her grandmother was smiling, but her eyes betrayed her anxiety. Zachary had been right after all, Ariel thought with a pang. In her haste to make the world a better place for all creatures, all mankind, she'd forgotten she also owed some consideration to those people closest to her. Forcing a chuckle, she reproved bracingly, "Oh, really, Ellie, do you think for one minute that Zachary Drake would let anyone get out of line on an expedition he was involved in?"

Eleanor searched Ariel's bland expression. "I...suppose not," she conceded dubiously after a moment. Glancing toward the bridge, she frowned. "Darn. I had hoped to speak to him, to welcome him back before we left. But he looks as if he'll be tied up for hours yet, and then there's that press conference...."

Ariel caught her breath. She didn't know how much longer she could maintain this surface composure. The effort was draining her already depleted energy at an alarming rate, and if she had to linger there longer, if she had to speak to the reporters and smile when Zachary put his arm around Laurette's shoulders and posed for the clicking cameras.... "Ellie, please," she murmured. "I—I'm so very tired."

Eleanor scowled as she studied Ariel's wan face.

Her eyes flicked intuitively toward the bridge and back again. Then quickly she turned her head toward the parking lot, where a small, three-wheeled vehicle was creeping past the long lines of cars. She forced a laugh. "All right, dear. If you're really ready to go, I think it probably would be wisest for us to get a move on before that meter maid gives poor James a ticket. He'd never forgive me if I were to besmirch his spotless driving record!"

James's driving record remained inviolate as, after exchanging a quick hug with Ariel and stowing her gear in the trunk, they drove away. It wasn't until the three of them were sitting once again in the graceful Victorian parlor, relaxing over green tea and Mrs. Fong's special almond cookies, that Eleanor broke the news. She glanced significantly at James, who sat close beside her on the horsehair sofa, and then across the coffee table at Ariel. Quietly she began, "I received a telephone call from your friend Marie Ryder two days ago."

Ariel's cup remained poised in midair as she stared at her grandmother. "Marie called you?" she queried breathlessly.

"She was trying to reach you, of course, but when I told her you wouldn't be back for another two days, she spoke to me instead. Poor child, she needed to talk to *someone*. . . ."

Ariel felt herself grow cold with apprehension. "How is she?" she demanded. "Where is she?"

Eleanor hesitated, her expression distressed,

and James answered grimly, "She's in the hospital in Palm Springs. Apparently, while she and Sam Walsh were driving across the desert, heading for Mexico, she went into labor. So he rushed her to the emergency room and then just...left her there."

Ariel flinched, her cheeks growing pale beneath the gilding tan. Long before Sam had decamped with the Goodearth treasure she had suspected he would someday let poor Marie down. Never in her most horrific nightmares had she imagined him being brutal about it. "Oh, God," she groaned as she searched her mind for a word vile enough to describe his reprehensible behavior; there was none. "That—that *bastard*!" she concluded inadequately.

After taking a deep breath to steady herself, she asked in quavering tones, "How is Marie? You say she had the baby? Is it all right?"

"She's well," Eleanor reassured her quickly. "She had a little boy. He's rather small—just over five pounds—but in good health."

Tears of relief welled in Ariel's eyes as she murmured a fervent prayer of thanks. "I'm so glad," she sighed. "Despite everything, I know how desperately she wanted this child."

Eleanor nodded. "Yes, I could tell.... Our conversation was naturally rather stilted—after all, that young woman has just been through an incredibly traumatic experience, and she doesn't know me at all. But as soon as I finished talking to her, I called the hospital administrator. I told him

I was a friend of the family and explained the situation as delicately as I could. I wasn't trying to meddle. It was just that I knew how concerned you would be, and while we were waiting for you to return, I just wanted to do what I could to make sure there would be no problems about insurance or money or that sort of thing.''

At this evidence of her grandmother's generosity to a total stranger Ariel's heart swelled with love. "Thank you, Ellie," she said sincerely. "That means a great deal to me."

Eleanor shrugged wryly. "Don't thank me, child. As it turned out, my grand gesture was unnecessary. The day after Marie was admitted, someone mailed the hospital an envelope containing a note and three thousand dollars in cash."

Ariel's eyebrows arched dramatically. "Sam?"

"Probably. At least he had that much sense of responsibility, even if it was someone else's money," James cut in darkly, obviously angered by this example of masculine insensitivity. "Not that it'll be much comfort to Miss Ryder when she and her baby have to start fending for themselves."

Eleanor patted his hand supportively. For a long moment the three were silent, thinking seriously about the problems of a woman two of them had never met. At last Eleanor asked, "Ariel, do you have any idea if Marie has relatives, people of her own who might be able to help her?"

Ariel shook her head. "I think there may be a couple of aunts in the Midwest—Nebraska, Iowa, somewhere like that—but as far as I know, Marie's had no contact with them for years."

"That's what I was afraid of. I guess it's up to us, then. It's so tragic when families break up...." Eleanor sighed, and in her brown eyes her granddaughter could read poignant lingering regret over another young woman, another family that had broken up many years before.... "Darling," Eleanor went on doubtfully, "I realize you've only just got back from this trip and you must be exhausted, but—"

"I know, Ellie," Ariel cut in. "I'll leave first thing in the morning."

Eleanor beamed approvingly. "I was sure I could depend on you." Turning to James, she said, "Sweetheart, would you mind telephoning the airport for reservations? I just hope—"

Suddenly Ariel knew exactly what she had to do. Setting down her teacup, she interrupted with quiet emphasis, "There's no need for plane tickets, Ellie. I'm going to drive down to Palm Springs."

She thought James nodded, but Eleanor stared blankly. "It's more than five hundred miles, ten or more hours by freeway from here to the desert," she declared. "Why on earth should you want to take your car when planes are so much faster and easier?"

"I'll need the Pinto because when I'm through in Palm Springs, I won't be coming back to San Francisco."

Suddenly her grandmother looked tired and

old, in marked contrast to her dashing clothing and youthful style. "You're going away?" she whispered.

"I'm going home," Ariel corrected her quietly. "Once I've helped Marie get things squared away, I'm returning to Mendocino. I've been gone far longer than I ever planned...." She smiled ruefully. "The grass in my front yard has probably grown up to the windowsills by now—I'm sure my next-door neighbor, who's such a careful gardener, is ready to shoot me!" When her grandmother didn't respond to this feeble attempt at humor, Ariel said gently, "I've loved staying here with you, Ellie, but it was never intended to be permanent. Mendocino is my home, and it's time I went back there. I have to start earning a living again, and before long there's to be a dinner at my father's old college. Anyway—" she chuckled dryly— "the last thing you two lovebirds need is me here underfoot while you plan your honeymoon!"

Eleanor started to protest again, but James silenced her. Watching the interaction between them, it occurred to Ariel that when her grandmother had at long last let down her guard a little, she'd ended up capitulating completely—and willingly; James was now very much the man in charge. Perhaps, Ariel mused wistfully, Eleanor found it a relief to let someone else shoulder the responsibility occasionally. She wondered when, if ever, there would be someone to help her bear her loads....

"You will come down for the wedding, won't you, Ariel?" James asked seriously.

She hesitated. Although she would dearly love to see Eleanor and James married, she wasn't sure she had enough emotional stamina left to stand near Zachary in the family-of-the-bride pew and listen to those sacred and solemn vows—especially not when Laurette would probably be clinging to his arm. "When's the date?" she stalled.

"We're not sure just yet," Eleanor replied slowly with a frown. "I'll be submitting my resignation to Seacliff's board of directors in a couple of weeks, and a lot will depend on how soon after that I can officially turn over the reins to Zachary." When Ariel still didn't reply, Eleanor cried, "Darling, you must come. It wouldn't be the same without you." She caught James's fingers in her own as she confided with an abashed grin, "I know it's silly at our age, but since neither of us has had a wedding in more than forty years, we've decided to go all out this time. James is threatening to ask his great-grandson to serve as ring bearer, and I...well, I was hoping you'd be my maid of honor."

Ariel gazed at her grandmother. Dear Ellie, the aggressive resourceful businesswoman whose success as a publisher had been equalled only by the sorrow and failure in her personal life. The same woman who was smiling at her lover with the serene radiance of a girl of eighteen. Pledging never to do anything to erase that smile, Ariel said feelingly, "Ellie, I would be truly honored to be your attendant at your wedding."

EVEN THE EXCELLENT AIR-CONDITIONING SYSTEM couldn't completely counteract the blast-furnace desert heat, and Ariel, who had spent her entire life basking in cool ocean breezes, found the hospital room uncomfortably warm. Or maybe, she amended wryly, it was Marie's pathetic narration that was making her uncomfortable.

Although Sam's dubious bounty could have provided for a private room, Marie had refused to spend any more of the money than necessary, so she was sharing a room with three other mothers. At the moment, however, the other beds were vacant, and the two women conversed undisturbed. A small wheeled crib stood beside Marie's bed, and someone from the hospital auxiliary had located a well-padded rocking chair. Marie moved slowly back and forth as she said, "He told me he was hired by a professional basketball team. He said the money was a bonus for signing the contract and he had been waiting to surprise me with it...."

Ariel took a deep breath. "And you believed him?"

"Of course I believed him," Marie retorted with soft irony. She had folded back the lapels of her elegant robe of blue green rucked satin, a gift from Eleanor, and now gently stroked the tiny head of the infant nursing at her breast. Shaping a silky blond curl around the tip of her finger, she repeated, "Of course I believed Sam. I didn't have much choice, did I?"

Ariel tried to think of something encouraging to say—and failed. The baby stirred and mewled like a kitten, and Marie soothed him expertly, crooning love words and snatches of lullabies. When he settled sleepily in her arms, Marie continued dispassionately, her pale, bronze-freckled face immobile. "I knew something was wrong right away. Sam was so nervous. He said he was going to take me on a vacation before he had to report to his team, but we never stayed in one place long enough for me to get any rest. Besides, I didn't think it was a good idea for me to be traveling so close to my time. In Sacramento I went to a doctor, who told me it would probably be another six weeks before the baby was born and that I ought to go home. But instead of taking me back to Mendocino, Sam traded our car in on a camper. He insisted it would be the perfect solution. I could sleep whenever I got tired, and he could still travel...."

She bit her lip hard as she declared shakily, "Oh, Ariel, it's been hell! I felt so rotten, and Sam was jittery and acting paranoid, and he started talking about going to Mexico. I thought he was out of his mind. I didn't want my baby born in Mexico! So finally I demanded that he cut out all the crap and tell me the truth, and when he did, I—I could have killed him. To think that after all those years of work he could betray you and all our friends that way—and then have the nerve to claim he was doing it for *me*." She closed her eyes for several seconds. When she opened them again she concluded baldly, "We argued. We argued a lot. The contractions started—and now here I am...." Again she hesitated, smiling adoringly at her son. "No, I mean, here *we* are—me and Steven Maclean Ryder."

When Ariel heard the middle name, her eyes shimmered. "That's—that's lovely," she choked. "I don't know how to thank you."

"It would have been 'Ariel' if he'd been a girl. After all, you're his godmother—and you're also the only person in the world who gives a damn about Stevie—or me, either, for that matter." She shivered. "You were... you were right about Sam all along."

"I wish I hadn't been," Ariel said sincerely. "I'd give anything to see the three of you settled safely and happily somewhere."

"Not much chance of that now," Marie muttered tersely. She put the baby on her shoulder and burped him with surprising skill. Then she laid him gently in the crib and checked his diaper. Soon he fell asleep, and she stood for a long moment, gazing down at him. Her red curls bobbed as she bent to tenderly kiss her infant son.

Adjusting her robe, Marie settled into the rocker again, and silence filled the room. Ariel yawned, the heat and fatigue of the day-long drive making her logy. "What about your family, your aunts? Is there any chance of—"

"No!" Marie interrupted sharply. Glancing

quickly at the baby, she repeated in a more normal tone, "No, I'd never ask them for help."

"But surely—"

"They threw me out when I turned eighteen," Marie said bluntly. "I hadn't *done* anything. It was just that they'd taken me in when I was five, after my mother died—my father disappeared years before that—and by the time I came of age they apparently figured they'd been saddled with me long enough...." Her hands clenched with fierce emotion. Bleakly she continued. "I'm not complaining about having to go to work and live on my own—anyone can understand why two spinsters would want to be relieved of the responsibility of a child who wasn't even theirs—but it was as if the moment I came of age they no longer needed to pretend to *care* about me anymore. I'd tried every way I knew how to make them love me, but they—" she floundered for a word "—they made me feel as if I were...irrelevant." She eyed Ariel squarely then. "I always knew what you thought of Sam, but one of the things that attracted me most about him was that he needed me. I was important to him—" her mouth trembled "—or at least, I thought I was...."

Quietly Ariel pointed out, "Well, now little Steven needs you."

Marie nodded. "Yeah," she said, lovingly peeking over the edge of the crib at her child. Her haunted eyes took on a resolute glimmer. "And for as long as he needs me I'm always going to be there, no matter what."

Shortly thereafter, Ariel stood up to leave. Worry about her friend had sustained her through the interminable drive from San Francisco down the length of California to Palm Springs. Yet now that she'd seen Marie and felt somewhat reassured about her state of health and mind, Ariel felt ready to collapse. As soon as she'd telephoned Eleanor to report what she'd found out and ask for advice—obviously Marie and her newborn baby were not yet capable of enduring the even longer drive north again to Mendocino—she thought she might just sleep for a week. Trying unsuccessfully to stifle yet another yawn, she headed through the door, looking back over her shoulder to wave goodbye to Marie—and cannoned directly into the spare lanky frame of Sam Walsh.

Just for a second she didn't recognize him. He was dressed as usual, his absurdly tall body garbed in casual athletic shirt and shorts, but when Ariel looked into his face, she realized that the stunning silver blond curls that had dangled past his shoulders for as long as she'd known him were gone now. His hair was trimmed so short, in a near-military style, that his scalp showed pinkish white through the bristled stubble that edged his ears and nape. He'd shaved off his drooping mustache, revealing a thin upper lip that trembled as he gaped first at Ariel, then past her into the room. In his naked face his pale blue eyes widened defenselessly. He looked very young and very frightened.

Ariel gasped his name, but he wasn't listening to her. He was staring with stark appeal at the small red-haired woman who sat in the rocking chair, beside his sleeping child.

Marie's freckles glared liverishly against the ashen pallor of her skin as she returned his gaze. He took a step toward her, but his progress was halted instantly when she demanded, her soft voice cold and unyielding, "Why did you bother to come back, Sam?"

Sam swallowed hard. Ariel could see the Adam's apple bobbing in his rather thin neck, and she thought with surprise how very ordinary-looking he was without his remarkable hair—unimpressive and almost...almost homely. He couldn't be the same man who had single-handedly organized Goodearth two years ago and then charmed tourists and Mendocinans alike into supporting it—and, even less likely, an accomplished seducer and embezzler.... His eyes never wavering from Marie's face, he swallowed again and said hoarsely, "I was so scared. The longer we were gone, the more certain I was that at any moment the cops would swoop down on us. I—I just knew they were going to find me, and I had to get away. I thought if I could make it to Mexico, I'd be safe—only you went into labor...." He drew a deep rasping breath. "After I—I dropped you off here, I got as far as the border, and then I couldn't go on, not without you. For days I just sat there in the van, thinking. I mailed some money, and then I called the hospital a couple times."

Marie's eyes flared, but glancing with concern at the baby, she tried to keep her voice low. Still it rose with each new indictment. "Am I supposed to be moved because you sent money for the doctor bill?" she countered accusingly, an audible quaver fuzzing her words. "Sam, it was *stolen* money—you stole it from our friends! You stole from them and betrayed them and then deserted me just when I needed you most." Tears of hurt and indignation beaded on her coppery lashes as she charged, "You say you were scared—what about me? I was in labor twelve hours, in a strange hospital, and I was frightened and bewildered and alone."

Suddenly Ariel couldn't take anymore. She spun on her heel and fled through the door, stalking down the corridor until she was met by a harried-looking male nurse moving toward Marie's room, who demanded to know what the commotion was. When Ariel tried to explain, the nurse shook his head grimly and exclaimed, "I don't care if he is the baby's father. He can't go around upsetting the patients!"

"No, of course not," Ariel agreed quickly. Realizing the man might blunder into a highly emotional scene, she turned with him, and together they headed back toward Marie's room.

Ariel reached the doorway just ahead of the nurse, and when she looked inside, she halted abruptly, staggered by what she saw. Sam was kneeling beside the rocking chair, his face buried in Marie's lap. He was clutching at the skirt of the vivid satin robe, and his words were muffled by the fabric as he sobbed again and again, "I'm sorry, I'm sorry, I love you, I'm so goddamned sorry...." It was a litany of remorse, the same tortured phrases repeated endlessly. "I'm sorry, I'm sorry, I love you...." Marie's needle-worn fingers stroked caressingly over the pale stubble that had been Sam's crowning glory, smoothing the short hair over his surprisingly fragile-looking skull. Somehow the movement reminded Ariel of the way Marie had soothed her baby....

When Marie's eyes lifted to confront Ariel's, beneath the red lashes they were bright with a curious mixture of emotions—acceptance, defiance, a plea for understanding—and gazing back, Ariel realized with a pang that she did understand. Marie had never had any illusions about her lover. She loved Sam not despite his weakness but because of it. While Ariel might be searching fruitlessly for a man who would ease her burdens—as she would his—Marie thrived best when her burdens and responsibilities were made heavier; she needed to be relevant, as she called it. She needed to be needed. Ariel sighed wryly. Well, Marie was certainly going to get her wish. Both Sam and tiny Steven were going to need Marie desperately—and somehow Ariel felt sure that her friend with the disarmingly vulnerable air would manage to guide her family past all the obstacles in their path.

With a faint nod Ariel signaled her acceptance to Marie; then she turned to the nurse, who still peered uncertainly at the man blubbering by the rocky chair. "Why don't we just leave them alone for a while?" she suggested with a smile, subtly urging him back out into the corridor. "I think—I really do think everything's going to be all right now."

MARIE GRIMACED SUDDENLY and said, "We'll be boarding the plane soon. I think I'd better change Stevie while I can." Propping the baby on her shoulder, she picked up the diaper bag and headed down the corridor toward the women's rest room.

Through the thermal-glass window, Ariel stared bemusedly across to the runway. After the forested seashore she was accustomed to, the desolate tortured terrain surrounding the desert resort of Palm Springs seemed like something from another planet, certainly not part of her home state. In the distance waves of heat radiated from barren mountain slopes, rippling the bright clean air, distorting the image of the small private jet that was just now approaching from the west, over the peak of Mount San Jacinto. As it banked to begin its descent, the dazzling sunlight caught on a tilted wing and glared into Ariel's eyes. She turned away, blinking.

Beside her Sam shuffled nervously. He looked remarkably ill at ease, and the unusual—for him—formality of his slacks and dress shirt, coupled with the new short haircut and clean-shaven upper lip, reminded Ariel irresistibly of a college underclassman summoned before the dean. Sweat beading his brow, he asked again, "You're sure your grandmother and Mr. Dunhill will be waiting at the San Francisco airport for us?"

"When I telephoned them last night, James said they would be there," Ariel replied sternly. "But if for some reason they're not, then it's up to you to go straight to Seacliff. The sooner you return the money, the better off you'll—" The piercing whine of jet engines penetrated the calm of the terminal, and automatically she consulted her wristwatch. It was still too early for Sam's and Marie's flight to depart, so she assumed it was the private jet that had just landed.

Swallowing hard, Sam laid his hand on Ariel's arm as he implored, "Once I've given back what's left of the money, do you—do you think they'll still prosecute?"

Sam's reappearance the previous afternoon, with its attendant phone calls and lightning-quick arrangements, had denied Ariel her long-sought rest, and now, aching with exhaustion, she felt far too depressed to be charitable. "I would," she said coldly. "But I'm not the person you have to—"

"*Ariel!*"

The harsh bellow was accompanied by the clash of glass doors being flung back, and throughout the terminal, lines of waiting passengers and startled ground personnel turned to stare. Ariel froze, instantly forgetting the man who stood beside her.

"Damn it, Ariel, I know you're here—I saw you

through the window!'' the deep voice shouted, closer, and her name echoed hollowly through the angled corridors. Above the crowd at the ticket counters she could see the top of a dark head jostling its way toward her, and she gaped vacantly as Zachary broke clear and galloped down the long carpeted hallway.

He was dressed as she'd seen him that very first day in Mendocino, in the impeccable gray pinstripe she thought of as his "executive armor." But now the armor seemed to be falling apart. As he ran toward her, he clutched an attaché case in one hand, while with the other he held his jacket slung over his shoulder, flapping behind him like a cape. His vest was unbuttoned, the tail of a wadded handkerchief protruding from the pocket, and the sleeves of his white silk shirt had been rolled to the elbow. His old school tie dangled from the loosened collar. Staring at him as he raced toward her, the only thought that formed clearly in Ariel's mind was a whimsical hope that those sleek Italian shoes were tightly laced, or else he was liable to trip and break something. . . .

But she found nothing even mildly humorous about the expression on his face when he slid to a halt in front of her and Sam. Beneath his tousled raven hair his craggy features were livid, sickly white. Behind his glasses only his sparking eyes had color, the hot luminous green of rage—or, Ariel suddenly realized in amazement, of fear.

Fear, she asked herself, gawking as she noted the visible tremor in the hand that gripped his jacket, the pulse that beat jerkily at his silver-streaked temple. Oh, God. Something horrible must have happened. Had Eleanor— Sick with trepidation, Ariel sputtered, "Z-Zachary—"

Cutting her short, he rasped, "I won't let you do this! He's not worth it!" Dropping his attaché case, he glared viciously at Sam.

She regained her breath with difficulty. "What on earth are you talking about?"

"I'm talking about you running away with this clown!" he shouted, still too agitated to modulate his voice, and Ariel was uncomfortably aware of the spectators who were avidly watching them. Zachary roared, "Ellie told me all about it this morning! I went to see you, to—to show you something, and she said you were gone—found Walsh—weren't coming back! I hired a plane—had to—to stop. . . ."

Ariel shook her head, trying to make sense of the broken phrases. Did Zachary think she was going to help Sam abscond with the Goodearth funds after all, or was he—could he possibly be. . . ? She wished she knew exactly what had been said between Zachary and Eleanor. Had he misunderstood her grandmother, or had she deliberately misled him in an effort to play Cupid? Whatever the reason for his harried arrival, Ariel knew she had to clarify the situation at once. His distress hurt her too much. "Zachary," she began gently.

She was unaware of Sam's hand still resting on her arm until suddenly Zachary growled, "Get your damned hands off her, Walsh! Don't ever touch her again!'' Roughly he shoved the other man away.

"Hey, now, wait a minute!" Sam squawked as he stumbled backward, but before he could right himself, from behind Zachary came yet another voice, a light feminine one that ordered fiercely, "You leave him alone!"

Startled, Zachary spun on his heel and almost knocked over Marie, who was clutching the diaper bag as if she intended to hit him with it. Scowling down at the petite, copper-haired woman with the baby in her arms, he asked blankly, "Who the hell are you?"

Pointedly she maneuvered her slight body between Zachary and Sam before she stated simply, "I'm Marie." Rubbing her cheek lovingly against the downy head of the infant she carried on her shoulder, she added, "This is our son, Steven."

Quickly Sam stepped to her side and threw his lanky arm around her in a protective gesture that Ariel found moving, if a little tardy. He met Zachary's incredulous gaze evenly. "Steven Walsh," he expanded. "As soon as I've straightened things out with Mrs. Raymond, Marie and I are getting married."

For endless moments Zachary stared at the couple. Then he looked at Ariel. As she watched, a flush of color began to rise under the harsh planes of his face, like water under ice, ever swifter, darker.... "Oh, dear God," he groaned in a thickened voice, and limply he sank onto one of the vinyl couches spaced along the walls, dropping his face into his hands.

Ariel gazed achingly at him. His embarrassment reached out to her, palpable and throbbing, and she longed to touch him, to cradle his dark head against her breast and soothe away the pangs of his wounded dignity as Marie might comfort her baby. Then, from speakers throughout the terminal, a metallic-sounding voice announced, "Flight Two-nine-three for San Francisco and Portland, now boarding at Gate...." Ariel's tawny eyes flicked questioningly toward the other couple.

"That's us," Marie sighed, hefting the diaper bag yet again. "I guess we'd better get going." She tried to hug Ariel, but she was hampered by the baby and the rest of her gear, and the two women could only touch cheeks solemnly. Sam stood silent, his pale eyes downcast.

The loudspeaker again announced the departure of their flight. Sam glanced at Zachary, then Ariel. Quietly she said, "Well, good luck, Sam. I know things are going to be rough for you, no matter what my grandmother decides to do about the money you took. It's never easy, learning to face up to your responsibilities."

"I guess it is at that," he said stonily. He looked toward Marie, who was trudging down the hall, her slender shoulders hunched by the weight of her load. Suddenly his grim expression lightened, as if he'd come to a decision. "Maybe I ought to start the first lesson right now..." he murmured. Striding after her, he called brightly, "Hey, sweetheart, wait up—you shouldn't be carrying all that stuff by yourself! How about letting me have charge of Stevie for a while?'' With awkward gentleness Sam took the baby from Marie. Handling him as if he were made of crystal, he settled his son in the crook of his arm and adjusted the receiving blanket around him. Then, catching Marie's small hand in his own, he led his family away, through the corridor to the waiting airplane.

After they'd disappeared around a corner, Ariel looked at Zachary again. He was still seated on the couch, but now he was gazing at her with a vulnerability and a naked longing that shook her to the very core of her being. Was he—could it be.... Tremulously she whispered his name.

His eyes were bleak as he said drearily, ''This morning Ellie told me it was high time I quit being a jerk. Now I know what she meant.''

He sounded exhausted, and the depression in his voice troubled Ariel deeply. She glanced around, noting with relief that now that the shouting had stopped, everyone seemed to have returned to his own business. Scooting Zachary's attaché case aside, she sat down beside him, laying her hand on his thigh in a gesture of reassurance. Instantly he caught her fingers in his own and clutched at them with urgent strength. She could feel him trembling. In a feeble attempt to make him smile she pointed out quietly, ''Being a jerk is a pretty common ailment, you know. Everyone gets a touch of it now and then.''

Her effort was rewarded when the corners of his mouth quirked faintly. "That's true," he agreed. "How I could ever have believed that you were involved with the theft—or that Ellie wouldn't find out about it. She was rather scathing on that point." He regarded Ariel enigmatically. "Of course, you haven't been too bright, either, thinking I was having an affair with Laurette."

"You mean you're not?" Ariel exclaimed, her golden eyes suddenly wide with burgeoning hope.

Zachary shook his head ruefully. "All I've ever done for Laurette is help her a little with her career since her parents refuse to. She's a very talented pop singer, but the senior Masefields seem to think that any music other than grand opera is beneath their dignity, possibly because Laurette's mother was a contralto before she married. Since Laurette is undeniably immature for her age and she does love her parents very much, this disagreement has created a lot of tension in her life. By the time I met her she was about to crack from the strain of trying to reconcile her ambitions with theirs. I was able to give her a little advice and encouragement." His face darkened. "I suppose Laurette's predicament appealed to me because I . . . happen to know something about what it's like to disagree with a parent's plans for you. . . ."

Ariel saw his mouth tighten, and she wondered if he would ever tell her about his childhood, about his flighty mother and the father who had deliberately packed him off to a prep school that was "like something from a Victorian nightmare." "Maybe it's foolish of me," she floundered, "but I still find it hard to believe you and Laurette never.... It seemed so...suitable. She's beautiful, she's fond of you, she's—"

"She's young enough to be my daughter," Zachary finished dryly. "She makes an attractive and convenient social partner when I need one, but cradle snatching has never appealed to me." For a second he paused. Then suddenly, as if the words were wrenched from him, he declared, "There's only one woman in my life who really matters. She, too, is beautiful and talented. She's also generous and loving and loyal and so incredibly courageous she makes me want to tear my hair out at some of the risks she takes—and, fool that I am, from the very beginning I've done everything in my power to drive her away."

Ariel blinked hard. "I—I don't understand."

"I realize that—" he began, but all at once his words were swallowed by a yawn. He covered his face with his hands, pushing his glasses up with his fingertips so that he could massage his eyes and the bridge of his nose. When he'd settled the glasses back into place, he grinned abashedly. "Pardon me! I'm sorry about that, but I've been working continually ever since we got back from the boat trip, and I'm worn out." He let out his breath in a hiss. "Actually," he murmured deeply, "I haven't had a decent rest since the night I slept with you in my arms...."

Their gazes locked, amber and jade, sun and cool green shadow. "I—I know just how you feel," she whispered hoarsely. With heart-stopping intent she stood up and extended her hand to him. "Come with me," she urged. "I'm staying near here, and we both need some sleep." She didn't breathe again until he slowly unfolded his long frame from the couch.

After the intolerable sunlight, the mind-destroying heat that had bounced off the pavement and back into their faces as the Pinto drove along palm-tree-lined thoroughfares, the curtained darkness of Ariel's motel room seemed almost unreal. Zachary set down his attaché case, and they faced each other almost gravely, the only sound in the room the soothing hum of the air conditioner. Ariel could see the fatigue weighing down his powerful body, the weariness aging his hard beautiful features, and she ventured, "I really did mean it about . . . sleeping."

"I know," he said as he slipped off his vest and shirt. "And believe me, I'm grateful." She watched him sit on the edge of the single bed and bend down to remove his shoes. He folded his glasses and placed them on the nightstand. Then, swiveling around on the coverlet, he settled back against the pillow. Wordlessly he held out his arms to her.

Ariel hesitated. "Are you sure there's room enough for both of us there?" she asked skeptically. "I don't think that bed was meant for two people our size."

"As a very wise woman once pointed out to me," Zachary drawled, "you can manage almost anything if you get close enough...." Again he smiled in invitation, and without further agrument Ariel lay down beside him.

She perched precariously on the edge, and Zachary shifted his weight to mold her against him. Kissing her lightly, he observed, "I know it's a little cramped, but it's still better than that king-sized waterbed of mine! God, darling, you have no idea how cold and empty that bed has seemed without you...." He cradled her head on his shoulder, and as she breathed the warm musky scent of his skin, she could feel the thud of his heart under her ear. Her curvaceous torso nestled into the contours of his body, and her long, denim-clad legs twined comfortably with his. She found the intimacy less provocative than reassuringly familiar, and with a sigh she relaxed. As she dozed off, she thought his fingers combed gently through her thick hair.

SHE WAS AWAKENED by the caressing stroke of long fingers cool against her breast, a broad thumb teased the nipple. Even without lifting her lashes she could tell that her shirt and bra had somehow been tampered with, that what she felt was the slide of flesh against silky flesh. Snuggling closer to the virile body beside her, she murmured, "I feel as if I've been asleep for a month."

Laughter rumbled in the broad chest beneath her cheek, making the hair-roughed skin tickle her. Zachary said, "It hasn't been quite that long, but it is after mindight."

Ariel's eyes flew open, blinking against the subdued light of the single lamp. She glanced at her
watch and groaned in dismay. "Oh, Lord, we've
slept almost around the clock!"

"So what?" he inquired calmly. "We both
needed the rest." When Ariel tried to pull away
from him, the hands splayed beneath her stopped
her. "Going somewhere?" he asked.

"No—yes—no—I don't know," she stam-
mered, still feeling drugged after such a long sleep.
She puzzled hard, trying to remember if there was
something she ought to be doing, but she couldn't
think of any tasks left incomplete. Eleanor,
Marie, the Goodearth voyage—everything had
been taken care of. But she'd been wrestling with
her obligations for so long that it felt wrong not to
be under pressure. Twisting awkwardly in Zachary's arms, she propped herself on her elbows and
peered intently into his face. His eyes were warm
and dreamy vague, and the expression in them
took her breath away. "I—I don't know of anything I have to do. I just thought you might be. . .
hungry or something."

"Or something," he said throatily. "I'm hungry for you, girl—starved for you. . . ." Brushing
her hair back from her temples, he framed her
face with his hands and drew her mouth down to
his. When they parted reluctantly, his fingers
trembled as he tugged her shirt over her head and
fumbled for the clasp of her bra. Her loosened
breasts rubbed with aching seduction against his
muscular chest, and he groaned and slid his hands

down the long curve of her spine to her waistband.

The limited surface of the narrow bed hampered their movements, and by the time they'd slithered clumsily out of the remainder of their clothing, they were both panting with good-natured frustration. As soon as Zachary had impatiently kicked away his shorts, he rolled onto Ariel with a triumphant leer. His considerable weight pinioned her seductively to the mattress, stopping her laughter, and she gasped, "Maybe there is something to be said for the waterbed, after all!"

Instantly he eased away from her, propping himself on his elbows. "Am I too heavy for you?" he asked, his voice gravelly with desire and concern.

Some thick strands of her hair were trapped beneath his arms, and her movements were restricted as she shook her head. Licking her dry lips, she soothed huskily, "No, sweetheart, you're not too heavy. I *love* the feel of your body on mine! I love having you...on me...in me...." The words died out in an incoherent groan as her tawny eyes grew glazed, and flinging her arms around Zachary's neck, she drew him inexorably back down to her.

The first night they'd made love they'd come together with fierce passion, their bodies merging in an elemental ritual that had given rapture even while it failed to address their anger, their unresolved conflicts. In time those conflicts had made a mockery of the ecstasy they'd shared.

Now they touched intensely but tenderly, hands

and lips relearning and inviting the silken wonder of their union. There was no haste, no conflict, and when, with open arms and open heart she welcomed him into the center of her being, their joy knew no bounds.

Afterward, boneless and still tingling, she rested her chin on his shoulder and drank in the sight of him. A hard flush of color still burned along his cheekbones, cooling with delicious slowness. Her fingertips traced over the reddened skin and moved upward to the fine crinkly lines that radiated outward from the corners of his eyes, white against his tan. She murmured teasingly, "You're too young for wrinkles. You shouldn't work so hard."

In matching tones he charged, "If I do work too hard, it's all your fault," and with a sigh he pushed himself into an upright position on the narrow bed and reached for his glasses. Ariel watched in surprise as he stood up and crossed the room to the table where he'd left his attaché case. His step was curiously unsteady.

Her eyes were still feasting on his glorious masculinity when he flopped back onto the bed beside her and drew a sheaf of papers from the case. "Here," he said. "This is what I meant to show you this morning—or yesterday morning, I guess it is now—when I went to Ellie's, before I found out you'd gone." When Ariel looked puzzled, he continued, "Now that Ellie's retiring and I'm taking over Seacliff, I intend to change the company's direction a little. We've always been noted for the exceptional quality of our graphic arts, but for years it's seemed to me that we ought to be able to use our superb photography and artwork more meaningfully, to produce books that are more than just pretty, that have real substance to them. I thought this might be a good way to begin...." He spread the pages out on the coverlet, and sitting up, Ariel studied them in wonder. On the first page, marked in a bold black script she would have recognized instantly even though she'd never seen it previously, was the title *A Proposal for AN OCEAN BIG ENOUGH: PICTORIAL JOURNAL OF THE GOODEARTH VOYAGE. Photographs by Gareth Gruenwald; Illustrations by Ariel Maclean.*

Ariel looked questioningly at Zachary, and he said, "I've been working on this idea ever since before we got back. Your friend Gary is amenable, and I thought that new project of yours sounded ideally suited for this sort of treatment. I talked to people I know on the East Coast, and I think I can get some pretty big names to write a couple of prefaces, one for background on the whaling industry, the other about the place of grass-roots organizations within the ecology movement. I figured that if the book's a success, you might want to use the proceeds to fund research or lobbyists or something along those lines."

As she turned the pages one by one, scanning the notes that already evidenced a considerable amount of thorough research, Ariel asked in bewilderment, "You'd do all this for me? Why?"

Zachary's face was shuttered, his voice low and intense as he clipped off each word. "Because I have to prove to you that even if our methods are different, I do give a damn about things after all," he said. "Because I love you."

She stared at him. His skin seemed stretched taut over the harsh planes of his face, as if the bones were about to burst through, and his eyes were narrowed with emotion. He said, "I didn't know I loved you until I watched you dive off the side of that trawler into a freezing ocean, determined to face down an armed ship all alone. I thought it was the bravest, most wonderful, most *foolhardy* action I'd ever seen, and I could have strangled you for putting your life at risk! Failing that, I knew that if anything happened to you I wouldn't want to live, either."

Scowling, he continued tonelessly, "Once you offered me your love, and I threw it back in your face. I'm sorry. I honestly didn't know what I was doing. You have to understand—love was not something that figured largely in my upbringing. In fact, lately I've come to realize there's a whole range of human emotions I know nothing about, and my ignorance makes me feel...defensive." He smiled sardonically. "Of course, from the very first day we met in Mendocino, I've been on the defensive with you. Even as angry as I was about that stupid letter from the lawyer, I couldn't help noticing how beautiful you were, young and bright and vivacious. You made me feel stodgy and... middle-aged...."

"For heaven's sake," Ariel protested in disgust, "you're not that old!"

"Pushing forty, my love," he pointed out cynically. "Old enough to recognize that there will have to be a lot of compromises on both sides if you and I are to sustain a relationship—where we live, how we live.... Old enough to wonder sometimes if I have the right to ask you to make those compromises."

Ariel frowned. "You're asking me to live with you?"

"Actually, I was asking you to marry me," he said quietly.

Her eyes widened dramatically. "Marriage? Why?"

One thick black brow arched as Zachary tilted his head quizzically to the side and chuckled. "Lots of reasons," he said, ticking them off on his long fingers. "Because we love each other. Because whenever you go diving into the ocean, I want the right to fish you out again. Because I would hate to think that I'd offered you less than an obnoxious creep like Sam Walsh is giving the woman in *his* life."

He paused, and his gaze skimmed over her. She could sense the tension radiating from him as his eyes clouded once again at the sight of her lush breasts partly veiled by her long sun-bleached hair, at the view of her tapering waist, the curving hips that enclosed the intimate triangle of dark blond curls.... She felt her own body stir in equal response to his obvious welling desire, and she knew it would always be like this for her. Whatever he felt, she would feel, also; she and Zachary belonged together. Despite their outward differences they were in harmony in everything that truly mattered—complementary, variations on a theme. They were two notes in the same chord, two phases of the same moon, two halves of one beautiful and indivisible whole.

Except for the low buzz of the air conditioner, the little motel room was silent for several moments. Then Ariel suggested diffidently, "My next-door neighbor in Mendocino commutes between there and San Francisco twice a week. You and I might be able to work out something along those lines, if you liked...."

His voice was strained as he clipped out, "Does that mean you're accepting my proposal?"

"Sounds that way, doesn't it?" she answered faintly.

Zachary relaxed visibly. Then with a shout of laughter he declared, "Of course, darling, you know the main reason I want you to marry me is purely selfish. I don't want to have to worry anymore about your asking strange men to pose nude for you!"

Ariel bit her lip to suppress a giggle. "That's a promise," she replied with mock seriousness. "No more strange men, no matter how attractive they are. The next one who shows up on my doorstep will be chased away with a broom. From now on

I'll never use any model but you." She held out
her hand to him as if to seal their agreement.
"Only you, ever," she repeated huskily.

He caught her hand in his own, firm and confident. Their eyes met and locked; their minds met
and locked. Then, with a sensual growl low in his
throat, Zachary pounced on her, dragging her beneath him as they sprawled together on the narrow
bed. "Only *us*..." he corrected thickly, his lips
warm and insistent against the slope of her breast.

There were no further words the rest of the
night.

About the Author

One of the things Sacramento author Lynda Ward enjoys almost as much as writing fiction, is whale watching! She has skillfully and lovingly combined the two in *A Sea Change*. Here Ariel and Zachary explore San Francisco and the choppy waters of the north Pacific, dropping their facades to reveal the true nature of lovers.

Lynda herself is a member of an Oakland-based antiwhaling group, and she occasionally sets sail to view these magnificent mammals in their natural setting. "Unfortunately," she confesses, "like Laurette in my story, I also get seasick...."

Married for eighteen years to the one love of her life, Lynda has three young sons who keep her occupied when she's not writing or organizing youth soccer or whale watching. Her fourth Superromance, coming up: the spicy encounter of a consumer advocate and a talk-show host.

Harlequin reaches
into the hearts and minds
of women across America
to bring you

Harlequin American Romance™

YOURS FREE!

Enter a uniquely exciting new world with

Harlequin American Romance ™·

Harlequin American Romances are the first romances to explore today's love relationships. These compelling novels reach into the hearts and minds of women across America... probing the most intimate moments of romance, love and desire.

You'll follow romantic heroines and irresistible men as they boldly face confusing choices. Career first, love later? Love without marriage? Long-distance relationships? All the experiences that make love real are captured in the tender, loving pages of **Harlequin American Romances**.

What makes American women so different when it comes to love? Find out with **Harlequin American Romance!**

Send for your introductory FREE book now!

Get this book FREE!

Mail to:

Harlequin Reader Service

In the U.S.	In Canada
2504 West Southern Avenue	649 Ontario Street
Tempe, AZ 85282	Stratford, Ontario N5A 6W2

YES! I want to be one of the first to discover **Harlequin American Romance.** Send me FREE and without obligation *Twice in a Lifetime.* If you do not hear from me after I have examined my FREE book, please send me the 4 new **Harlequin American Romances** each month as soon as they come off the presses. I understand that I will be billed only $2.25 for each book (total $9.00). There are no shipping or handling charges. There is no minimum number of books that I have to purchase. In fact, I may cancel this arrangement at any time. *Twice in a Lifetime* is mine to keep as a FREE gift, even if I do not buy any additional books.

Name _____ (please print)

Address _____ Apt. no. _____

City _____ State/Prov. _____ Zip/Postal Code _____

Signature (If under 18, parent or guardian must sign.)

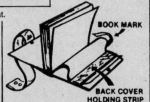

A Harlequin

ROBERTA LEIGH

Collector's Edition

A specially designed collection of six exciting love stories by one of the world's favorite romance writers—Roberta Leigh, author of more than 60 bestselling novels!

1 Love in Store　　　4 The Savage Aristocrat
2 Night of Love　　　5 The Facts of Love
3 Flower of the Desert　6 Too Young to Love